TRIAL
RUN

Books by Thomas Locke

LEGENDS OF THE REALM

Emissary

FAULT LINES

Trial Run

FAULT LINES

TRIAL
RUN

THOMAS
LOCKE

Revell

a division of Baker Publishing Group
Grand Rapids, Michigan

© 2015 by T. Davis Bunn

Published by Revell
a division of Baker Publishing Group
P.O. Box 6287, Grand Rapids, MI 49516-6287
www.revellbooks.com

Printed in the United States of America

Library of Congress Cataloging-in-Publication Data
Locke, Thomas, 1952–
    Trial run / Thomas Locke.
        pages ; cm. — (Fault lines)
    ISBN 978-0-8007-2433-7 (pbk.)
    ISBN 978-0-8007-2434-4 (cloth)
    I. Title.
  PS3552.U4718T75 2015
  813'.54—dc23   2015003245

15   16   17   18   19   20   21   7   6   5   4   3   2   1

In keeping with biblical principles of creation stewardship, Baker Publishing Group advocates the responsible use of our natural resources. As a member of the Green Press Initiative, our company uses recycled paper when possible. The text paper of this book is composed in part of post-consumer waste.

green press
INITIATIVE

This book is dedicated to
Mason F. Matthews,
whose passion for quantum physics inspired this project.

⫙

The most beautiful experience we can have is the mysterious.
It is the source of all true art and all science.
—*Albert Einstein*

1

When Hal Drew turned off the Pacific Coast Highway, his wife took that as the moment she'd been waiting for, and reached for the real estate brochures. Again. Hal told her, "Don't get those out. It's too dark to read."

"I'll just turn on the inside light."

"Leave it off. I don't know these roads and I need to see what's going on."

Mavis Drew watched Santa Barbara slip away, the brochures clutched in her lap. "Tell me which development you liked best."

Hal waited until he was headed east out of town to say, "Remind me which one had that view of the ocean."

"Oh, you."

"It's a fair enough question." He pointed to the top brochure. "The Pacific is right there on the cover."

"So they dressed things up a little." She lifted one he didn't need to see. Again. "This is my favorite."

Mavis had begged him to make this trip. Just visit Solvang for a look-see. She'd been going on for months about how these California housing developments were going bust. She claimed they could get a steal on a home and live her dream of retiring near the ocean. Which was why they'd taken this miserable excuse of a highway from Solvang to Santa Barbara. So Mavis could have a look at the Pacific. Soon as they drove along the harbor and saw all the pretty sailboats bobbing in the blue Pacific waters, Hal knew he'd lost his wife to the California myth.

He said, "I'm thinking we're better off staying in Phoenix."

"Why does that not surprise me."

"Who do we know in California? Not a soul. It's just six hundred miles farther from the kids."

"Hal, both our children live in *Georgia*. There are *airports* in Santa Barbara. We fly to see the children now, what difference does it make?" She stared out her side window, seeing a lot more than the dark night ahead. "I loved that townhouse with the lake and the view."

"We got lakes out by where we live now."

"And the mountains. You said they were nice."

"We got mountains too." When she did not respond, Hal added, "I've put down roots. I like where we live, Mavis."

"And I'm ready for a change."

Hal drove in silence and fumed. The road heading inland was in wretched shape. Get away from the money and the robbers that lined the coast, and California treated their own state like an afterthought. The pockmarked highway stretched out before them, veined like a cadaver. Beside him, Mavis gave a dreamy sigh. Hal thought of the arguments to come and sighed as well.

Then it happened.

Mavis screamed so loud he slammed on the brakes before he even knew the reason. A souped-up Japanese car appeared out of nowhere, no lights at all. Hal almost took a bite out of the trunk. The shadowy car crawled along at something like twenty miles an hour, utterly dark.

Hal turned into the oncoming lane and hit the gas. The road ahead was black. Hal felt like he drove through an empty tunnel. The night just sealed them in.

As he started to overtake, his wife screamed a second time. Why, Hal had no idea. But he felt it too. A weird sensation, like the dark had grown claws that scraped the skin off his spine.

Hal slammed on his brakes again and pulled back behind the night crawler. He turned to his wife and started to ask her why she was making all the noise and freaking him out.

When it happened a *second* time.

A shadow roared past them. It had to be a car. No missile could fly that low. This second car was doing 120, maybe more.

And no lights.

The car ahead of them roared to life. It pulled a smoking wheelie and accelerated to warp speed and roared off after the other car. Still with no lights.

Hal stopped and pulled over to the side of the road. He needed a couple of minutes to pry his shaking foot from the brake pedal. And a while longer to stop his heart from stuttering over how they'd just been handed a tomorrow. Because his wife had screamed at an empty night.

When it happened a *third* time.

Two SUVs and a van roared past. Their lights were off as well. All three looked painted in shadows. Hal's headlights revealed that all the passengers wore night-vision goggles.

Then they were gone. And the night was empty. Black. Silent.

Hal turned to his wife and said, "I'd rather retire on Mars."

⫸

The woman who led the operation was seated in the first SUV's passenger seat. She knew the men had expected her to take the safer middle car. The lead vehicle was always the one to catch the worst incoming fire. Particularly in a situation like this, flying down the highway in the dead of night with the lights off. The agents from the local FBI office probably thought she was riding in the most vulnerable position to show she was as tough as any of them. They were wrong. The woman would have to care what they thought to make such a move.

She spoke for the first time since they had started off. "Are the police in place?"

The guy seated behind her said they were.

"They know what to do?"

"We've gone over it with them in detail."

"For your sake, I hope they follow orders," the woman said. "Call it in."

The driver picked up the radio on the seat between them and said, "The ops is a go. Repeat, go."

The woman said, "Light us up. Keep the siren off. I want to hear myself think."

They stripped off their night goggles as the driver turned on the headlights, then set the bubble on the dash and hit the switch.

The man in the rear seat said, "Sooo, they have a name for this midnight madness?"

The woman replied, "The car running hot is called tricking. The setup car is trolling. They trade back and forth."

The guy in the rear seat said, "Redline down an empty highway looking for death—this is a game?"

The driver said, "I guess if I had enough drugs in my system I wouldn't care either."

The woman said, "They do it straight. That's part of the deal. Straight or not at all. It amps the fear factor."

The guy behind her asked, "How did you find out about this anyway?"

The driver agreed. "I've been stationed out here for nineteen months, and this tricking hasn't ever surfaced on my radar."

"Radar," the woman said. "Cute."

"Is that your answer?"

The woman pointed ahead. "Here we go."

The road ahead was suddenly illuminated by police cars flipping on headlights, spotlights, flashing top lights. The two racing cars spun about, only to find the trio of followers had stretched out, running in flanking position, blocking the entire highway.

For once, the local police did exactly as ordered. The officers stepped forward, guns drawn, but they held their fire.

There were two kids in each car. Three guys, one girl. Aged nineteen to twenty-three. They were cuffed and searched and crammed into the unmarked van. The kids watched through the van's open door as two agents got into their tricked-out cars and drove away.

The woman opened the van's passenger door, then turned and said, "Thank you, gentlemen. That will be all."

"That's it?" The senior agent exchanged astonished glances with his men. "What happens to the culprits?"

"Your commanding officer did not find it necessary to ask any questions when he received the call from Washington," the woman said. "I suggest you do the same."

The agents and the police watched the van drive west, into the night-draped hills.

·|||·

The unmarked van drove to a blank-faced building in the industrial zone east of the Santa Barbara airport. The building was rimmed by fencing designed to look like a sculpted garden of metal staves. The fence's razor tips were blackened to mask them from curious eyes. The infrared cameras and ground sensors and electronic attack systems were carefully hidden. The building's windows were a façade. Behind them were walls of steel sheeting.

The van's driver coded them through the unmanned entry and pulled up to the loading zone. Three security men came out. They brought the kids inside.

The kids were photographed and fingerprinted and led to individual rooms. Actually, one was led and the other three were dragged screaming and fighting. It made no difference. They were sealed into rooms fashioned like an officers' barracks, tight spaces with narrow foam mattresses and a six-by-six shower room and a small fold-down desk and a three-legged stool. The door was plastic-covered steel and had a little ledge at eye level. Two hours after they arrived, the slit was opened and a tray was passed through with food. Otherwise the kids were left alone. No one spoke to them. There was nothing to read. There was no television. There was no sound except what they made themselves.

The woman let them cook overnight. She would have preferred to make it longer, but she was in a hurry. Outside events were bearing down.

Besides which, in her tradecraft these kids were classed as disposables.

The kids were brought into another featureless room, this one with a conference table. The woman took fractional pleasure in how they moved as they were told and seated themselves where directed. She took her time and inspected them carefully.

The girl was dark haired and beautiful in the manner of a crushed rose. She exuded the scent of undiluted sex. The woman seated on the table's other side did not need to check her file to know the girl's name was Consuela Inez.

The girl said, "I want a phone call and a lawyer."

The woman took her time inspecting the three guys. Two of them aped how the girl slouched in her seat. The pair did not actually look at her, but still they mimicked her motions and her attitude. The exception was Eli Sekei, aged nineteen. He was tattooed like the others, same spiked hair, same piercings. Same sheet of juvie offenses. But he remained very alert, very self-contained.

"Hey." The girl thumped the underside of the table with her shoe. "I'm talking here. I know my rights."

The man standing in the corner of the room started to reach forward, intending to grip the girl and straighten her. The woman said, "Let it go, Jeff."

The man resumed his position. The girl swiveled her chair. "Yeah, Jeff. Back off." She faced the woman. "About that phone call."

The woman said, "Officially you no longer exist. Your cars have been wrecked and burned to a crisp. Your families have been notified of your deaths. The newspapers carried photographs. You are gone. If you don't do exactly what we say, we will make that happen. Take a good look at me, and see if you believe I mean what I say."

It was all a lie, of course. But by the time they discovered she was not telling the truth, the outside world would have lost its hold. Either that, or they would not ever have a chance to make the discovery.

The woman knew how she appeared to them. She had been beautiful once. But now she looked blasted by some furnace, melting her down to an ultra-hard core. She spoke with a rough burr that might have been sexy on someone else. On her, it was like listening to distilled hate, or purpose, or an intent that turned her eyes into pale lasers. She gave them thirty seconds, then said, "Now sit up straight and pay attention."

The two older boys were born followers. In the time it took for them to settle properly into their chairs, they had switched their allegiance from the girl to her. The woman had no idea whether this was good or bad. She made a mental note. Over time, if her project proved successful, such items might prove vital in making future selections.

She turned her attention to the girl. "This is your last and final warning."

The girl scowled and cursed but obeyed.

When the woman turned back, she saw that Eli Sekei was smiling. She resisted the temptation to smile back. She hoped he was the one she was looking for.

"My name is Reese Clawson. I need two people who are utterly without fear. Only two. Two people who are willing to explore the impossible. Two people who have nothing to lose. People who will be utterly mine. In return, I'll give you anything you want. Money, travel, sex on command. But no drugs. That's the key. Anything else, name it, and it's yours."

The girl gave her a sullen look. "So how about my freedom?"

"No problem."

Eli spoke for the first time. "After all this, you'll just let us go?"

"If you make the cut, absolutely."

"So what keeps me from going home and blowing your cover?"

"Forget that, man," the girl said. "What happens if we don't make the cut, that's what I want to know."

Reese kept her gaze on the kid seated directly across from her. "Eli Sekei, what kind of name is that, Persian?"

"Turkish."

Reese knew that already. She just wanted to know if he would respond in a decent manner. "Well, Eli. The answer is, if you were so happy being home, you wouldn't be spending your nights out tricking on the Chino highway. But that was then and this is now. What I have is so amazing, you'll never let go or do anything that would risk your chance to do it again." The woman hesitated, then added, "That is, assuming you survive."

It might have been just the two of them in the room. "How about slipping a television in my room? Nintendo, something. I'm going nuts in there, staring at the walls."

"Sure, Eli. I can arrange that." Reese stood and motioned to the two men standing guard. "But after next week, I doubt you'll be much interested. Not ever again."

2

Trent Major dreamed he was eight years old again, and very scared.

In his dream Trent was back in Ojai, a hundred light-years from his present home in Santa Barbara. He hid under the neighbor's mobile home. Steel tie-downs formed a web around the concrete crib holding the water heater and the AC. Trent had made it his very own haven from the bad times. Like now.

Trent's mother liked her men. Some of her visitors didn't notice the kid at all. A few complained over her half-breed son hanging around, watching them with his solemn unblinking gaze. The worst men just barked. Some, though, like the man Trent hid from now, were just plain bad. Trent couldn't understand how his mom didn't see that also. Or maybe she did, and that fueled the manic laugh she only used when bad men were around. Trent heard her laughter rock the trailer across from where he hid, a screeching mix of pleasure and rage and pain that twisted Trent's guts.

Trent didn't need to see this particular guy's pistol to know he was trouble. Or his switchblade. Or the snub-nosed hold-down he kept strapped to his ankle. Trent may have been eight years old. But he had been raised on the streets of Chino. He knew his guns. And the men who carried them. He knew what his Latino neighbors said about guys like this. How the man was building his own coffin, one bullet at a time.

The sand Trent crouched on was cool. Sunlight never made it down inside the concrete cave. The neighbor's cat liked Trent, and most of the times when he slipped in here the cat curled up beside him. The cat was there now, a caramel tabby with a purr so loud it almost made Trent's fear go away.

He had no trouble being alone. He played games inside his head, pulling up books he'd read or math puzzles he'd been working on, spreading them out until they blocked most of what was going down, out beyond his safety zone. The doctor said Trent had an eidetic memory. But Trent's memory games vanished when the door across the dusty lane banged open, and his mother stumbled out, and there was blood everywhere.

The cat did a cat thing, there one moment, gone the next. Then the guy came out. Waving a gun in one hand, his knife in the other. He spotted Trent. And took aim.

Which was the point at which Trent always woke up.

Only not this time.

This time, the dream shifted.

Trent knew he was still dreaming. Instantly he recognized the setting. He was seated behind his desk at one corner of the podium in the lecture hall where he now taught two undergrad classes a week.

This new dream-image was crystal clear. In a way, the image seemed more vivid than reality. Because Trent was able to look at things inside himself from a dispassionate distance. He realized the Ojai nightmare had been growing in frequency, following a trend that he only now saw was logical. Strange how he needed to be inside yet another dream to perceive this. He was a scientist. He was a specialist at identifying trends. But he had remained blind to this one. Until now.

Which was when things grew seriously twisted.

Trent realized there was another guy standing in front of the blackboard. And this other guy was himself. Trent Major. Only older.

The older Trent turned toward him and said, "Pay attention."

Trent did not *think* the voice. He *heard* it. The voice was not loud. But it held such power Trent's entire body resonated from the force. Like a nuclear whisper.

He watched himself write a string of mathematical symbols on the board. Trent was captured by the idea of how vividly real this all appeared, sitting at his desk, feeling the scarred wood beneath his fingertips, watching an older version of himself write on his blackboard.

Then the older self was finished. He turned to Trent and said, "Check it out."

Trent studied the symbols awhile and decided, "That is amazing."

"You want amazing," his older self replied, "get a load of this."

Suddenly a computer screen floated in the air before Trent's face. Only there was no computer attached to the picture. Applied physicists had been working on this for twenty years, how to do away with the need for a physical screen of any kind. The world was desperate for a way to project true three-dimensional images. In order to do this, the picture had to be separated from the current two-dimensional surface. Trent reached out and pushed his hand through the image. He felt a faint tingle run through his fingers. Which, given the fact that he knew he was still dreaming, defined bizarre.

"Stop fooling around," his older self said. "This is important."

Trent was carried through five scenes. With the appearance of each new image, he expelled a sudden breath. The pictures were so powerful they punched him straight in the soul.

Then the images were gone. Trent watched as the older version of himself crossed the dais. Trent heard the scrape of his shoes across the wooden floor, a sound he knew vividly from his classes.

The older Trent moved in so close he filled Trent's field of vision entirely. His words now carried the same impact as the images. "Are you listening to me?"

Trent wanted to ask, "Like I have a choice?" But the older version of himself held such force, he couldn't even nod his head. He just shivered. Or tried to.

The older Trent moved closer still, and rocked his world with the words, "What you just saw? Make this happen. Do it now."

3

Charlie Hazard stood in the Lugano airport parking lot. Campione, the village where his team was now based, was a tiny Italian enclave surrounded by Switzerland. Milan was the closest major airport. The municipal airport was intended mostly for private jets. But four times a day, small regional carriers arrived from Zurich, Paris, Frankfurt, and Rome. The Lugano airport's setting was idyllic, pristine, extremely Swiss. Snow-capped peaks clutched at passing clouds. The April wind was laced with glacial ice. The parking lot separated the airport from a five-star spa hotel. Even the trees bordering the hotel grounds looked manicured. The place was so quiet Charlie could hear a radio inside the hangar on the runway's far end.

Charlie had worked in Switzerland any number of times. The orderliness had always struck him as artificial, a lid that could not quite seal the seething cauldron underneath. Ticino, the province of Switzerland where Italian was the principal language, was a haven for dirty money. Charlie's memories of the place were filled with killers who assumed they could mask bloodstains with tailored suits and expensive cars and lakefront villas.

The flight from Rome descended from a deep-blue sky. Charlie waited by his Range Rover as the jet wheeled toward the miniature terminal and powered down. The Tibetan woman was the last to emerge. Her face was pinched, her look as resentful as her tone.

Dor Jen handed Charlie her lone bag and said, "I am not coming back, Charlie."

"Thank you for making the trip."

"I mean what I say." She pulled herself up and into the Range Rover's high seat. "It doesn't matter what Gabriella feels like she needs to tell me."

Dor Jen was a medical doctor who had formerly served as Gabriella's chief scientist. Their team had been together almost two years before the split, which had been diplomatic and quiet and explosive. Dr. Gabriella Speciale was a psychoanalyst who had developed a concept so revolutionary they had hired Charlie Hazard to keep them alive. Dor Jen and her group had objected to Gabriella's slow, measured approach to the process. Dor Jen was still concerned with survival. But she also wanted to complete her research before the enemy tracked them down.

Charlie shut her door and went around and slipped behind the wheel. As he started the car, Dor Jen told him, "We are doing important work. Vital."

Charlie pulled out of the parking lot and took the highway south.

"I've talked it over with the others," Dor Jen went on. "We all agree. We're better off staying where we are."

The highway skirted Lake Lugano. The still waters reflected a mirror image of the sky and mountains. The city was a jewel nestled in green and blue.

Dor Jen said, "We have established a very careful cover. We have told no one of our real purpose. This serves us well. We do not need to worry about impacting our research through the power of suggestion."

Charlie did not respond. He figured it was better for Dor Jen to get the arguments out of the way before they arrived. She had obviously spent a lot of time practicing. Better she release them here and now.

"Even if Gabriella did manage to resolve the other issues, there is no Swiss clinic that would serve our needs. This region is simply too tightly controlled for us to do our work." Dor Jen glared at him. "It doesn't matter what Gabriella says. We are staying in Rome."

The research team led by Gabriella Speciale had begun with trial subjects drawn from two neighboring universities. Within six weeks, their quiet little enclave was inundated. Word spread through the university systems of three countries. An invading army of eager students overwhelmed everything and everyone. They filled the local campsites. Their clamor alerted the enemy. Something Charlie had always assumed was inevitable. So they relocated to Switzerland, where the ultra-cautious Swiss police offered the hope of safety. At least for a little while.

Anyone who arrived without being invited would never be accepted as a trial subject. Strict protocols were set in place. But by then it was too late. Their work had come to the attention of the local authorities. Questions were asked, and asked again. The chance to work in relative secrecy was lost. Which meant moving beyond the most basic level of research was dangerous. The unwanted attention threatened their very existence. They felt eyes everywhere.

Dor Jen and her small team found the atmosphere stifling. She was a medical doctor licensed to practice in Italy. She had been designing a series of experiments intended to apply their work in the field of holistic medicine. Holistic medicine was the point at which Western and Eastern medicines came closest to functioning in parallel.

But there were problems. What Dor Jen proposed was, to say the least, extremely controversial. Charlie doubted there was anything that might have raised the Swiss alarms any faster.

Gabriella ordered Dor Jen to hold off. She insisted the team maintain its cautious pace until, hopefully, the authorities turned their attention elsewhere. Dor Jen chafed for four months. Then she opted to move. She did so with silent efficiency. Taking six others with her. Including Julio, Charlie's number two on the security detail. Charlie had no idea it was happening until the morning they left. So much for his powers of observation.

Dor·Jen said, "If Gabriella starts arguing with me again, I will leave immediately for the airport."

Charlie took the Campione turnoff and did not respond.

"I mean it, Charlie. You can't keep me here against my will."

Charlie drove through the village and climbed the winding road that rimmed the lakefront. He took the electronic control from the compartment between the seats, pointed it through the windscreen, and hit the button. The tall metal gates slid open. He drove around the front grounds and parked beside the ornamental pond.

Dor Jen stared at the villa's blank exterior. "I should not have come."

Charlie walked around and opened her door. He led her around to the side door. "You did right."

Dor Jen entered, tasted the air, and sensed it immediately. "What's the matter?"

"This way."

"Where are the trial subjects?"

"Gone."

"Gone where?"

He pointed her down the hall. "Give me thirty seconds more and you'll understand everything."

The villa had been built in the late sixties. Downstairs, a central hall dissected the house into front public rooms and rear private chambers. The downstairs bedrooms had been turned into offices, technology support, and records. The remaining team ate and assembled around a long refectory table that dominated the living room. The formal dining room and smaller parlor now served as test chambers. These two rooms were connected by a narrow butler's pantry. Charlie had stripped out the mahogany cabinets and installed monitoring equipment and one-way mirrors. Normally the kitchen and the front parlor were jammed with excited test subjects and bustling team members. By this time of day, the front porch and rear gardens contained the overflow. Today, however, the villa held an oppressive stillness.

"Charlie, what has happened?"

He knocked on the door leading from the hallway into the small parlor. At a sound from within, he opened it and said, "She's here."

Gabriella rushed out. She gave no sign she noticed how Dor Jen flinched away from her approach. She was too busy reaching for the Tibetan lady, embracing her, holding her with fierce desperation. Whispering, "Thank God. Oh, thank God. I was afraid you wouldn't . . ."

Dor Jen's remaining defiance vanished at the sight of Gabriella's tears. "What is it?"

Even when caught in the vise of impossibilities, Gabriella had the power to light up the room. She had almond eyes tilted at an impossible angle. Dark hair. A body that turned jeans and a T-shirt into a magnet. Charlie had loved her from the very first breath. Maybe before.

Which made her professional distance a burden that grew heavier with every passing day.

Gabriella wiped her face, took hold of Dor Jen's hand, and said, "Come with me."

⁂

"How long has he been like this?"

Charlie checked his watch, did a rapid calculation. "Fifty-eight hours and counting."

"Has a doctor seen him?"

"Impossible." Gabriella resumed the position Charlie had drawn her from. She had scarcely moved from the chair pulled up beside the bed. She reattached herself to the hand lying limply upon the covers and addressed the figure lying in the narrow bed. "To make this public would ruin us and destroy everything."

Charlie said, "One of our new team members is a nurse. She's seen to him so far."

Dor Jen leaned over the supine figure. She checked his pulse. "Slow but steady. I did not bring my instruments. I thought . . ."

"We've got the basics." Charlie held up the nurse's emergency kit. "Make a list of anything else you need."

Dor Jen peeled back one eyelid. "Can you bring that lamp in closer, please. All right, that's enough." She checked the pulse in his neck. Then she unbuttoned his shirt and fitted the stethoscope into her ears. "Breathing steady, lungs apparently clear." She rose and made a process of straightening his clothes. "Tell me what happened."

"We're not entirely sure," Charlie said.

"We know enough." Gabriella did not clear her face so much as smear the liquid. She had aged twenty years in two days. "Brett signed himself in for a trial."

"Who counted him up?"

"Jorge. They've been working together. Brett has been trying to measure the difference between physical time and temporal observations made during a trial. He thought perhaps . . ." Gabriella stopped. "It's all my fault."

Charlie started to argue. As he had been for the past two days. Dor Jen watched him stifle his comments, then asked Gabriella, "How could this possibly be your fault?"

"I was supposed to record a series of controlled instructions for him. I let other things get in the way."

Charlie said, "Brett gave her almost fifty pages. Detailed stuff, counting down at specific time points. It would have taken hours to record it all. Days. She's been swamped. You know what the students have been like."

"I know." Dor Jen checked the leads attached to Brett's head and chest. "Were the monitors running?"

"They've been on since he started."

Dor Jen stepped into the former butler's pantry. Charlie remained where he was, holding up the wall beside the door. He didn't need to see the screens again.

Dor Jen emerged. "His vital signs have remained constant?"

"What you see is what you get," Charlie replied. "The guy hasn't changed since it happened."

She checked the IV. Saline and glucose. Standard therapy for shock. Charlie remembered that much from his bad old days.

Gabriella looked at Dor Jen. "Is he dying?"

Dor Jen sat on the side of the bed. Her weight was scarcely enough to crease the covers they had laid over Brett. "Tell me what Jorge said."

"They were trying out his new instructions. Jorge is very careful. He followed the clock, read out what was written. I know because I've listened to the tape. He hit the instructions Brett laid out as precisely as humanly possible. The trial lasted eighteen minutes. Jorge counted him back down." Charlie pointed at the bed. "Brett never returned."

Dor Jen said to Gabriella, "I know what you want. It could be very dangerous."

Gabriella nodded. "Will you try and bring him around?"

Dor Jen studied the figure on the bed. "Of course."

4

Shane Schearer came out of her final class at the University of California at Santa Barbara's business school and steamed down the main hallway. Beyond the building's entrance beckoned California's idea of paradise. Palm trees lined the two-lane road that rimmed the UCSB's inner campus. The road was jammed with two-wheeled traffic. Thousands of bicycles flashed in the sunlight. Cars were not allowed on these roads. The campus was as eco-friendly as an imperfect world permitted. Shane had no problem with the California lifestyle. Just the attitudes that came with it.

She checked the time on her cell phone. The only people on campus who still used watches were the older professors and the sorority queens who sought any reason to add more bling. Shane pushed through the glass doors and parked herself in the shade. Ten minutes and the streets would empty out. Right now, at the end of classes, the bike traffic was borderline suicidal. UCSB undergrads cycled with the same self-centered blindness that they applied to most of life. The thousands of other bikes were inconsequential. Cyclists cut and swerved without a glance. The previous week Shane had seen an accident that took down over a hundred bikes, resulting in three broken arms and a chorus of bruised egos.

Shane had come to UCSB because the business school had offered her a free ride. Times like these, after she had coasted through another wasted day of classes she could do in her sleep, the admittance letter from Yale still branded her soul. But she had maxed out on her student loans. She had also received a truly nasty letter from the federal government after pretending she was a man by the same name and borrowing still more so as to attend Oxford's international finance summer school. The feds' letter had arrived the same week as Yale's scholarship committee had turned her down. The feds had basically threatened her with public dismemberment if she took out a cent more in debt or even thought about skipping town.

These days, Shane didn't like herself all that much. She remained trapped in one of two speeds. Either she coasted with everybody else, caught inside a world that lacked any hint of sharp-edged reality. Or she had her bumper shoved up tight against whoever was ahead in line, pushing and shoving and shouting at them to speed up. Seven months into her MBA, Shane moved around the university in her very own isolation bubble. UCSB's business school was all about teamwork. The word had become a little poison pill shoved daily down her throat. Shane couldn't decide which would kill her first, her inability to fit in or her loneliness.

Then the guy rose from the bench on the other side of the road.

She noticed him for two reasons. First, because he studied her with a gaze that could only be described as intense. Second, because of how he crossed the road as though the bikes were smoke. The cyclists shouted and braked and swerved and shouted some more. The guy didn't even blink. He just kept watching her and walking.

When he was close enough, she asked, "Are you positively suicidal?"

"I've wondered that myself." He stopped directly in front of her. "My name is Trent Major. I'm a graduate student in theoretical physics."

"Well, Trent Major, could you move to one side or the other? I've got to stare straight into the sun to see you."

"Sorry." He kept to the stair below where she sat, and squatted down so that his head was below her own. As though he wanted to make himself as unthreatening as possible. "We need to talk."

"Do I know you?"

"No." He drew out a sheet of paper filled to the max with mathematical symbols. "I need you to set up a company and register this for a patent."

"Wait. Stop. Back up about six miles and explain to me exactly how it is we're having this conversation."

"Do you mind if I sit down?"

"Are you dangerous?"

"Not to you. Not to anybody."

Oddly enough, she believed him. He looked like exactly what he claimed to be. Trent Major was dressed in the grad student's uniform of Ecco sandals and clothes that had never, in their very long life, made the acquaintance of an iron. His skin was a shade darker than olive. His hair was straight and dark and full, the kind of hair that many women would have killed to possess. He did not wear it long so much as not bother to cut it. He shook his head to clear it from his face, calmly waiting, letting her look, not pressing. Shane figured he was part Native American. He had strong features and the latent intensity of a restful cat. His eyes were a hue of grey so light as to appear luminous. He was tallish and big-boned and gaunt in the manner of a half-starved animal. The hand that held the sheet of paper was twice the size of her own.

"Sure, Trent Major. Take a load off."

He set the sheet of paper with its dense writing between them. "Thanks."

"Now tell me why you're here."

"You're a business student. You're bored. You're an orphan. You're broke."

Shane had not been this knocked back since the winter her parents were killed. "Are you stalking me?"

"Absolutely not. I didn't even know you existed until . . ." He took a long breath. "About an hour before dawn this morning."

Shane pulled out her cell phone. "I'm going to take your picture now."

"Go ahead."

"Then I'm going to show it to campus security. And ask them if you're as nuts as you sound."

"I'm not a threat."

"And I want to hear how you know about me."

He waited until she snapped his picture to say, "My answers don't even make sense to me. I'm asking that you trust me long enough to see for yourself that this is for real."

"Turn to the left." She snapped a second picture. "Now the other way. Get your hair out of the way."

Shane shut her phone. And stared at him some more. Taking the pictures had somehow drawn the guy into a different focus. As in, Trent Major seemed to go out of his way to hide the fact that he was actually good-looking. He was also extremely patient. He did not move, not even blink. Just waited.

Shane said, "I think you should go away now."

He rose to his feet and descended the stairs. "My phone number and email address are on the back of the sheet."

"Hold on a second." The guy's passivity only added to the intrigue. Shane motioned to the sheet of paper. "What is this?"

"An algorithm."

"Which is what, exactly."

"An algorithm is a mathematical interpretation of reality. A computer algorithm provides physical input through a series of instructions that form an electromagnetic structure the computer can understand."

The guy might be a psychopath, and her alarm bells might still be ringing. But she liked his voice. "Sure. Okay. I understand that."

"This is an algorithm for computer games. Do you game?"

"I'm the one asking questions here."

He nodded as though he found her brusqueness totally acceptable. "Online gamers download a series of algorithms that set up the game's background structure. Otherwise the game would move too slowly. The online data stream shifts them in relation to this base algorithm and to other gamers. This means every algorithm comes in two parts, the downloaded base and the reactionary data stream."

His delivery was as calm and unthreatening as his stance. She said, "So?"

"This is a two-part algorithm for game music. It is totally new. There is nothing like it anywhere. Formulas like this are called interactive or parallel algorithms, because they restructure results based upon incoming data. If we ever manage to design thinking computers, these interactive algorithms will most likely form the basis."

She broke in with, "You don't look like a Trent to me."

He stopped in mid-flow. And waited.

"You look like you've got Native American blood. What's the name of that tribe east of here?"

"Chumash. I get that a lot."

"Are you?"

"No. I'm half Afghani. Probably."

"You don't know?"

"I know my father was Pashtun. The border area is pretty fluid."

"So you don't know."

"Not for certain. I never met him."

She didn't know what to say, so she settled on, "Oh."

"My mother claimed he was an Afghan freedom fighter. More likely, he drove a construction truck. They were building a big development near where she worked as a waitress. She stole his commercial driver's license. I found it in her purse when I was a kid. His name was Reza.

Reza Shah. I know about the Pashtun connection because I had a friend in the genetic labs test my DNA."

Shane studied him. "You're so open about anything except what I really need to know, is that it?"

"Give this a chance. See if it's for real. That's all I'm asking."

"That's a lot."

He took a huge breath. Expelled it. "I know."

She gave that a beat. Coming to terms with the thought that she actually might do this thing. And something else. The way he stood, how he waited for her, it was as though he had already given her control. "You were saying. About the formula here."

"This interactive algorithm allows the game designer to input a basic melody. All computer games have background music. Only with this one, the gamer will *redesign* the melody through his or her actions. What role the gamer chooses, the armor they wear, their weapons, the attacks they win or lose, everything will impact the base melody. The music becomes transformed into a personalized signature."

Shane watched him grow increasingly animated. His big hands began weaving a pattern in the space between them as he said, "This means you can identify another gamer by his or her sound before they actually appear. And when gamers come together to form a combat team, the music of each gamer *combines*. It becomes a personalized symphony. Each individual supplies a new electronic component to the total."

She knew she shouldn't respond. But she couldn't help it. "That's pretty interesting."

"It is more than that. It is groundbreaking." He motioned at the sheet on the step beside her. "We can sell this for real money."

"I'm still having trouble with this 'we' business."

"I know. But we've got a lifetime to have that conversation. If you'll just hold off with the questions for a while longer and do what you've spent your entire life dreaming of doing. And help me take this to the next level."

5

harlie Hazard joined Dor Jen in the kitchen of their Campione house. Dor Jen ate toast with marmalade and drank strong black tea. She explained that Rome's Fiumicino airport was three and a half hours from the village where her clinic was situated, and she had not eaten since dawn. A woman named Katrina, from Albania by way of Vienna University, was boiling eggs. Fifteen of their team were spread about the kitchen's perimeter, perched on ledges and cabinets and leaning against the walls. Only Charlie and Dor Jen were seated at the central table.

Gabriella maintained a policy of complete and utter openness within her team. Being admitted as a member meant being included in every aspect of their work, every component of the research, every discussion. Nothing was kept confidential. No meeting was held in secret. The only time a door was shut on the public rooms was during ascents. Charlie had feared that, as their numbers grew, so too would the backroom disputes. But their respect for Gabriella and their enthusiasm for the project was too great.

Until now.

Charlie had attended funerals with lighter moods. The kitchen was rimmed with grim expressions and frightened looks. Brett Riffkind had been their resident biologist since the very beginning. His specialty was the blood-brain barrier and the chemistry governing the neural net.

Everyone knew of the earlier friction between Brett and Charlie. Most had assumed this was in the past. Gabriella remained an aloof mistress to them all, applying affection in almost equal doses. Charlie pretended that it was enough and kept his private yearnings tightly sealed deep inside.

As Charlie sat and watched Dor Jen drink her tea, the one person who caught his eye was Elizabeth Sayer, their resident pharmacologist. Elizabeth carried her standard aura of inapproachability. But she had been shadowing Charlie ever since his return from the airport. He glanced over, giving her a chance to say something. She remained isolated behind her spiky hair and glacial gaze.

Dor Jen ate with calm impassivity. The Tibetan doctor was very slight yet gave off an air of tensile strength. Her intelligence charged the atmosphere. As did her anxiety. Charlie could feel it, could see it in the way she avoided his gaze. Her moon face and glowing features with their yellowish cast were made to hide secrets. But Charlie knew this woman. And he knew she was afraid.

He sipped his own mug and said, "Would you tell me about your research?"

"We're not stopping."

"I would never ask you to. I made the request simply for the sake of our new team members." Charlie took another sip. "We hold no secrets here."

He saw the flicker to her gaze, the quick flash of tension below the impassive surface. And he knew he had guessed correctly.

Dor Jen said, "I am a medical doctor, trained in both Western and Tibetan medicine. We are working at a clinic outside Rome that specializes in conditions that defy standard treatment. No cancers, at least not yet. The clinic focuses on undiagnosable pains. Ailments that have burdened a patient for years. When they have tried everything else, they come to this clinic. If nothing else, the clinic offers comfort. One of the wings is dedicated to long-term care. It operates like a hospice, only most of these patients will not die from their ailment. Because of this, these patients have often bounced from one hospital to another, doctor to doctor, and they have given up. Now all they want is partial relief from their distress."

"So you work with the hopeless."

"Yes. We do not offer them a possibility of healing. We are not ready for that. We explain that we are simply doing experiments in finding a reduced level of pain medication. That is enough. We do not work with everyone, of course. We avoid the patients who do not want to hope again. Many have become enamored with their drugs and their routine and being the center of so much attention. We isolate our volunteers away from such patients."

"You want people who are still willing to try."

"We want patients who will *fight*. We seek people who are willing to look *beyond*. We intend to join together Western and Oriental medical directions into a new holistic system. We want to find the root causes for their afflictions."

"Even if these causes are not physical."

"Especially if the cause is not a standard illness as defined by Western medicine. Yes."

Charlie figured she was relaxed enough now to spring his trap. "But that was not why Brett came down to see you, is it."

Dor Jen froze in the act of raising her fork. And Charlie knew his suspicions were all correct. And that he had in fact been right to call Dor Jen and demand that she return. It was all tied together. The woman's departure, the conflict, Brett's coma. Everything.

6

"People around here are so thoroughly into the good life I could scream."

Trent sat across the wrought-iron table from perhaps the most amazing woman he had ever met. He did not know her name. He was careful not to stare directly at her. Even so, she filled his senses. She was angular in the manner of a long-distance runner, with copper hair streaked lighter in places. He assumed it was not color from a bottle. He had no evidence for such a postulation. But this woman did not appear the type to concern herself over alternate hair colors. Everything about her was direct, straight ahead, forward looking. She was turned slightly from him, as though she too was determined not to focus overmuch on Trent. Which made his peripheral inspection less intrusive.

She went on, "Two weeks ago, UCSB was ranked the nation's number one party school. But you already know that."

"No. Sorry."

She glanced over, a lightning bolt, there and gone. "You don't get out much, do you."

"Hardly ever. Especially not since I started my doctorate two years ago."

"Anyway, the business school dropped tools and put together a party to celebrate the honor. If they'd put half as much energy into their studies, we'd bump the grade curve forward a semester. I went because everybody else was going. The profs included. My school is very big on teamwork. I've never felt more out of place in my life."

Trent didn't know what to say, so he remained silent. He knew she kept talking because she was nervous. He could feel her unease radiating like friction off a high-tension line. But there was nothing he could say or do to make things better. Certainly not tell her the truth. She would bolt. So he made himself as small as he could and waited.

"This place is exactly what I'm talking about, only more so." She encircled the sports café where they sat with her forefinger. "You bring my classmates in here, they'd salivate like Pavlov's puppies. This is why they're in school. So they can exercise in a place that would look gaudy in Vegas."

"So what are you doing here? I mean, why you're studying at UCSB."

"I know what you mean." She gave him another lightning glance. "I'm still not comfortable with your questions, Trent Major."

"Of course. Sorry."

The sports club was located in an upscale outdoor mall between the university and the closest business park. There were a number of these industrial islands rimming the Santa Barbara airport. They tended to attract high-tech groups that used the university's specialists as part-time consultants and the postgrads as researchers. Trent had hoped he could line up some work with one of them. But the professor supervising his dissertation had axed the idea straight out. Trent had initially thought the man was concerned about a business tainting results or encroaching on cutting-edge work. Now he knew better.

The sports club occupied its own building. The central atrium was marble tiled. The café tables were separated by full-grown palms planted in wooden tubs. The ceiling towered eighty feet above them. A balcony ran around three sides and held the exercise machines. Hit music drifted down from overhead.

She and Trent had biked over from the campus. He had scarcely believed it when she had agreed to come with him. He had kept to the main roads and let her trail behind him. Trent knew where to come because he had cycled here straight from his apartment that morning. Finding the sports club exactly where his dream-image had shown was why he'd had the courage to meet this woman. Trent risked another glance. He had so many things he wanted to say, starting with asking her name.

She was dressed in standard student garb, an off-the-shoulder sweatshirt worn over a dark tank top. The sweatshirt was a faded grey and draped down over pale blue tights. On her, the outfit looked regal. She asked, "So are you going to tell me why we're here?"

Trent pointed at the glass wall directly in front of them. On the other side were a trio of squash courts. "We need to speak to that man."

"Which one?"

"The tall one with dark hair."

"Who is he?"

"A corporate lawyer."

She shot another look. "In case you missed the fact, I'm actually in the business school. Where there just happens to be several lawyers. People I know. And who know me."

"No," Trent replied. "It has to be this attorney."

"Oh." She crossed her arms. "Well, that clears up everything, doesn't it."

"I know you have questions."

"Oh, and that's supposed to make me feel better?"

"What you need to do is treat this like an experiment."

"As in, I sit on a petri dish while you poke and prod? I don't think so."

Trent liked that. He liked her spirit. He liked how she fought to keep her nerves under control. He especially liked how she was willing to come over here with him.

"What are you grinning at?"

"When he comes off the court, go over and speak with him."

"You're not coming with me?"

"No. You have to do this alone."

"Why?"

Trent pressed against the table. He saw the flicker of alarm in her gaze. He forced himself back in his chair, keeping his distance, holding his voice to a calm that was itself a lie. "Do this one thing. Please. Go over and show him the paper and tell him what I've told you. If it goes like . . . He should agree to work with us on the spot."

"What, a corporate attorney who's never seen me before will accept us as clients on the basis of a howdy-do?"

"Yes. And tell him that we're broke and he won't be paid until we are. He will agree to accept payment on a contingency basis."

"That," the woman said, "is impossible."

"I know. But if it happens like I say, I'll tell you everything. And you'll believe me, precisely because it has happened. If it doesn't, well, I'm sorry for wasting your time, and I promise I'll never bother you again."

She started to say something, but the squash court's glass door banged open. She eyeballed the man laughing his way toward the café's main counter. "What's his name?"

Trent's voice sounded strangled to his own ears. "I have no idea."

He expected her to bolt then. She had every reason to. Instead, she flashed a grin as fleeting as her glances and rose to her feet. "That makes about as much sense as me standing here."

Trent watched her approach the man and thought, *The lady has a fabulous smile.*

7

"Brett traveled to Rome nine days ago," Charlie said to Dor Jen. "You offered him the chance to do some cutting-edge research. Work that Gabriella would never have approved."

Elizabeth spoke for the first time. "Brett told me he was going glacier skiing."

"Brett lied. He traveled down to see Dor Jen. Isn't that right."

With slow, deliberate motions, Dor Jen set down her utensils and pushed her plate aside.

"I found this very interesting." Charlie held to a very calm tone. "Brett's research has been very tightly focused. Isn't that right, Dor Jen."

The Tibetan did not respond.

"His goal has always been the same, ever since he first met up with Gabriella. His aim has been to use these experiments to prove, once and for all, some of the most contentious issues related to human brain activities. Brett decided that if he could develop evidence that our experiments operate *beyond* time, *removed* from time, then he could introduce our work as evidence that human consciousness can be separated from Newtonian physics. This would be worthy of a Nobel Prize. It would place his name in lights throughout the scientific world. Isn't that right, Dor Jen."

The doctor stared at her hands resting on the scarred table and did not speak.

"What I couldn't understand, though, was how could Brett's work on the nature of time help you down in Rome? Then it hit me. You were working on something else entirely."

Dor Jen said softly, "Everything I have told you is the truth."

"Sure. Of course. But that's not the issue. You have *two* experiments running simultaneously, don't you. One related to the living, and the other to . . . what?"

From his place by the window, their key techie breathed a soft, "Whoa."

"You wanted to look at the dying, didn't you. You wanted to examine the moment of final transition. But there were problems. Because how could you possibly know this moment in advance? So what do you do? Do you just sit and wait? You can't, can you. We all know there are finite boundaries for our experimental states. So if you are looking at pending death, you first have to identify the exact moment. Which would prove Brett's hypothesis. But if you move backward, then you can name the moment, but you are still breaking the bounds of time. Which was it to be?"

"Both," Dor Jen murmured to the tabletop. "We wanted to try both directions."

The entire room murmured. Charlie started to speak, but stopped when he saw Jorge turn to Elizabeth and mouth the words, *Tell him*. Elizabeth met his gaze and gave a minute shake of her head. Charlie did not press. Elizabeth was not someone who would ever give in to outside pressure. She would talk when she was ready, and not a moment before.

Charlie turned back to the Tibetan and said, "So you contacted

Brett. And he came down because he thought he could use your work as a proving ground for his own."

She lifted her gaze and, in so doing, revealed the rising terror. "Did I do this to him?"

Charlie turned to Jorge, who was already shaking his head. "The instructions he gave me before he went comatose were simple in the extreme."

These ongoing instructions remained part of the protocol Gabriella had laid out in the early days of their very first trials. One person, the monitor, was responsible for giving the ascender precise instructions. This was where Dor Jen's first disagreement arose. Gabriella used the monitors as a means of restricting. Do this and nothing more. Dor Jen and her team wanted to use the monitors as a means of *expanding*.

Dor Jen asked Jorge, "What did you tell Brett to do when he ascended that day?"

"Exactly what he wrote down. Go forward. Look at where he would be in two weeks. Try and leave himself a message, but only if it was safe. Come back. Finish. Nothing else."

Charlie said, "I'm not bringing this up to make you feel guilty. I want you to see that it doesn't matter whether you move six hundred miles south or six thousand. We are all still connected. At the core, at the most basic level, we are all after the same thing. Do you understand what I'm saying?"

Dor Jen nodded slowly.

"Good." Charlie rose from the table. "Now let's go see if we can bring this guy home."

Shane's first thought as she approached the counter was, *I must be insane.*

Her second thought was, *Beefcake.*

As in, the guy she was moving toward. Prime cut of filet. Tall. Early thirties. A model's legs. Great smile.

Then he had to turn toward her and give her that look.

His expression was the one handsome California guys had perfected. The look said it all. How he liked what he saw. But he had known better, and he probably would again, maybe even tonight. But if she was interested, hey, take a number, he might be able to fit her in.

Which was why Shane halted before him and spoke with the crisp clarity of a woman who had surgically removed all nerves. "My name is Shane Schearer."

He set down his spritzer and said, "Shane, as in the cowboy hero?"

"My mother was from Deadwood. She loved Westerns more than just about anything."

"Well, Shane, if that's a line, I'll buy a ticket to the whole show."

He offered a long-fingered hand and a full-wattage smile. "Murray Feinne. My buddy here is Kevin Hanley."

Even dressed in sports togs, the guy she faced was too polished for Santa Barbara. "Mr. Feinne, I'm here to discuss a business proposition."

Murray Feinne's opponent was still struggling to regain his breath. Kevin Hanley coughed and wiped his face with a drenched towel and said, "Good. You do that, Ms. Schearer. Keep him from billing me for this hour. He's already gotten his pint of blood on the court."

"You let me win, Kevin. As usual." Murray's gaze was dark, his features saturnine. He was not even breathing hard. "I'm sorry, Ms. . . ."

"Schearer."

"I don't generally interview new clients outside my office."

"This won't keep." Shane launched straight into her spiel. The words were clear enough. Before she rose from the table she'd been uncertain whether she could recall anything Trent had told her. But standing there, facing this tall, handsome lawyer and his sweating overweight opponent, she found herself basically reciting all that Trent had said. She might as well have read the stuff off a script.

What she didn't expect was the sweating guy's response. Kevin Hanley went from near-collapse to full alert. All in the time it took her to rewind on Trent's pitch.

Murray noticed his opponent's change as well. He asked, "You know about this?"

"Not the application to gaming. But interactive algorithms, sure. It's the new hot thing." He pointed to where Trent sat watching them. "Is that your partner?"

She started to object to the term, then went with, "Yes."

Murray asked, "Why doesn't he join us?"

"He's . . . shy."

Murray snorted. But Kevin nodded, as though the description fit his expectations. "Why don't I go over and have a word."

"Wait." She reached into her purse and came out with Trent's sheet of paper. "This is his work."

Murray said, "I'm not sure that's a good idea, Ms. Schearer."

Kevin said, "Give it a break, Murray. What connection do I have with gamers? That is, other than having lost my two nephews to World of Warcraft." Kevin snagged the sheet of paper. "I'll have a look at his work and see what the guy has to say for himself. Maybe save you some time."

Murray watched him move away. Shane asked, "Hanley is a scientist?"

"Something like that." He shifted his gaze back to her. "I am still not comfortable having such a conversation with a person I don't know under these circumstances, Ms. Schearer."

She caught the note of disdain. That in and of itself would probably have been enough. But the waitress behind the counter chose that moment to glance at her. And smirk.

Shane gave them both a flinty smile and replied, "You're going to like this even less, Murray. My partner and I? We don't have a cent. You do this, you're going to have to wait for payday with the rest of us."

The barrier slipped over Murray Feinne's gaze. She had seen other people in business who had that sort of polished power of denial. Usually they were much older, top-level execs in to give a guest lecture or pick up some honorary prize. They'd get hit on by some eager young student, and the veil would slip down. They would hand out the professional rejection that did not require volume to crush. Just as Murray was about to do.

But before he could form the words, Shane surprised them both by saying, "Tell you what, Murray. Let's go for the best of three at your own game. I win, you work with us."

He showed surprise for the very first time. "You play squash?"

"That's the question, isn't it. Whether I can meet you on the court."

He liked that. He tried not to show it. But she could tell. Murray glanced over to where his former opponent was heads down with Trent. Shane's mystery guy prodded the handwritten sheet and talked with more animation than Shane had seen before. Kevin frowned over the page and nodded in time to Trent's words. The two of them were totally lost to the world beyond their table.

Murray conceded, "It looks as though your partner may have the goods."

"I'll have to bike back to my apartment for my equipment."

"I don't have time for that. I'm sure the pro shop has something in your size."

"Sorry, Murray. I'm just a poor grad student."

Murray reached over and fished a credit card from his gym bag's side pocket. "I'm not that far removed from my own starving student days."

Shane liked the guy's style. A lot. But she said, "I couldn't possibly."

"My time is money, Ms. Schearer. It appears you're going to cost me one way or the other." But the bite was lessened by his smile. "One thing we didn't discuss was what happens when you lose."

"I like your optimism, Murray. Misplaced as it may be."

"*When* you lose, Ms. Schearer." He handed her his card. "You'll have dinner with me."

She accepted the card and replied, "Isn't it a shame how you're going to have to miss that train."

⑾

It had been a long time since new clothes had felt this good.

Murray Feinne held the squash court door open for her. Shane knew he wanted to check out the rear view, and to be honest, he almost deserved the favor. Seeing as how the package was dressed in his money.

Almost, but not quite.

"This is your court, Murray. After you."

"Don't tell me you're captain of the university's squash team."

"UCSB doesn't have one. And if they did, I wouldn't be interested."

He took position on the right quadrant and slapped the ball to the front wall. "You played competition?"

"Never have."

"You're telling me the truth?"

"Rule one in doing business. Never lie to your partners."

He liked that one too. "I could name a few clients who missed that day at school."

Murray took it easy. Lofting his shots, cutting her slack. Shane held back, giving him nothing. Just limbering up, stretching more than she needed to, flexing her back and legs, swinging through the ball.

When it came to sports played in a tight wooden room, Americans tended to go for handball and racquetball. Both of which were oriented toward American mentalities. Handball was brutal, smacking a small hard ball with nothing but a light glove for protection. Racquetball was a bruiser's sport, where body blows were common and the ball bounced enough for the player to anchor himself and fight to control their space. Squash, however, was a dancer's game. It required a lithe body and a long reach. Physical contact was forbidden. An increasing number of women were going in for squash, which had recently been shown to provide the strongest aerobics workout of any competitive sport.

No, she never had played competition squash. But she could have. Easily.

Growing up, Shane's passion had been gymnastics. The mats, the parallel bars, they were her very own private universe. One of the few mementos Shane kept from a fractured early life were the two silver medals from Junior Olympics. Won at age fourteen, the summer before her parents died in the crash and her world fell totally apart.

When she entered university as an undergrad, she had gone in for freshman gymnastics. But the fire had been extinguished. She was so totally detached she could stand at a distance and watch herself perform with the objectivity of a robot. Despite not having trained for almost four years, Shane had been good enough to make the team. But the passion required to reach the top ranks was absent. Her mother had been a gymnast of modest ability and had nurtured her daughter's talents from a very early age. Her mother had never been emotionally demonstrative. The closest Shane had ever felt to her had been in the gym. Her mom had never missed a trial, a competition, an event. Standing on the university's mats had brought back all the lost and lonely days after the accident. Shane had stopped competing before the end of her freshman year and never looked back. Squash had been an afterthought, just a way to release the pent-up energy. And the rage.

Squash was an odd sort of game. The sport was far too intense to be constrained within a tight little wooden box, even one with a rear glass wall. The sport required reactions so swift the best players did not think out their movements at all. The responses went directly from eyes to limbs, bypassing the brain entirely. Shane loved that part of the sport, how thought was an impediment to good play. She loved the electric combination of frantic speed and lithe motions. Both were a gymnast's stock and trade.

Toward the end of their warm-up session, Murray lowered his strikes down to near the bottom rail, powering into the corners, forcing her to move out of her space on the left side of the court. Shane met his strokes but continued to hold back. She saw his smirk and knew the guy was already busy writing her off. A girl with some skill, but not enough force to offer any real competition.

"Okay," she said, catching the ball. "I guess I'm ready."

He spun the racket. Shane called the smooth side and won the serve. She knew she should give it a few points, lull him further. But that smirk of his brought it all back.

She moved to the serving box, turned, asked, "Ready?"

"Fire away."

She showed him a smirk of her own. "You sure?"

He motioned at the front wall. "The clock is ticking, Ms. Schearer."

She crouched, tossed the ball, and unleashed.

Early on she had learned to apply a standard gymnast's move, using her entire body as a catapult, twisting from the hips first, then swinging all her upper body, and finally whipping her arm around.

The ball did not fly so much as explode.

Murray did not even get his racket up in time.

Shane caught the ball on the rebound, said, "I believe that is my point."

9

Kevin Hanley drove Murray Feinne back to ProTech in his new Lexus. Murray was regional outside counsel to ProTech, a specialist electronics firm based in Santa Barbara, Los Angeles, Silicon Valley, and North Carolina's Research Triangle Park. Kevin was his primary contact on the technical side. His job was basically to keep Murray in the dark. Murray had been working with ProTech for three years and he still wasn't clear on everything the company did.

Normally they'd play a few games then have lunch at the club. Kevin usually spent the time complaining over how hard he'd been worn down. Murray knew it was bad form to beat a client as badly as he beat Kevin. But he was extremely competitive. It was one of his defining characteristics. Whatever Murray did, he did it to win.

Which was why he sat in the passenger seat and winced over the scalding he had just received.

Shane Schearer had not just won. She had bullied Murray into one corner of the squash court and beaten him to a sweaty little pulp.

No matter how Murray had schemed and fought and battled, she had just amped up her play.

Murray had barely been able to walk off the court, his legs had been that tired.

Kevin asked, "Did you hear a thing I just said?"

Murray shifted. "Sorry. I was drifting."

He grinned. "Yeah, she whipped you pretty bad."

Murray just ground his teeth.

"I urge you to take them on."

"Not a chance." Murray didn't have to think that one through. "They don't have a cent. They want me to work on a contingency basis. I left that behind years ago."

"What are we talking about here, a phone call? E-Games is still your client, right?"

Murray glanced over. "How did you know about that?"

"What, you think we'd retain you without a background check?"

This was totally new. And far from welcome. "What else did you dig up?"

"Hey, you're clean. Otherwise we wouldn't be having this conversation. Answer the question, counselor."

"Yes, I represent them." E-Games, one of the majors in the interactive games business, was his largest client. "I don't know how long I'd still hold that position if I waltzed in with some off-the-wall idea."

"If this thing is as big as I think it is, they'd be kissing your hand."

Murray rubbed a rising welt on his thigh. He had eked out a win in the second game, grinding it down to a tie break, then pulling off two impossible shots. As he started to serve the third game, he realized his strength was waning. So he tried to take her out with a body shot. Shane not only avoided the blow but spun around and hammered his thigh with her racquet, then spent ten minutes apologizing, her expression telling him she knew *exactly* what he'd just tried to do. No way was he going to do business with that woman.

"I'll think about it."

Kevin drove up to the automatic gate, flashed his badge, and pulled into the lot. He turned off the motor, then sat where he was. "I want you to pay careful attention. ProTech is working with DOD on solving the artificial intelligence puzzle. Recent developments suggest the answer lies in interactive algorithms. What Trent Major showed me back there is miles beyond anything my team of highly paid specialists, working day and night for two years, have managed to develop."

"You never thought it might be worth mentioning to legal counsel that you hold contracts with the federal government?"

"Your remit is commercial. Our DOD work is highly classified."

The guy behind the wheel had undergone a seismic shift. Gone was the somewhat pudgy middle-aged corporate clone. In his place was a man who clipped off his words with scalpel sharpness and whose gaze suggested he would quite happily chop Murray Feinne off at the knees.

Murray said, "So offer Trent Major a job."

"Won't fly. He's a UCSB student, the most liberal campus within the California university system. He's got some exotic blend in his veins, Persian or Arab or something. We could spend years waiting for security clearance. And my team is fully aware of their remit. They have to be."

"Which is?"

"Here's a question for you, counselor. What could possibly require a guidance system that needs to respond to changes in its environment at lightning speed, with a time frame so limited it can't revert back to its point of origin?"

"You're talking self-guided missiles."

"I'm talking directives you can't possibly know about."

"If I take them on as counsel, I'd be legally bound not to discuss anything that transpires within their operation."

The top half of the steering wheel was solid burl. Kevin kneaded the wood so hard his knuckles whitened. "So field an offer from me to buy into their start-up company."

"What?"

"I'll pay your fees. The guy already knows I'm interested. I'll front them capital. Me. Privately. Not my company." Kevin reached for the handle, then turned back to give him another blast of arctic freeze. "Just make it happen. Are we clear on this? If you value ProTech as a client, you will call the lady and connect. And Murray? You are to phone me the *instant* you learn anything more about this guy's work. Especially if you hear anything to do with cryptography or quantum computing."

"But you just said—"

"Remember those words, Murray. Quantum computing. Anything to do with code breaking or cryptography." He thumped his ring against the wheel in time to his words. "Your future with my group depends on it."

10

Kevin Hanley feigned interest in the meeting that followed. Ninety-three minutes later he finally managed to shake Murray Feinne's hand and see him out the front door. Murray tried to start another conversation about the two UCSB students and how they fit into Kevin's other work. For the second time that day, Kevin was forced to show the attorney what he called his secret face. The one he normally covered with the bland mask that the outside world found comforting, safe, dismissible. Kevin had made a profession of letting the outside world write him off. He could see Murray was shaken by this sudden change. Normally Kevin would be angry with himself over revealing the hidden side. But right then he didn't have time.

ProTech's principal facility did indeed have a division that designed guidance systems, both for missiles and jets. That particular group was located in Florida. Kevin didn't have anything to do with their work. The Santa Barbara division was supposedly focused on specialist applications of semiconductors. Kevin was listed as a senior vice president.

But the majority of his work was done in a building that stood to the northwest of the ProTech campus. This particular building was not identified as being part of ProTech at all. A "For Sale" sign stood in the building's front garden, just outside the perimeter fencing. The realtor's number had a Washington area code but in fact was directed to an office at NSA headquarters.

Kevin entered the elevator and used his ID to access the restricted bottom level of their underground parking garage. At the back was a door marked "Supervisory Personnel Only." It was one of those meaningless signs that nobody really saw. The door was grimy and smudged and everyone probably figured it was for janitorial supplies. Nobody spent a second longer in an underground garage than was absolutely necessary.

Kevin paused so that the camera hidden in the roof crevice could get a good look. The door clicked open. He let himself in. He walked to the room's opposite side, where a scanner extended from its perch in the rear wall and took a reading of his retina. The steel door sighed open, revealing a long concrete corridor and a trio of electric carts. Kevin slipped behind the wheel and started off. The corridor was a quarter mile long. It was one of three underground entrances that ran to this building.

The entry on the other side was manned only by a pair of cameras and an electronic voice that ordered, "Identify."

"Kevin Hanley."

"Voice ID accepted." The door clicked. "Welcome, Kevin Hanley."

He climbed the stairs and entered the massive atrium. The ceiling was the building's roof, six stories up. Since the building had no external windows, the atrium was designed to offer the technicians and residents a false sense of space and freedom. All the floors were rimmed by irregular-shaped balconies that faced inward and were rimmed by ferns and flowering shrubs. A kitchen and dining area lined one wall. There were pool tables and large-screen televisions with cordless headsets lying on empty sofas. Beyond a glass wall stood an array of exercise equipment. A lone woman sweated on a Stairmaster. Even without windows or visible clocks, the technicians and residents tended to hold to outside time. By seven that evening the lounge area would be packed.

He went through yet another ID check to enter the eastern lab. Nine years dealing with intel bureaucracy had left him immune to federal paranoia. Until that morning, however, he had assumed this particular lab was an utter waste of time.

He used the phone in the empty reception area. To his relief, the supervisor was both there and available. When Kevin said they needed to talk, Reese Clawson gave him the standard line of being tied up. Kevin begged because he had to.

To Kevin's eye, Reese Clawson appeared so consumed by the flames of ambition that every ounce of other human emotions had long since melted away. She had been distilled down to an essence that left her only half alive. The government was filled with such types.

He drummed his fingers on the counter and went back over his conversation with Murray. He disliked having been forced to show as much of his hand as he had. But that couldn't be helped now. What was crucial was that his disinformation had worked.

Kevin was absolutely not interested in algorithms for the gaming industry. Silicon Valley and Caltech were both full of hyper young brains expanding the world of gaming possibilities.

Kevin had just been blowing smoke in Murray's face. What had him resisting the urge to pace the empty lobby was what had come up in his private conversation with Trent Major. The lies he had spun in the car were simply a means to force the lawyer to act.

Because they had to. Act. And fast.

The door leading back to the labs sighed open and the woman walked out. "Okay. I'm here."

Kevin said to Reese Clawson, "We have a problem."

11

"Coma is a catch-all term," Dor Jen said. She used the kit the nurse had supplied to extract several vials of blood. "In its most basic terms, comatose simply means that the patient shows no sign of interaction with the outside world."

Which perfectly defined Brett's condition, as far as Charlie was concerned. The guy had not shifted position or opened his eyes or changed his breathing patterns once in sixty hours and counting.

Dor Jen pointed with an empty vial to the laptop standing upon a table pulled up beside the bed. Brett's body-feeds formed a series of disturbingly regular lines across the screen. "His brain stem controls heart and respiration. That is the baseline you see there. But activity within the upper lobes is virtually nil."

Gabriella had taken up her station by the foot of the bed, giving Dor Jen and the nurse room to maneuver. "What could be causing this?"

"Certain severe viral attacks can cause comas. Meningitis is the most common form. Has Brett exhibited any flu-like symptoms?"

"No."

"Viral meningitis is only transferred one way, through impure milk products. Has he eaten anywhere with a poor health record?"

"Since he returned from Rome, he left the clinic twice," Gabriella replied. "Both times to eat in Campione village with some of the others."

"Has anyone else become ill?"

"No."

Dor Jen handed the nurse the last vial of Brett's blood, extracted the needle, swabbed the vein, and applied a plaster. "Trauma to the head is the most common reason for a patient becoming comatose. Has Brett fallen? Slipped in the shower? Banged his head somewhere?"

"Not that we have been able to determine. The nurse said the same thing. We checked. Thoroughly."

Dor Jen slipped her fingers behind Brett's head and probed the base of his skull, then along the upper spine. "No sign of external trauma. Which leaves a possible metabolic cause. We need to analyze his blood for possible toxic substances. He doesn't use drugs?"

"No."

"Routine blood tests will scan for possible renal failure or severe liver damage." She straightened and pulled off her latex gloves. "We also need to perform a CT scan and check for raised intracranial pressure. It's possible an artery has burst inside his skull. If so, intracranial bleeding could interfere with normal brain activity. We could also perform a lumbar puncture and check his spinal fluid for any sign of infection."

Charlie heard her doubt. "But you don't think that's the reason, do you."

"Brett is young. He is in extremely good shape. He has not been in an accident or suffered a fall. He does not smoke or take drugs. There have been no warning signs that might point to a heightened risk of stroke or embolism." Dor Jen addressed her words to the motionless man on the bed. "Can you arrange for CT and MRI scans?"

"Not without risking everything," Charlie replied. "We would have to officially register Brett as a patient. We're already under tight observation. I know this for a fact."

"But we'll do it," Gabriella said. "Without a moment's hesitation. If you think . . ."

"No." Dor Jen spoke very slowly. "I don't believe it will reveal anything of use to anyone. Most especially not to Brett."

Charlie said, "Which leaves just one option."

Dor Jen took a long breath. "I suppose I might as well begin."

"You don't understand. I didn't ask you here to go hunting for this guy." When all eyes in the room turned his way, Charlie finished, "That's my job."

⊹⊪⊹

"All I want," Charlie said, "is everything you can give me on what to expect and how to make this happen."

"We've only just started our research. It's far too early to know anything for certain."

"Listen to what she is saying," Gabriella pleaded.

"But we don't have time to wait until the process is perfected," Charlie replied. "Do we." When neither woman responded, Charlie went on, "What have you learned so far?"

"Almost nothing," Dor Jen replied. "Brett helped us design a series of suggestions to project forward to the moment the patient expires. If we could determine a time of death before it actually happened, we could record this in advance. His work would take a huge step forward."

Charlie supplied, "But this hasn't been successful."

"Not so far. We can't seem to move forward temporally at all. We begin the trial. The instructions are received, but the observer remains stationary. Every time we have failed."

Gabriella broke in with, "I dislike hearing you use that word. Failure. We have faced obstacles at every stage, and yet one by one they are overcome. You will do the same."

Charlie was very glad to observe this moment and see the months of friction dissolve in Dor Jen's simple question, "Would you take a look at our data?"

"Other than having Brett safely returned to us," Gabriella replied, "there is nothing that would give me greater joy."

Gabriella had spent the better part of six years researching the brain-wave patterns of people at prayer. Her studies had included Coptic monks in the western Sahara, Dominican priests, Orthodox monks, evangelical pastors. She sought to identify specific brain-wave patterns identified with deep prayer and meditative states. Then, in her sixth year, Gabriella made two discoveries that altered her life forever.

Multiple research studies had shown that if patients were played a pure tone in one ear and another tone minutely different in the other, they did not in fact hear two tones. Instead, the brain registered the sound as a *wave*. And the frequency of the wave depended upon the difference between the tones. The subject could then be given a name for this tone. And once they were brought to a restful state, they could be returned to that very same brain-wave pattern. Simply through suggestion.

But there were problems.

Higher brain frequencies were not simply one pattern. They were a *combination* of frequencies that moved in very complex order, forming this alternate awareness. Brain-wave patterns were notoriously complex and difficult to read. Scientists had spent decades trying to identify patterns associated with specific thoughts or emotions. They failed completely.

Which was where Brett Riffkind came in.

Brett had approached the issue from a totally different perspective. He rejected the notion that they needed to work with certainties. Black-and-white results were impossible, in his opinion, just like no two individuals had the same personality. In brain-wave analysis, Brett suggested, there was only grey. He applied a statistical concept called chaos theory, which states that some patterns in reality are simply too complex to predict a certain outcome. This was where Newtonian physics collided head-on with the quantum world. Newtonian physics demanded that for every action there was a *predictable, measurable,* equal, and opposite reaction.

Chaos theory said nuts to that.

Chaos theory was a series of algorithms designed to show the *probability* of outcomes. Weather forecasting, hurricane tracking, bird formations, all were examples of chaos theory applied to real-life situations.

From the analysis, Brett designed a series of harmonic frequencies that mirrored the *probability* of brain-wave patterns over a multitude of test cases. The result, when applied to trial subjects, was nothing less than astounding.

Gabriella and her team referred to their experimental state as ascents. Controlled, measurable separations of body and consciousness.

The problem was, word got out. It was inevitable. People felt threatened for any number of reasons.

Which was where Charlie came in. Charlie's background was security, by way of some very hard knocks. But nothing, not a landmine in Anbar Province nor saving a UN special ambassador's life in Darfur, prepared him for the first time he met Gabriella. The lady just plain knocked him out of the park, heart first.

⫻

Charlie knew Gabriella was gathering herself, readying all the arguments why they should not try this. And he knew as well as she did that they had no choice. He said to Dor Jen, "Here's what I want you to do. Take Brett's plans for the backward ascents."

"But we haven't even tried—"

"I know that." Speaking calmly, showing all the patience he didn't feel. "But you and Brett spent a lot of time working this through. So it's as clear a direction as we can get right now."

"Charlie." Gabriella swallowed hard. "What if doing this is why Brett is gone?"

"You heard Jorge the same as me. Brett was aiming forward."

"But what if moving against time in *either* direction creates an anomaly?" Dor Jen's voice rose in time to her heightened fears. "What if—"

"How many times have you ascended and returned safely?"

Dor Jen blinked. "It's not the same."

"You've followed Brett's instructions. You've ascended. You return. And no problems."

Gabriella moaned, "I can't lose you."

"You won't."

"But why can't—"

"Think of me as a test pilot. A good test pilot is crazy enough to love risks. It's the law." Charlie raised his hand to stifle further protests. "Something else is at work here. I'm going to find out what it is. And then I'm going to bring our boy back."

12

Charlie stood on the front porch staring over the Chiasso Lake to the peaks beyond. Unlike the previous April, the weather this spring was almost perfect. The air held the incredible mix that was possible only here, in southern Switzerland. The sun carried the Mediterranean punch of heavy heat and low humidity. But the slightest breeze, so long as it came from the north or the west, held an alpine edge. Afternoons like these carried the incredible mix of fire and ice.

He wasn't out here to admire the view. He just wanted to avoid any further arguments with Gabriella. Her face danced in the air before him. She flashed in reflections off the pond's surface. She was there in the flowers. Birds sang, but Charlie heard her voice from happier times. Moments when he managed to hope that they might actually find a way to be together.

Times like these, he feared each day only pulled them farther apart. He could not say exactly why. But Charlie had learned to trust his gut. And right now, his gut was telling him that the lady was lost to him.

Their paths might remain in parallel for a time longer. But the gulf between them was impassable. Sooner or later, she would go her way. And that new way would be along a path he could not follow. What that might be, he had no idea. But standing here, isolated by what was about to come, Charlie found himself staring into a void that the woman would probably never fill.

"Charlie." Elizabeth Sayer walked down the villa's stone steps and followed the path around the lake to where he stood. "We need to talk."

"Can it wait?"

"No."

"All right." Charlie pointed them to a bench out of the sun. Most of the team found Elizabeth Sayer hard-going, a prickly pear whose center offered no real reason to take the trouble. But Charlie knew enough of the woman's past to admire her for making it this far intact.

"Not here." She led him around the southern side of the house.

"I need to get back."

"This won't take long." She stopped where a narrow strip of green separated the villa from the stone wall. This side of the house held no windows. It was as isolated a place as they were going to find on the grounds. "Is Gabriella going to shut us down?"

"Of course not."

Elizabeth's hair was so white as to appear silver in the shade. Her features were an odd mixture of femininity and cold refusal, as though everything delicate and pliable had been frozen into a rigid core. Her gaze was as direct as her words, and as unbending. "Don't be so sure. She's scared enough to go off the deep end. She's already sent away the students scheduled for this week's trial runs."

"We're facing a crisis. We will deal with it. Life will go on. And our work with it."

Her gaze was intent enough to peel away his skin. She must have found what she was looking for, because she nodded once. "All right."

"Is that what you wanted to see me about?"

"No. I have a problem."

Charlie searched his memory, could not recall another time when she had even suggested such a thing. He came up blank. "Tell me."

"Something's been happening inside my ascents."

"Since when?"

"This is day three."

He felt the cold sweep up from his gut to grip his throat. "It started the same day Brett did his disappearing act?"

"The same hour. He was in one chamber. I was in the other."

"What's happening?"

She apparently found it easier to address her words to the side wall. "I ascend. But when I hear the instructions to open my *other* eyes—you know the point, right?"

Charlie recalled the first time Gabriella had spoken those words to him. And shivered tightly with want. "Of course."

"When I do, I'm in a room. It's all white. There aren't any windows or doors. There's no way out. Jorge's been talking me up. When he says to go do what I'm slated to do, I bang on these invisible walls. It feels like I'm bruising myself at some core level. So I told him to stop. Now I just stay. There's a white table in the middle of the room. On it is an envelope." She stopped and blinked hard.

Charlie could hear the breath passing through her clenched teeth. "What happens then?"

"Somebody else is in the room. It's me. At least, she looks like me. She's standing on the other side of the room. She's smiling at me. She says, 'Take it.' That's all. Just two words. When I don't, I feel as though I'm crammed back inside my body."

"How many times has this happened?"

"Seven times. Well, six like I described."

Charlie realized what she wasn't saying. "You opened the packet."

"Envelope. Yeah. I did."

"You should have checked with us first. Especially with Brett like he is."

"Gabriella would have said not to do anything."

"You don't know that."

"I did what needed doing, Charlie. And the only way it was ever going to get done. By myself. What other option is there? You have some way to climb in the white room with me?" She looked away. "So today I went in and I opened it."

"And?"

"There was this flash of images. Each time I felt like I was hooked into a power station. Each image detonated like a bomb. I have no idea how long each lasted, and it doesn't matter. They are tattooed on my brain. When it was over, the room was gone. And so was the woman. Like I had been kept in that room for a purpose. And now I was free."

"Do you want to tell me what you found?"

"Why do you think I'm standing here?" She described what she needed.

When she was done, Charlie summarized just to make sure he understood. "You want Jorge to reprogram an iPod so that it contains both the vibratory patterns and the instructions for an ascent."

"Does that sound crazy?"

"I think it sounds brilliant. Did you ask Jorge?"

"He'll do it if you give the okay."

"Tell him I said it's fine." He waited. "What else?"

"I have to take a trip. Los Angeles. And then Santa Barbara. I need to leave tomorrow."

Charlie could see Elizabeth was very scared. This was totally new. Elizabeth was their in-house warrior lady. All armor and cocked weapons. He asked, "Do you want some company?"

Only when Elizabeth released the tension she'd been carrying did Charlie realize how frightened she'd been that he would let her make the trip alone.

13

S hane was still seated in the sports complex café with Trent two hours later when the call came through from Murray Feinne. Shane lifted her cell phone from her battered shoulder bag, checked the readout, and asked Trent, "It's the lawyer. So how does this conversation turn out?"

"I already told you." If Trent was weary from Shane's repetitive questions, he did not show it. "I saw what I was shown. Nothing else."

She hit the button, said, "This is Shane."

She watched as across the table Trent turned toward the rear door and said her name to the sun-splashed glass. *Shane.*

"This is Murray Feinne."

"Hold on just one second, please." She lowered the phone. "Look at me, Trent."

Trent turned back. "What?"

"You didn't know my name?"

"Not until you just said it."

"You didn't think it might be good to know who I am before you offer me a partnership?"

"You said you weren't comfortable with my questions."

Shane stared at him a moment, lifted the phone, and said, "I'm here, Murray."

The lawyer said, "I think it would be good if you and your partner came to my offices in LA."

"Why not meet here in Santa Barbara?"

"I have just one client in your area. My offices are here."

She felt a certain shift in the atmosphere, as though a tornado was forming, one only she could see. The air grew dense with the friction of compressed energy fields. "Los Angeles is a long way to come for nothing."

"You want to do business with me, but you're unwilling to travel two hours down the freeway?" Murray waited. When she did not respond, he pressed, "Maybe you're not as professional as I thought, Ms. Schearer."

"Here's what I think. You didn't call to set up a meeting. You called because you've already checked out my partner's work. And you want to do a deal."

"I told you before. I don't feel comfortable—"

"This isn't about comfort zones, Murray. This is about profit."

The attorney was silent a moment. When he came back on the phone, his voice carried the same metallic tint she had last heard after whipping the lad all over the court. "Will three o'clock tomorrow afternoon work?"

"Hang on." She cupped the phone. "Any reason why you can't take a meeting tomorrow afternoon in Los Angeles?"

"I teach a class. It finishes at twelve. But I don't have a car."

"Neither do I." That time of day, the journey from Santa Barbara to downtown LA should not take more than two hours. But she said to the phone, "Sorry. My partner and I are free from noon onward, but we don't have transport and it'll take—"

"I'll send a car. The driver will be in touch." He hung up.

Shane made a process of settling the phone down on the table. "He's agreed to work with us. In a manner of speaking."

Trent exhaled a long breath. "So it's happening."

"You doubted it?"

"Not exactly." He drummed his fingers on the tabletop. "Well, yes. In a way."

"You're not a closet nutcase, are you? I mean, there's not some mental or emotional deficiency I need to know about."

"No."

"You don't self-diagnose major diseases on a daily basis."

"No."

"Or consider yourself a witness to alien abduction."

"No, no." He froze. "Unless you think . . . No."

"You think this was aliens?"

"I told you. All I can say is, the algorithm and the images were delivered by what appeared to be an older version of myself."

"In the classroom where you teach physics."

"Tensor calculus. Yes."

"I didn't mean to offend you, asking about mental defects. But I need to know. I mean, we're talking about a partnership."

"You can ask me anything you want."

Shane leaned back in her seat. From recessed speakers, the Steve Miller Band sang an anthem to living in the USA. The jogging machines and Exercycles and Stairmasters lining the balcony were filling with the after-work crowd. Beyond the glass wall at the café's far end, another crew fought it out with racquets and balls. Trent sat motionless, watching her with eyes like frozen smoke.

She knew she should be talking about paperwork, probing more deeply, trying to get a better handle on what had just happened. But what she said was, "When I was a kid, I read a cartoon about some cowboy who lassoed a twister and rode it into the sunset. I haven't thought about it in years."

Trent nodded with his entire upper body. "I know exactly what you mean."

14

The Campione Institute's formal dining room was twenty-eight feet long and nineteen wide. The high ceiling was fashioned from broad mahogany boards that matched the pillars between the three tall windows. The view of sun-dappled peaks and blue waters was hidden behind heavy drapes. Recessed lighting rimmed the ceiling. Normally this chamber was reserved for multiple test subjects, or when Massimo and his group did a joint ascent. Otherwise lone ascenders used either the room now occupied by Brett or one of the upstairs rooms. But Charlie wanted to stay close to Brett, and the monitoring equipment and leads snaking across the floor would have made it impossible to move a second bed into Brett's room. Now that he was lying down, though, he wondered if he had made a mistake.

Gabriella noticed his unease and asked, "What's the matter?"

Charlie didn't want to say what he was thinking, which was, he felt like a Ping-Pong ball inside a packing crate. Just waiting to get bounced around the big empty space. "Elizabeth has to go to America. She wants me to travel with her."

"Why?"

"She's scared."

Gabriella stopped in the process of uncoiling the leads. "Elizabeth? Afraid?"

"Yeah. That's what I thought." Charlie related what she had told him about the ascents. "I don't know if there's anything to her concerns. But I want to be there to offer what support I can. And there's something more."

But Gabriella wasn't hearing him. "Why hasn't she said anything about these ascents?"

"She was worried you might tell her to stop."

"She was correct." Gabriella gestured to the man imprisoned within the room next door. "What was she thinking?"

"Elizabeth was right to do what she did. Her only mistake was to go it alone."

"Has it even occurred to you that there might be a connection between her experiences and what's happened to Brett?"

"Yes, and I've discounted it. And has it ever occurred to you that the last thing we should do is allow our actions to be dictated by fear?"

"What if the fear is justified?"

"What if there is no connection whatsoever between Brett's condition and his ascent? What if we need to keep this isolated problem in perspective and not go flying off the handle?"

The coils of leads lay forgotten in Gabriella's lap. "Is that what you think? That I'm overreacting?"

"Not yet, no. But you would if you tried to freeze further research."

"Perhaps we should. At least until we know what has happened here."

"That would be a terrible mistake. If we let our enemies stop our research, they have already won."

Gabriella looked down at the bundle of wires. "We should not be discussing this now."

Charlie kept his response to himself, which was, *Actually, we're not talking about the real problem between us at all, we never have, and it looks like we never will.*

Gabriella said, "What we're trying to do is already dangerous enough without adding a disagreement to the mix." She reached over and checked his pulse. "You need to be focused and relaxed."

Charlie resisted the urge to pull away. "I'm good to go."

"Perhaps we should wait."

"No. I'm ready." And now he was.

This entire discussion had never been about Elizabeth. At least, not for Charlie. He needed to separate himself from his feelings. He had to take an emotional step back from the draw he felt every time he was in Gabriella's presence. Especially now, when just looking at her was enough to force the flowers of remorse to bloom.

Facing the unknown threat, confronting whatever had locked Brett down tight, was dangerous enough already. He needed to focus. There was room in his world for just one thing. Emotions would only cloud his judgment.

Gabriella said, "Are you sure?"

Charlie settled back on the bed. He had never been after resolution. He was after distance. "Let's lock and load."

Gabriella walked him through the ascent's stages. She could do nothing about the soft musicality of her accent or the allure of her fragrance. Charlie shut his eyes and recalled other ascents, hearing her almost sing the words that counted him up and out of his body.

"Charlie?"

"I'm ready."

Charlie's headphones filled with the now-familiar rush of sound. Gabriella said, "I am beginning the count now."

15

Reese Clawson said, "You're telling me a kid you only just met, what's his name?"

"Trent Major."

"He has somehow mimicked your research."

"No." Kevin Hanley had never had a serious conversation with this woman before. A few words exchanged in the hall, comments shared at joint conferences, sure. But this was different. This was extensive, and it covered a highly sensitive issue. And he didn't know Reese Clawson well enough to understand her speech patterns. He couldn't tell whether she repeated what he said because she needed to claim the ideas as her own, or because she genuinely didn't understand the ramifications. And he needed to get this right immediately. Time was crucial. If she couldn't comprehend the potential crisis, he needed to go over her head. Find someone who understood just how critical this situation actually was. "That's not it at all. If he was copying, it wouldn't matter. He has *surpassed* us."

"One lone kid. Operating out of a second-rate university lab."

"Stop calling him a kid. Most of the top researchers in this field are his age or younger. Quantum computing basically requires the researcher to throw out everything they've learned and start over."

She eyed him coldly. "Explain."

"We don't have time for that."

"You're the one who came to me. I'm not asking for a crash course. I just want to understand the reason for panic."

He wanted to bark at her. Or just stomp out and find somebody who was willing to move at his speed. Which was borderline panic. But he couldn't. He had been involved in the intelligence bureaucracy most of his life. If he didn't give this a serious try, a superior would just shunt him back here again. And then he'd have to deal with Reese's resentment as well as her questions, which were maddening enough already. "If a researcher has been trained in standard computing, everything they know basically has to be tossed out. The challenge of relearning is bad enough. But what's worse is how older researchers feel threatened. Nothing is the same. Right down to the basis upon which the interpretative code is formed. Their entire lives have been wasted."

"So quantum computing threatens the status quo."

"No, no, no." He tugged at what hair he had left. "That's not it at all."

"Kevin, look at me."

"Maybe I should run this by Washington—"

"I know you're one degree off full boil. And I know you're desperate for my help. Which I'm going to give you."

Her flat statement stopped him. "Really?"

"Yes, Kevin. But I have people I need to answer to. And they're going to ask why I allocated time and resources to your problem. I need to show why we're attached at the hip here. And that means I need to comprehend where we're going with this."

The reason he stood here at all was simple enough. Kevin's directive was strictly research-oriented. It might be highly secretive. His team might be under constant surveillance. He might carry a top-level security clearance, and his work might be supervised at the highest level of national intel. But he had no security detail of his own. He was not ops. Reese was. He knew that for a fact. And in order to make this work, he needed someone whose remit included getting their hands dirty.

Kevin said, "My team is working on a specific application of quantum computing. Quantum computing occupies a totally different universe from anything we know in today's world. Okay, yes, someday there might be a quantum laptop in every home. But that is a generation away. Maybe never. Even then, it probably means having a central computer linked to home terminals. But that probably won't work either." He knew he wasn't making sense, but that was the trouble with trying to explain the concept to somebody without the math. "Look. First of all, quantum computers already exist. But there are problems in lifting them beyond a very small number of operational units, called qubits. Huge problems. And there are other problems related to linking the computational functions to the definable world. The world we call reality."

"So while quantum computers might operate at near light speed, the difficulty is in the readout."

"Well, yes. In a way."

Speaking of readouts, this woman was utterly impossible to gauge. She was even more attractive close up like this, the two of them standing within touching distance, separated by the curve of the empty reception desk. Talking in near whispers, keeping secrets inside an empty room. Reese Clawson's face held the frigid splendor of a Nordic goddess, utterly composed, full of a passion that defied mere human desires.

Kevin said, "Quantum computations are almost immediate. Some say the answers exist the same instant that the question is asked. But if you grow the quantum computer beyond a certain point, their ability to compute is marred by what we call interference."

"You *grow* the computer?"

"Right. Quantum computers operate at the sub-molecular level. We grow their structure in a chemical bath. Our work has been with a type of complex carbon structure called prions. We thought we were the only ones operating in that field."

"But this—" She caught herself just as she started to say the word *kid*. And smiled. Her entire face was subtly transformed, from frost maiden to vixen. Then the smile vanished. Leaving only a sultry residue at the pit of Kevin's gut. "This researcher at UCSB shows up, working on the same structure."

"Yes."

"Right under your nose. And you've missed him."

"Totally. He came to us today talking about an algorithm for the gaming industry. It was only when I asked a simple question, as in, what are you doing otherwise, that I learned what his doctoral research was on."

"He's working on the same issues as you."

"Trent Major is *miles* beyond our work." Kevin swiped his face with both hands. "His three-minute overview basically knocked me into next week."

Reese said slowly, "So the crucial problem you're facing is how you've missed him until now, when he apparently pops up out of nowhere."

"Exactly."

"Unless, of course, there is *another* group out there somewhere. In which case you've caught a major break. Because this Trent guy could lead you straight to them. But only if we act fast." She stared up at the camera plugged into the corner opposite her. "Did you tell him who you worked for?"

Kevin felt the tendrils of panic begin to ease. She got it after all. "Not a chance."

"Keep it that way."

"Don't worry." He found himself growing uncomfortable under the intensity of her gaze. Kevin wondered if this was how bacteria felt, trapped on a lab slide beneath the glare of a microscope. "What?"

"How do you know the whole thing wasn't a setup?" she asked. "What if he arrived for that meeting clued in to who you are?"

"Why go to all that trouble to identify my lawyer and pitch him the idea?"

"Is that common knowledge, this attorney working for the games industry?"

"Murray never spoke about it personally. But LA is one giant fishbowl."

"Still, it's worth considering."

"I'm telling you, those kids know nothing about me."

"They're researchers, not kids," she corrected, giving another flash of that smile. "Can you keep an eye on him without drawing attention our way?"

"No problem." Kevin related his offer to acquire a share of Trent Major's new company.

Reese nodded approval and headed for the door. "I'll arrange checks on the woman as well. What's her name?"

"Shane Schearer. How long—"

"I caught the urgency, Kevin. I'll be in touch."

16

Charlie's ascent began normally enough. Gabriella's voice remained steady, a constant metronome counting him through the various mental stages and finally extending his awareness beyond his physical body.

Charlie did as she instructed, hovering there in the room. Always before he had exited his physical form with the objective already in mind. This time, he drifted balloon-like just above his bed and forced himself to look beyond Gabriella and her magnetic appeal. The room vibrated to the emotional turbulence that surrounded him. All attention in the villa was directed their way. Silent, somber, expectant, tense. Everywhere except through the wall beyond Gabriella, the room that held Brett. In that chamber, there was nothing. Charlie studied the wall without reaching out and sensed only a vacuum.

Not a good sign.

Even so, he was fascinated by this extension of his senses. He had never experienced anything like this before. Charlie wondered if this was what happened when the ascender was invited to pause and take stock without taking aim. He needed to discuss this upon his return.

"At my count, you will extend yourself back in time. You will transit to the point at which Brett Riffkind entered into whatever caused his current state." Gabriella was forcing herself to speak in a flat, unemotional tone. Charlie could sense her tension radiating beneath the surface, however. "You will remain in complete control and in total safety at all times. If there is any sign of discomfort or distress or risk, you will return immediately and end the ascent. I will begin the count now, from five to one. At one, you will arrive at that point. Five, four, three, two, one. You have arrived."

The only problem was, he hadn't.

Charlie had only shifted to the room next door. The transition was as straightforward as any he had experienced. What the team referred to as interference, when multiple avenues opened in a storm of images, did not occur. Instead, he had a very clear sense of standing at the foot of Brett's bed. Otherwise, the room was empty. The sense of tension and worry that Charlie had felt emanating from the rest of the villa was gone.

Then he heard another voice.

The shock was so great, Charlie felt his powers of observation waver. This had *never* happened. It took him what seemed like forever to realize that he knew who was speaking.

Jorge said, "You will now extend yourself outward. Go forward to your next ascent. Address yourself. Give yourself a clear signal that a communication has passed between you."

Charlie realized he had shifted back to three days ago. The transition had been so simple, so straightforward, he had not even known it had happened.

But there was no question of this having occurred, not with Jorge saying, "You will now return to the here and the now."

Only, Charlie remained exactly where he was. Observing the still figure upon the bed.

Then it happened.

17

harlie was certain the moment Brett's disembodied form returned to the parlor. He could not actually see the other ascender. But the man's presence was unmistakable. It was as though Charlie could *smell* Brett. A fragrance that was as distinct as the man's voice, or his physical image. Brett was there.

Charlie wondered if he could communicate in some way. He started to move over. He wanted to at least try to make his presence known.

Then he froze.

What if he was the one who had caused Brett to vanish? What if the physicist was so shocked by the sudden arrival of another ascender that it caused him to lose focus?

Charlie remained where he was.

He heard Jorge say, "You have returned to the ascent chamber. I will now begin the count bringing you out of ascent mode."

It was the standard routine Gabriella had worked out with the other team members. The beginning and the ending of every ascent used precisely the same words. There was a reassuring constancy to hearing the terms. It always reminded Charlie of his military days and the homing signal his teams heard when returning from free-fire zones. It was the moment he could breathe safely, knowing they had escaped from danger once again.

Only this time, things did not go according to plan.

The room's opposite side vanished.

The image was so vivid, Charlie wondered if perhaps it had actually taken place on the physical realm. But then Jorge began counting down in his neutral tone. And Charlie knew that whatever it was that was happening, it was restricted to this ill-defined realm.

An emotion reached out. The term was not meant to fit what Charlie experienced, but there was nothing else to describe it. Emotion certainly played a role in the new force that entered the room. Charlie knew it was directed at Brett and not at him. Even so, the lure was enormous. He felt himself being drawn forward. Called by what sounded like Brett's own voice. Only it wasn't Brett. Even as Charlie found himself losing contact with Jorge's droning chant, he knew what tugged at him was not Brett, but some sort of construct. A myth. A lie in the form of a raging cyclone.

The furious energies fashioned themselves around a voice that *imitated* Brett. The lure carried a cyclone of rushing force, a vortex that mawed open, revealing a myriad of dark and lonely halls. Branching and opening and weaving. It was like Charlie could look into the formation of dozens of tornadoes. All sucking and weaving. All dark. One force, one emotion, mimicking Brett's voice and calling him to enter the maelstrom.

The driving force, the lure sucking him forward, was guilt.

Charlie was drawn by a torrential recollection of all his misdeeds. All his selfish acts. All his failures. Pulling him into the maelstrom.

The intensity was so great, Charlie almost missed the voice calling him home.

Gabriella said, "You will return now to the chamber. You remain safe and in total control."

The words were almost sucked away by the maelstrom. Charlie could sense Gabriella's voice being frayed around the edges. Then the voice strengthened. And Charlie returned.

18

The driver assigned to take Shane and Trent to LA was named Manuel. He waited beside a gleaming black Town Car as Shane emerged from the business school. There were a thousand of these limos clogging the LA arteries. A million. Still, Shane found herself wanting to giggle like a teen going to the prom. She covered it by saying, "Aw, I was hoping Murray would spring for a Rolls."

A cluster of her fellow students watched the driver usher Shane into the rear seat, then pull smoothly away from the curb. The cyclists parted like minnows making way for a predator. Shane was dressed in the only business suit she owned, a dark off-the-rack Versace from the Bakersfield discount mall. She had last worn it for a meeting with a court-appointed lawyer handling her sister's most recent mishaps. Billie was not a bad girl. She simply invited trouble. Shane's sister was a magnet for problems that were never her fault.

Shane brushed those thoughts away. Billie wasn't here. Shane was. End of story.

The physics building was attached by a second-story walkover to the newer engineering school. Situated next to the gleaming new structure, the physics department looked like a dowdy old aunt. Shane didn't wait for the driver to come around and open her door. That was only fun in front of the business-school types who took such pleasure in putting her down. She bounded from the car, saying over her shoulder, "Five minutes."

Trent's office was on the third floor, a typical postgrad cubbyhole crammed with books and computer gear and lab printouts. The walls were scarred and blanketed with more paper. The door was open, and Shane could observe Trent talking with an attractive undergrad bent in close enough for Trent to drown in her perfume. Shane could smell the girl from the hallway. Spurred by the young woman's obvious flirtation, Shane stood by the side wall and for the first time saw beyond the oddity of how she and Trent had met.

Trent was dressed in what would pass for a student's idea of formal—ironed denims, stock navy jacket, white oxford shirt with a slightly frayed collar. Shoes old but polished. Clearly the guy had made an effort for today. The student was seated in the room's only other chair. Shane wondered idly if the young woman thought Trent had gone to all that trouble on her account.

His desk was jammed against the side wall, and the student's chair was pulled around beside Trent's. Her skirt was hiked up to mid-thigh and her dark hair shadowed the textbook on the table between them. Shane resisted the urge to walk into their space. She had spent half the night worrying over what it meant to take this guy on as partner. His online records had revealed almost nothing, except that everything he had told her checked out. Now she was feeling jealous? She stayed where she was.

The student frowned at something Trent said, gathered up her books, and steamed out, casting Shane a tight glance as she passed. Then Trent spotted her and said, "Shane! You're early."

The student punched at the linoleum flooring with her clogs. "Yeah,

Shane. Give us a break, why don't you." Then she turned a corner and was gone.

Shane said, "Actually, I'm right on time."

"Which means I'm running late. Sorry." Trent scrambled through the papers on his desk and came up with an elongated notepad. "You won't believe . . ."

Then Trent looked behind her, and went away.

That was how it appeared to Shane, standing now in his doorway, staring into his windowless office that could have used a cleaning crew and a bulldozer. One moment Trent appeared genuinely excited to see her. The next, and the guy was just gone. The body remained. But the light in his face was snuffed out.

"You're here. Good." A man brushed past Shane without glancing her way.

Beach freak was Shane's first impression. She had seen enough of them. Santa Barbara was a haven for deadbeats who hit on the tourists and slept under the palms. The guy wore a tattered surfer shirt, slaps, three days' growth, wild grey hair, ultra-dark Ray-Bans. Apparently Trent's windowless cubbyhole was too bright for this dude.

"Got something for you." The guy dumped a pile of papers on Trent's desk. A few slipped onto the floor. The guy either did not notice or did not care.

Trent stood by the rear wall. Watching without seeing. "When are they due?"

"Tomorrow."

"Which means you've been sitting on them for a week."

The guy was already shuffling toward the door. "Forgot."

Shane entered the office and bent over and picked up the papers. She realized she was holding exams. She set them back on the pile on Trent's desk.

The guy entered the hallway, then turned around. "Oh. My journal article. They need it. Get it done."

Shane waited until the guy's sandals slapped their way down the hall to say, "In the business school, a prof using a grad assistant to grade exams is a firing offense."

Trent picked at a blister on his hand. "Lucky you."

"And you're writing his journal articles. Will your name be on it?"

Trent continued to probe the blister.

Shane finished the thought. "That guy is responsible for approving your doctoral thesis. And he's holding that over you like a Damocles sword. You do his work while he trips away on his next little pipe dream."

"Actually," Trent said, "the professor has developed a taste for prescription drugs."

"You're dying in here." Shane walked over and grabbed him by the arm. "Come on, sport. Your limo awaits."

·|||·

Trent remained silent and withdrawn. He held a steno pad in his hands, the pages filled with calculations. He flipped through them from time to time, then stared out the side window. Shane had no idea what Trent Major was like under normal circumstances. Maybe the guy was lacking the social gene. So she held herself in check until they left Santa Barbara on the 101 and took the curve around Rincon Point, then she asked, "You think maybe you could set your problems aside for thirty seconds?"

"Sorry."

"I know things are rough. But the UCSB physics building has disappeared into the sea mist outside our rear window. And we've got something pretty awesome in the works."

Trent set his steno pad on the seat between them. "You're right."

"Sure I am." She indicated the ocean gleaming a hundred feet beyond the window. "Blink and it's gone. Sort of like life."

He kept shooting glances at the notes he had made. "It happened again."

She needed a minute to understand. "You got another . . ."

"Image. Yes."

"When?"

"An hour before dawn."

She pointed at the pad. "Is that it?"

"Yes."

"It looks, well, complicated."

"It is. Extremely."

"Are you sure you got it down right?"

"Yes. I have an eidetic memory."

"You mean, like, photographic?"

"That's the street name. The correct description of eidetic memory is, a clinician shows the test subject a sheet filled with dots. The dots are in a computer-generated random pattern, usually set in perpendicular and horizontal lines, but not always. The subject has twenty seconds to study the page. Then the sheet is taken away and another is given, this one also covered with dots. But the random pattern is different. Then the subject is given a blank sheet of paper and told to set out all the dots that are on the first page but not the other."

The image beyond her window was lost now. "Why does that make you sad?"

"When I was a kid, I got tested. Eidetic memory is associated with a number of very serious mental disabilities. Severe autism is one. There are others. Much worse. Because I was quiet, they thought . . ."

Shane noticed the driver shooting her glances in the rearview mirror. She leaned forward and asked, "Is there a problem?"

The driver replied, "I just wanted to say, there is a thermos of coffee in the wicker hamper on the floor there."

"Do you want a coffee, Trent?"

"Maybe later."

"We're good, thanks." The driver turned his attention back to the road. But Shane was certain he took in everything they said. "Maybe we should talk about this another time."

"No." Trent kept his gaze on the pad between them. "We can't wait."

She caught the unspoken. Only later did it occur to her how she was moving into sync with this stranger. "Part of the image?"

Trent nodded. "You need to present this to Murray Feinne. Today. He'll know what to do with it."

"You want me to make the presentation again this time?"

"This time, every time. In public, I'll play the ghost."

She disliked how the driver kept shooting her glances. Shane asked Trent, "My taking charge is part of the image?"

"No." Trent's expression was so grave he looked tragic, like a martyred saint she had seen during her one visit to the Getty. "It's just who I am."

19

The driver reported to Murray Feinne by phone, "They talked about some formula most of the way."

At a knock on his door, Murray said, "Hang on a second." He cupped the phone. "Yes?"

His secretary said, "Your three o'clock is here. Shane Schearer and Trent Major."

"Have them wait." When his door shut again, Murray said to the phone, "I already know about the formula."

"This was about a new one. I heard that distinctly." The driver was Honduran but had lived in Texas for eight years and spoke English with an odd Southern drawl. "It came to the guy last night."

Murray used this driver whenever he was ferrying clients who might be hiding something. The resulting information had saved him a bundle more than once. "That's what he said, it *came* to him? Like somebody passed it on?"

"Not exactly. More like, he was up all night checking this thing out."

"A sudden flash of inspiration."

"I guess. They called it an image. The guy's got a photographic memory. Only he called it something else."

Murray wrote the word *image*. Circled it. "Eidetic."

"Yeah, that's the word he used. He said he got tested a lot as a kid. Talking about it really brought him down."

"Did the two of them act like they're an item?"

"Hard to say. They don't know each other all that well, is what I'm thinking. Most of the talk was about this new formula. The guy wants the lady to make the pitch."

No surprise there. "What else?"

"The lady's got your number, man. She's checked you out down to your back cavities. She knows you work for the gamers. She knows where you went to school, how long you been with that firm, she even knows you're up for making partner this year." When Murray did not respond, the driver asked, "You still there?"

"Give me a second." Murray recalled standing on the squash court, waiting for what he knew was going to be a gentle lob. Figuring he could eat this lady like salad. Once again he saw that first service, the girl using her entire body as a whip, the ball rocketing past him so fast he was still gaping when she launched the second service. Five aces in a row. Five.

The driver said, "I got my next pickup waiting."

"One more question. Did they mention the name ProTech?"

"They talked the whole two hours, man. Maybe. But I don't remember hearing that one."

Murray hung up the phone and stared out his side window. His office was on the eighteenth floor of the Universal Tower, the tallest building in Brentwood. He faced straight west. On clear days he could see the Santa Monica Pier extending into a horizon of blue waters and Pacific sunsets. Today the rooftops and green palms melted into the LA haze.

There was nothing unusual about a new client checking him out. But that wasn't the problem. Murray was still coming at this like a game of twenty questions. He hadn't used the driver because he considered these two students potential money spinners. He wanted to know why Kevin Hanley, his largest client after the gamers, flamed on after five minutes with this guy. Murray assumed he'd figure out what was going on, then drop these kids off a cliff. He had never even called the gaming company. Why risk contact with his biggest client over a pair of loser kids?

Meanwhile, the girl was checking out his shoe sizes and working on her next ace.

Murray reached for his phone, said to his secretary, "Show the pair in."

◦│┃│◦

Shane's meeting with Murray Feinne had started off well enough, even after he kept them waiting almost an hour. When they had finally been shown into his to-die-for office, he had come around his half-acre desk and shaken their hands and asked if they needed anything. Treating them like real clients. Trent had hung back, shooting her glances, looking for guidance.

Like she knew how to handle this.

Murray had been cautiously optimistic. He had actually used those words. He had spoken to some possible backers, and one particular gentleman was interested. The executive wanted to know if Trent was interested in a job, because they might be willing to make—

Trent had spoken for the first time since they'd entered the law firm. Absolutely not. No way. Keep that from ever coming up again.

Murray had studied him. Clearly he wanted to ask some questions. But he didn't. Why, Shane had no idea. Instead, Murray had changed the subject and asked if they might be interested in selling a portion of their company.

Shane had been so shocked she had found herself unable to respond. All the possible replies just clogged up her throat.

Murray took that as his cue and said that when he had mentioned their concept to this third party, the executive had expressed an interest in buying shares. Murray thought he could perhaps raise the offer to, say, fifty thousand dollars. For a half interest.

Shane's first thought was, they didn't have a company to sell a part of. But one glance at Trent was enough for her to reply, "Not interested."

Murray took the response as just another opening gambit. The lawyer entering into negotiations, billing by the hour, in no hurry to go anywhere. He pointed out that one good idea did not make a future. At least this way they could relieve some of their obvious financial pressures and—

"Actually," Shane interrupted, "we are here to present a second idea."

As she placed the pages from Trent's notepad on the desk, she had the distinct impression that Murray already knew about it. And recalled glances cast in the limo's rearview mirror.

Murray dismissed the handwritten pages with a flick of his hand. "It may be in our favor to wait and let the gaming firm respond to your first idea before—"

"This new idea has nothing to do with the gaming industry." She smiled around her smoking ire. "I guess the details were over the head of your pal the driver."

Something flickered deep in those dark eyes. The same sort of latent rage she had noticed on the court after she had won the first game. As if the guy hated being forced to take them seriously. "What is it this time?"

"Do you know anything about quantum computing?"

Which was when everything changed.

Murray Feinne was already moving before she finished relating what Trent had said about the new algorithm. Ushering them back out into the lobby. Making sure they would hang there and wait. As if they could go anywhere without another company limo. Murray said he had forgotten about an urgent matter, one that required his immediate attention, stumbling over excuses he didn't even bother to hear himself.

Even Murray's secretary was astonished by their return to the eighteenth-floor reception area.

When they were alone, Shane asked Trent, "Does this make any sense to you?"

"You mean, getting sent back to the waiting room? None at all." Trent stretched out his long legs. "But sitting around this place sure beats playing slave to a drugged-out professor."

◦⫾⫾⫾◦

Dale Partell, senior partner to Murray's firm, was not a man to hurry. He expected the world to slow down to his speed. In Dale's eyes, his primary job was to show the world an air of sublime control. He was the man with all the answers. He could resolve every dispute. Smoothly, discreetly, calmly. Dale Partell liked to see himself as the perfumed oil that could still any troubled waters.

He entered Murray's office without knocking. "We need to have a word."

Murray tried to recall the last time Dale had ever just popped by and came up blank. Dale liked his little formalities. The senior partner's secretary had a honeyed way of turning even a summons into a well-wrapped gift.

Murray replied, "I've got clients waiting."

"The two students from UCSB. I know all about them. Where are they now?"

"In the waiting area. What—"

"I feared that might be them. Really, Murray, the firm's reception area can't be used as a holding pen."

Murray watched in astonishment as Dale opened the door, called for Murray's secretary, and quietly instructed her to offer their guests refreshments. He then shut the door and glared at his junior partner. "I just received a call from Kevin Hanley at ProTech."

Murray felt a chill congeal at the base of his spine. "Oh?"

"Hanley was most concerned. He wanted me to assure him that your new clients were being received with the utmost courtesy and the highest level of service. Naturally, I assured him that the level of assistance offered to all our clients was second to none. What I didn't tell him was, I had no idea what clients he was referring to."

"Actually, Dale, I haven't yet agreed—"

"Kevin Hanley said he'd called just to let me know that if these two students decided to ever take their legal business elsewhere, ProTech would follow them."

Murray said weakly, "I don't understand."

"That makes two of us." Dale pointed at the closed door. "I do not understand how you could leave such important clients stranded in the reception area."

"No. What I mean is, I don't understand what's so important about them. They're just two kids who have come up with a couple of ideas."

"That's where you're wrong, Murray. Whatever else they might be, they are *not* just a couple of *kids*."

"Dale, believe me, I'm doing exactly what Kevin told me to do. His exact words were, soon as they mentioned anything to do with quantum computing, I was to give him a call. Which is why they are waiting in the reception area. So I could call. Kevin told me to sit here and wait until he completed passing on a vital message. I had no idea that meant phoning you . . ." Murray wiped his forehead, felt his hand come away wet. "This is nuts."

Dale crossed the office so that he could glare down without the desk separating them. "How long have you been working here, Murray?"

"Nine years."

"And you're coming up for partner, do I have that correct?"

Murray swallowed. He thought it was all done but the announcement. "Next month."

"So am I correct in assuming that you're interested in remaining here with us?"

Murray wanted to ask, *What am I, chopped liver? I put in nine years of eighty-hour weeks for this?* But Dale Partell's gaze held all the warmth and concern of a guillotine. "Of course."

"Good. I'm glad to hear it. Now why don't you walk me through just exactly who these two *clients* are, and what we can possibly do to improve our standing in their eyes."

20

hane and Trent watched an older man rush past Murray's secretary. He was dressed in pin-striped trousers to a fancy suit and a brightly colored tie and red suspenders and a striped shirt with white French cuffs. His collar held a golden stickpin that glittered in the hazy sunlight as he cast Shane and Trent a worried glance. He entered Murray's office without knocking.

When they were alone, Shane asked, "Do you have any idea what is going on?"

Trent shook his head. "You think this is about us?"

"I don't see—"

The silver-haired gentleman opened the door to Murray's inner sanctum and called for someone named Grace. Murray's secretary hurried over. They exchanged whispered words. The older gentleman disappeared and the door clicked shut. The secretary forced a smile in their direction as she hurried past.

Shane asked, "The image told you to tell them about this formula?"

Trent nodded. "He said it was important we discussed it today."

"You got this formula from yourself again?"

"I already told you in the limo. Same classroom, same older me."

"If it happens again—" Shane stopped because the secretary returned.

This woman set down a polished silver tray on the coffee table. On it were little plates of crustless sandwiches. "Mr. Partell thought you might like to have some refreshments while you waited."

"I'm sorry, we're here to see Murray Feinne."

"Yes, ma'am. Mr. Partell is the firm's senior partner." The secretary hurried away and returned with a silver coffee service. The cups were so delicate Shane could see the woman's fingertips through the china. "How do you take your coffee, Ms. Schearer?"

"White, one sugar. Thanks."

"You are most welcome, Ms. Schearer. Mr. Major, could I pour you a cup?"

"Black. Thank you."

"It is my pleasure." The secretary motioned to the sandwiches. "Smoked salmon is on the brown bread, cheese and cucumber and relish on the white. I do hope that's adequate, Ms. Schearer, Mr. Major. I'm sure the chef could make you something warm, but I don't know how long it will be before Mr. Feinne and Mr. Partell are ready—"

"No, no, this is great."

"Please don't hesitate to inform me if there is anything else you might require." The secretary gave them another nervous smile and departed.

Shane whispered, "You think this is how they treat all new clients?"

"I have no idea." Trent bit into a salmon sandwich, sighed with pleasure. "Perfect."

"Especially clients who can't pay." The napkins were damask and starched. She was almost afraid to lift the cup, it was so delicate.

Trent finished his sandwich, took another, asked, "You were about to say something about the next midnight image."

"Right. If it happens again, you think maybe you could ask what we're supposed to expect when we do what he says?"

"I tried to this time."

She turned in her seat. "You didn't think that might be worth mentioning before now?"

"He only gave me one word." Trent showed her wide eyes. "Boom."

⫸

When they were ushered back into Murray's office twenty minutes later, the attorney appeared on edge. Murray watched nervously as the older guy moved forward to shake their hands. "Shane Schearer, do I have that right? Dale Partell. I'm the firm's managing partner. And Trent Major, a pleasure and an honor, sir. I hope you don't mind if I join you for a moment. Why don't we make ourselves comfortable over here. Ms. Schearer, perhaps you would care to sit with your partner, Mr. Major, on the sofa? Splendid. Can I get you another coffee?"

"We're fine, thanks."

"Excellent. Ms. Schearer, Mr. Major, I am here to assure you that our firm stands ready to do whatever it takes to make you both completely satisfied that your legal requirements are fully met. We offer a standard of service and attention to detail that is second to none. The firm of Parker, Partell, and Bowes is known throughout California as a preeminent . . ."

The older gentleman continued to drone on. In the chair to his right, Murray listened with an intensity that bordered on manic. Shane found herself shivering slightly. Mentally she repeated one word over and over.

Vision.

21

Reese entered the facility's central atrium. The entire building was windowless. The threat of claustrophobia was lessened by muted colors and sweeping ceilings and inward-facing balconies. The sense of space was deceptive. Each segment of the building was tightly restricted. The absence of patrols meant nothing. Every corner, every inch, was monitored.

She found Karla, her chief techie, drinking coffee with Jeff, her security chief. Karla Brusius was half German, half Persian. She had been raised by her father, a mathematician at the University of Cologne. Her mother had returned to Tehran when Karla was nine, searching for a sister who had been picked up by the religious police. Karla's mother was never heard from again. Her father had never stopped mourning. Karla had attended the University of Maryland in an attempt to escape her father's suffocating sorrow, which was where she had been recruited. Her hatred for the Revolutionary Council was cold, reptilian, unending.

Karla greeted her with, "The colonel is in the Treatment Room."

Reese already knew that. "Let's take a walk."

As they started away, the security chief said, "The natives are getting restless."

"Good." This was what Reese had been waiting for. But she couldn't allow herself to be diverted just now. Not with her job on the line. "Take them to the Departures Lounge. Get them ready for one more trial run. Tomorrow we'll test their limits."

Reese had been assigned the building's second and third floors. Her section included a self-contained dormitory, security rooms, labs, electronic monitor stations, and the area known as the Departures Lounge. No one had anticipated needing the additional rooms where she was now headed. Perhaps they should have. But hindsight was for the bureaucrats warming chairs in Washington. Here on the front line, you played the hand you were dealt. The upshot was, one unexpected segment of Reese's group was now located in jury-rigged rooms on the ground floor. Needless to say, these new rooms were where the Washington brass visited first.

She went through the process of vocal and retinal scans before being passed through the two sets of doors. The hospital odors that awaited her were a silent and constant rebuke. As were the pair of hard faces that ignored her approach. "I wasn't expecting to see you today, Colonel."

"You're not the only item on my agenda, Clawson." He used his chin to point through the glass wall. "I see you've managed to lose another trial subject."

Reese turned to stare through the plate-glass wall. She had no need to study the supine figures in the row of beds. She saw them in her sleep. She simply wanted to divert her attention away from the man. "No one is lost, Colonel."

"Dress it up in whatever fancy term you want. We've still got another body to account for. How many does that make?"

"I assume you can count."

"You might think your buddies on Capitol Hill have got your back. But soon as I complete my report, they'll see this for the debacle it is." Colonel Mark Morrow was a human bulldog, right down to the stubby square build and the face that was all jaw and bad attitude. "Nothing would bring me more pleasure than to have you brought up on felony charges. You and all your team. You hear what I'm saying, Clawson? Delighted."

"I still have four days."

"That's right. You do. Enjoy them while you still can." He tapped his Marine Corps ring on the window, pointing to the comatose figures by the nurse's station. "You cost me two of the few and the proud."

"You ordered me to use those soldiers as trial subjects, Colonel. Against my express—"

"Four days from now, Clawson, I'm gunning for you. Coming, Kevin?"

"In a minute."

"Don't waste your time with this one, that's my advice. I don't care who she knows or who she might have once been. Four days from now, she's toast." Colonel Morrow marched down the hall.

Kevin Hanley pointed at the two empty beds at the room's far end. "Expecting more casualties?"

"We're doing the final set of trials this morning. It's where we lost the others."

"Are you sure it's worth the risk?" He surveyed the nine beds. "I mean, how many failures does it take for you to raise the white flag?"

Reese hesitated. Kevin Hanley was a mystery. She had accessed his file and found whole years had simply been expunged. The man had apparently spent his life dealing on the borderlands between national intel and private industry. He was trained as an electrical engineer and had worked on a dozen different projects, mostly related to cryptography and code breaking. That was just what she had been able to access.

Kevin had the ability to vanish in plain sight. He was in his late forties and stood an inch under six feet. He was slightly overweight and tended toward ill-fitting jackets and mismatched ties. Reese knew he was divorced, with two sons who lived with their mother in Chevy Chase. Kevin had the bland features of a pudgy little boy who had never fully grown up. There was nothing to suggest he was anything more than a bureaucrat with scientific training who was now grinding out the years until he could pull his pin and vanish from the face of the earth.

Except for the missing years.

Which was why Reese decided to reveal, "They're not all failures."

That turned him around. "What?"

"We have the initial components of a team."

"Why haven't I heard about this?"

"Because there is success and there is success. And I don't want the colonel out there running around the Pentagon, shouting about half measures."

He nodded slowly. "You're trusting me with a lot here."

"That's right, Kevin. I am."

His smile was perhaps the most attractive thing about him. "If I can get rid of the colonel, you mind if I come by, watch you in action?"

She thought that one over, decided, "This time, day after tomorrow. Upstairs."

"Thanks. Appreciate it." Kevin started to pat her shoulder as he departed, then thought better of it and made do with a nod.

Reese spent another few minutes gazing at the room beyond the glass wall. It had been intended as a lecture hall. Now it held eleven beds, two of which were still vacant. The other nine held six men and three women. They were all hooked up to identical equipment. Reese could hear the beeping monitors through the glass partition. At the room's far end, a bored nurse sat behind her desk and turned the pages of *Vogue*. Her nine charges were all stable. Their heart rate monitors chimed almost in cadence. Their breathing was steady.

Beside her, Karla murmured, "Why won't they wake up?"

Reese did not respond.

Karla said, "Where do you think they are?"

She glanced at the techie. Karla Brusius was not particularly attractive and did little to improve the basic components. Her brown gaze was framed by large tortoise-shell eyeglasses that had gone out of style thirty years ago. Reese could not have cared less. Karla was loyal, diligent, and very sharp.

Reese said, "We've got four days to find out."

22

C harlie Hazard dreamed of Gabriella's eyes.

He and Elizabeth flew cattle class from Zurich to Los Angeles. Charlie had a professional soldier's ability to sleep under almost any conditions, which was good, because their departure had left them little time for rest. The instant their flight hit cruising altitude, Charlie cranked his seat back as far as it would go, which wasn't much. He shut his eyes and was gone.

In his dream, he spoke to a new member of their team. Most of the male subjects tracked Gabriella's every movement, their expressions a unified plea for her to make them her very own personal lap dog. In his dream, Charlie talked with one such subject. Charlie shared what he found most enchanting about the lady, how her eyes held an almost Oriental cast, an upward slant framed by perfect cheekbones and hair like spun onyx. He was pointing out the long eyelashes, the way her eyes cast languid glances his way, soft invitations to stay close, to care for her, to be her favored protector. Then the dream altered, a quiet flash of insight, and Charlie was standing before her. Just the two of them now, and Gabriella stood revealed. He saw how her aloofness was essential to holding their team together. She cared for everyone and was there for them all. Whatever she wanted at heart level was secondary to what the team required.

In his dream, Charlie spoke with a force that resonated through his entire being, a gentle grenade of insight. He said, "You will never be mine." And she responded as he knew she would, with the same look, the same yearning, the same silent message that she had made her choices long ago. All that was left was for him to make his own.

When he opened his eyes, he realized that Elizabeth was watching him. "You okay there?"

"Sure." Charlie dry-scrubbed his face. "Just tired."

"All of a sudden, you started making sounds like you were crying." When he did not respond, she dropped his tabletop and slid over a meal. "They came by a while ago with food. I didn't want to wake you. Not for this stuff."

"Thanks."

"I got you chicken. It was that or congealed pasta."

"Chicken is fine." He was not hungry, but he peeled off the container top and ate anyway. Charlie could feel her eyes on him. He did not mind. They had lived in each other's pockets for almost a year now.

Elizabeth was a biologist who specialized in pharmacology. Her beauty held no welcome, for she met the world sharp-edged and constantly armed. Any trial subject or crew member foolish enough to try their Italian charms was swiftly evaporated. But Charlie found her intelligent, focused, perceptive, utterly trustworthy, a rock in times of crisis. Like now.

She said, "Would you go through that last ascent of yours again?"

"Yes." He waited until he had finished eating. When the flight attendant passed, he asked for a cup of coffee. He folded his paper napkin and set it on the plate. Elizabeth sat and waited. That was another thing Charlie liked about her. She was utterly comfortable with silence. She showed a warrior's ability to wait.

Charlie described the ascent. He did not mind doing so. This was the fourth time he had talked it through, and each time he thought of something new. The flight attendant returned with his coffee, then another offered them water. Otherwise they were not disturbed. The flight's noise created a cocoon within which they talked in utter privacy.

When he was done, she nodded slowly, then began drawing a design on the tabletop with one finger. "So the power sucking you into this tornado was guilt."

"Call it remorse. Regret. Sorrow tied to a wrong deed. They all work just as well."

"I've got to tell you." Elizabeth spaced out the words. "That really rocks my boat."

Charlie sipped at his coffee.

"I mean, if anybody has a reason to be trapped by guilt, it's me."

"Get in line," Charlie said.

"What if it happened to me next?"

He wanted to offer comfort. But he also wanted to remain honest. All he said was, "We don't know if there ever will be another. We've been working on this now for over a year. This is the first time anything like this has ever happened. The question we need to be asking is, why Brett, and why now?"

Elizabeth kept drawing her invisible design. "Do you think what's happened to me has anything to do with this?"

"I've been wondering about that. I don't see a connection. But it just won't leave me alone. How maybe the timing was important."

Elizabeth did not speak again for the rest of the flight. They landed in LAX, picked up their luggage, and took a taxi to the airport hotel she had booked for them. As they stood in line for check-in, she asked, "So what's your thinking on the timing issue?"

Charlie had to smile. Eleven hours and six thousand miles, and the woman's laser focus did not waver. "You're the scientist here. You know the drill. You don't discount a possible correlation. But you also don't let coincidence create links that aren't there."

She waited until they signed in and picked up their keys and were in the elevator to say, "That was the mistake of medieval medics. They tied healings to whatever was closest. And didn't search out the underlying cause."

"Exactly," Charlie said. What he thought was, this was a lesson he needed to keep in mind.

They had been assigned rooms next to each other. Charlie slipped his key in the lock and asked, "What's the plan?"

"The ascent was specific. This afternoon at five, I make the first step."

Charlie's watch read nine in the morning, LA time. "In that case, I think I'll catch a few hours' sleep, then hit the gym."

"Give me a call, I'll go down with you." When he started through his door, she added, "Thanks, Charlie. For not making me do this alone. And for not asking questions I can't answer. I mean it. Thanks a lot."

He turned back. And saw in her expression something he could not identify. "It's what I do."

⫷

Three hours later Charlie woke and phoned Elizabeth's room. He dressed in gym gear and found her waiting in the hallway.

They stopped by the snack cart in the front lobby. Charlie bought her a muffin and a coffee. Elizabeth stood beside him at a narrow circular table. The lobby was on the second floor, above a conference center and a gym that catered to the surrounding businesses. Outside the lobby's massive windows, the sun shone in a pale blue sky. Charlie could see the tops of several dozen imperial palms. The lobby was large and very full and framed in marble. The noise was a cacophony that isolated them completely.

Elizabeth broke off a segment of her muffin and said, "You need to go back and observe Brett in the lead-up to his vanishing act."

He nodded. "I thought of that."

A trio of businessmen approached the coffee cart. They paused in their discussion to inspect Elizabeth. Charlie could understand why. Her gym shorts accented legs that looked sculpted. If the woman carried any excess body fat, he could not see it. Her hair was a silver-blonde spray. She stood very erect, her frame both muscled and intensely feminine. If Elizabeth even saw the businessmen, she gave no sign. "You should probably investigate what Brett was doing before his ascent. See if there's any connection."

"I asked Massimo and his team to cover that base."

She broke off another piece of her muffin. "Massimo. Great."

Elizabeth's attitude toward the Italian students was shared by most of the other team members. The group remained the only ones who could ascend and co-mingle. If they could do anything else, either jointly or individually, no one had identified it. All ascent instructions were ignored in their quest to come together. Otherwise they were friendly, cheerful, and ever eager. They helped the cook and washed dishes and scrubbed floors and broke into song as they worked. The rest of Gabriella's team treated Massimo's group like mascots.

Charlie said, "Give them a specific task, they do just fine."

Elizabeth lifted her coffee cup and huffed softly.

"Gabriella thinks they are going to play a vital role."

Elizabeth drank her coffee and did not respond. The whole team knew what Gabriella thought about Massimo and his group. Charlie knew they thought Gabriella doted on them to a ridiculous degree.

Charlie directed them to the rental agency in the hotel lobby and booked a car. Then they went downstairs. The gym was as vast as everything else about the hotel. A battalion of Exercycles and jogging ramps marched down the outer glass wall. Elizabeth draped her towel on an empty Stairmaster, unfolded a warm-up pad, and began stretching. Charlie moved to the free weights. He had no interest in bulking up. He used free weights as part of his own warm-up system. He used light weights and did forty, fifty reps of each position. Shoulders, lats, chest, arms, thighs. Charlie avoided his reflection in the surrounding mirrored walls. He disliked the scars that emerged from his tank top and the memories that were bound to them with the intensity of flash grenades. A woman on the nearest mat angled toward him and spread her legs, then smiled as she gripped one foot. Charlie wondered if he would ever consider such unwanted offers as anything more than reminders of past mistakes.

When he was sweating and breathing deep, he walked over to the empty space by the mirrored rear wall. The area was clearly designed for exercise classes but was empty now except for a long-legged woman using the bar to perform dancers' stretches. He paced off the free area, his head down, making a careful sweep of how much space he could safely take up. He moved over to the side wall. He stared out the lone window at the sunlit traffic and held the position until his mind cleared. There was no crowd, no blaring music. No room.

He did a series of stomach exercises. Then he began a series of simple strikes, taking it slow, working them like stretches. Charlie held each pose to where his body was forced to find impossible balance. Drawing everything down to the center. To the core. Planting himself in the earth of LA. Being entirely where he was.

He moved into a series of katas. Gradually he accelerated. Allowing himself to extend his reach, flying up on the kicks, launching himself fully now. Spinning and weaving until the light took shape and became his adversaries, and even they could not match his speed.

He finished by decelerating, then moving back into simple strikes, then a series of stretches. A long continuous flow that he maintained until his breathing and his heart rate were back to normal. At which point he realized the entire gym was watching him.

Elizabeth stepped off her machine, wiped her face with the towel, and walked over. "Ready to go?"

⠼

They had the elevator to themselves. They were silent until Elizabeth pointed at a spot above Charlie's collarbone where the sweat-drenched T-shirt revealed a deep cavity. "What caused that?"

"IED. Iraq, sixteen klicks from the Syrian border." Normally Charlie hated any attention drawn to his various injuries. But something about this woman and her conflicting mix of feminine beauty and prickly strength erased his normal reserve. "I had been up country for less than a week. We went out on patrol. Benny Calfo, my NCO, was on point. He claims I smelled the blast before it happened. I remember a click. Benny swears there wasn't any sound. I shoved him into a ditch. I caught a frag."

"Those burn marks on your neck are from the blast?"

"Some of them. The rest are from a traffic accident." The one that had killed his wife.

The elevator doors opened. Elizabeth followed him down the hall. When he stopped in front of his door, she said, "You don't have any idea at all, do you."

"Sorry, I don't track you."

She punched the plastic key into her door, like she was angry. Furious. With him. "You want to step in here a minute?"

"I should shower."

"This won't take long." She didn't wait but entered the room. When Charlie followed her inside, he found her standing in the middle of the room. Her arms were banded about her middle so tightly her shoulders and her neck were corded and bunched. Charlie figured he was about to catch incoming fire. But for the life of him he could not figure out what he had done wrong.

"Did you ever wonder why Julio left for Rome like he did?"

"Yes, as a matter of fact." Of all the people to depart with Dor Jen, losing his number two security guy had shocked him the most. Charlie had been more than a little hurt that Julio had taken off without a word or backward glance. In fact, Charlie had not even known Julio was considering the shift until a team member told him the man was gone. He had not heard from Julio once since then. This from a man he still considered a close personal friend. Charlie recalled, "You were the one who told me he'd taken off."

106

"That's right."

"You said he had a thing with Dor Jen."

"He did. Does."

Which had been good for another total surprise. "I always thought, well, you two . . ."

"He wanted it. I couldn't." Her shrug was a fullback's move, pushing aside the opposition. "He left."

Charlie's confusion left him only able to say, "I'm sorry."

She burned him with her gaze. "Did it ever occur to you why I couldn't be the lady he wanted me to be?"

"I figured it was—" Charlie stopped. "Are you saying . . . me?"

"Gabriella really has left you blind."

"I hope not," Charlie said. "For all our sakes."

"Yeah, well. That's how it is. I just thought you should know."

"Elizabeth . . ."

"Don't say anything. This is awful enough already. And don't worry. I won't make a fuss."

Charlie tasted several comments. But nothing he could think of would make any difference at all. He nodded and turned and opened the door and stepped into the hallway. When the door clicked shut behind him, he released a quiet, "Oh, wow."

⫶⫶⫶

Charlie tended to travel very light. He showered and dressed in the one decent outfit he had brought, the standard uniform from his corporate security days—grey slacks, dark single-breasted jacket, white shirt, rep tie. He examined his reflection in the mirror. He had never much cared for clothes, another reason why the civilian life had fitted him like somebody else's suit. He thought he looked exactly like what he was, a tough security agent trying to disappear. The burn scar still crawled from his collar, and his shoulders still bunched the jacket in an unsuitable manner, and his eyes were still agate hard.

But nothing, no hours of anticipation, would have prepared him for what he found waiting for him when he knocked on Elizabeth's door.

Gone was the bad attitude and the radical clothes and the spiky hair. In its place was a woman whose short hair was styled and coiffed, her makeup perfect. Charlie had never seen Elizabeth wear cosmetics before. The result was beyond striking. The hard-edged features and the unspoken threat were smoothed and refined and distilled into pure allure. She wore a suit of café con leche silk. The skirt was short, her stockings patterned, her heels high.

Charlie said, "Whoa."

Elizabeth winced in the manner of receiving what she most feared. "Ready to go?"

"What I mean is, you look great."

She strode past him and out the door and down the hall. Charlie followed to the elevator. At least the silence was the same.

Elizabeth's genuinely fine looks and short skirt acted as a magnet for virtually every male's gaze they passed. Charlie assumed the show was for his benefit, and he wondered what could possibly have been the right response to keep the woman from being hurt more than she already was. They left the hotel and crossed the parking lot to the rental agency's numbered spaces. The car was a grey Maxima.

Charlie unlocked the car and held Elizabeth's door. He slipped behind the wheel and started the engine. "Where to?"

Elizabeth even sat differently. Gone was the powerful ease of a lazy cat. She sat with the careful composure of a lady headed to her own funeral. "I need you to know what happened in the ascent."

"Sure thing."

"I went home." She shook her head. "Wrong word. That place was never my home. I went back to the house where I was sent off from. I was dressed in this outfit. Not clothes like this. This exact suit."

Charlie huffed a quiet laugh. At himself.

Elizabeth might look like a totally different woman. But her skills of perception were still precise. "You thought I dressed like this for you?"

He nodded. "Put it down to typical male ego."

She studied him a moment longer. "If I thought it would make a shred of difference, Charlie, I would burn my whole wardrobe. For you."

That shut him up.

She turned back to the front windshield. "Turns out our hotel has a small clothing store in the lobby. It caters mostly to the tourist trade, but there are a few outfits for travelers coming in for conferences. I found this. In my size."

"It looks like it was tailored for you."

"I know."

"What happened then? I mean, in the ascent."

"I went home, like I said. My father was dying."

"I'm very sorry, Elizabeth."

"Don't be. In the image, you weren't with me. Do you think that matters?"

"I have no idea. I can drive over and wait outside."

"If I get to the house and he isn't there, or he isn't ill, we can cut things short and head back to Switzerland, right?"

"We can do whatever you like." Charlie watched her face constrict and realized she was fighting back tears. He had never seen the woman cry. "You sure you're up to this?"

Her nods grew to where they rocked her upper body. "Seeing Daddy is one thing. I can handle that. But what came after gives me nightmares."

23

Murray Feinne pulled into the UCSB admin parking lot, wondering not for the first time what he had gotten himself into, and why.

He had done his undergraduate work at Yale, then returned to his native Bay area for law studies at Stanford. He had edited the prestigious *Law Review*. He had spent a year clerking for the head of the California Supreme Court. He had fielded offers from every major firm in the western United States. He was on the cusp of making partner.

And now this. Playing flunky to a couple of UCSB students. Who couldn't pay him. And yet had the power to threaten his career.

For today's meeting, Murray's senior partner, Dale Partell, had wanted him to rent a suite at a resort spa in the hills above Santa Barbara. The spa catered to the Hollywood crowd, and a standard room cost over a thousand bucks a night. Murray had pointed out that such a setting might be a tad over the top for a couple of starving students. Dale Partell had acquiesced, but only after phoning the university president and personally describing their keen interest in this pair. Since several of their clients were alumni with deep pockets, the UCSB president had offered them his own private conference room.

The secretary knocked on the open door. "Your guests are here."

Murray rose to his feet. "And right on time."

The words sounded lame even before they emerged. But he doubted either Shane or Trent heard him. They were too busy taking in the opulent fittings, the high-backed leather chairs, and the massive oval table. The room was as close to a royal audience chamber as the California university system possessed. The view was out over Del Playa Park and the tidal pools. The Pacific glowed a fierce blue in the afternoon light.

Shane took in the trio of chandeliers, the high-tech video conference center on the far wall, the damask drapes in the university colors, the president's own silver coffee service resting on the antique sideboard. She said to Trent, "Maybe you should have gone with the tie after all."

Murray dismissed the secretary and personally served them coffee. Which was overkill. But he could feel his senior partner's breath on the back of his neck. He opened the first file and walked them through the basic articles of incorporation, the structure of shares, all the things he had done a million times before. Hoping they did not notice the occasional quiver to his voice. Trent Major sat back in his chair and watched with calm disinterest. But there was nothing detached about Shane Schearer. The lady was totally on, her questions precise.

He asked the president's secretary to witness their signatures and notarize the documents. When they were alone once more, he opened the second file, swallowed hard, and said, "I haven't been as successful with the gaming company as I would like."

Shane and Trent exchanged a glance. "They didn't go for it?"

"No, no, not at all. But they say it's going to take months to see whether the algorithm performs as you describe." Murray had lain awake all night worrying over how to handle this next bit. He still wasn't certain. But the recollection of being assaulted by the lady's service echoed through his brain. So he gave them the truth. "I've worked with this group for over three years. I consider the company president a personal friend. And I could not read him. I couldn't tell whether we're getting jerked around or they genuinely don't know what to do with your concept." Murray slid the unsealed envelope across the table. "This was their best and final offer."

Shane pulled out the slip of paper. Didn't speak. Trent leaned over. Read, "Ten thousand dollars."

"It's peanuts. I agree. But they wouldn't budge. The best I could do was one percent of revenue from any game that employs your concept. Which is paltry."

Shane said, "Take it." She looked from the check to her partner. "Right?"

"Absolutely."

Murray found himself sweating. Which was nuts. "I could approach another group—"

"No," Shane said. "We stay with this company. You know them. The deal is a good one."

"It's hardly what I would call—"

"How much does a new game make?"

Murray checked the pages just to give his hands something to hold. "Their last hit was Mars Attack. It was released last June and has sold six million units."

"There's your answer," Shane said. "How much do their gamers pay for online access?"

"A monthly fee of nine dollars. Which doesn't sound like much, but . . ."

"Most of these players are in their teens," Shane supplied. "Nine bucks a month is a major financial hit. The residuals are huge. At one percent of the gross—that was gross, right?"

"I did manage to negotiate that. Yes."

She said to Trent, "The game retails for seventy bucks a pop, half of that goes to the company. Say a third of the gamers are online any given month. If we were part of a game this big, our payout would be . . ." She looked out the side window. "In the first twelve months we'd walk away with two and a half million dollars."

Trent said, "Take the deal. Definitely."

Once they had signed the documents and Murray's secretary notarized their signatures, Shane tried to return the envelope. Murray said, "The money is yours."

"What about your cut?"

Here it came. "All initial fees have been set aside. A goodwill gesture on behalf of my firm."

"Is that normal?"

"It happens occasionally," Murray replied carefully. Every inch the cautious attorney. "When we are seeking to establish long-term relationships with clients whom we deem of particular interest."

Shane looked at him. "Did you practice that all the way up from LA?"

"Excuse me?"

"Come on, Murray. Put yourself in our shoes. One minute we're struggling to get in the door, the next and your company is comping us? Doesn't that sound just the teeniest bit weird to you?"

In response, he opened the third and final file. "You remember Kevin Hanley?"

"Your squash partner." Shane smiled. "Sort of."

The lady had a beautiful smile. It transformed her from stern and mysterious to childlike. All by the shifting of her facial muscles. Even Trent was mesmerized by the sight. Murray had the sudden impression that she did not smile often. Which was a shame.

He said, "Kevin Hanley is a very important client. He has made a second offer to acquire an interest in your newly formed—"

"No," Trent said.

Shane turned in her seat. "You don't want to hear the guy's offer?"

"No other partners. That's final."

Shane shrugged. "You heard the man. Sorry, Murray."

Murray closed the file holding the first agreement and replaced it with the second. "In anticipation of your rejection, Kevin Hanley has tabled a different offer. He is very keen to work with you on an ongoing basis, however you want to see this happen. Kevin has found your second concept to be of extreme interest."

Trent asked, "You showed him the algorithm related to quantum computing?"

"Your instructions as I read them were to patent the concept and find someone willing to acquire the process outright."

"Trent isn't complaining. Are you, partner?"

"No. It's just . . ."

Shane studied him. "What?"

"Nothing."

"You sure?"

"Yes. I just wasn't expecting anything this fast."

Shane wanted to ask him something else. Murray could see the strain it caused to hold back. But she turned to him and said, "So Kevin Hanley is interested in my partner's work."

"Interest doesn't begin to describe it." Murray slid a second unsealed envelope across the table.

This time Shane was longer in responding to what she found inside. "A hundred thousand dollars."

"Actually, if you'll look once more I think you'll find there are two checks. Each for the same amount."

Shane pulled out the other. Set them beside each other on the table. Trent watched her fingers trace their way around both borders. He did not speak. Or move.

"The first check is to acquire sole proprietary rights for the usage of your formula. The second is initial payment for a long-term arrangement. Kevin Hanley wants first rights to whatever you discover next."

"So this is an advance on future work."

"Exactly. In exchange, Kevin wants your promise that you will show your work to no one else. He has six weeks to examine—"

"That's too long."

Trent said, "No it isn't."

"Six weeks is an eternity. He could rework your next concept and claim it was his all along."

"Then what happens to the concept after that one?"

Shane clearly didn't like it. But all she said was, "Since Hanley is such a power around your firm, how can we be certain you'll act in our best interests?"

Murray nodded. It was the right question to ask. "You are my clients. I am required by law to represent your best interests in all matters."

She asked the next question to her partner. "And if there's a conflict between Hanley's interests and ours?"

Trent shrugged. "We've got to trust somebody, Shane. And this guy came highly recommended. To say the least."

Murray started to ask where they had gotten his name. But Shane chose that moment to rise from her chair. She asked Trent, "You mind if I have a word alone with Murray?"

"Of course not."

"Hang tight. This won't take long." When they were outside, Shane lowered her voice and asked Murray, "You think maybe you could work it so I speak with the university president?"

The secretary was on her feet behind her desk. "Actually, Ms. Schearer, the president has mentioned that he would very much like to meet you and Mr. Major both."

"It'll be just me and our attorney." She motioned with her chin. "Let's go, counselor."

24

In California, university presidents within the state system held less power than elsewhere. Statewide regents retained most authority over budgets and investments. Even so, the UCSB president's office was suitably grand, done in shades to match the seal woven into the carpet and the drapes. The president was the former CEO of the largest bank still based in San Francisco, a smooth operator long used to hosting powerful egos. Murray had met him on a number of occasions and knew the man could lie with utmost sincerity.

Shane gave the president three minutes, scarcely enough for the guy's standard windup. Then she interrupted with, "I asked for this meeting because we have a problem."

The president's face was a marvel of modern medicine. He had been Botoxed and de-lined and stretched and chiseled so much that not even his million-dollar tan could hide the scars bordering his hairline. "Actually, Ms. Schearer, I was the one who requested—"

"My partner, Trent Major, is doing his doctoral work under a menace."

He blinked. "I assure you, madam, that the UCSB faculty are drawn from the highest echelons of their specialties."

"Maybe when you hired him. But that was then and this is now. Trent's supervisor is hooked on something. Trent says it's painkillers, but my money is on a stew of his own personal blend. Trent Major is teaching the professor's classes. He's writing the guy's articles, and he's being denied credit. He is grading the druggie's exams. He is being held hostage because this prof has the power to shred Trent's thesis and chop my partner off at the knees."

When the president began his polished protest, Shane glanced at Murray and mouthed two words. *Your turn.*

Murray had not clawed his way up the legal ladder without learning how to ad lib. "If I may interject, sir. Two of your major donors are most concerned that everything possible is done to ensure that this problem disappear."

Shane said, "Reassigning Trent to a sober professor would do for a start."

The president made a process of adjusting his spectacles and tapping keys and inspecting Trent's online file. "I see that your partner is researching an issue related to quantum physics. Certainly we could look into some sort of alteration in his present circumstances, but as you can imagine, these things take time."

"Take all the time you like," Shane replied. "So long as Trent is reassigned by tomorrow morning."

Murray halted the president's protests with, "My clients are not interested in pressing charges against the professor in question. Nor do we have any desire to see the university's good name dragged through the mud. But we do intend to see this situation rectified immediately."

"And Trent needs a better office," Shane said. "One with a window."

Murray lifted her with his eyes. "And I can personally assure you, sir, that this issue will not have any detrimental impact whatsoever on the level of my firm's donations to your fine institution." He offered the president his hand. "Just so long as the matter is seen to by the close of business today."

Shane shook the president's hand. "It's been great. Really."

When they were back in the president's outer office, Shane gave Murray another of those full-wattage smiles. He was expecting something in the manner of a job well done, pat on the back, maybe an invitation to dinner. Instead, she said, "About the second part of Kevin Hanley's offer. We'll take his second hundred thousand. And we will agree to giving him full initial rights to the next formula only. Beyond that, we will need to have a serious conflab."

"I doubt Mr. Hanley will be thrilled with your decision."

"Tell him it's that, or we will return the check and put the next concept up for public bid."

"I am sure that won't be necessary." Murray studied the woman. And finally accepted that he had met his match. "I'll need to make a quick phone call to confirm."

"Be my guest. Meanwhile, I'll pass this by my partner. But before we sign on the dotted line, I'm worried about just one thing. And you know what that is, don't you."

The sense of cold dread returned. "Ms. Schearer, I assure you that your interests are my foremost concern."

"I'm glad to hear it." She patted his arm. But her smile was all for the secretary's watchful eye. "I'd hate to ever need a word with Mr. Partell. Wouldn't you agree?"

Murray didn't realize he'd forgotten to ask where they got his name until he was on the 101, almost at his exit for Malibu Hills. He made a mental note to get that information the next time they met up.

But by then it was far too late.

25

Charlie took the 101 to the Sunset exit and headed east. Elizabeth directed him through Bel Air's main gates. They drove down velvet-smooth roads sheltered by flowering shrubs and imperial palms. The air through his open window was heavy with exotic blooms and eucalyptus and heat. The LA haze cast a thick pallor over the sky. A swan hissed at Charlie as he drove past the Bel Air Hotel. Elizabeth directed him into the second entrance past the country club. Charlie pulled up to the wrought-iron gates and waited as Elizabeth stepped from the car. She stood before the recessed camera, spoke a few words, then watched as the gates cranked open. Not moving. Staring down the drive. As grim as Charlie had ever seen her.

The winding lane carried them through acres of sculpted gardens. A pair of hummingbirds swooped in for a close look through Charlie's open window, as though astonished that he had the gall to enter the grounds.

"Welcome to the house that pain built," Elizabeth said.

The manor was gargantuan, a stone and brick monument to an LA-sized ego. Elizabeth unclenched one arm from around her middle long enough to point at the tallest of the three turrets and say, "My prison."

Charlie's tires scrunched over combed gravel. He halted before the sweeping stairs. Before he cut the motor, two dark-suited security were already moving toward the car.

Elizabeth said, "Stay in the car."

"I can come in with—"

"I told you. The problem isn't here." She rose from the car. "I won't be long."

⫿⫿⫿

In fact, she was gone almost two hours. When she emerged, one of the security detail shepherded her over to where Charlie stood holding her door. By the time he started the car, Elizabeth had wrapped her arms back around her middle and resumed her tight rocking.

Charlie retraced his way out of Bel Air, taking it slow. He did not speak until they arrived back at Sunset. "Which way?"

"Left. Downtown." When he accelerated into traffic, she said, "It was harder than I thought."

Charlie rolled up their windows, shutting out the city noise.

"Daddy's tombstone ought to read, 'He never met a pain he didn't like, long as it wasn't his.'"

"What about your mother?"

"She left him. And me. I was four. She married an Austrian baron. He didn't like me."

"You mean, he didn't want kids."

"No, Charlie, my stepfather despised me. It was very personal with the baron."

Charlie drove them through Beverly Hills and gave her the silence that statement deserved.

Elizabeth said, "In the ascent, I saw myself apologizing to Daddy.

And then I forgave him for everything. Those were the words I used. In the image, it all came out smooth as silk. Easy. Like I almost sang the words. In there, I felt like I was choking. Saying the words cut off my air."

"But everything else was as you observed in your ascent?"

"The room, the bed, my father, everything. He was awake. He watched me but he didn't say anything. I don't know if he could even respond. We never talked unless we were fighting. In my entire life, up to this moment, I have never apologized to him. For anything. Maybe the shock is what kills him." She glanced over. "Bad joke. Sorry."

Charlie passed through the invisible barrier separating Beverly Hills from West Hollywood. The road lost its silky polish. The palms wilted. The buildings grew tawdry. Billboards sprouted. The traffic turned aggressive.

"My grandfather started the company. Sayer Pharmaceuticals turns pain into gold. That was actually how my grandfather described it. The company's sole focus was on identifying a pain and manufacturing a drug that stopped it. Everything from hospital anesthetics to over-the-counter tablets. My father hired PR companies to weave a nice set of lies, but he was the same thug as his old man."

"Where are we going now?"

He could actually see the shudder wrack her frame. "To meet the company's latest villain-in-chief."

⊹║⊹

The Sayer Pharmaceuticals headquarters occupied an entire city block in downtown Los Angeles. It rose in a spiral of steel and glass, like the tip of a spear ninety stories high. Charlie must have looked impressed, because Elizabeth said sourly, "*Architectural Digest* called it the world's largest pickle. I always thought the shape was fitting for a company that stuck it to the human race when they were weakest."

She directed him into the underground lot, and he parked in a visitor's space. Elizabeth said, "I need you with me this time."

"No problem."

They took the elevator to the main lobby. A clone of the guards at the Bel Air house was there waiting for them. "Mr. Sayer is expecting you."

The guard led them to the last elevator fronted by a velvet rope. He swiped a card over the controls and unclipped the rope. He waited for them to enter, joined them, and used the swipe card a second time before hitting the button for the penthouse. Elizabeth stepped over close to Charlie's side. He stood very still, feeling her tension and her heat.

The elevator deposited them in a small antechamber, where yet another dark-suited guard stood waiting. "This way."

The penthouse foyer had a spectacular view of the LA haze. The ceiling peaked some eighty feet over Charlie's head. The glass must have been polarized, because the clouds and sky were tinted a dusky bronze. The guard escorted them to an empty waiting area. The entire area was very minimalist. The secretary's desk was a single slab of onyx on legs colored to match the sky.

Elizabeth said, "In my ascent, two men come up now. They both wear pin-striped suits. They are the company's senior in-house attorneys."

"Is there anything you want me to do?"

"You didn't figure in my ascent, remember?"

"Who are we meeting?"

"My elder brother, Joel." She was silent for a moment, then added, "Don't be fooled by his smile. He is a fiend."

The elevator pinged. Two men emerged. One wore a navy suit with chalk stripes, the other slate. They walked past without acknowledging Charlie or Elizabeth.

When the secretary rose from her desk, Elizabeth whispered, "Here we go."

The president of Sayer Pharmaceuticals occupied a suite of offices decorated in a color that Charlie could only describe as mink. Not brown and not grey, but a lot of both, with some gold mixed in for good measure. The desk was smoky quartz. The lone decoration was a sculpture of the building done in gold and gemstones.

A sleek wolf was seated behind the desk. The two lawyers stood behind him and to his left. The wolf did not smile so much as expose his teeth. "My dear sister. How lovely you look. And what a marvelous suit to hide your tattoos."

Elizabeth did not move toward the desk so much as drift across the room. Charlie walked a half step behind her, ready to offer a supporting hand if required. But she remained erect and steady. There was no visitor's chair. She did not seem to care. Charlie was not certain she noticed the insult at all. He walked over to a conference table by the far window and brought back one of the leather chairs.

"Thank you, Charlie."

The wolf did not like it, but he didn't say anything. Just cast a languid glance in Charlie's direction. A silent promise. "And does your Charlie have a last name?"

Elizabeth crossed her legs. "Yes."

Then she waited.

The wolf smirked. "I know you went by the house. I know you forced the nurse to leave my father's side. I also know that he did not speak. You see, we anticipated your arrival. We monitor the room twenty-four hours a day. I found your little speech very touching, by the way. Quite a performance, considering the source. But even if you had extracted something from Father, it would hold no legal force. Is that not so, Bernard."

The elder of the two attorneys said, "There are any number of legal precedents."

Elizabeth did not reply.

"So you can pack up your nasty little aspirations and have your associate here carry them away for you." Joel Sayer made a dismissive motion, as though clearing the air. "Good-bye, sister. Don't feel obliged to return for the funeral."

Elizabeth said, "I want fifty million dollars."

The two lawyers shifted. The younger man started to say something. Joel shot him a look. The lawyer froze.

Elizabeth said, "In return, I will relinquish all rights to the family company and my shares."

Joel offered her a professional sneer. "You have conveniently forgotten, dear sister, that you've already been disowned."

"Your lawyers started checking things out the instant I showed up at the house. And they've told you that I could make a lot of trouble."

"And trouble is something you've always been very good at, isn't that the next part of your threat?"

"In the hands of the right judge, I could get as much as half. Your lawyers told you that too."

Joel snapped, "Who talked?"

"It doesn't matter. If you pay. Today only. Special price. The whole shooting match is yours free and clear. The price is fifty mil."

"Impossible."

"There is also the matter of the incident. I'm sure you remember the one I'm speaking about." Elizabeth uncrossed her legs. "The records of minors are sealed. But you know how porous the police system is these days. It's amazing what you can get your hands on, if you're willing to pay."

Joel Sayer studied his sister with the impassivity of a scientist inspecting a laboratory animal. "I suppose I could go as high as five. The nuisance value is certainly worth that much."

"Not a chance."

"Five million and not a penny more. Don't even think of negotiating. My attorneys urged me to give you nothing. I've half a mind to agree. But you know what a softie I can be."

Elizabeth said quietly, "All too well."

Joel's features and tone both hardened. "Five million. You walk out with the check today, or you walk out with nothing."

"Agreed."

"You and your associate can wait downstairs in the lobby. My men will bring the documents to you." His features continued to tighten, as though he no longer had any reason to hide his true nature. "Goodbye, sister."

Elizabeth rose from her chair. Her face had gone ghostly pale. Charlie followed her across the vast office. At the door, she turned back. She stood looking at her brother, her hand on the doorknob.

"Well, what is it?"

Charlie could hear her swallow. Her breath sounded like it was forced through an invisible vise. "I . . ." She swallowed again. "I just want to say . . . I forgive you."

"I have no idea what you're talking about. And couldn't care less." Joel Sayer looked like a skull in a toupee. "Now get out."

26

When Gabriella answered, Charlie said, "It's me."

"I asked Elizabeth to phone."

"She's had a hard day. She asked me to fill you in."

"I see. Just a minute, please. I need to record this conversation."

"How is Brett?"

"No change. All right, I'm ready. Will you tell me what happened?"

Charlie related the day's events. When he was done, Gabriella said, "So Elizabeth offered two concrete predictions of the events before they occurred?"

"She didn't state them as predictions."

"But that's what they were."

"Actually, there were more. Her father being ill and laid out in a certain room. That was one. Her brother writing a five-million-dollar check while she waited, that's two. And then the dress."

"I was not referring to the check or the amount, Charlie. She described that after the meeting with her brother was finished. The only

126

two clear foretellings were her father's illness and the company lawyers. She told you about the dress after she had purchased it."

"Okay. I see what you're saying." But his mind was hooked by the recollection of a woman who had willfully erased her armor. "I wish you could have seen her. It's like I was dealing with another woman inside Elizabeth's skin."

"Certainly we are talking about more than changing the way she was dressed. Did the vision require this change?"

"She doesn't like that term. Vision."

He could hear Gabriella's pen scratching six thousand miles away. The distance was heightened by her clinical tone. Detached and intent in equal measure. "Did she say why?"

"No, but I think she prefers to keep things on a clinical level. Like you."

He heard the pen stop. "I need to maintain careful records of this, Charlie."

"Sure thing."

"We are breaking new ground here."

"I'm not arguing with you."

She was silent for a moment, then, "So in both cases, with her father and then again with her brother, she offered them what she had spent her lifetime refusing. An apology, and forgiveness."

"Even though it was a wrenching ordeal."

"Because the vision told her to do this."

"Because the *image* in her ascent *revealed* her doing precisely that. Only, in the image, she said it came easily. Her exact words were, she sang to them."

"What do you think that means?"

Charlie hesitated. "You're asking for my opinion?"

"You were the only other one of our team who was present. I would appreciate knowing what you think."

The words emerged slowly. "I think maybe she was actually singing. On a level other than there in that room." He stopped, then added, "It sounds ridiculous, what I just said."

"No, Charlie. It is anything but." The pen scratched in Charlie's ear for a time. Then, "The money surprises me. I have never met anyone who is less interested in money than Elizabeth."

"She's giving it to us. The five million. All of it goes to our institute."

"She can't—"

"She already has. I drove her by the LA branch of our bank. When I told her she should sit on the decision for a while, take time to recover, she said someday she'd have to tell me just how happy money had made her."

"The poor lady."

"Also, Elizabeth says we need it."

"For what?"

"She doesn't know. But she said the image was definite about that too. She says we'll need more. A lot more."

He listened to Gabriella's soft breathing. Then she said, "Is there anything else you think I should know?"

"Another hunch. Nothing more. Maybe it should wait until we return."

"No, no. Tell me, please."

"The timing."

"You mean, how the image came on the same day as Brett's situation."

"Actually, it was closer than that. She thinks she started her ascent pretty much at the same moment that Brett vanished. At first I thought it didn't mean anything. Now I'm beginning to wonder if I missed something."

"You're suggesting the timing was not coincidental."

"No, Gabriella. What if the purpose was *positive*? Let's just assume for the moment that this really is Elizabeth at some future point in time who is communicating with herself. What does that mean to you?"

"I'll have to give that some very serious consideration. But for now—"

"What if this future Elizabeth used the timing as a means of communicating with *all* of us. What if she was aware that you are thinking about shutting everything down until this mystery regarding Brett is solved. But she knows that can't happen. So she sends this message as evidence. To all of us."

Her voice deepened with the intensity of her concentration. "What evidence do you see that suggests a possible tie between Elizabeth's experience and Brett?"

"Come on, Gabriella. Brett was searching for a means of denying the chains of time. He saw this as a means of confirming that our ascents shift the human consciousness to a level defined by quantum theory. Elizabeth's experience proves Brett is right in his quest. The image's message might have been meant to say we need to continue with this. It's our responsibility."

27

The next morning, as they passed through the security doors, Karla Brusius asked Reese, "Why are you allowing Kevin Hanley to watch the test transit?"

"A hunch."

"I'm not sure that was smart. You saw how tight he was with the colonel."

Reese noticed the security chief on the balcony overhead, waiting for her. She gave Jeff a thumbs-up. She asked, "Do you ever operate on hunches?"

"No."

"When I was your age, I didn't either."

"You're not that much older than me. You make it sound like we're generations apart."

Reese smiled at her reflection in the elevator doors. "You have no idea."

·||·

Washington loved its labels. The more misleading, the better. The clinic with the comatose patients was designated the Treatment Room.

Which was absurd. They had no idea what the patients' problem was, there was no treatment, and the patients were not getting any better. Reese and Karla passed through another set of security portals and entered the area called the Departures Lounge. Who came up with these names, Reese had no idea. Although, if they were successful, this particular label might actually fit.

Reese would have preferred Launch Site. But Departures Lounge was better than some of the things they might have come up with. As in calling the subjects' tight, windowless cells the Barracks. The kids would no doubt have some choice things to say about that.

The Departures Lounge was split into four rooms. There was no actual need for a reception area, but they had one anyway. Reese assumed it was a throwback to the days when security personnel manned front desks. But the electronic systems they had in place were more efficient. The security systems never got bored and harassed the female staff. They could not be bribed or slip away for coffee and restroom breaks. The electronic system operated to a series of very strict protocols. Every incoming individual was to be double scanned and checked against records. Any unauthorized access was to result in immediate and total eradication. No warnings. No mistakes.

The foyer opened into two rooms. To her right was the control room. The security chief waited by the left door. "Hanley phoned through. He's on his way."

She heard the question in his voice, and Karla's sigh of displeasure. Reese said, "Meet him at the portal and code him in."

"You're the boss."

Reese amended, at least for another two days. She asked Jeff, "They all here?"

"Ready and waiting."

The room she entered held two rows of plush leather seats rimming the curved rear wall. The chairs faced across a carpeted expanse to a long bank of electronic displays and controls. Above them stretched a glass window. Where the window met the ceiling hung a row of flat screens. Karla slipped into the left-hand seat and fired up the controls.

The four kids she had picked up the previous week were clustered in one corner. Reese studied them carefully, looking for cracks. To her astonishment, the young woman had held up well. Consuela Inez stared at nothing. Which, Reese had decided, was a very good thing. The ones who made it back tended to start each transit with a period Reese secretly called *changeover*. They disengaged from one life, making room for another.

The youngest of the four, Eli Sekei, was the only one who appeared totally alert. He rocked in his chair, scoping the room. When he caught Reese's eye, he grinned. This time, Reese responded with a tight smile of her own.

The other two kids had shrunk into themselves. They did not so much sit in their chairs as crouch. They cast repeated glances to the room's other side. Where Reese's team was gathered.

Team was probably too strong a word for the other seven. But her crew was better than nothing. A lot better. As in, the difference between getting dumped and having a future. A chance at attaining her real aim.

Reese pretended to study the seven who had made it this far, and made an effort to hide the hunger that threatened to escape. The desire strong as lust. The reason she was here at all.

Washington wanted a team to steal secrets.

What she wanted was the best-kept secret of all.

Kevin entered, followed by the security chief. Reese said, "Seal us in."

The chief coded the wall keypad. Through the open door came the sigh of a pneumatic lock sealing the main entrance. Kevin Hanley's gaze drifted upward as the air conditioning overhead shut down and then sighed back, operating now as a self-contained system.

Reese addressed her new group. "You have now all been through twelve transits."

"Twelve!" The loudest of her seven was a computer geek and convicted hacker named Neil Townsend. The other four hackers who had made it called Neil the Goremaster. "We got six!"

"You're lucky, dude." The guy seated behind Neil was Corporal Joss Stone, a seriously buff former Marine with razor-cut features and enough death in his gaze to freeze the kids seated on the other side of the room. Joss sat next to the lone member of Reese's security crew who had volunteered for the team and made it. So far. Joss said, "We got three."

"This is new to all of us," Reese said. "We don't know if additional transits make any difference."

"Twelve, fourteen, two hundred, you do whatever it takes." Joss cast another look across the room. "Long as you bring Lolita over there back safe and sound."

The crushed rose burned him from beneath long lashes. "The name is Consuela. Not that it's any business of yours."

"Sweet. Why don't you dance on over here, Consuela. Give me some of that Cuban sugar."

"Not in a million." She tossed her hair. "Besides, this lady's from Nicaragua."

Joss kissed the air.

From his place on the front row, Eli said, "I seem to remember something about getting the keys to the kingdom."

Joss snorted. "You fell for that one?"

"I didn't fall for nothing, dude."

"Whatever."

Reese addressed the four. "The preliminary trials were designed to make you increasingly accustomed to the experience of transiting. That phase is over. Today begins your real work. If you succeed, you get precisely what I promised."

"Anything I want."

"Yes."

"I say the word, I get up and walk out the door back there."

Reese looked at Joss. "Tell them."

"Dude, you make it through today, there ain't *nowhere* you'll want to be but here."

"I got a life, unlike some people."

The Marine's laugh was as sharp as the rest of him. "Man, you don't got nothing, and you don't even know that much."

Reese said, "Karla."

Her techie hit the controls, dimming the lights both in the Departures Lounge and in the room on the other side of the glass. A map flashed onto the screens rimming the ceiling. Reese said, "This is your destination."

Neil snorted. "That old place?"

Reese told the four, "This is a palace inside Baghdad's Green Zone."

Neil's whine was particularly invasive. "Why are you sending them back there? We already got that place down cold."

Reese went on, "Inside the main ballroom, which you see here, is a safe. That is it there. As you can see, the safe door has been welded shut. Inside the safe is an envelope. Your job is to go to this room, enter the safe, read the sheet of paper in the envelope, and return back here."

"This is nuts."

Joss said, "Neil."

"Don't start on me. We did this—"

"You want me to put a sock in it for you, just keep it up."

Neil slumped in his seat. "Boring."

"That's what I thought." Joss waved a hand. "Go for it, boss lady."

"This is not merely a test of your abilities," Reese said. "This is vital work. The future of our program depends upon your being able to successfully achieve this task. Do this, and whatever you want, *anything* you want, is yours."

Eli said, "Except no drugs, isn't that what you said?"

"You do drugs, you can't do this," Joss said. "And once you do this, man, you'll know the same thing I do."

"Which is?"

But the Marine had already turned away. "Sorry. I don't talk about the field with recruits. You want the scoop, you come home with the goods."

28

When Karla led the four new recruits next door, Reese said to her seven tested team members, "We're still working on the attrition level."

Joss said, "As in, why my buddies are out prone in the room down there."

"I want a volunteer," Reese said. "Somebody to monitor their transit."

Neil said, "Is that possible?"

Reese glanced at where Kevin Hanley stood frowning by the back wall. "I have no idea."

"So we could go out there, follow the wrong crew, and never come back?" Neil shook his head. "I don't think so."

"You've all lost friends. We need to know *why*. Where do they go?" Reese gave that a beat. "If we track their progress, can we discover what's going wrong? And if we find that out, can we bring them back?"

The final member of Reese's team was the quietest person Reese had ever known. Elene Belote was a former mid-level CIA staffer and the oldest of the team, an operations analyst who had chafed at her desk, so much so that she had volunteered for a project that had neither name nor description attached. Elene was from a south Louisiana parish and spoke English with an accent that rang of shadowy bayous. "I'll go."

⦚

Kevin caught Reese by the coffee machine in the kitchen alcove off the front foyer. "Did I understand what that hacker said?"

"His name is Neil."

"I want to know if it's true. Have you already cracked that safe?"

The question confirmed Reese had been right to let him come. She hid her satisfaction in her cup. "Yes."

"Your orders were to inform the colonel the *instant* you got inside that safe. Why in the world are you sitting on this?"

"That's an interesting question, Kevin. Here's another one. My assistant said I was taking a foolish risk, letting you in here. Is she right?"

Kevin shook his head. "What you really want to ask is, am I of any use to you."

"I knew you were smarter than you looked."

"Where did the technology for this project originate?"

"Not with us, if that's what you're asking. It was sold to us by one of the original research group. They have no idea we've obtained their technology. No one does, except the agency funding us, and now you."

"So you stole it."

"Actually, when we first learned about their work, we tried to shut them down. We failed. So yes. We used an inside source and stole their research. And we copied it. Do you have a problem?"

"No, Reese. There are times when 'whatever means necessary' actually applies. This is one of those times." He glanced at the wall separating them from the Departures Lounge. "If it actually works."

"It works." Reese caught movement out of the corner of her eye. "Yes?"

Karla said, "We're ready to go."

"Two minutes." She waited until the foyer was theirs, then went on, "This whole experiment was never about getting inside the safe."

"Colonel Morrow has repeatedly stated—"

"The colonel is a parrot in a uniform. He'll say whatever order is passed down from on high. You want an answer to your question, Kevin? Fine. Here it is. I don't *know* what Washington is after. But even more important, I don't know how far I can take this. What I do know is, there's more at stake than reading some note in a Baghdad palace. And whatever that is, I want to have the answer for it before I walk into that Pentagon briefing."

Kevin studied her. "You were right to trust me."

Reese met his gaze. "Prove it."

⫯⫯⫯

Reese knew it was against protocol to have her entire team observe these transits. And she didn't care. Either she trusted them or she didn't. Besides which, she had two further reasons for this inclusion. She wanted to build a tightly cohesive unit. And she wanted to develop a sense of normalcy within this core group. Perhaps someday when they'd discovered a way to stop losing so many subjects, her admin staff would want to volunteer themselves. It would be good to have team members who weren't drawn from the more unstable fringes of society.

As she started to enter the main control room, Kevin asked, "Have you ever, you know, done it?"

Reese had no interest in ever discussing her own internal cauldron, or all the ghosts she could never confront. Which added cold force to her response. "You are here to observe. You don't open your mouth. You don't budge from your chair. You don't make a sound. Is that clear?"

She turned away before he could respond. Karla Brusius cast Reese another of those looks, the one that said, *This is insane, letting a stranger and possible enemy observe.* Reese ignored her too. "How are the monitors?"

"All within the green, but number three is spiking on the heart rate."

"I'm going to go down and have a word with them."

"Are you sure that's—"

"Open the door, Karla."

Her number two unsealed the side door, and Reese took the stairs down to the transit room. The chamber was a muted cream color—floors, walls, ceiling, even the frames rimming the reflective glass windows to the control room. The control room was positioned half a floor higher, so that the monitors could observe all the subjects at once. Reese had never entered this room before a transit. But the loss of so many trial subjects bothered her a great deal more than she revealed.

The four trial subjects were laying twenty degrees off full prone in adjustable leather chairs. Padded straps were fitted around their waists and chests. These four were the youngest trial subjects they had yet used. Reese had no problem with their age. The vectors for a number of cutting-edge technologies were constantly shifting down the age scale. But laid out as they were, the four appeared both childlike and terribly vulnerable. Which was why she had insisted on coming down and speaking with them.

"We'll start this the same way we have all your trial runs. I will count you up, then you will disengage and transit. I will hold you in the room here for final orientation. Then I will give you your destination. Five minutes later I will call you back."

The youngest kid, Eli, asked, "Is five minutes enough?"

She knew she shouldn't like this boy as much as she did. Their success rate hovered below 25 percent. Until they made it through the first real transit, Reese normally kept her distance. But something about Eli tugged at her heart. Especially now, strapped as he was in this chair. The room's muted light masked his tattoos and made him look about twelve.

Reese replied, "Everything we have determined thus far suggests that time has no real importance."

"You mean, like, we can control time?"

"Let's leave these discussions until you return." She included the others in her look. "And that is the key here. Our experience thus far shows this transit to be the real cutoff. Those who survive control their destinies."

It was much too flowery a way to describe what happened. But she was shooting off the cuff here, and she wanted to have them identify the real goal. Which was, plain and simple, making it back.

Reese went on, "I want you to focus on one thing and one thing only. Each transit, the only voice you've heard through the earphones has been mine. One purpose of these trial runs has been to familiarize you with the need to recognize my call. It is vital that you remember this. Whatever you discover out there, whatever you face, follow my instructions and I will *bring you home*."

With every other initial transit, at least one of the subjects had chosen this moment to bug out. Just go into a screaming fit, clawing at their straps like they were chains, demanding to be let out. Reese could see they were all very scared. But they also remained planted in their chairs. She allowed herself a tiny sliver of hope.

"You heard what Joss said. There is *nothing* like the high of making a successful transit. You all have had a taste of this. Now it's time to discover the real thing." She gave that a beat, then continued, "The night we brought you in, you were on the road hunting death because the world you knew held no meaning. But that is a different world, and you are about to become different people. You have a purpose now. You were chosen for this project because you have trained yourselves not to fear death. You understand what most people in the world spend their entire lives running away from. You know that death is inevitable. You *seek* it. Not because you want to die. Because you want to overcome mankind's deepest terror. Why? Because it gives you *power*. And that is what you will find out there today. A power that is all yours. Exclusively. A power that will transform a life you once called worthless into something that holds not just value, but potential." She gave that a moment, then finished with, "Good luck, and good hunting."

The transit room was large enough to hold a dozen chairs. Reese's shoes squeaked softly as she crossed the padded floor to the rear left corner, where a fifth chair rested by itself. She looked down at Elene Be-lote and tried to put some genuine feeling into her voice. "Thank you."

"No problem." Elene's voice was scarcely above a whisper.

"Your headphones will be on a separate line. I will count them up and instruct them to hold while I lead you through transit. Then I'll send them off. After they're on their way, I will give you instructions to follow and observe only. Do not approach."

"Roger that."

"If something does go wrong, your instructions will be clear. Go after them, but only so far as it is safe. At the first sign of danger, you return immediately. Is that clear? You do *not* go forward if you feel threatened in any way. I do not want to lose you."

"That makes two of us."

Reese patted her arm. "Stay safe. Come home."

She exited the transit room and climbed the concrete stairs. The control room's lighting seemed overbright. As she entered, Joss said, "I thought I'd been sent off on missions by the best. But that little speech you gave in there, that was top of the list."

"Nothing but strong," her security chief added.

"You were right to go down there," Karla agreed.

Reese settled into her chair before the monitor panel. She pulled the mike's metal cord over close to her mouth. "You have the kids and Elene on different channels, right?"

"The newbies are on one, Elene on two."

"Okay." Reese willed her hands to stop shaking. She took a steady-ing breath. Another. Then she keyed the mike and said, "Here we go."

29

Reese did not need her notes to guide the four new team members through their transit. "You are going to transit now. Remain in the transit room. You are in complete control. You are completely safe."

The Italian scientist, Gabriella Speciale, and her research group referred to these events as ascents. Reese had dismissed the name out of hand. She wanted to disassociate her operation from theirs. Plus the term reeked of higher aspirations. Reese had no interest in searching out the higher possibilities of anything. Her orientation was much baser.

Thus the term *transit*.

The panel's monitors showed the EKG patterns for each trial subject. Ditto for heart rate, oxygen consumption, the works. Cameras focused on each face. All these images were repeated in the flat screens that rimmed the ceiling. Reese gave the four a moment longer, repeated her instructions for them to hover and remain where they were, then keyed the mike's controls and said, "Okay, Elene, I'm counting you up now."

A year earlier, Reese had considered herself as close to invulnerable as was humanly possible. She had been second-in-command of security and intel at one of the world's largest industrial groups. A new high-level threat had been identified, in the form of a research team led by Gabriella Speciale. Her security had been limited to one former Ranger named Charlie Hazard and a motley collection of untrained aides. Reese had been ordered to take them out. With all the forces at her control, the task should have been straightforward. She had done it dozens of times before. A simple eradication. Instead, Speciale and Hazard had demolished her team. Sixteen months later, Reese remained in recovery mode, trying to refit her fragmented life together and erase the nightly dose of tremors. Dawns were minefields. Remnants of memories still erupted with destructive force.

This project had come to Reese via one of the shadow organizations that operated in the grey zone between DOD and the outside world. One of the Italian scientist's team had asked for Reese by name, then offered to become her own personal in-house spy and supply them the complete package—technology, full instructions, research data, the works. In return, he wanted his own lab, total control over his research, total freedom to publish, and a full professorship at UCLA. Reese said yes to all but the last. She had no swing inside the UC system. Her spy accepted the terms without a quibble. Clearly he was thinking the same as she. If the project was as successful as initially indicated, he could name his ticket to any school on the planet.

Then just as they planned an extraction, their spy within the research organization had gone silent.

Reese and her associates could only assume the spy had been caught by Charlie Hazard and eliminated. Given what Hazard had done to Reese, she felt a real pang of sympathy for the scientist she had never actually met.

Reese's superiors were mildly concerned about this possible threat to their clandestine world. More than anything, they wanted it to all just go away. Colonel Morrow represented the faction that felt Reese and her team were nothing but an expensive waste of time. There were others, however, who were not so sure. Preliminary findings from numerous interviewed trial subjects suggested that Gabriella Speciale had actually managed to establish and control situations where human sensory awareness was no longer restricted to the human body. Reese's bosses needed to know if this impacted their ability to hold and maintain secrets. They needed to determine if these experiments could be channeled to stealing other people's secrets. And they needed to know this *first*.

The intensity of their concerns, and the opposition Reese faced inside the group, came through loud and clear. As well as their unspoken aim. And it was at this point, the issue that was never discussed, where Reese and her new bosses were in complete harmony.

The ultimate goal was simple. If it worked, no one else could be permitted to obtain this capability.

Reese needed to annihilate the opposition. Obliterate Gabriella's entire group. Wipe them off the face of the planet. Erase their very shadows. Salt the earth. And walk away.

‑|||‑

When Elene Belote had transited, Reese keyed the mike to the off position, shifted the page of instructions over, took another breath. And still hesitated.

Karla glanced over. "We're good to go."

"I know."

"You've done everything you can." When Reese continued to hesitate, she said, "Green lights across the board."

Reese keyed her mike so she spoke to the four. She said, "Follow my instructions. On my say, transit to the Baghdad palace. Enter the safe, read the sealed document, come home. Accomplish the job and return. Remain perfectly safe and in control throughout. Those are your orders. Stick to them."

She keyed the mike over, said, "Elene, I am about to send them out.

You are to track their progress, but only so far as it is comfortable. That is the primary objective. To go where it is absolutely safe. To observe. And to return. Safely."

She returned the mike to the position for the new team members and said, "Here we go."

⫶

There was actually almost nothing for the observers to see.

The first few times, Reese had regretted her decision to allow her team not transiting to observe. But when they moved from the initial trials to the first attempt to infiltrate the Baghdad safe, and two of the three subjects remained in a coma, Reese's tension became shared by everyone. That was the one good thing that had come from losing her people to comas. Those team members who survived became as intent and focused as frontline troops.

The group inside the control room was utterly silent. There was nothing to see through the glass except the five inert bodies, four clustered together in a tight row and Elene by herself against the rear wall. The monitors showed no change. Heart rates steady and very slow, oxygen levels down 80 percent from normal wakeful state. Brain-wave patterns steady and particularly strong in the alpha signals. Everything in sync with a deep meditative state. The left-hand wall held a large clock. There was also an electronic timer between the control panel's two center terminals. Karla had started the timer the instant Reese launched her team. Everyone watched the second hand. When it hit five minutes, Karla lifted one finger in a silent alert, but Reese was already keying the mike so that her voice was heard by both the four and Elene.

"You will now return to home base. You will do so in utter safety and complete control. You will return home now. You are home. You will reenter your bodies. The transit has been successfully completed. You are safe and in total control. You are now counting back to full wakefulness. I am counting you now. You are coming awake. You will open your eyes. Welcome home."

And for once, she could say the words with total sincerity. Because for the first time since she had started her trials, four sets of eyes opened and stared upward. Four sets of limbs moved in jerky motions. Four voices chattered in vivid excitement. This was another of the discoveries Reese had made, how *thrilled* the returning transiters were. No matter that some of their mates did not awaken, the mystery and the danger on vivid display. The thrill, the excitement, the electric high was so intense that in that first moment all they wanted was to shout, to scream, to dance. In that instant of wakefulness, they were no longer trial subjects confronting the greatest of all human mysteries. They were a *unit*.

Just like the four of them were doing down below.

And for once, Reese wanted to join in. Though she wasn't sure how, clearly she had taken a major step toward achieving her goals.

Then Karla said, "We have a problem."

Reese looked beyond the four. And instantly her elation was demolished.

Elene Belote was not moving.

30

'm going after her."

"Joss, no, wait."

"Woman, you got one choice. One. Either you help me or I toss you out the way and find somebody—"

"I'll help you. Calm down."

Joss was not a big man. But there was a new quality to him now, a murderous cold that darkened the chamber's energy. He did not raise his voice. He spoke in little more than a rasping whisper. But the man's other nature was laid bare. The same nature that had stained his personal file with the six men who had tried to take him down in a bar fight. All six had been blooded members of a San Diego gang. Joss had been the only one to walk away. But the bar had been filled with the gang's buddies, and they all claimed Joss had started the fight. It was a bogus charge, but the SD police had been forced by strength of numbers to file charges. Which was how Joss had wound up standing in the center of the monitoring room, breathing deadly danger. His two comatose buddies had come to Reese by similar routes.

The security chief said, "Take it easy."

Joss did not even glance at Jeff. "I'll give you easy. You rise from that chair, you'll find out easy death can come your way."

"Stay where you are, Jeff. Joss, look at me."

"My code is my code. I don't leave a buddy behind." Joss did not raise his voice. "I've got two mates downstairs lost to comas. I didn't know enough to go back for them. I do now. Elene needs me and I'm going."

"Of course you are. And I'm going to help you." Reese kept to a similar calm, something she would never have thought possible under the circumstances. "I'm glad to see you think it's important to be there for your team. Really. But first there's one thing we need to do."

"There's nothing happening here but me going out and bringing the lady home."

"This is about saving her, Joss. We need to debrief the survivors. Do you see? We're in uncharted territory here. We need to find who the enemy is and where he's hiding. You with me?"

Joss decompressed slightly. Enough to say, "We need to hurry."

"I know." She said to the security chief, "Bring the crew up here."

"But—"

"Do it, Jeff. Fast."

But as the security chief passed through the side door, Karla pointed through the observation window and cried, "She's coming out!"

Joss moved faster than Reese thought humanly possible. When Kevin and the rest of her crew started to follow, Reese snapped, "Stay where you are."

They watched Joss leap down the stairs and fly across the room and scoop up Elene, who clutched at him frantically and sobbed so hard her body convulsed.

Reese was still watching when Jeff brought the four crew members into the room. She said, "I want you to tell me what just happened."

"It was *amazing*." Consuela was alight now, almost singing the words. "I went out there—"

"I could *smell* you," Eli said.

"I knew you were there! I went to the safe, and I read the note, and I felt you reading it with me! How amazing—"

Consuela stopped speaking because Reese stepped in close enough to freeze her solid. "Calm down. I want you to listen very carefully. We've had a crisis. We don't know how, but the agent we sent to monitor you almost didn't make it back. Now, I want you to skip over how cool everything was, and how great you feel, and *focus*. Can you do that? Okay. Now tell me what happened after I told you to come back."

Eli was the first to answer. "I did exactly what you said. Came out, stayed downstairs for a second, then took off. Got to the palace, knew exactly where the safe was, went in, read the note, then you called me home. I came. End of story."

"Good. Anybody feel otherwise?" Reese saw how the girl grew sulky. "Look at me, Consuela. No, not like that. Those days are over. I'm not the cops and you're not in trouble. We're a team. You're *vital* to our work. Raise your face. Good. Now tell me *exactly what happened*."

"I left the palace like you said. Then something happened and I started to move away."

"When precisely did this happen?"

"You said come back. I came. I was almost inside the room down there. I felt like it was just up ahead. Then something called to me."

"Who?"

Consuela shrugged. "I got *no* idea. I don't even know if it was a *who* at all. But . . ."

"Tell me."

"It sounded like my own voice. Kind of, anyway. But different." She shrugged a second time. "I can't say it any better than that."

"I heard it too," Eli confirmed. The other pair nodded. "Kind of."

"Consuela's voice, or your own?"

"Mine. But now, I don't know, it wasn't me. It was like an echo. But deadly."

Reese noticed Kevin and the others closing in but resisted the urge to snarl them away. "Describe the danger zone."

The two kids who rarely spoke shared a look, their gazes hollow. Eli said, "Like a giant tornado turned on its side."

"More like an octopus," Consuela said, trying hard to keep her voice steady. "All these different arms, wanting to suck me in."

"For one moment, it was all I could see," Eli recalled.

Consuela said, "I felt like I was being dragged away. Not dragged. But it was easy to go. And it was so totally hard to hear you."

"I got sooo scared," one of the other kids said softly.

"But you're here now, and it's all good," Reese said. "Tell me what happened then."

"The other person showed up."

"Was it Elene? Look down through the window. Was it her?"

"I'm telling you, I don't have idea one." Consuela sounded certain enough about that. "I didn't actually see anything except that thing waiting to eat me."

"But this other person was there."

"Oh, totally. I could smell her. Or him."

"Me too," Eli confirmed. "I thought it was an angel."

"What happened then?"

"The other person said, 'Go back.'" Consuela shrugged. "I went."

Reese turned back to the window. She watched Elene clench Joss in tight and repeat something over and over. Reese said, "Turn on the speaker. I want to hear her."

Over and over and over, Elene said one thing. "Thank you."

Joss clearly felt uncomfortable with being cast as the hero, when he had done nothing except offer to put his life on the line. But he stayed where he was, locked in her frantic embrace, and said, "I'm here and you're safe. It's done."

But Reese knew the man was wrong. The problem was not behind them.

In fact, the danger was only just beginning.

31

"Let me get this straight." Kevin Hanley leaned against the monitor station to Reese's right. To her left, Karla's chair was empty. Through the glass Reese could see her down on the floor, prepping Joss. Reese wanted to be down there as well. But she knew Kevin was going to raise a stink. And this was something she needed to handle herself.

Kevin went on, "You're sending the guy into a red-alert situation, and for what? To rescue a woman who is *already safe?*"

Reese replied, "You're too locked into the twentieth century. Isn't that something you have to tell your computer geeks?"

"We're talking about a man's *life.*"

"Actually, it's two lives." Reese had never been affected by other people's anger. It had been one of her earliest traits. Her mother had found it absolutely infuriating, how Reese had never shown any response to shouts or fury or even spankings. Her reaction to rage was uniform and cold. Just like now. "I want you to take a deep breath. And calm down."

Kevin started to snap at her. But something in her expression gave him the clarity to ease off a notch. "This is *serious*."

"Listen carefully, because this is absolutely crucial to what we're facing. *Time isn't linear*."

He blinked. "That's just theory."

Reese turned to where the crew huddled beside Jeff. They were wrapped in blankets and drinking coffee. That was another common result of transiting, the sense of communal weakness once the initial high wore off. Some felt cold, others simply disconnected from reality. As though a strong wind might separate them permanently from their bodies. The blankets were pashmina, a silk and cashmere blend, soft and reassuring. The coffee was hot and sweet and strong.

Reese said to the four, "Tell this man how long you were out there."

Eli replied, "Days. Weeks."

Consuela could not quite suppress her shivers. "Longer."

Kevin said uncertainly, "So the sensations were intense enough to distort perceptions. It happens all the time under live fire."

"This isn't just an awareness issue, Kevin. Time *changes*."

He didn't like it. But he was listening intently to her now.

"We haven't conducted controlled experiments to prove this because we operate under the gun. Maybe later. But not now, while the colonel is breathing down our necks. All I can tell you is, every debriefing, every transit, every trial, the results are the same. Time as we know it ceases to hold control over the matters at hand."

Reese stopped, struck by the sudden thought that she needed to insert the instruction into her initial commands for the transit crews to hold to a proper perspective on time. Or not. At least to control this like they did their destination. She made a note to herself on the pad. When she looked up, Kevin was watching her intently. She had to think a moment to remember where she'd been headed. "Okay. So what we're facing is this. When Elene made it back, what was the first thing she did?"

"She could have said it because he was there in the room—"

"Come on, Kevin. We're talking about a highly trained CIA agent with years on the clock. You're suggesting Elene was so totally shattered by a guy being there to hold her she falls apart?"

Kevin did not speak.

"Elene *thanked* him. She was desperate. Why? Because he *brought her back*."

Kevin was still mulling that over when Karla said over the speaker, "We're ready down here."

As Reese started for the door, Kevin demanded, "What are you going to do?"

"That's simple enough. I'm going to make it happen."

⊸⊪⊸

When she entered the transit room, Karla greeted her with, "It was a mistake to let Kevin observe us."

The transit room's central pillars effectively split the room into two long segments. The pillars held the electronic cables, fiber optic lines, and controls that linked the chairs to the monitoring chamber. Reese reached over and switched off the mike feeding the control room's loudspeaker. "Full marks on lip. Failing grade on subtlety."

Karla's face reddened. But she held her ground. "You're the one always going on about secrecy."

Reese did not mind her objection. In fact, she welcomed having a reason to focus momentarily away from the danger they faced. Because the threat was both real and extreme. There was a risk she was trading one seasoned operative for another. Her best. She replied, "What is Kevin's responsibility here?"

"Research into quantum computing."

"Come on, Karla. Do you really think the head of this ultra-secret and ultra-expensive facility is some aging engineer? One whose remit is overseeing a group of nerds operating on the fringes of reality?"

"His title is a name on a door," Karla replied. "He wasn't permitted into our section until you invited him."

152

"Do you really think the government would stick us with computer geeks working on something with a zero success rate and a timeline stretching into the next century? Kevin Hanley is into something as secret and as potentially huge as our deal. My guess is he's working on cryptography. Which means he's a professional keeper of secrets."

"You don't know that." But Karla sounded uncertain now.

"What I know is, the last time Colonel Morrow showed up, he wasn't here to pull my string. He was here to talk with Kevin. Far as the colonel is concerned, we're just a sideshow. Somebody he's planning on shutting down when I travel to Washington. But Kevin's group is totally safe. Why is that, do you think?"

Karla shrugged. "The bodies in the clinic are our guillotine."

"Colonel Morrow is your typical officer," Joss Stone said, listening carefully now. "Officers have a different word for a man down. They call it acceptable losses."

Karla frowned at the floor and did not respond.

Joss bent down and fastened his leg and waist straps. He lay back and said, "Morrow isn't shutting you down, not when you tell them what we've done here."

"Maybe not. But what happens afterward?" Reese kept her eyes on Karla. "You haven't worked with Washington. I have. And one thing I know for certain is this. We need allies. People who will make sure we get credit for our successes and protect us when we fail. We've got a roomful of failures that won't be wiped away just because we bring in the goods. I'm also thinking the colonel is going to be intensely unhappy that we succeed. Why? Because he's already been prepping his superiors, telling them what a bunch of losers we are. We need allies to make sure our success isn't buried, and us with it. That's why Kevin is standing up there watching us argue."

Joss grinned. "You got a way with a point."

Reese looked down at him and wished she could return his smile. She reached over and turned the loudspeaker mike back on. Then she said, "Your primary objective, soldier, is to make it home."

"Roger that."

"We're in totally uncharted territory. So I'm going to give you as tight and precise instructions as I possibly can."

She watched Karla settle a hand on the guy's shoulder. Up high enough to where she could trace a finger through the hairs on his neck. Reese found mild humor in learning this Marine had another notch to his gun.

Joss must have seen something in her face, because he drawled, "There's room for one more."

"Let's be serious here."

"Always am, when it comes to the ladies."

"I am going to count you up. You will transit and remain here in the lounge. I will direct you to depart only if you can already see your safe return."

Joss sobered. "This is new."

"I told you. Everything about this is new terrain. So I will then order you to find Elene and direct her home. I will instruct you to be away for fifteen seconds only."

"That's tight."

"Fifteen seconds. And you are to hear the time counted down. No stretching it out at any level. Elene said in her debriefing that the instant you showed up, she remembered where to go and what to do. So you find her, you get in her face, you return. Clear?"

"Five by five."

Reese hesitated, then added, "You're my number one, Joss."

He met her gaze. "You go up there and do your job. I'll do mine."

32

The silence in the control room had never been more intense. Air had never been harder to find.

Reese keyed her mike and said, "On my signal, you will depart the transit chamber. You will find Elene. You will redirect her away from the danger and toward home. You will return. You have fifteen seconds. I will maintain the count. You will keep a clear connection to me and to my time-count throughout the entire transit."

Joss lazily showed her a thumbs-up but did not open his eyes. The monitors showed a lazy heart rate, calm breathing, all the biological lies Joss had learned to fabricate when entering Indian territory.

Reese moved through the standard exit routine, then said, "You are good to go. I am beginning the fifteen-second count now." The electronic timer between the monitors was utterly silent. Even so, Reese felt as though she could hear each passing second chisel into her brain. "Fifteen. Fourteen. Thirteen. You have twelve seconds left. Ten. Eight."

Beside her, Karla had stopped breathing. She heard footsteps cross the room behind her. Elene had probably moved up. And Kevin. Maybe Eli. The other three midnight crew members were sacked out in the foyer. Just too drained to keep their eyes open, no matter what load of tension the rest of them were feeling.

"Six. Five. Four. Three. Two. One."

With the hand not holding the monitor controls, Karla reached over and gripped Reese's hand. Reese said, "You are returning. You are back. You have reentered your physical body. You are counting down. You are opening your eyes."

When Joss did exactly that, Karla covered her mouth as behind them Elene took a broken breath. Even Reese found it hard to hold herself steady as she said, "Welcome home, soldier."

·ı|ıı·

They all came down with her into the transit room. Kevin. Jeff. Elene. Eli. Even her hacker, the hostile and ever-aloof Goremaster. A clear breach of protocol. Reese could not have cared less.

"Tell me what happened," she said.

Joss replied, "The whole thing was five by five."

"You transited."

"Came out easy as a smile. Stood there looking down at myself."

Kevin asked, "What is that like?"

"Save it," Reese snapped. "Go on, Joss."

"You told me to go. I went."

"Any difficulty due to this movement into past tense?"

"Couldn't tell any difference at all. You said go, I went. You kept counting." He shivered. His complexion was pale. Waxy. A sheen of perspiration covered his body. "The only trouble is now. I feel like I've just run a twenty-mile obstacle course with a full pack."

"Focus on the issue, please. You found Elene. You turned her around." She stopped because Joss was shaking his head hard enough to rattle the monitor cables. "What?"

"That's where it gets a little weird. I never found her."

Elene cried, "But I *saw* you."

"Sorry, babe. Wasn't me."

Reese said, "You're not making sense."

"All I can tell you is, I heard you say, 'Find her.' I started off. And there he was."

"Wait. You mean—"

"Another guy. Or *something*. Blocking my way. Turning *me* around. And I knew it was all solid."

The room was as tight and still as the control room. "A *third* person."

"This somebody or something didn't speak. But I knew just the same. It was all taken care of. My job was to focus on getting home. I followed your count back. I reentered. I woke up. End of story."

33

The next afternoon, Reese sipped from her disposable cup of coffee and told Kevin, "I think I've resolved the issue regarding how you didn't hear about Trent Major's thesis project."

Reese sat in the passenger seat of Kevin's Lexus. They were parked on Cota Street, half a block off Santa Barbara's main shopping avenue. They faced the Hotel Santa Barbara. The hotel's corner shop housed a Starbucks. They could look through the coffee shop's glass walls and see almost everything. Their car was shaded by a large elm and the adjacent building. Reese had ordered Kevin to circle the area four times before they found the spot she wanted. The shade helped block them from view.

Kevin said, "Explain to me what we're doing here."

"I wanted to get a look at our targets. They're meeting here in a few minutes."

"You've tapped their phones? Why aren't I in the loop?"

"We just got this up and running last night. Besides which, we've been a little busy, remember?" Reese opened the file she had just downloaded. "We have no useable intel so far. A few hours back, Shane Schearer called

Trent Major and set up this meet. Soon as I heard, I called you. That's it. I would have run it up the flagpole if there was anything worth an alert."

"Did you go through channels for this?"

"Of course not, Kevin. I assume that's why you came to me in the first place. Because I'm not in the official loop. If the colonel decides to ax me at our meeting tomorrow, I'm dead in the water." She shot him a glance. "Just like you might be, if Washington ever found out there was a guy working down the block on your own project and you didn't have a clue."

"I might be able to help you out with the colonel."

Reese nodded satisfaction. The guy had gotten the message. "Trent's background check uncovered a few anomalies. But before we get into that, tell me exactly what it is you want from me. Skip over the preliminaries. Give me a best-case scenario."

"We need to know how far Trent Major has gotten with his research. We can't access it. For his thesis, Trent uses a laptop that has no internet connection. He splits his work into two encrypted files and stores them on different drives. One he carries with him at all times. The other he stores in the department safe."

"Sounds like major-league paranoia."

Kevin shook his head. "Chinese companies have a history of patenting discoveries in computer technology that we assumed were highly confidential and totally ours. Their stuff parallels research going on at Caltech and MIT. We cannot prove a theft. But years of research and several major discoveries have been lost. Trent Major is following what has become standard protocol for cutting-edge research."

Reese opened the file in her lap. "According to this preliminary workup, the targets actually share some surprising commonalities. Both spent time in foster care. Shane Schearer's parents were killed in a traffic accident when she was fourteen. She and her younger sister were bounced around by the courts until an aunt gained custody. Trent Major's father is a mystery, we're still working on that. When Trent was eight, his mother was injured in a dispute with her boyfriend, a multiple felon. Trent was shot in the same dispute. He was placed in foster care. No other living relatives on record. Another shared trait, both raised in Central Valley towns. Trent Major is from Ojai, Shane Schearer's aunt lives in Bakersfield."

"You were going to tell me how Trent Major's research remained under our radar."

"Last year, his former doctoral supervisor broke his leg skiing and was put on OxyContin for the pain. The prof has had problems with substance abuse before. This time, lost his driver's license for a year and his wife filed for divorce. Apparently he's become a parasite masquerading in professorial clothing. Trent Major was teaching his classes, grading his exams, writing his journal articles. All this ended yesterday. When I spoke with the prof this morning, he was seriously steamed over losing his lackey. And even hotter over being forced to sober up and work. He was delighted to dump on Trent."

Kevin was nodding now. "So the professor buried Trent's work in order to keep him chained in the dungeon."

"Which is where he'd still be, except Trent's business partner and the lawyer you put them on to, Murray Feinne, met with the university president. Apparently they strong-armed the president to override departmental protocol. Trent's doctoral work has been reassigned to . . ."

Kevin looked over. "What's the matter?"

Reese opened her mouth, but no sound emerged. She had lifted her gaze from the file when the sunlight caught the café's glass door as it opened. She had possibly glimpsed an anomaly. But she couldn't be certain. The image had been too fleeting. A slender white-blonde young woman, holding to a long-limbed stride, had entered the Starbucks.

"What's going on?"

"Probably nothing." Southern California was filled with long-legged blondes. "I just thought I saw one of our opposition. Which is impossible. They're all in Switzerland."

"Maybe we should go over, check things out."

"Stay where you are. Here comes Trent now."

34

Trent Major walked down Santa Barbara's main shopping avenue in a daze. He never used drugs. He was reluctant to take aspirin. The memories from his early years remained piercingly vivid. His mother had downed whatever drug on offer with an abandon that bordered on frantic glee. Trent feared some latent chromosome might be triggered by anything he took and, once awakened, consume him.

But as he walked the sunlit street, he wondered if this was what it meant to get high.

The previous day he had met Shane at her favorite smoothie bar on Camino Del Sur, just beyond the university borders. She had made a process of standing in line for him, bringing over a drink he didn't particularly want, playing the solicitous friend. Talking about the weather. Clearly about to burst with excitement.

When her phone rang, she answered, listened, thanked the caller, rose from her chair, said, "You going to nurse that thing all day?"

"You were the one who brought us here."

"That was then and this is now. Let's go, sport."

She bounced down the road beside him, acting like a balloon on a string. Trent did not know Shane well enough to understand what was happening. All he could say was, this was a new side to her, an aspect he had never seen before. One he liked very much.

What was more, she really did have a lovely smile.

She tried to hide it, but the effort only poked holes in her cheeks, dimples that lit fires in her eyes and made her half skip, half dance down the sidewalk. He wanted to ask what was happening, but he was enjoying her act too much to speak.

Then she turned toward the physics building, and the moment was pretty much wrecked.

But she was expecting that too, because she grabbed his arm and pulled him forward. "No hanging back."

"Can we please not go in there today?"

"Sorry, sport. It comes with the package." She was immensely strong, a lithe composite of muscle and energy and determination. Shane pulled him up the stairs and down the hall holding the faculty offices. She unlocked an office whose nameplate was empty and flipped on the lights. "Ta-da."

"What is this?"

"You're the genius. You tell me."

The room was shaped like an *L* and lined with empty bookshelves. There was even a quartet of padded chairs surrounding a narrow coffee table. A new desk and ergonomic chair.

Trent whispered, "No."

"Believe it, sport." She dangled the keys in his face. To Trent's mind, they rang like crystal bells. "What's more, your new thesis professor wants to meet with you in thirty minutes. So if you want me to help you move, we've got to jump."

"This can't be real."

"It's real, all right." Shane moved in close enough for him to catch a hint of her scent, a heady mix of shampoo and wildflowers. "Your days of being locked inside somebody else's idea of a good time are over."

⽁⽁⽁

Trent pushed through the glass doors and entered the Starbucks attached to the Hotel Santa Barbara. Three hours ago, Shane had called to say she'd meet him there at five thirty. The checks had cleared, they had money in the bank, dual accounts, the works. Trent's only job was to show up with an appetite. In the meantime, Shane had said, she was headed off for some serious Santa Barbara therapy. Trent had made out like it was a major pain, breaking his routine, he needed to stay where he was and settle in, get back to his research. Not meaning a word of it. Just seeing what it was like to play on this new reason to smile. Shane had replied, "Five thirty, sport, it's your time to do some research on real life."

Shane was not in the café, but Trent was not troubled. If anybody had earned the right to keep him waiting, it was his partner. Just thinking that word, *partner*, caused him to grin. The barista must have seen something good there, because she smiled back with a lot more than just professional courtesy. Trent took his coffee to a window by the side street.

Then he noticed the woman.

She was seated by herself at the table beside the rear wall. She kept looking his way. She was *studying* him. Trent was certain he had never seen her before.

The lady was seriously fine. She was beautiful with a very aggressive edge. Her white-blonde hair was cut butch-short, her clothes new and expensive and as sharp as her features. She was definitely not the sort who would normally give Trent a second glance.

Trent forgot his coffee, the lady's interest was that strong. She alternated between staring him down, then glancing at her watch, then back again. Trent was about to walk over and ask if there was something he could do for her when she beat him to it.

The woman rose from her chair and looked around the café. She stared out the front doors, very worried now, very tense. Then she walked swiftly across the café, her motions catlike. She leaned against the concrete pillar beside Trent's table. She dropped a beautiful shoulder bag on the chair next to his and asked, "Where's the lady?"

"Excuse me?"

"The lady. Your girlfriend. She's late."

"Shane said she'd meet me here."

"She's called Shane? Cute." The woman was so tense the skin around her eyes and lips were parchment-white. "The lady is late, and that's a problem. I can't stay."

She indicated the shoulder bag. It was large and shaped somewhat like a briefcase, with a beige leather handle and matching shoulder strap. The body of the bag appeared to be the skin of some reptile and was dyed a chalky yellow. The clasps were gold plated. As was the emblem on the side. It looked very expensive.

The lady said, "When your *Shane* gets here, tell her she's got to leave with just one bag. And she needs to play with the toys inside. Not you. Her."

"You're not making any sense."

"I know. But I've gone to the trouble of getting this bag so your Shane will accept this as totally real." She started for the door, then turned back and leaned over and got tight in his face. Showing Trent the fear behind the terse words and the tight motions. "From now on, the only place you'll be alone is in your dreams, and maybe not even there. But you already know all about that, don't you."

Trent felt the breath freeze in his chest.

The woman asked, "What's your name?"

"Trent."

"So tell me, Trent. Did you really figure you'd get those three bonus dreams and not pay the price?"

He managed, "Two."

"What?"

164

"There've only been two."

She grimaced, or perhaps it was her best try at a smile. "Which means the next one will be coming at you tonight. My bad. The facts stay the same. There's no such thing as a free lunch, Trent. Not even in your dreams."

35

Kevin drummed on the steering wheel as he said, "Basically, the objective of quantum computing is the same as a regular computer. To manipulate data and arrive at real-time solutions. From that point on, everything else is different. A quantum computer makes direct use of subatomic phenomena known as superposition and entanglement."

Reese only half listened to Kevin. She stared at the Starbucks, trapped inside the thought that perhaps one of Gabriella's team had suddenly just appeared here in Santa Barbara. Everything to do with the Swiss group, as far as Reese was concerned, defined entanglement. Little flashes of uncertainty jerked Reese about, like a beast in a mental cage. She had no idea how far ahead of the curve they might be. The fear that Gabriella's group might be scoping them out, here and now, left Reese severely spooked.

She realized Kevin was waiting for her response and searched her brain for what they were talking about. "So what makes a quantum computer different?"

"Traditional computers are built around transistors. They manipulate bits of information. These bits carry an electronic charge of either positive or negative. In numerical terms, these bits can be either a zero or a one. Nothing else. All these ads you read about how microchips grow faster and smaller and more powerful, they're still based upon the same concepts of transistors and binary bits.

"A quantum computer works on the manipulation of qubits. A single qubit can represent a one or zero, and on top of that, a superposition of four more states. These additional states are based upon probabilities, also known as spin. But here's the thing. If you increase a quantum computer from one qubit to two, the number of possible answers rises at an exponential rate. A three-hundred-qubit quantum computer would hold more potential states, or possible answers, than the number of atoms in the observable universe. This offers us huge potential to resolve questions that standard computers just can't handle."

"Like encryption, right? That's what you're working on, isn't it?"

"My team is working on several issues. But encryption is definitely top of the list. Virtually everything on the internet, all online banking and shopping and supposedly confidential file sharing, they're all based upon what is known as RSA encryption. This is also known as open-key security, because it allows the passage of the security key, or access code, from one person to another. Without both of these keys—the user's ID and the password—the system remains basically invulnerable. It's calculated that our fastest supercomputer would require six centuries to break an RSA-encrypted code system. But using what is known as Shor's algorithm, a 128-qubit quantum computer could break this in eight seconds."

On the level of logic, Reese knew she was probably removed from any possible threat that Gabriella and her Swiss group might pose. But Reese had glimpsed the concept's potential and saw a bit more every time her team went out on transit. She knew it really didn't matter whether the blonde woman she had spotted actually belonged to the Swiss team. The threat was real. They had to be taken off the grid. Now.

Kevin spoke with the quiet passion of a typical engineer. As though nothing in the known universe was more important than taking the next step along the scientific ladder. "Quantum computing faces huge difficulties. Our team focuses on the two biggest issues. The first is interference, sometimes referred to as decoherence. Each qubit must be able to transfer data to another qubit without outside interruption, otherwise they come out of superposition and the calculation is lost. This means separating our system from the slightest interaction with the external environment. We're building isolation chambers, and we're working with particular molecules that have very special qualities." Kevin glanced over again. "Imagine my surprise when we discovered that our boy in the coffee shop there was working on the same concept."

Reese searched her memory and came up with the correct term. "Prions."

"Right. These are very special protein molecules. Very complex, so long they create their own internal electromagnetic state, which results in the molecule folding a particular way. If you look at the atomic makeup, prions are the same proteins that form the essential structure in the human brain. But these prions are folded differently. We think there is a unique relationship between this pattern of folding and the manner in which the brain stores data and calculates responses. We are hoping that our work with quantum computing will someday duplicate the brain's essential power."

Sunlight through the tree beside their car etched slow-motion shadows across the windscreen. Santa Barbara's main street was filled with tourists and locals enjoying a perfect California afternoon. The air through her open window was laced with Pacific salt. Normally Reese did not care for Santa Barbara at all. The place lacked everything she fed off, the edge, the energy. But just then she found great comfort in the city's tame feel.

She took a deep breath, released the remaining strands of tension, and glanced at her watch. "Shane Schearer is late."

Kevin shrugged. "Our guy doesn't look bothered."

168

"Is Trent talking with someone?"

Kevin squinted through the windscreen. "There's nobody else at his table."

Reese could not see the blonde. But the room's back recesses were lost to late afternoon shadows. She was about to ask what made Trent's work so special when a shape appeared by the front windows. Reese flung the file at the backseat and shrieked, "That's *her*!"

"What's the matter?"

"Start the engine!" Reese stabbed the windscreen. "Drive, drive!"

"Why? Trent is still—"

"*Do it!*"

Elizabeth Sayer had pushed through the café's exit and rounded the corner and was gone. Fast as a pro. Like she knew she was under surveillance.

"Straight ahead. We're losing her!"

Kevin slid through the intersection and started past the hotel. He flinched when Trent Major turned toward the window, as though he watched their progress. "I think we just got made."

"Forget Trent Major. Our target is a female in her late twenties, five nine, 120, white-blonde hair worn short and spiky, wearing a red leather jacket and black skirt with matching stockings." Now that the target was identified, Reese was coldly together and functioning on full alert. "Take this left! Can't this thing go any *faster*?"

Kevin goosed the engine. The alley was so narrow he dragged Reese's door against the first of two hotel dumpsters. "Tell me what is happening!"

"We are in pursuit of a highly dangerous operative. Elizabeth Sayer is one of the opposition's original team. Did you catch my description of the target, Kevin?"

"Of course. Sayer. I know that name." Kevin frowned. "The pharmaceutical giant."

"Same family. Elizabeth is the black sheep. Disowned. Turn into the parking lot. Slow down. I need to check . . ." She leaned out the window, checking the shadows beneath parked cars for any sign. "She's gone."

"I never even *saw* her."

"Stop the car." Reese climbed out. "I'm going to cover the terrain again on foot. You use the car and circle the block. I'll meet you back where we were parked."

"I thought we were here to watch the pair."

"Do it, Kevin." She walked through the lot, checking under each car. When she reached the empty alley she pulled out her cell phone. Held it to her chest long enough for a couple of tight breaths. She had to call this in.

36

Fifteen minutes later, Trent Major was still watching the coffee shop's front door when Shane Schearer entered.

Actually, it was more like a controlled dance. The lady floated across the floor, high on whatever lit up her face from the inside.

She wore a new outfit of beige and white, a skirt and matching jacket, very simple, very elegant in a businesslike fashion. Her legs were sheathed in tights a shade lighter than the suit. She wore new shoes with mid-level heels. They matched the beige-gold bag that was slung over her shoulder.

Shane set the bag in the middle of the table. "Ferragamo's finest. It's designed to serve as a briefcase as well as a purse. What every successful woman will give her eyeteeth to carry this season."

She was happier than Trent had ever seen. Her hair had been done. Trent knew she was not doing this for him, at least not directly. He was simply the audience that she needed. Which was wonderful. It was not merely that she trusted him. She considered him part of something real. Something she could rely on.

Such a shame, Trent thought, that he had to burst that bubble.

He said, "Put your bag on the chair."

Shane looked hurt. She recovered swiftly, but the light had faded from her features. She pulled out the chair to his left. "What's the matter?"

"Not that chair." Trent pointed at the one by the window. "Set it over here."

Which was when Shane saw the other bag. Identical to the one she had just bought.

She whispered, "What's going on?"

Trent shook his head. "I have no idea."

37

Charlie Hazard entered the alley behind the Hotel Santa Barbara. He scoped out the streets at either end. He saw no parked car with multiple heads pretending not to observe him, no pedestrians loitering too long, nothing. When he decided the threat was either gone or invisible or had never existed, he reached for his phone and dialed Elizabeth's number.

The dumpster to his left chimed.

A very shaky voice called softly, "Charlie?"

"It's me. Come on out."

Which was when he spotted the warning sign.

"That is the absolute worst place to spend a hot California afternoon." Elizabeth took hold of Charlie's hand, gripped the dumpster's edge, and pulled herself out. Her legs came free with a sucking sound. "And it was probably all for nothing."

Charlie continued to scope out the alley and the surrounding buildings. "Tell me what happened."

"Can we get out of here?"

"Not yet." He fitted them both in between the two dumpsters. "This is as safe as anywhere."

She picked a wedge of vegetable goop off her skirt. She stank of fish and fry oil. "I was sitting in the back of the café, waiting for Trent's lady to show up."

"I thought you didn't know his name."

"We talked. He told me."

"Tell me about the threat."

"I was sitting at the table in Starbucks where I'd been in the image. Just like I told you. Trent sat by the window."

"Which one? The café is lined with glass."

"Halfway back from the front door. Just past the coffee machine. He was by himself. The lady was late. Which was what I said when I walked over. And that was when I spotted the threat."

"Describe the setup for me."

"There was a car parked across the street. Two people were sitting in the front seats. The woman shifted just as I was moving toward Trent's table. Suddenly there she was."

"Reese Clawson."

Saying the name was enough to put Charlie in combat mode. Two months after Gabriella started her research, a shadow organization had tried to take them out. It was the first concrete evidence Gabriella had that their power of awareness extended beyond earthbound parameters. They had survived the attack. Barely. And then done their best to move off the grid. Thus the shift to Campione. Knowing Reese Clawson was back on their trail, hunting them down in Santa Barbara, was the worst possible news.

Elizabeth said, "I don't remember her name. All I know is, she was the one you warned us about."

Having Reese Clawson show up here, when none of them had any idea they would be moving in this direction, could only mean one thing. She was hunting beyond the horizon.

Charlie said, "Go on."

"I stood behind a pillar while I talked to Trent. Afterward, as I left the café, I got another look at her. I raced around the corner and down this alley. I couldn't find any other place to hide. The hotel's rear entrance was locked. It was just me and the sunlight. So I climbed inside that dumpster. Then I heard the sound of a car engine. I thought maybe it was them, but now I'm not so sure."

"The car," Charlie said. "Was it a light metallic green?"

Elizabeth stared at him. "How did you know?"

Charlie pulled her out far enough to point at a strip of new paint down the side of the first dumpster. "You were right to run."

"Oh, man."

"Wait here."

"You're going to leave me alone?"

"Three minutes. You're not exactly dressed for Santa Barbara." He decided not to add that they might have watchers in place. Charlie jogged back to their rental car, drove around, waited for her to slip inside. He said, "Show me where the car was parked."

"Take the right up ahead. Okay. Across the street, down that side lane, beside the building."

The position offered a tree's shade and was ideal for scoping the coffee shop. A pro's setting. "Did you get a look at the other person in the car?"

"Some guy." Elizabeth studied the empty parking space. "I could have been imagining things."

"No, Elizabeth. You saw her. Reese Clawson is here. And she has targeted the lady you came to meet, or this guy. What were their names?"

"Trent. The lady is Shane." She watched him intently. "What are you going to do?"

Charlie put the car in gear. "Whatever it takes."

38

Trent said, "Six hundred bucks."

"That's just for the room. Don't forget the meal."

They were in the Hotel Santa Barbara's top-floor suite. The hotel was an art deco masterpiece. The public rooms were a graceful combination of Spanish heritage and Western modernity. The downstairs floors were tiled, the high ceilings adorned with hand-painted redwood beams. The suite was filled with antiques. The luxury left Trent feeling uncomfortable inside his own skin.

Not to mention the blonde ghost who had gotten tight in his face and poured acid all over his dreams.

The room-service waiter had set their table overlooking the French doors and wrought-iron balcony. Footsteps and nighttime chatter echoed up from below, soft as rain. Farther down the street, a band played excellent jazz.

Shane said, "We need to talk about what we're not talking about."

The equipment from the strange woman's briefcase was spread out on the living room coffee table. The shoulder bag contained an iPod, a charger, one page of terse instructions, and a pair of Bose headphones. While waiting for dinner, they had circled the table like cats, touching nothing.

Trent said, "I'm still not comfortable with us being here at all."

He expected argument. Instead, he got a look that he could only describe as soft.

Shane said, "There's a big reason for tonight. I want you to think very seriously about what I'm about to tell you. Are you ready?"

"Yes."

"Two things. First, we are partners. Second, you have money."

Trent pushed his plate to one side. "That's a lot to take in."

"I know."

"But six hundred dollars for a room, Shane, it's . . ."

"It's wild. I've never done anything like this either. And we might not ever do it again. But I felt like we needed to hammer the point home for both of us. This is real. This is also bigger than what we're seeing."

Trent nodded. Crazy as it seemed, uncomfortable as it felt to spend the money, he understood. "So what's the other big reason for us being here?"

"The lady said you're going to have another experience tonight. I'm not missing that. I'm also assuming your room at the university doesn't have space for me."

"There is no way," Trent said, "you will ever see where I live."

"That's what I thought. And I doubt my roomie would be very excited over you doing your thing on her floor." She pushed her chair back. "You want to have a closer look at the lady's bag of tricks?"

The instructions were both precise and explained almost nothing. Shane was to put on the earphones and lay down. The iPod contained a new app marked simply by an X. Shane was to key that app and shut her eyes. She needed to be alone. She would hear an auditory program that would introduce her to a meditative state and a specific set of experiences. She would be guided by instructions embedded in the program. She would remain in total control and could stop this at any time.

Shane was tempted to try the thing then and there. But she decided, "Maybe we should wait."

"Whatever you decide is fine."

"One mind-bending phenomenon at a time." Shane turned the iPod over in her hands. "Do you think this might give me experiences like what you're having?"

Trent shook his head. "I'm still trying to get used to the idea of a woman I've never seen before walking over and telling me about things going on inside my head."

⁂

There was a double bed in the suite's only bedroom. Trent insisted Shane take that and made a pallet for himself on the living room floor. He was already laying down when Shane emerged from the bathroom. She wore an oversized T-shirt from the hotel's gift shop. With her face washed and her copper hair hanging free, Trent thought she looked like a pixie.

Shane gave him a very solemn look and said, "I don't have to worry about you, do I."

"Not now," Trent replied. "Not ever."

"I knew that. I just needed, you know."

"You needed to put it out where we both could see it."

Shane danced across the room and bounced into bed. She propped up a second pillow so she could look down at where he lay. "Anything?"

"I'm still awake."

"Just checking. I wonder if I'll know. A beam of light from above. Green aliens flitting around your pillow. Something like that."

"I think other people in the graduate dorm might have noticed."

"You never know. They might have figured it was just another student flying off to the OD Corral." She studied him for a time, then said, "Okay. Go ahead and ask."

"Excuse me?"

"We've moved beyond phase one here. It's time to let you ask your questions."

"Anything?"

She crossed her arms. "Within reason."

Beyond the open balcony doors, the night continued to buzz with unfamiliar sounds. Trent thought he caught a whiff of her fragrance, soap and toothpaste and fresh hopes. "Will you tell me about your family?"

"My parents were killed in a freeway pileup when I was fourteen and my sister was ten. We were split up and got bounced around the foster care system for about six months."

Trent forced himself to stop thinking about her being there in the bed and listened intently to what she was saying. "I'm really sorry, Shane."

"Thanks. It was awful for me, but worse for my sister. She's never talked about what happened. But she came back a different person. Twisted up inside."

"What's your sister's name?"

"Billie." Shane reached behind her and punched her pillows into submission. Then she lay flat and said to the ceiling, "My aunt finally won custody. We were never that close. When we were young, family gatherings were battlegrounds. And my sister was a real handful. But Aunt Emily saw us both to eighteen."

"Where is your sister now?"

"Still in Bakersfield. That's where my aunt lives." Shane was quiet for a time, then, "Billie never made it out. Now she's just counting the days, withering on the vine."

Trent nodded to the shadows made by the streetlights. He realized she could not see him, so he said, "I understand that all too well."

Shane reached over and cut off the light. "I don't want to talk about my family anymore."

"I totally understand."

The silence lasted long enough for slumber to emerge from the corner shadows and creep across the room to where Trent lay. Then Shane whispered from the other room, "Anything?"

"Good night, Shane."

39

Trent had no idea when it happened. Only that afterward, everything had changed.

His shout had woken Shane. Now she sat on the couch, watching him with a wide unblinking gaze. She had the blanket from her bed wrapped around her. "Why don't you sit down?"

"I don't *want* to sit. I want to *pace*."

"Fine. So pace."

"You can't imagine how nice it is to have the room to pace. It's worth wasting six hundred dollars to have room to move around. I live in a dorm room the size of a packing crate. The flies don't have room to pace."

"We didn't waste anything."

He swatted the air. "That's inconsequential. I went to bed as one guy, and I wake up and I'm in a different dimension. A different *universe*."

"Tell me what happened."

"I've already told you."

"Tell me again." When he didn't respond, she said, "I'm only asking because I'm pretty spooked by the whole thing."

Trent kept stalking from one end of the room to the next. "The image started the same as every time before. The same nightmare."

"You never mentioned a nightmare before."

He didn't want to answer. But the words flew out of their own accord. "I was eight. My mom was in the trailer where we lived. She was keeping company with a bad guy. We're talking seriously evil."

"Wait, you're telling me this really happened?"

Trent dragged down the collar of his T-shirt, revealing a deep crevice at the point where his neck joined his shoulder. "That real enough for you?"

"What *is* that?"

"Thirty-eight."

"He *shot* you?"

"Shot us both."

"Oh, Trent."

He let the collar slip from his fingers. "I've had the nightmare for so long it doesn't bother me anymore. Well, it does, but not a lot. After each nightmare, the scar burns when I wake up. Then it fades with the memory."

Shane slipped from her cocoon. She pulled the blanket off his pallet. Draped it around his shoulders. "Come over and sit down."

"I don't want to." He sounded petulant to his own ears.

"I know. Do it for me." She settled him down, wrapped him up tight, then slipped back into her own nest. She turned to face him. "So you had the nightmare."

"Then I was back again in the classroom. Seated at my desk on the corner of the dais. And the older me is there at the blackboard. He doesn't speak, just starts his projector—"

"Sorry, the what?"

"That's my name for it. A three-dimensional image system. It just hangs in the air between us. And every time I see a new image, it feels like nuclear fission." He clenched his fists and pounded his thighs. "Only this time, I see myself destroying my doctoral research. Demolishing two years of my life, then walking away."

He looked at her. And whatever it was he saw in her face was enough to launch him from the sofa. It was either pace and rage at the night, or weep. "But that wasn't the worst. It was how *calm* he was. He *smiled* at me. Like this was nothing."

Shane watched him make another pair of crossings. "Then what?"

"Then he wrote out another formula on the board."

"Do you think maybe you should write it down before you forget?"

Trent choked on a laugh.

"What's so funny?"

"I never forget *anything*." He fought with the air before his face. "I feel like I'm trapped again, just like the bad old days. Once again I'm stymied by life. They dress it all up by using a mirror image to hand me this myth of freedom. But they're still thieves, and I'm still getting robbed."

"Partner, I'm trying hard as I know how to understand. But it seems to me that you're forgetting one big thing here. You've just been handed chapter three in our corporate saga."

He rounded on her, so tightly furious he hardly saw her at all. "You're saying I should just admit defeat? Give in to this bait and switch? Sacrifice two years of my life so I can parasite off this stuff from another galaxy?"

Shane studied him. "You think this is coming from aliens?"

Trent stared at the carpet, breathing hard. "I never yell."

"I'm glad to hear it."

"I got all the yelling I needed growing up."

Shane smiled. "So now you're saying I'm this great influence, bringing back all the worst of your early years?"

"Oh, no." When he looked at her, it seemed to Trent as though she was illuminated from within. "You're the only reason I'm sure this whole thing is even partly good."

40

Kevin greeted Reese with, "The colonel ordered me to join you today. It's not my idea. I just want you to know that straight up."

Reese had taken the red-eye from LAX straight into Reagan National. Kevin had left the previous afternoon. He'd received an urgent summons while they were still scoping downtown Santa Barbara for the blonde ghost. He'd departed an hour later by private jet.

Reese asked, "Do I want to know why?"

"I was flown over for some high-powered conflab on encryption and national security." Kevin pointed her toward an olive-green sedan waiting at the curb and followed her into the rear seat. "Imagine my surprise when I'm pulled out of the meeting by a call from Murray Feinne."

Reese guessed, "Trent Major has come up with another concept?"

"The best so far."

"You don't sound pleased about it."

"The kid has another algorithm. Specifically designed for code breaking."

"Which you receive while sitting in a meeting about that very same thing. Spooky."

"My team is supposed to be the best out there. Then here comes this kid. Not only is his work miles ahead of where we are. But he's *fast*." Kevin ground his heel into the sedan's carpet. "It's impossible, is what it is."

"So he's getting help."

"It's the only thing that makes any sense." Kevin looked more than grim. He looked dangerous. "I offered him a job. His own lab. Signing bonus. A team to work for him. The kind of deal a young postgrad could only dream of. Trent Major turned me down flat. Wouldn't even discuss it. The people I've been seeing are convinced he won't come in because he's getting fed this stuff by the outside. Moving into space we control would reveal his sources."

Reese realized where this was going. "You let them in on Elizabeth Sayer's sudden appearance?"

"I had to. I want to wrap this kid up." Kevin looked at her. "Trent Major has shaken my world."

Reese understood with a pro's clarity. "Now the colonel wants to know how my enemies are your enemies. He's using this as another reason to shut us down. He thinks I'm potentially breaching your security."

"He didn't actually say that. But I'm fairly certain you've pegged him to the board with your first dart."

The cherry blossom season was long gone. The parks lining the 395 were framed by minty green. Reese seldom noticed California's largely monochrome landscape until she was somewhere else. She sighed. "Swell."

"For what it's worth, I've done my best to make an end run around Colonel Morrow. We'll soon know whether I've had any . . ." Kevin frowned at a passing sign.

Reese asked, "What's the matter?"

Kevin leaned forward and addressed the driver. "Corporal, you're in the wrong lane."

"No, sir. I am not."

"This will take us over the Fourteenth Street Bridge."

"That is correct, sir."

"Our meeting is at the Pentagon."

"Sorry, sir. The location of your conference has been shifted."

"Where are you taking us, Corporal?"

"Sir, my orders are specific. Deliver you to your destination in no time flat."

"You're not going to tell me, are you."

"Sir, I am very good at following my orders."

Reese watched the road rise above the Potomac. In the distance she could make out the towers of the Smithsonian castle. They crossed the river and headed down Fourteenth Street. When Reese had first come to Washington as a teen, Fourteenth Street had been one of the worst neighborhoods in the country. Fourteenth and U was the capital's den of iniquity. Drugs, hookers, guns for hire, it was all there. Then the city spent a ton revamping the whole district. Now it was known as the U Street Corridor. The yuppies and the power groupies crammed the sidewalks.

"Are we headed where I think we are?" Reese asked.

Kevin nodded slowly. "It appears our meeting has been shifted to the center of the universe."

"Is that good or bad?"

He directed his shrug to the side window. "We'll soon find out."

◁|▷

The soldier deposited them outside the Pennsylvania Avenue entrance to the Old Executive Office Building. The wedding cake structure was attached to the White House by an underground concrete umbilical cord and the restricted parking area for the president's limos and his official guests. Colonel Mark Morrow waited for them just inside the OEOB entrance. He wore a formal dress uniform, his vast array of medals as imposing as his scowl.

The colonel greeted Kevin without taking his gun-barrel gaze off Reese. "Glad you could make it, Hanley."

"What are we doing here, Colonel?"

The officer offered Reese a predator's smile. "It appears Ms. Clawson's crash-and-burn exit is about to become an extremely public event."

A young blank-faced bureaucrat stepped forward and handed them badges on cords. "Wear these at all times, please."

Once they had signed in and passed through security, the young man led them up a flight of cracked marble stairs and down a long corridor. The hallway was wide as an avenue, a throwback to a different era. The marble tiles were grooved by a century and a half of use. Reese tried not to be impressed, but the place was designed to impose. They were led into a conference room overlooking trees of springtime green and the pearl-white palace beyond.

A small woman sat at the head of the oval table. She was in her late fifties and wore a civilian-style suit of midnight blue. Reese doubted she weighed more than ninety pounds. Her hands looked fragile as a small bird's claw. But her stature was rigidly erect, her grey-brown hair cropped tight to her skull. Her skin was taut across her features, her lips nonexistent. Her expression was military in its severity. She read from a stack of files. Otherwise the conference table was empty.

The young man shut the door, walked to the corner behind the woman, seated himself, and vanished in plain sight.

The woman said, "Have a seat, everyone."

"And you are?" the officer said.

"Just a witness to the execution, Colonel." She initialed a page, shut the file, set it aside, opened another. "Carry on."

"Am I not allowed to ask your name?"

"I'm here representing the people who pull your people's strings. That's all you need to know." She waved the hand holding the pen. "This is your baby, Colonel. Rock away."

Reese walked around the table and put the view behind her. The last thing she wanted was the White House as a distraction. Kevin hesitated, then walked over and joined her. The move said a lot about the man's character. Most Washington types would flee the scent of fresh carrion. Reese did not look his way. But what she thought was, *I owe you one.*

The colonel seated himself, opened his file, said, "Before I shut you down, Clawson, review for us exactly what it was you were supposed to be working on."

There was no logical reason for Reese to feel any sense of hope. The unnamed woman had not even glanced her way. The colonel sat across from her, watching her with the expression of a satisfied executioner. Even so, Reese was fairly certain the show was not over. Not by a long shot.

She said, "We are studying a potential cross between telepathy and teleportation."

"Well, which is it supposed to be?"

"Both," Reese replied. "And neither."

The colonel turned to the woman seated at the table's far end and said, "Exactly the sort of answer I'd expect from this project. Nothing but smoke and mirrors."

The woman's pen scratched through a line. She wrote something in the margin. Signed the bottom. Shut the file. Did not look up.

Reese said, "A telepath can read minds. My team can't do this. A teleporter would transfer their physical body from one place to another."

"Which your group can't do either."

"No."

"So remind me why I was ordered to waste my time with you at all."

"Our stated objective was to achieve a measurable extension of conscious awareness beyond the body's physical confines."

"Which you haven't done."

Reese did not respond.

"There was a specific test designed for your team," Colonel Morrow said.

Reese reached into her pocket. "That's right."

"A message was put in an envelope. The envelope has your name on it. The message was set inside the communications safe in the US embassy in Baghdad. The safe was then sealed. Your team was ordered to read that message. And report back."

Reese made a process of unfolding the sheet of paper. She slid it across the table.

The colonel turned the paper around. And huffed softly.

The woman looked up. "I'd like to see that."

When the colonel's only response was to study the sheet, the woman turned to her aide and said, "Jason."

The young man rose from his chair, walked over, and pulled the sheet of paper from the officer's fingers.

The colonel said, "This doesn't mean a thing. They could have obtained this data a thousand different ways. The whole idea is a total waste of time, and resources that could be used—"

"I agree." The woman reached out her hand. Her aide had the file ready for her. "Ms. Clawson, your project is hereby terminated."

Reese watched numbly as the woman signed the sheet, tore off the top copy, and slid it down the table to where the colonel smiled.

Reese protested weakly, "But we did what you wanted us to."

"Correction," the colonel replied. "You managed to circumvent our guards. This whole detail was a mistake from the get-go."

The woman wasn't finished. "You too, Hanley. You're done. You and your team. We're axing the project."

The colonel registered genuine shock. "I wasn't informed this was even on the agenda."

"I'm notifying you as of now." Another signature, another sheet slid down the table. "I won't keep you any longer, Colonel. Thank you for your time."

He gestured at the shell-shocked pair seated across from him. "But they're—"

"I want to debrief them a moment longer. A car is waiting to take you back across the river. Good day."

41

Trent packed his research materials for the second time in three days. His movements were robotic, his brain spiraled through useless data. A robot felt nothing because there was no way to program emotions. In the human experience, intellect and emotions were separate functions. Thus knowing and experiencing followed completely different parameters. Trent had heard a psychologist explain this was why scientists often felt like fish out of water when leaving their labs and entering the external world. They could design an algorithm to describe a basketball player's muscular structure, the gravitational restrictions, the air resistance, the calculations required to put the ball through the hoop. But put them on a court, especially when there were other humans in opposition, and they fell apart.

Trent knew his mind was running in circles as tight and useless as a gerbil on a metal wheel. He felt no emotions because he had shut down. He had returned to the same mental cage he had dwelt in as a kid. What he needed was an algorithm that would eliminate his emotions entirely.

Shane reentered his office and asked, "Why are you smiling?"

"No reason." He dumped another shelf's worth of books into the next box. "Not a single, solitary thing."

"You were the one to say this was what we needed to do." When he did not respond, she added, "Don't bug out on me, Trent."

He started to say that he was okay. But he stifled the words before they emerged. He would not make the day worse by lying.

Shane said, "Murray Feinne called again."

"I'm not taking any job." When they had delivered the latest algorithm, Murray had called back within half an hour. Kevin Hanley was desperate for Trent to come work for his team.

"Your own lab," Shane said. "Pay and perks out the kazoo."

"We weren't told to start this partnership just to dissolve it a week later." Trent fed a pile of research documents into the departmental shredder. He winced at the sound. He might as well feed his heart through the metal teeth. "I'm not working for some company Kevin Hanley hasn't even bothered to name."

"In that case, Murray says the group wants to get a lock on your future work. All of it. Murray has negotiated a flat up-front fee of one million dollars." When Trent's only response was to feed more paper into the shredder, she asked, "Did you hear what I just said?"

"Yes." He knew he should be ecstatic. He had never imagined possessing such a sum. But just then, it was all he could do not to rage at the sky. He fed the last of his research documents into the shredder, then sat down at the computer. He plugged in the two external hard drives, the one from the office safe and the other he kept with him at all times. He told himself to get it over with. But his hands would not obey.

That afternoon, at what was to be his second meeting with his new thesis advisor, Trent had resigned from the doctoral program. Or at least, he had tried to. His new advisor was the former head of the physics department, who had returned to teaching in order to have more time for his own research. But the man retained a dean's ability to read the winds. He had excused himself, apparently to phone the president's office. Five minutes later, he had returned to the office and informed Trent that his request to *delay* his thesis work had been accepted. The university intended to maintain a very close connection with their new rising star, the professor told him, clearly repeating what the president had said. Trent was urged to take whatever time he needed. And then return. His position would be waiting for him.

Shane broke into his thoughts with, "Those external drives are all that's left of your thesis?"

Trent stared at the two hard drives. "Yes."

He reached for the mouse. If only he could remember what he was doing this for.

Shane covered his hand with her own. "I have an idea."

Trent listened to her plan.

She asked, "What do you think?"

Trent licked his lips. He tasted something, a fragrance so faint he could not actually name it as hope. Even so, he said, "Let's do it."

42

When the door shut behind the departing colonel, the woman said, "Jason."

The young man reached into the briefcase beside his chair and set another file before her. The woman opened it, scanned two documents, and signed both. As she wrote, she told them, "Your projects are hereby reinstated under my direct supervision. You will report to me and me alone. Tell me you understand."

Reese asked, "Who are you?"

"My name is Amanda Thorne." She gave Reese the full force of her steel-blue gaze. "You may consider me as the only person who matters. Are we clear on this?"

"Yes. Absolutely."

"Good." She shut the file. "So, Ms. Clawson. You have achieved a controllable extension of human awareness. Spooky."

"You have no idea."

"You're working with technology that was stolen from a foreign source, is that correct?"

"Their system was passed to us by a dissatisfied team member. Some of the team is American. The leader is an Italian psychologist, Dr. Gabriella Speciale. They are based in the borderlands between Italy and Switzerland."

"What tie do they hold to foreign governments?"

"I am almost certain that there is none whatsoever."

"If they're in this room, would we know it?"

"No. Definitely not."

"So how do we know they're not here right now?"

"To date, every known non-physical contact with the group has been tied to a specific risk identification. Something or someone has directly targeted their team."

Reese waited then, dreading the woman's next question. Which would be, what specifically had happened for Reese to know all this. And the answer was, she had failed. She had never met this woman before. But she knew the type. Amanda Thorne hated failure above all else. Reese might as well put a gun to her head.

Instead, the woman asked, "You still have your mole inside their team?"

Reese did not know how to answer that.

Amanda Thorne nodded, as though she had wanted no other response than silence. "I'm glad not to hear it, Ms. Clawson." She turned her attention to Kevin. "Let me make sure I have this straight. How far down the road are we looking before your team can break standard 128-bit encryption?"

"Maybe ten years," Kevin replied. "Maybe never."

"You are facing serious problems, then."

"Huge. Maybe impossible to resolve."

"But recently you were contacted by this young researcher." She glanced at her assistant.

Jason supplied, "His name is Trent Major."

"A student at UCSB suddenly offers you one completely new construct after another. And in the process, he accelerates your progress. But you are still some distance from your objective."

"Affirmative."

"Then yesterday, you obtained concrete evidence of Trent Major's direct involvement with this Swiss team."

"Trent Major and the woman known as Elizabeth Sayer met in Santa Barbara," Reese confirmed. "Sayer has been part of the Italian scientist's team since its inception."

"Sayer, as in the pharmaceutical company?"

"Daughter of the chairman. Disowned."

"Let's focus on Trent Major for just a moment longer. His obvious connection to anyone or anything outside our scope is certainly troubling."

Kevin replied, "Trent Major's research is beyond cutting edge. Whatever his source, we need to tie him up. We offered him a job. He refused outright. His attorney has countered with an offer to give us exclusive rights to all future research. It cost us a million dollars up front."

"Do it."

"I already have."

The woman turned back to Reese. "Say we determined that this Swiss team is an unacceptable risk to the security of our nation. Say we wanted to take them out. What would you advise?"

"Make no advance planning." Reese had thought of this long and hard. Her response was immediate. "Give no warning. Decide and go. Attack from all sides. Use overwhelming force. And one other thing."

"Yes?"

"Anticipate serious casualties."

43

This is as faceless as I could find," Shane told him.

They were seated in her rental car outside a bank in downtown Goleta. UCSB was not actually inside the city that bore its name. Instead, it was three towns away, where it had acquired a former military base. But the regents of the California university system were not total dodos. The name University of California at Isla Vista held no draw whatsoever. If they could name the airport after a town nineteen miles to the south, why not the university? And so a lie was born.

The quiet middle-class town of Goleta was located midway between Isla Vista and Santa Barbara proper. Downtown Goleta was a hodgepodge of fifties-era family companies wedged between all the big-box stores that Santa Barbara refused to admit. The Goleta State Bank was a throwback to earlier days, a two-story hacienda-style structure with a polished, moneyed air.

"The deposit box is registered under my name," Shane told him. "I've had it ever since my sister went down for the ninth time. Or maybe the tenth. It holds the last remnants of our lives before the shredder. My father's watch. Mom's earrings. Our birth certificates and my passport. A bracelet. Everything my sister couldn't find and pawn." She brushed the flies of memory away from her face. "There's plenty of room in there for your hard drives."

Trent said, "Thanks. A lot."

"It's not really breaking the rules, right? I mean, you've stopped your research and you're hiding away your results. Sticking it in a bank's basement is as good as frying the drives. Almost, anyway."

Trent did not correct her. But he could do nothing about the dream memory. The crystalline-edged image had shown him demolishing the two hard drives and walking away from his research. For good.

Shane said, "When this is over, I need to see what's on that iPod. Why it was important for that woman to rock our universe."

Trent had been thinking the same thing. But all he said was, "Let's do this thing."

※

When they landed in LAX, Reese and Kevin turned on their cell phones. The chimes came instantly. Reese listened to her messages and shut her phone and wished she could smash it on a rock.

Kevin cut his own connection and announced, "Our new ops team has just reported in."

Amanda Thorne had placed enough agents under Kevin's direct supervision to maintain constant tabs on Trent Major and Shane Schearer.

"They're already in place?"

"And not a moment too soon. Trent has resigned from the UCSB doctoral program. The university is calling it an interim sabbatical. But the kid is gone. He destroyed all records, all files. Or so we would have assumed, had our team not observed him going straight from the physics building to a bank in Goleta, where his partner keeps a safety deposit box."

Reese waited until they entered the airport terminal's din to reply, "Maybe Trent has another formula in the works. Bigger than all the rest."

"Maybe he's got a dozen. Or maybe he's become a repository for that group in Switzerland. Or maybe he's uncovered something awful. I don't care. I want it all, and I want it now." Kevin checked the monitors for their Santa Barbara flight, steered them down the hall, and said, "I don't want to go back to Amanda and ask for more favors. We need something concrete to demonstrate we're worth the trouble."

"I can handle this."

"It's a safety deposit box in a private bank, Reese." When she did not respond, he said, "You've got trained thieves on your payroll?"

She had actually thought of that and discounted it. "Too noisy. I told you I'll handle it and I will."

They arrived at the departures gate just as their connecting flight was called. Kevin said, "You want to tell me what's got you looking so grim?"

"One of my team went out for dinner last night. Elene Belote. She hasn't checked in."

"How late is she?"

"Fourteen hours."

He shrugged. "That's nothing. Fourteen hours is one decent hangover."

Reese shook her head. "This has never happened before. Especially not with this lady. Elene Belote lives and breathes for her next transit."

Kevin studied her. "What aren't you telling me?"

She hesitated, then shrugged. Why not. "Elene and Joss Stone, the former Marine, they're who I consider my primary crew. I was hoping to shape them into something more than just hunter-seekers." Reese followed Kevin into the flight for Santa Barbara. When they settled into their seats, she said, "I've got a bad feeling about this. Very bad indeed."

When Gabriella called, she must have caught Charlie's guarded tone because her first question was, "Can you talk?"

"In principle."

"Where are you?"

"A realtor's office. Elizabeth says it's important."

"This is another component of those images she received during the ascent?"

"Apparently so."

Elizabeth glanced over. "Gabriella?"

When Charlie nodded, Elizabeth picked up a magazine. She flipped the pages hard enough to make them pop.

Charlie asked, "What time is it over there?"

"Almost one in the morning," Gabriella replied. "The students just left. They have a message for you. It's why I called. Massimo says to tell you we have to move away from here."

Charlie shifted in his seat, drawing in closer to Elizabeth. "Massimo gave you the message that we have to leave Campione?"

Elizabeth stopped turning the pages and stared at him.

"He and the other students together. They all received the same image."

Charlie returned Elizabeth's gaze. "Did Massimo say what form the image came in?"

"They ascended. It was waiting for them. He said it was a very powerful experience."

"Did Massimo say where we were supposed to go?"

"Only that you and Elizabeth would know. They saw a square enclosure covered in sand. Very large. Surrounded by a rock wall. They were high up. He could see the ocean in every direction. He says it is very important and you should look for this."

Charlie directed his words at Elizabeth. "Massimo's image says we're supposed to find him a giant sandbox. On top of a hill. On an island. In the middle of the ocean."

"Massimo and all the others. They said something else, Charlie. He said to tell you that spies are coming."

"Did he say when, or who was behind it?"

"No. He said it was another image. A warning. It carried a sense of dread. He said the spy was a ghost. We were speaking Italian. That was the word he used. Or specter. Massimo says to tell you that the specter will be attacking us very soon." Gabriella waited for Charlie to respond. When he remained silent, she asked, "When are you returning?"

"Hard to say." Actually, Charlie was uncertain about a lot of things just then. Including what they were doing in this office. All he knew was Elizabeth had ascended the previous night. Without his knowledge. Alone. "I'll call as soon as I know something definite."

Charlie said his farewells and shut his phone and relayed Gabriella's message. When Elizabeth did not respond, he asked, "Is there any particular reason why you didn't ask me to help with your ascent?"

She stared at the magazine. "I couldn't sleep. I didn't want to disturb you. The iPod's instructions are meant to be used alone."

Charlie knew she wasn't telling him everything. But Elizabeth was back in tough-girl mode. He had arrived for breakfast to find her dressed as she was now, in an outfit of black silk with two flashes across her padded shoulders and her hair spiked and her expression hard. Elizabeth's outfit and attitude was a distinct contrast to all the other wealthy women in the realtor's office.

He asked quietly, "Is there anything else from the ascent you think I should know?"

Elizabeth spread her hands over the magazine still open in her lap. She said, "The older me was there waiting again. Same envelope on the table. Just like last time. I opened it and got struck by three images. Hard. First, we're going to have to leave Switzerland, and soon. Second, we needed to come here and do this thing."

Charlie waited, then asked, "And door number three?"

Elizabeth clenched her entire body, like a fist turning to stone. She trembled. Or perhaps she merely shook her head.

The receptionist walked over and said, "Mr. Credwell will see you now."

⊪

Santa Barbara's main shopping street passed beneath the Central Coast rail lines before ending at the entrance to the pier. Right of the pier, the Santa Barbara harbor formed a clamshell design holding million-dollar yachts. South of the pier was a waterfront park with jogging lanes and bike paths that rose to join the oceanfront cliffs. The park was lined by beachfront hotels and private houses and high-end offices. The Christie's real estate office occupied the penthouse of a gleaming white cube at the park's northern end.

"Ms. Sayer? Nigel Credwell. So sorry to have kept you waiting. How nice to make your acquaintance. And you, sir, are . . ."

"My associate," Elizabeth replied for Charlie.

"Of course. Delighted. Please, do be seated. Can I offer you refreshments, a coffee, perhaps?"

"No thank you."

200

"Splendid. Well then, perhaps you'd be so kind as to share with me what I can do for you."

The British realtor had done what he could to transform the sterile cube into something suitable. Charlie's chair was French and old and finished in silk. He was fairly certain the coffee table was rosewood. As was the desk. The chamber itself was framed in walnut wainscoting. Two display cases held antique scientific instruments. The oil behind the realtor's chair appeared to be a Gainsborough landscape. Beyond the damask drapes, sailboats drifted across a turquoise sea.

Elizabeth said, "I want to buy an island."

"Do you indeed. How fascinating." Credwell was dressed in what Charlie assumed was that year's mode for the yachtie set, a cream blazer with solid gold buttons, woven linen shirt, matching trousers. His Rolex was oversized and rattled on his bony wrist. "Might I say, Ms. Sayer, you have come to the right place. Christie's has more—"

"Not just any island. I want one with nation status."

The realtor studied her. Then Charlie. Then back to Elizabeth. "You wish to acquire a property which comes with sovereignty."

"That is correct."

Credwell gave her a long look. "Such properties are extremely rare."

"But you have one."

"Might I ask how you obtained my name?"

"No," Elizabeth replied. "You may not."

"This is most astonishing." Credwell steepled his hands. "As it happens, I am personally in contact with one family with a property that is not officially for sale. Or perhaps you are already aware of this."

Elizabeth did not respond.

"Yes. I see. Well. The family patriarch passed away some eight years ago. Since then, the property has been used during the summer months only. There is an ongoing feud between the surviving family members. However, I am led to believe that a suitable offer might be welcomed."

"How much?"

"Somewhere in the neighborhood of thirty million dollars."

When Elizabeth glanced doubtfully at Charlie, the realtor lifted his chin slightly. "Might I say, Ms. Sayer, these days such a hefty premium means the property is really only suitable for an entity with very special needs. Such requirements, if you don't mind my saying, that are not—"

"Our reasons for needing the property are our own." Elizabeth reached into her purse and came out with the Los Angeles bank documents. "We're good for the money."

The realtor's eyebrows lifted at the size of their opening deposit. Five million dollars. "Would you mind terribly if I phoned the bank and confirmed this?"

"Go ahead."

He started to rise, then settled back into his chair. "There is something you should know in advance. The property in question is a Channel Island, some eight miles off the northern tip of Guernsey. It is not, well, how shall I put this. To describe the accommodations as basic would be a vast overstatement."

Charlie glanced at Elizabeth for guidance. She did not respond.

Credwell went on, "The island in question measures three miles long and two wide. But less than sixty acres are anything approaching level. The remaining landscape is quite hilly. Steep, actually. There is only one road, and that is of compressed shale. There is a manor, completed in the eighteenth century. Plumbing and electricity were added in the early twentieth century. Since then, very little has been done to the place. There are seventeen other permanent dwellings on the island, mostly cottages occupied by crofters and fishermen and shepherds." He looked worriedly from one to the other. "I am told that in the summer it is quite nice. Welcoming, in fact. But between September and May the island holds a rather forbidding aspect."

Elizabeth asked, "When can we do the deal?"

"Don't you wish to view the property?"

"I'll fly to London tomorrow. Go make your calls." Elizabeth glanced at her watch. "We must leave for another appointment."

45

Shane did not want to be on her own when she tried the iPod. Trent could understand that. But the instructions were clear enough. The single handwritten sheet said she was to be alone in a room where she could be absolutely certain she would not be disturbed, either by noise or by an intruder. Trent had studied that final word with a scientist's care. The issue was clearly related to concentration, something that required such an intent focus that any outside interference was not merely a distraction but a threat. Even so, Shane had been adamant.

"I'm not doing this alone."

"I might interrupt the process."

"Then again, you might keep me from disappearing." She was very solemn. "I need you here with me, Trent."

He tasted the words several times before saying, "I like hearing you say that."

"Will you stay?"

They were in her apartment, a typical student affair two blocks from the ocean cliffs. The building had been thrown up in the seventies and poorly maintained ever since. The place smelled of unwashed clothes and dust and cosmetics. Each apartment contained a cramped living/dining area, three closet-sized bedrooms, and one bath. But it was a five-minute cycle ride from the business school, and it was cheap. The waiting list for such apartments was three years long.

Trent walked to the French doors. The balcony was a foot deep and overlooked a scruffy bit of lawn and the West Campus Lane. He set his chair so that the two rear legs were outside the room. "How's that?"

She settled onto the bed and leaned her back against the side wall. "Thank you, Trent."

"No chance of your roommates barging in?"

"They both work afternoons." The bed was narrow even for her. Even so, there was scarcely enough room to open the door or fit in the desk jammed by the far wall. Shane must have been thinking the same thing, because she said, "One night in luxury, and I'm ready to leave this place forever."

"You can afford it." For a brief moment, he wondered if she might consider taking an apartment with him.

She studied him, as though testing whether she might say the same thing. When she spoke, it was to say, "I'd be breaking the family mold, moving into something decent."

"Sorry. I don't follow."

"My aunt's happiest days were playing hippie. She never found a reason to work very hard or look for very much." Shane picked up her pillow and bundled it into her lap. "My sister took that attitude and distilled it down to an essence made for the new millennium. She's determined never to extend her horizons one inch."

"I understand."

"You really do, don't you." Her normal rigid strength, a determination that kept her entire body taut, was gone now. Her face was scrubbed clean. Her hair was loose and tumbled around her shoulders. She looked about twelve years old. Shane asked, "Do you find it strange, how we feel so comfortable around each other? I mean, given how weird it was the way we came together."

"I know what you mean," Trent replied. "And I think it's great."

"I guess I might as well do this thing." Shane settled the pillow back in place and stretched out on the bed. "Remind me what I'm supposed to do."

Trent did not need to read the page again. "Put on the headphones. Press the tab marked simply with an X. Close your eyes. Follow the instructions."

He watched her adjust the headset. She looked his way, then keyed the controls and set the iPod on the covers beside her, and shut her eyes.

After that, there wasn't anything to see. Not that Trent objected to being there. Normally the only way he could study her openly was from behind, when she didn't know he was watching. From the back, her neck was a vase holding a perfect bouquet of copper hair. She usually wore it caught in a band, pulled back tight from her face and ears. He had come to think of them as fairy ears, delicate and perfectly formed and so pale as to be translucent. As he watched her now, a trace of hair trembled upon her right ear, beckoning him to lean forward and lick it away.

Ten minutes passed. Her breathing grew so shallow he could not see her chest move. Trent wondered if she had fallen asleep. A warm breeze pushed through the balcony doors, carrying the spice of eucalyptus and Pacific salt. A car drifted past, music spilling from the open windows. A pair of women cycled by, their tires slipping softly over the asphalt. One of them laughed. They turned the corner, and the world was silent except for the rush of wind through the trees. Trent checked his watch. Twenty-two minutes had passed. He wondered how long he should give her.

Shane took a long breath. Another. She opened her eyes and rose to a seated position. And stared at the wall opposite her. Frowning.

"Are you okay?"

"Yes."

"Do you need a drink of water or something?"

"No. I'm good." Shane started to rise, then dropped back hard. "Whoa."

He was instantly there beside her. "Steady."

"I feel like I've run a marathon."

"Maybe you should lie down."

"No. We need to get back to the bank before it closes. My passport is in the box with your data." She gripped his arm and pulled herself upright. "I feel weak as a kitten. And dizzy."

He steadied her as she left the bedroom and made a tight circuit of the front room. "Do you want to tell me what happened?"

She looked at him. "I have to go to London tomorrow."

He caught the worry in her voice. "What's the matter?"

"You weren't with me."

46

Charlie called Gabriella in the park across the street from the realtor's office. It was the middle of the night in Switzerland, but Gabriella did not sound at all sleepy. Elizabeth strolled beneath the imperial palms while he described the meeting. Gabriella absorbed it quickly, then said, "I should travel with her to this place. What is the island's name?"

"Starn. Eight miles off Guernsey." He knew Elizabeth wouldn't like it much. But Charlie said, "I think you should go too."

"When is this happening?"

"Elizabeth leaves tomorrow morning for London Gatwick. She'll make arrangements to travel on once she arrives. Christie's has an office on Guernsey. They've been alerted and will be ready to take her over."

"Tell Elizabeth I'll meet her in London." Gabriella hesitated, then asked once again, "When will you be returning to us, Charlie?"

"I've got to see about the kid and his girlfriend. And what role Reese Clawson plays in all this."

"I can't get over how that woman has resurfaced. Are you safe?"

"I used a false ID from my security days to check us into our hotel here in Santa Barbara. I masked myself from the security cameras with a cap and sunglasses. Elizabeth waited in the car." His customary precautions were probably enough. Even so, once he was alone, he'd find another hotel with better back-door access.

"Return as soon as you are able, Charlie. This place is not the same when you are gone. Especially now."

Charlie said his farewells and stood staring into the sunlight, compressing the cell phone between his hands. Wondering if he should have just come out and said how he felt about her, and about her distance. Knowing he had not spoken for fear of how she would probably reply.

⫴

Elizabeth directed him north along the coastal road. They skirted Santa Barbara's harbor and passed the art deco pool complex anchoring the port's northern end, then drove through a neighborhood of overpriced sixties-era tract homes.

Elizabeth said, "Turn here."

The parking area was nestled in a forested valley separating the city from Hope Ranch, a quiet enclave of multimillionaires, towering redwoods, and jaw-dropping homes. The park was clearly a locals spot, with no road sign indicating that it led to a beachfront playground. The lot was filled with pickups and builders' vans and the sort of family vehicles that were largely absent from Santa Barbara's better-known locales. The beach was wide and filled with kids. To the north, a rocky promontory extended into the Pacific, forming a point break for an overhead swell. The cliffs of Hope Ranch towered above the surfers clustered south of the rocks.

The Boathouse Restaurant was a throwback to a simpler era. The booths were covered in cracked vinyl, the floors linoleum, the tables scarred. Behind the counter and the oblong chef's window, cooks hustled. The place was crowded and noisy and cheerful. The view was spectacular.

Elizabeth snagged a passing waitress and asked if they could take a recently vacated window booth. Charlie waited until they were seated to ask, "What are we doing?"

"All I know is, the third image showed us sitting here. In this booth." She pointed at the clock above the chef's window. "At noon."

"If this happens again, do you think you could ask yourself when she comes from, and why?"

"I tried to this time." She resumed her tightly distraught expression. "All she said was, 'Pay careful attention.'"

"Look at me. Please." Charlie leaned across the table. "If you won't tell me what's wrong, I can't help you."

Her gaze was as shattered as her whisper. "I wanted to lie to you about the third image."

Charlie leaned back. He had no idea how to respond.

"I wanted to say I saw us going back to the hotel from here. And I saw me doing what I've longed to do since the first time we met."

Charlie met her gaze. Which cost him. He searched for something that might diminish the moment's discomfort but came up empty. Maybe because of just how tempted he was. That, and knowing how he kept trying to climb his own glass mountain.

When the words did not come, Charlie reached over and took her hand and sat there. Silently helping Elizabeth knit her world back together.

Eventually her breathing eased. But her voice held the same fractured note as she said, "I ascended to see if we would ever get together. Or when. If not, I thought maybe I could walk away. That's why I didn't ask you to help me out. But all I got for my troubles was another visit to the white room, another look at my older smiling face, another letter."

Charlie sat with his back to the Pacific and facing the door. Which was why he was the first to see the woman enter. He released Elizabeth's hand and straightened. "Heads up."

"What is it?"

The woman saw him then. She focused on Charlie so tightly she almost collided with a bustling waitress. The woman did not even hear the waitress's sharp warning. She just kept coming.

The woman stopped before their table. She stared at Charlie for a long moment.

He asked, "Can I help you?"

She replied, "It's you, isn't it."

Then she burst into tears.

·|||·

Elizabeth did not like sitting next to the tear-streaked woman, but Charlie insisted upon it. He wanted the table between himself and this woman's traumatized state. A waitress had spoken with the cooks through the kitchen window, and now they were all giving him the stink eye. Elizabeth was too captivated by what she was hearing to notice the glares. Twice she started to interrupt the woman, but Charlie silenced her with a fractional shake of his head. He did not even know the woman's name. He watched her fight for control and let her ramble.

When the woman finally ran out of steam, Charlie asked, "Do you want something to eat?"

"No, thank you. A tea would be nice."

Catching the waitress's eye was never easier. "Elizabeth, you want anything more?"

"Sure thing. Some answers."

When the waitress was gone, Charlie said to the stranger, "Let me make sure I understand what you're saying. This team run by a woman—what was her name again?"

"Reese Clawson."

"Okay. So Reese operates a project under federal jurisdiction that utilizes a stolen program to elicit—what was the word you used again?"

"Transits."

"When the subjects transit, they go to specific targets that Reese lays out. To steal secrets."

"Yes." She sipped her tea. "So far."

The woman was a professional ghost. Charlie had met a number of them in his former life. They fashioned an unremarkable physical appearance into a cloak that masked them utterly. They could transcend danger in plain sight and go unnoticed.

Charlie asked, "What were you, DOD intel?"

"CIA. I had moved as far up the analysis ladder as I was going to climb. Then one day word was quietly passed, suggesting volunteers were being sought for a new form of field duty. I had just been through a nasty divorce. I didn't even think about what I was doing."

Elizabeth asked, "What is your name?"

"Elene. Elene Belote."

"I'm Elizabeth Sayer. This is Charlie Hazard."

The act of meeting his gaze caused Elene to leak more tears. "I thought I recognized you when I came into the restaurant. But I couldn't be certain. Then when I was close, I caught your flavor. And I knew."

Looking back later, Charlie realized this was the moment when he became aware of what was coming down the pipe. He did not know how he could possibly have understood this far in advance. But his gut became twisted in the manner only a warrior ever knew, when the unlit cordite and the unspent bullets emitted a funk as real as terror.

Elizabeth asked for them both, "What did you know, Elene?"

"That you were the one who saved me from the horror." She gave that a long beat, then continued, "The last time but one that I transited, I was almost swallowed by the same thing that has devoured others from my team."

Elizabeth was watching him now. Waiting for him to explain. But Charlie was too busy dealing with the surging dread. He made do with, "Go on."

"I didn't want to transit again, but I had to. Because I knew someone had come and saved me. For a time, I thought it was Joss, another member of Reese's team. But something told me I was mistaken. I'm an analyst. I've spent my entire professional life valuing precision. That night, after the panic eased, I knew I had been wrong to thank Joss. It wasn't him. It was someone *like* him. Another warrior. Only this one was concerned enough about others, even strangers, that he would risk the horror to come for me."

"What horror was this?" Elizabeth asked.

Elene's gaze never left his face. "You know, don't you."

Charlie tasted the air. "I know."

"So I snuck into the transit room on my own. And went up again. And this time, I asked a question of my own. I was shown this restaurant, today, right now. So I came. And here you are." She began shedding more tears. "I need you to tell me what happens next."

Kevin watched the swarm of activity and said, "I'm impressed."

The Goleta State Bank's forecourt was jammed with dark-windowed SUVs. Two men and a woman, all in black suits, spoke with people just inside the bank's main doors.

Reese said, "Normally I'd prefer such a seizure to take place in the middle of the night. But the regional team just cleared a bank closure and had an unexpected opening. It was this afternoon or in three days."

"Three days is too long," Kevin agreed.

"The Federal Deposit Insurance Corporation is a quasi-private group." Reese returned her attention to the bank's front doors. "Which means they are open to pressure from somebody higher up the banking food chain."

Kevin pointed at the three stern-faced men and two women in blue nylon jackets surrounding the bank's entrance and ushering out the day's final customers. "But those guys are federal agents."

"Standard operating procedure. Any time a bank is taken over by the FDIC, the sheriff's office and the local feds are alerted. One or the other takes care of security during the handover." Reese watched as a trio of red-faced bankers were ushered through the front doors. The executives protested angrily as they were directed to move away. "It turns out the bank's been under FDIC watch for several months. Same old story. Bad loans, bad economy, too small to obtain bail-out funds, sinking under the weight of its debts. All I did was move things forward."

Kevin's words carried a genuine sense of approval. "Way to get things done, Reese."

"What if Trent Major has encrypted his research data?"

"I'm hoping my team can break through any firewalls he's inserted. In that case, we'll copy his work, replace the drives in the safety deposit box, and nobody is the wiser. But if need be, we'll bring him in. Give him the choice. A rock or a hard place."

Reese watched another news van pull into the lot. Two agents in standard nylon jackets unwound police tape to establish a perimeter. "I wonder what Trent has locked away in there."

"I've been thinking about that." The agents blocked one of the announcers who wanted a close-up of the bank's entrance. "These days, there are two totally different kinds of physicists, theoretical and applied. Quantum theorists operate on the edge of reality. In many cases, they've lost touch entirely. The applied physicists are people who are interested in seeing their work realized on the physical plane. They want *action*. But theorists accuse the applied group of being little more than engineers, incapable of coming up with anything genuinely new. This dichotomy is what makes Trent so different. He is taking an applied physicist's view toward the outer borders of the theoretical realm." Kevin glanced over. "Do you understand what I'm saying?"

"Trent is a rare beast."

"He is *unique*."

"So which camp do you belong to, theoretical or applied?"

"Neither." Kevin aged ten years in the time it took to shape that one word. "I'm the third kind. The prehistoric animal who's survived by moving into admin. The guys doing the real work put up with me because I control the checkbook. Most of the time, I'm not even sure what they're talking about."

Reese smiled, not because she found what he said humorous. Because she liked his willingness to be open with her. "We were talking about what's inside Trent's hard drives."

"My gut is telling me he's come up with a means of breaking the barrier of superposition."

"Explain."

"The prion molecule used for shaping the quantum computation must be totally isolated from its environment. The slightest interaction with the external world causes the molecule to decohere. The effect is irreversible. So long as that doesn't happen, while the only stimulus operating within our quantum field is our own algorithmic calculation, the molecule remains in superposition. Expanding this superposed period is crucial. We're looking in particular at something called the transverse relaxation time. The only ways we've managed to expand this period are through a combination of supercooling and vacuum isolation of the individual molecules. But there are indications that prions can be held in superposition through strong magnetic resonance generated within tightly controlled wavelengths. I'm hoping Trent will supply—"

Kevin stopped speaking because one of the agents walked over to their car. Reese rolled down her window.

The agent asked, "You Clawson?"

"Yes."

"Can I see your warrant?"

"Sure thing."

The agent took her time inspecting the documents, then handed them back through the window. "They're ready for you now." She waited for them to rise from the car, then handed over two navy windbreakers. "Put these on."

Reese handed one of the jackets to Kevin. "All I can say is, I sure hope Trent's research is worth the trouble."

48

Shane and Trent argued the entire way to the bank. Shane said, "We can bend things a little bit. What's the problem? We'll just say your traveling with me to England is part of the package."

"You're missing the point."

"That's absolutely not true. I know exactly what the point is. I don't want to go anywhere without you." Shane put her hand to her mouth. "Did I really say that?"

Trent's smile felt too big for his face. "Boy, did you ever."

"The point is, we're in this together. That's what I meant."

"Whatever."

"Stop grinning."

"Yes ma'am. Absolutely." Trent pulled up to a stoplight. "Take me through this ascent thing again. That's what they called it, right?"

"Yes. I've done that already. Three times."

"Please."

"I was counted up. There was this background hiss, almost like music. Or the wind."

"But it sounded nice."

"Really pleasant. I drifted further and further as this guy counted me up. He explained everything in this very steady voice. He had an accent."

"You didn't mention that before."

"I forgot. French, maybe. Or Portuguese. It was nice too. He talked about how my heart rate and breathing were slowing, and how I could stop this ascent any time I wanted. I felt that, you know. Really clearly. That was why I didn't get scared. And because you were in the room."

Trent waited, then pressed quietly, "Then it happened."

"It must sound crazy."

He was glad for another stoplight. "You want crazy, let's talk about me meeting myself in a dream and coming back with an algorithm. And us meeting. And you coming up with a whole pile of dough."

She crossed her arms. "I know what you're going to say."

He told her anyway. "This is bigger than we can possibly understand at this stage. And it's growing all the time."

She did not respond.

"So what happened then?"

"You know what. I moved up to where I was floating somewhere above my body. I saw you sitting on the balcony. You were watching me. And smiling. A small smile, but it looked nice."

Trent shivered. This was the fourth time she had described seeing him. It still freaked him out.

"I could still hear the guy talking, even while I was floating there, looking down at myself. He said, if there is anything vital I needed to gain from this ascent, I needed to realize it now."

"Ascent," Trent repeated. "Realize."

"One second I was there in the room with you, the next and I was in an airport. Standing in line for immigration. I knew it was London. And a blonde woman was standing beside me. I'm assuming it's the same woman who spoke to you in the Starbucks."

"Spiky white-blonde hair, very pretty, but tough build with an atti-tude to match. There can't be two of them." Trent gave her a moment, then said it for her. "And I wasn't there."

"I didn't see you, is all. Maybe you were somewhere else."

"No, Shane. That's not what you said before. You knew I wasn't with you."

Her face was pinched tight. "I might have gotten that wrong."

"You didn't, though. Did you."

She swiveled in her seat. "What about your data sitting in the box with my passport?"

He nodded slowly. "I've been thinking about that. I need to do what I was shown. Destroy it."

"Trent. No."

"The bigger this is, the more precisely we need to move."

"Two years of work."

He searched for something to lighten the moment. But the ache bloomed in his chest like a tainted rose.

Then he pulled into the bank's parking lot and was blocked by a trio of news vans. "What's going on here?"

Shane was up and moving before the car stopped. When a woman in a blue jacket tried to halt her, Shane exclaimed, "I've got to get in there!"

"Sorry, ma'am. The bank is closed."

"But my passport is in—"

"Step back, please. You can't get inside the bank and that's final."

Trent could see she wanted to argue. He took hold of her arm and pulled her back. Shane let him move her but continued to argue with the agent. "I have *got* to make that flight."

"Steady." Trent led her around the periphery of the taped entrance area. Another news van was parked at the lot's opposite end, the roof-top satellite dishes unfolded and aimed skyward. A technician leaned against a bumper and smoked. Trent asked, "Can you tell me what's happened here?"

"FDIC seizure." The guy flipped his cigarette across the lot. "The bank's gone bust. They're searching the documents."

"My friend has a flight to England tomorrow, and her passport is inside the safety deposit box."

The guy shrugged. It wasn't news and he wasn't particularly interested. "I've covered eight of these closures. Day after tomorrow they'll have the bank up and running under new management and probably a new name. Three days tops. Until then, you're not getting inside those doors."

"But—"

"Trent. Save it." Shane was pressed against the van's rear door, angled so she was out of sight of the bank entrance. "Get over here."

"What's the matter?"

"Kevin Hanley is inside."

The name was so unexpected Trent needed a minute to place him. "That can't be."

"Oh really. And what else just happens to be inside that bank?" She was the one moving now. Her hand in his. Pulling hard. "We have to get out of here."

Which was when he saw the watcher. Trent accelerated until they were jogging together, back around the taped perimeter. He slipped behind the wheel of the rental and started and accelerated away. Almost clipping a truck as he pulled from the lot.

"Slow down. They didn't see us."

"We're being followed."

Shane looked at him, frightened now. "What?"

"A woman was talking on the phone and watching us. I saw her before. Outside the physics building this morning just as we were driving away."

"You're certain it was the same woman?"

"I'm the guy who never forgets, remember?"

Shane turned around, stared out behind. "Are they following us now?"

"My guess is, probably."

"What are we going to do?"

Trent floored it through a yellow light. "I have an idea."

⫰⫯⫰

Kevin slapped his phone shut and said, "Step away from the doors."

"What's going on?"

"The kids. They're outside."

"What?" Reese turned her back to the entrance. "Why?"

"Most likely they returned for the hard drives in my hand. You want me to trot over and ask them?" He gripped the two drives so tightly his knuckles turned bloodless. His phone rang. He slapped it open, listened, shut it again. "Okay. They're gone."

"I can't believe they showed up like that."

He pushed through the entrance and headed for the car. "Let's shift things to the lab and see what we've got."

Shane heard the party long before she could see it. The noise carried a manic quality, like a cheap carnival on a Saturday night. But it was the middle of the week here, and the sun was only now settling into the Pacific. Classes were supposed to be in session. But the university was empty. The party had been going on for several hours already. UCSB was unofficially shut down for the holiday of Floatopia.

Isla Vista Beach ran north of University Point and could only be accessed at a few spots. Which was how the students liked it. Anybody who wanted to scope out whatever they were doing could be seen a long way off. For a public place, nowhere in Isla Vista was so private as the beach.

The cliffs were very high and unscalable in most places. The beach itself was broad and flat enough to cycle on. But not today. Fifty thousand people jammed the beach and the surrounding area. Atop the cliffs, Del Playa Drive was effectively closed to traffic, and every yard fronting the shoreline was packed.

Like many things at UCSB, Floatopia was a good idea gone bad. It had started as an environmental protest. Bring together all the university groups concerned about the quality of the sea—the whale watchers and offshore drilling opponents and surfers battling pollution runoff. The groups waited for a calm day. Then they fashioned a floating rig of recycled materials. They paddled beyond the surf line. And passed a resolution to secede from America. The rest of the day was spent voting into policy all the things that would make for a better world. They named the project Floatopia. That first year, a hundred people showed up. The university rag gave them three paragraphs.

The second year, someone had the bright idea to bring beer.

After that, Floatopia grew like a toxic red tide.

Shane and Trent strolled down Del Playa Drive to a postage stamp of oceanfront green called Window To The Sea Park. As they descended the ramshackle stairs to the beach, Shane started to scout for watchers. Trent touched her arm and said, "Be cool."

"Sorry."

"You're doing great." Trent adjusted the straps of his backpack. He was carrying her makeup kit and an extra pair of shoes and her laptop and a book for the flight. Shane's backpack was filled with clothes. She had started to protest over him taking the heavier stuff. But he had been so solemn and intent upon doing right by her and taking care of her. Shane had never known the luxury of relying on another person before. She felt slightly weightless, as if all the forces that surrounded them were kept at bay by Trent's concern. Even gravity.

When they reached the beach, Trent asked, "Ready?"

She took his hand. "Sure thing."

Floatopia was a colorful island of junk five hundred meters offshore. A steady stream of homemade rafts and surfboards trekked back and forth from the beachside party. The island was perhaps a quarter mile wide, a massive floating junk pile topped by thousands of flags and kites and balloons. Music blared from hundreds of portable players. People danced all around them as they walked along the shoreline, but it was hard to say which music the dancers heard. If any. Faces carried a sunburnt glaze from hours of hard partying.

The university spirit had never left her feeling more out of place.

Trent headed south. The partiers shouted and pointed as the sun's final rim slipped below the horizon. Trent steered them back toward the cliff, where the crowd was less packed and they could move more easily. Twice they stopped and pretended to watch the waning light. Around them people argued over whether there had been a green flash. Shane kept her face directed at the sea while she searched the surrounding throng. "I don't see anyone."

"Unless our watchers were already decked out like drunken students, I doubt they'll risk coming down here and being spotted."

Shane caught an edge to his voice. "What's the matter?"

"I didn't bring anything for us to eat."

She laughed out loud. "We've got secret agents on our tail, some shadowy group has invaded a bank because of your data, and you're worried about me getting peckish?"

"Well, sure."

She wrapped her arms around him. "You're something else."

He looked down at her. "Is that good?"

"Yes, Trent. That is very good indeed."

He hesitated a long moment, then lifted one arm and settled it onto her shoulders. Shane strengthened her own grip in reply. She felt a tension ease from his frame, something he had been carrying for so long she only noticed it when it was gone. She took it for the right moment to say, "I want you to come with me."

"I can't."

"If you should stay, then so should I. We're partners. I'm not going without you."

She readied herself for all the responses she could imagine. The longer he took, the more she felt isolated from the surrounding hilarity. The only two somber faces on the entire beach.

Trent said, "Do this for us. Not for me. Not for you. For us. So we can hope for a future together."

She locked on to him more tightly. "How can you possibly speak the only words that will break down my walls?"

He lowered his face into her hair. "I've dreamed of doing this. All my life."

Shane said, "Promise you'll come join me as soon as you can."

He held her closer still. "The very nanosecond."

·¦¦¦·

They walked down past the point and then turned east on Ocean Road, the street that bordered the university. They had left their bikes there that afternoon before walking back to the apartment, having a bite, going for a drive, apparently drifting through a slow day in typical student fashion, while the party got under way. Abandoned bicycles formed a metal forest along the university's border and the park fronting Ocean Road. They waited in the shadows until a cluster of semi-sober students wandered past. Then they mounted up and headed south, through the university.

The university's southern border was rimmed by Lagoon Road. Where the street turned inward, a paved bike path branched off. The path continued along the top of the beachside cliffs. Trent held to a steady pace, passing a number of slower-moving cyclists returning to Goleta from the party. Five miles later, the path emptied into the parking lot fronting Goleta's main public beach. Their tires hissed past the shorefront restaurant and locals playing beach volleyball beneath the streetlights. Trent did not push it hard.

Where the parking lot ended, so did the streetlights. Their bike lights illuminated a small path of asphalt. If Trent had not known where the path started again, he would have missed it entirely. It was an inky river beneath a quarter moon. Once they left Goleta's shore- line behind, the only sound was the hiss of their tires along the path.

Seven miles farther south, they climbed the steep rise up to where the path joined the main shoreline drive. He stopped at the top, using a stumpy cedar for shelter. "Everything okay?"

"Fine." Shane was not even breathing hard. "That was fun."

Trent searched the night. Fifty yards farther on, Highway 101 ran through a concrete cavern. The traffic noise was thunderous in the night. "We'll cross that bridge and then be back in shadows."

"Let's do it."

Trent checked the night once more. A few cars passed. None slowed or gave any indication they were aware of two bikers hovering behind the tree. "Here we go."

The traffic noise rushed up at them. Then they were over and back on the empty path. After two miles and another rise, they entered into the rarified realm of Hope Ranch.

The main avenue was broad as the highway and rimmed by imperial palms. The streetlights cast a gentle glow over their progress. Trent knew there was little risk of their being followed. But he pushed it hard just the same. He swung into a cul-de-sac and cycled to the end. A stairwell opened through a grove of pines. The tang of kelp and sea salt was very strong.

Trent said, "We'll hide your bike in the trees."

Shane stepped from the bike. "How did you know about this place?"

"I started coming down here my first year. It's about as far from the university scene as I could get on two wheels. The beach below here is almost always empty. I've never seen anyone use these stairs." Trent descended three steps and lifted her bike over the railing. A trio of pines formed a natural wall. He had hidden his own bike here many times. Unless someone knew where to look, the bike was lost from view. "I guess they're too busy playing golf or off spending money."

Shane hissed, "Car."

"Come down here." As the car swung around the dead end, a street-light illuminated the vehicle's lone passenger. "It's Murray."

The attorney watched them approach the car with stone-like gravity. He inspected them and the night before unlocking the doors. When they slipped inside, he said, "I want to know what's going on, and I want to know now."

50

Gabriella sighed the name over the phone. "I can't believe someone on our team betrayed us and sold Reese Clawson our experimental protocol."

"And records," Charlie added. He stood by the window of his Santa Barbara hotel room. The bedside clock read three minutes after eight. Charlie could hear the television playing softly in Elizabeth's room next door. He also heard a shower running. "At least we now know what Reese is doing with her group. But it still doesn't answer what role Trent and Shane play in all this."

Gabriella pondered silently, then asked, "This woman who approached you in the restaurant did not specifically name Brett as the spy, did she?"

"Her name is Elené Belote. No, she did not hear who was behind the theft." Charlie recalled standing before the maelstrom while guilt and remorse snagged every wrong memory, pulling him toward the swirling dread. "But I know it was Brett."

He expected Gabriella to argue with him. But instead she said, "Belote sounds like a French name."

"She's from south Louisiana. Very quiet. But precise. A typical intel senior analyst. Able to sift through junk and find facts. I'm convinced she's telling us the truth. Elene Belote has ascended. Or transited, as they call it. Many times. And she did it according to the system you worked out."

"If you are convinced, Charlie, that is good enough for me." But her compliment was robbed of potency by her tone, which was utterly detached. "What do you think Clawson and her team are after?"

"First, infiltration and secrets. Belote told us that much. So far they've focused on transit points they themselves controlled. But their goal is to penetrate enemy territory and escape unseen." Charlie hesitated, then added, "We need to keep in mind what Massimo told you, how observers were returning to attack us. That sounds like Clawson and her team. It's the way they think."

"You know this for a fact, do you? How they think?"

"I know what I know."

Gabriella hesitated, then asked, "Will you tell me what is wrong?"

Charlie leaned against the side wall. The wallpaper was fabric with a rough weave. He could sense Elizabeth's feelings for him. They pulsed through the wall separating his room from hers. He could feel his own answering desire, woven into the wallpaper's design.

"Charlie?"

He dropped his hand. "You haven't asked the critical question yet. How did Elene know to come meet us? The answer is, she transited. And broke ranks. And asked her own question. Can you think what that question might be?"

Gabriella's silence was an admonition against his tone. Charlie knew he was being overly harsh. And he could not stop it. He went on, "Belote asked how she could help the others trapped like she almost was. The coma patients filling the ward they've set up. Elene Belote has seen for herself the horror they faced. There are nine of them, Gabriella. Nine more people trapped in comatose states. Just like Brett."

She moaned softly, "What have we done?"

"We didn't do this, Gabriella. Don't make things worse by taking on guilt you don't deserve. Belote knew that Reese Clawson might give lip service to keeping their casualties at a minimum. But if push came to shove, she would sacrifice them all to her goals. And I'm convinced her ultimate aim is to attack us. On our terms."

Gabriella grew subdued now. Thoughtful. "I don't understand."

"Elene Belote transited or ascended or whatever you want to call it. And she asked who would save her teammates from the same cauldron that almost swallowed her. And she was shown me and Elizabeth seated in that restaurant by the sea. Waiting for her. Only when she was close to us did Belote realize I was the one who had saved her." When Gabriella remained silent, Charlie spelled it out. "It could only mean one thing. I go and I bring her back. And then I try to save the others."

"No, Charlie. You yourself said how dangerous—"

"This isn't a Q&A. We're not talking options. This *already happened*." Charlie could hear the longing and frustration in his own voice, laced together with fear. "I have to do this, Gabriella."

"But not alone."

"That's how I always am. Even when I'm in Switzerland. Isn't that right? Out on the rim. With the other disposables."

He knew he was being unfair. He knew and could do nothing about it.

Gabriella, however, said merely, "You are our guardian. And when we move, you will become our island chieftain."

Charlie knew he should thank her. But all that came to mind was, *It's not enough.*

Gabriella went on, "You cannot risk our future on what this woman has told you. Promise me you will not do this alone."

Charlie returned his hand to the wall. "I have to go."

"Charlie. Please. Let me do this with you."

She was right, of course. Even in his state of ultimate frustration, he could see that much. "All right. We'll set it up by phone."

"You promise me?"

"Yes."

Even her sigh carried a musical quality. "Come back as soon as you can, Charlie. I miss you. We all do."

He hung up the phone and stood touching the wall. Wondering if there had ever been a life where things looked simple, and all choices did not seemingly lead to loss.

51

Unless I get answers I like, I'm walking." Murray Feinne's face was tightly cavernous in the glow from the car dash. "I don't care what kind of pressure you think you can lay on me. Managing partners, clients, whatever. I'm done being played with."

Trent sounded surprisingly calm to his own ears. "Who is pressuring you, Murray?"

"Oh, like you don't have a clue what I'm talking about." The attorney's laugh was brassy with strain. "I should never have gotten involved with you two."

Shane said, "Is that your answer?"

"I'm not in the answer business. Not tonight. Now tell me what's happening."

Trent was in the rear seat. It was his normal position when connecting with strangers. Stay low, stay out of range. Only now he leaned forward and told Shane, "I think we should tell him."

The leather seat rustled as Shane turned around. "You mean, everything?"

"Yes." Trent asked the attorney, "What we say is confidential, right?"

"Everything you tell me is covered by attorney-client privilege unless I learn that you have committed a felony. I cannot be party to covering up a serious crime. Have you broken any laws?"

"No. Absolutely not."

"Then I would lose my license and possibly face jail time for divulging the contents of our discussion."

"Shane?"

Her voice went very small. "If you're sure."

"I am." Trent settled his elbows on his knees and launched in.

When he was done, the lawyer powered down the windows and turned off the car. The night breeze felt refreshingly cool. He spoke to the night beyond the front windscreen. "To recap, you dreamed you were seated in a classroom in the physics building, where an older version of Trent Major offered you access to new algorithms."

"These experiences are more than a normal dream state," Trent said. "The difference is unmistakable and instantaneous. And I have no idea if this character I meet is actually me."

"Have you asked him?"

"I've tried." The attorney had shifted to what Trent assumed was his courtroom persona. Crisp and incisive and tightly focused upon the facts. Which resulted in a heightened ability on Trent's own part to see and assess. "But I am not in control of either the experience or the conversation. I am too involved. The encounter is simply too intense."

"You're certain this could not simply be your unconscious self projecting your current state of work forward to the next level?"

"You are forgetting how I met Shane," Trent replied. "And then there is how we knew to come meet you at the sports club."

"You had never seen Shane before that day?"

"I did not know she existed."

"Ms. Schearer, do you concur?"

"With everything he has said."

Murray tapped the steering wheel, frowning intensely. "Then this woman, whose name you do not know, and whom you insist you have never seen before, accosted you in the Starbucks on State Street in downtown Santa Barbara. She deposited a duplicate of a handbag that Ms. Schearer was in the process of purchasing. In it was an apparatus containing a software package we can only assume is not something generally available to all iPod users. Ms. Schearer—"

"I think it's time you called me Shane."

He looked at her for the first time. "You elected to follow this unknown woman's instructions. Which resulted in your own dream state."

"It was not a dream. It was an ascent."

"I have as much trouble with the name as I do the supposed process. Whatever actually happened—"

"It happened, Murray. I ascended. I hovered above my own body. I traveled. I returned."

"—you received a message asserting that you must journey to London."

"The trip is vital," Shane replied. "So is the timing."

"So you can meet this strange woman who accosted your partner."

"Vital," Shane repeated. "Just remembering the experience fills me with that same intense pressure. I have to do this."

Trent added, "Don't forget how the woman warned me before leaving Starbucks."

Shane said, "And the threat was confirmed this afternoon."

Murray asked, "You are certain it was Kevin Hanley you saw inside the Goleta State Bank?"

"Absolutely positive," Shane said.

"And we were being followed," Trent added.

Murray did not so much sigh as huff a hard breath. "I've got to tell you. Under different circumstances, I would call this the perfect time to cut my losses."

"But you believe us," Trent said. "Don't you."

"Ever since we met, I've been facing a torrent of incoming fire. And for reasons I don't understand. My managing partner is furious. Not with me. I'm just the whipping boy. He's scared. I've never seen him scared before. He won't even tell me who's pulling his strings. Which means it has to be so far up the food chain he is afraid to even spell the name."

Shane asked, "Does that mean you'll help me?"

Murray looked at her. "Where were you born?"

"Sacramento."

"You will spend tonight in my guest room. I will make an urgent request for the hospital to supply us with a copy of your birth certificate. Tomorrow morning you and I will hand-carry it to the regional office of the State Department. I will explain that you have lost your passport and the nature of your trip is so urgent I am postponing a hearing in federal court to walk you through this process. Which I am."

"Thank you, Murray," Shane said solemnly. "Very, very much."

He turned to face Trent. "You're not traveling with her?"

"I can't."

"Do you have somewhere safe to stay?"

"I haven't thought that far ahead. I was mostly concerned with getting Shane off safely." There were several hotels around the school that were lax when it came to ID's. "I'll find somewhere."

"Do you have any money?"

"Some."

Murray reached for his wallet. "Here's six hundred bucks. This is going on your account. And I'm billing you for these hours."

Trent didn't like accepting the man's money but knew he had little choice. "Thanks. A lot."

"When you get settled, phone my private line. Leave your address. Don't give your name. Do I need to tell you to avoid ATMs, credit cards, cell phones, all that?"

"No." Trent folded the money and slipped it into his pocket. "You don't."

"Why can't you accompany your partner to London?"

"Yeah, Trent," Shane said. "Why not?"

"I have no idea."

The attorney nodded slowly. "Given the circumstances, that almost makes sense."

52

The mattress beneath Trent was lumpy and smelled of old sweat and spilled beer. The bare pillow stank of cigarette ashes. Radiohead thumped through the wall to his left. Shadows flickered across the slit of light below his door. His chest ached from Shane's absence. Now that he was alone, his reasons for staying behind felt empty as the room.

When he had arrived back at campus, Trent had been afraid to approach one of the cheap motels adjacent to the university. Courage was much easier to find when Shane was around.

He had decided to avoid the physics building for fear of reconnecting with the trackers. Using a coffee shop computer, Trent had hacked into the university residence files and identified a vacant room in the freshman dorm, the university's largest. He had slipped into the dorm as students had bounded out on a midnight snack run. Entering the room had been a snatch, as virtually none of the door-locks worked. All had been so repeatedly jammed with screwdrivers they were little more than decoration.

Trent showered in the stalls down the hall and dried off with his T-shirt, ignored by everybody. He returned to the room, lay on his bed, and rested. He did not expect to sleep. The noise bothered him, and the room was crowded with memories from his own freshman year, which had been awful. He had arrived at university at the age of fifteen and a half, the youngest in his dorm by over two years. He had been shunned. He had not known such loneliness since the first year of foster care. Now he lay on his back and missed Shane with a longing that wrenched him over to his side. He would move tomorrow. Where to, or for how long, he had no idea. He needed to rest and figure things out.

Finally he began to slide into sleep. The day's events and the long nighttime cycle ride left him able to push aside the din and the light streaming under the door and even his own uncertainties. He drifted away.

Trent had no idea how long he had been asleep when it happened.

There was no preliminary nightmare. His sleep state simply shifted, he focused with the now-familiar crystal clarity, and Trent found himself in the classroom.

Standing by the scarred front desk, Trent had the sudden impression that the nightmare's recurrence had served to separate him both from his normal dream state and from his external reality. Now the nightmare was no longer necessary. Some transition had been made. Trent sensed that the nightmare would not come back, at least not in preparation for another dream session.

He stared at his older self and saw a sense of approval, as though commending him for this newfound awareness. But all his older self said was, "You must have questions."

"You could say that."

"Remember that any scientific investigation is only as good as the initial inquiry. If you start with a bad question, your result is bad data."

"You're saying my questions don't go far enough." He watched his older self smile. "But that doesn't mean my questions don't have merit."

"I wish you could hear yourself. This isn't the time for defensiveness. This is your chance to focus on the big picture. Which you can't see."

"Without you."

"That's right."

"And just exactly who are you? Or should I say, *when* are you?"

The mirror image shook his head, the gesture carrying a sense of sorrow. "So little time together, and you insist on these tiny glimpses into a shattered reflection."

"So what is it I *should* be asking?"

The mirror image smiled. "Now you're talking."

When the three-dimensional image maker floated into the space between them, Trent protested, "I'm not done."

He heard his own voice respond, "You can say that again."

The images carried the same explosive force as before. But they had nothing whatsoever to do with new mathematical discoveries. This time, they were awful.

Trent watched in mounting horror as two scientists in some faceless corporate lab analyzed the data from the hard drives containing his doctoral thesis. Kevin Hanley watched approvingly from the background, accompanied by two truly bizarre-looking women. One was an ice goddess with eyes of burning wrath. The other was a stunted scarecrow who wore about her a shadow shaped like a specter. Kevin Hanley and the women listened as the two scientists described gleefully what they had discovered in Trent's research.

The next image showed the same two scientists working with a team of technicians, reshaping the prion molecule to fit Trent's design.

The next, and the redesigned prion molecule ate through the supposedly impenetrable isolation tank. The glass wall simply dissolved. As did the rubber seals around the door. And the wire leads bonded to the metal walls. And the filtration system. All gone.

The redesigned prion escaped into the lab. And killed everyone inside.

It moved into the building outside, replicating at an exponential rate. It remained an invisible gas unseen by anyone except Trent. It moved into the outside environment. It engulfed the university. And the city. And kept going.

It killed.

And killed.

53

The hour before dawn, Charlie left his hotel room and knocked on the next door. When Elizabeth appeared, he said, "It's time we headed for LAX."

"I'm ready."

Charlie looked over to where Elene Belote was seated in the room's far corner, doing her best to disappear behind a floor lamp. "You'll need to come with us. We won't be returning here again."

Elizabeth wore faded jeans and lace-up boots and a T-shirt and navy jacket. Charlie thought she had never looked more alluring. She must have spotted something in his expression, because she added softly, "I could stay."

Charlie said, "Step out into the hall for a second, will you?"

Elizabeth let the door shut behind her. "Gabriella can handle buying the island. What difference does it make whether I'm there or not? I won't make the decision for the whole team. That's not my role."

"You need to go."

But his response only accelerated her words. "I don't like leaving you here alone. You might need backup. I'll be six thousand miles away, along with the rest of—"

"Just hang on a second and listen to me." Charlie took a hard breath. "I know what you're not saying. And I appreciate it more than I can say."

"Oh. Right. Let me guess what comes next." Her mouth twisted. "You're going to drag out the 'let's be friends' spiel."

"No," Charlie replied. "You know I was married before."

Her face lost its parody of a smile. "I heard that."

"We got married for all the wrong reasons. We were headed for divorce court when she died in a traffic accident." Charlie had never expected to use a windowless hall as a confessional. But as soon as he had looked into her eyes, he had known the answer. The only one that made sense. Bitter as it tasted to shape the words. "I never want to disappoint another woman I care for, Elizabeth."

"When I think of us, the last word that comes to mind is *disappointed*."

"Because you see how you want it to be. Me and you. Unhindered. And I know that's just not going to happen."

"You're not the only one who's hauling around ghosts, Charlie."

He moved an inch closer. Staring into that lovely fractured gaze, seeing a woman raw with honesty. Giving her the same in return. "Gabriella is not a ghost."

"But your love for her is."

"It might be," he corrected. "But I have to deal with that first."

She swallowed. The act compressed her lips. "And after?"

"I can't predict. I can't lead you on. I can't promise. I can't."

Her lips only compressed further, a jagged line of regret that sliced across her strong and lovely face. She nodded, a jerk of her head, and turned from him. She fumbled in her pocket for her key. Charlie watched her take two hands to fit the plastic card into the lock. He stood for a long moment after she had disappeared inside her room.

Searching the empty hall for some sense that he had just done the right thing.

⫻

They arrived in Los Angeles before rush hour. The early morning traffic was dense but moving fast. Charlie pulled up in front of the international terminal and halted in the drop-off zone. A cloud of disquiet consumed the car's interior. He turned in his seat and asked Elizabeth, "Can I have your iPod?"

She reached for her purse, then stopped. "You're not thinking of going after her alone."

"Gabriella made me promise I wouldn't. Will I understand the controls?"

She handed him the apparatus and the headphones and the charger. "Hit the app marked with a simple X. Lie back and shut your eyes and go."

"Thank you, Elizabeth. For everything."

"I hope you know what you're doing."

He nodded. He had spent the entire journey south thinking the same.

Elizabeth opened her mouth. Then she stopped herself before the words emerged. She jerked the car door open and rose and slammed it shut.

Charlie pulled into traffic. He caught sight of Elizabeth watching him in the rearview mirror. Elene's presence in the rear seat kept him from saying the words out loud. But what he was thinking was, *You are such a fool.*

54

eese had not waited planeside for an arriving official in years. This was a peon's duty. She had always delegated such trivialities to security. No matter who it was or how important they assumed they were, there were more important things on her agenda. Only not this morning.

Kevin's phone call had plucked Reese from a slumber so profound he had hung up before she could shape a decent protest. And now here she was, standing on the tarmac beneath dawn's pale wash as a Gulfstream wheeled toward them.

The jet powered down, the door opened, the stairs descended. Amanda Thorne climbed down, followed by her Washington clone, Jason. Reese remained standing where she was as Kevin moved forward to greet Amanda, who treated the formalities with the same impatience Reese would have shown in her place.

Amanda walked over and pointed to the steaming cups balanced on the car's front hood. "One of those mine?"

"If you like. How do you take it?"

"This time of day, hot and strong." She let Kevin hold her door. Jason walked around the car and settled into the backseat beside Reese. When they were moving, Amanda went on, "Let's get the preliminaries out of the way. Trent Major and Shane Schearer are off the grid. My people are good. They know what is at stake. Even so, last night two grad students gave them the slip. What does that tell you?"

"They're getting help," Kevin said. "I said that yesterday, when they showed up at the bank."

Amanda sipped from her cup. Nodded her approval. "Are your people ready to brief us on Trent Major's doctoral research?"

"They better be," Kevin replied. "They've been at it all night."

Reese asked, "Is that why you're here, to determine the value of Trent's research?"

"Partly." She turned so as to inspect Reese directly. "Is your team ready to go to work?"

"Standing by."

"What about the missing member of your transit team? What's her name?"

Jason spoke for the first time since stepping down. "Elene Belote. CIA."

Reese liked how Amanda Thorne spoke that word. Transit. As though it was already part of her standard vocabulary. "My team is shaken by Elene's vanishing act. No question about it. But we're good to go."

Amanda turned forward again. Sipped from her cup. Said, "That's what I came three thousand miles to hear."

⫿⫿⫿

Kevin's two senior scientists were waiting and ready. They might not have known Amanda. But they were scientists on the federal payroll. They had a nose for power. And danger.

The senior of the two was tall and bearded and wore the standard

243

white lab coat. The other man was portly and frowning. He wore jeans and a faded Cancun sweatshirt with what looked like tomato stains spattered down his front. The two scientists stood before a white greaseboard covered with calculations. Beneath the window was a long bench filled with electronic apparatuses and coffee cups and two pizza boxes. Six oversized computer screens were filled with text and graphs and more math. Reese assumed it was Trent Major's thesis work.

Kevin rolled over a padded stool. Amanda Thorne was so small she had to hike up a bit in order to make the seat. "What have you got for me?"

To their credit, the two scientists looked to Kevin for approval. He said, "Spell it out."

The taller scientist said, "The student has laid a golden egg right in our lap."

The fat scientist said, "Maybe."

"No maybe. This is a major breakthrough."

"We don't know if it works yet."

"And I'm telling you—"

Amanda halted the exchange with one forefinger. "Skip the debate and get to the core."

"Right. Our current thrust focuses upon the prion molecule as the basis for a quantum computer. The two major problems we face, *everybody* in quantum computing faces, is—"

"Decoherence and interference," Amanda supplied. "I've read the file."

"Right. So we've been focusing on magnetic resonance as a means of heightening the molecule's stability in isolation. Meaning we gain more time to both program the algorithmic calculation and take our readings. We were expecting to find that he had determined a resonance frequency, probably in conjunction with a supercooled state. But instead, the student has gone in a completely different direction."

"Explain."

The tall scientist waved at the greaseboard. "He's supplied us with a *different structure* for the molecule."

"Theoretically," the portly scientist added.

The tall scientist glared at his mate, then continued, "We've always taken the molecular structure as a given. A prion is a prion. But Trent Major is saying, hang on, a prion is *already* redesigned. A prion has the same atomic structure as highly complex proteins in the brain. Which is why it's been so carefully studied. Only the prion has been refolded."

Amanda was nodding now. "In a totally toxic way."

"Right. Sure. But that's not the point." The tall scientist did not actually dance in place. But his caffeine-induced excitement was such that the air around him vibrated. "What Trent Major has done is taken the prion, worked back to the basic atomic structure, and calculated a totally new design."

"The purpose being?"

The scientist waved at graphs on the computer screens. "This is what's so incredible. He based his work on a question we've never thought to ask. What if we could have a molecule that doesn't respond to outside stimuli?"

The portly scientist huffed his opinion but did not speak.

The tall scientist continued, "The time it holds superposition would shift from nanoseconds to hours. The problems we have with molecular isolation would vanish."

The portly scientist said, "Theoretically."

Amanda said, "I am all for scientific debate. And I accept that the data is meaningless until proven in the real world. But for now, I want you to swallow all further sidebars. Are we clear on this?" When she was certain the portly scientist was silenced, she turned back to the tall scientist and said, "Is it possible to redesign a molecule?"

"Oh, sure. It's been done any number of times. The most spectacular was with the creation of C_{60}, also known as buckminsterfullerene or the buckyball. Organic chemists were trying to understand the method by which long-chain carbon molecules were formed in interstellar space. Up to this point, it was generally accepted that elemental carbon only existed in two states, known as allotropes. These two states are graphite and diamond. But the scientists vaporized graphite using laser irradiation, producing a third allotrope. It held a remarkably stable cluster of sixty carbon atoms, arrayed in the shape of a soccer ball."

"So this change is theoretically possible. And you're suggesting that Trent Major has calculated a new shape for prions that does away with some of your problems."

"In a totally groundbreaking fashion."

The portly scientist dragged his hands in a nervous gesture across the front of his sweatshirt, revealing how the stains had occurred. He glanced at Amanda, then said, "The risk is, this realigned prion won't function in real-world conditions."

"We've been at this all night. Have you detected a flaw in his calculations? No you have not."

The scientist stared at the greaseboard and kept streaking his hands across his sweatshirt.

The tall scientist's Ecco shoes slipped across the floor as he traced a hand across the greaseboard, smearing the calculations. "Think of a car spring. The spring compresses whenever pressure is applied. But once the pressure vanishes, what happens? Its form and tensile strength mean the spring returns to its original shape."

"All right. I've seen enough." Amanda Thorne slid from her stool. "Thank you, gentlemen. Very good work. I suggest you go get some sleep."

When the lab doors slid shut behind them, Amanda turned to Jason and said, "Contact our people. I want Trent Major found. And I want him brought in. Now. And if he won't come in, take him out."

55

When Charlie and Elene returned to Santa Barbara, he shifted them to a hotel he had spotted earlier in Goleta. He checked in wearing his customary cap and shades. The motel had been built in the sixties, with the ground-floor rooms opening straight to the cars parked in the forecourt. Charlie chose two rooms at the back of the middle block, with a side window that did not open. But in a pinch, he could cover himself with a blanket or drape and leap through the glass and come up running.

They ate lunch at a diner just off the interstate. Charlie asked Elene to repeat her description of Reese Clawson's operation, but Elizabeth's fractured gaze kept inserting itself.

Afterward he drove back to the motel and circled the block twice. He parked in a space easily reached from his room but not directly in front of the door. He saw Elene safely inside, then entered his room and closed the drapes and locked the door and put a chair under the knob. He pulled the spread off the bed and set Elizabeth's iPod on the table.

He lay on the bed and fitted the earphones in place. He reached over and picked up the iPod. And lay there, staring at the closed curtains.

He had not ascended since observing Brett being swallowed by the maelstrom.

Charlie traced a finger along the iPod's polished surface. When he thought back to the moment he had sensed Brett's presence, the maelstrom always appeared with an enormous amount of noise. Charlie knew that the moment's only sound had been that parody of his own voice, calling to him, giving form to his guilt. Yet the storm's fury had been too intense to remain soundless. So mentally he had inserted a roaring clamor, a great sucking ferocity. Just like a tornado. Tearing through everything with shattering force.

Even so, he had to do this.

If Elizabeth had asked why he wanted the iPod, he had been ready to tell her that he needed to locate Trent and Shane. But that was for later. Right now he had a different purpose. He did not know if honesty played any part in his remaining safe. But he knew he had to do this thing.

Charlie had known he was going to do this from the instant he had heard Elizabeth confess her secret reason for ascending. He was going to go up and go out. And ask if Gabriella would ever be his. And if so, when.

And if not, when he could be free.

He ran his finger over the symbol marked by a simple X. Breathed in and out. Forcing the fear down and clamping the internal lid tightly in place. Just like he would before combat.

He pressed the button. Set the iPod on the bed.

And shut his eyes.

·||·

The sound of Jorge's voice was very comforting. Charlie may have been alone in a faceless motel room. His nostrils tingled slightly from the smell of bathroom disinfectant. The mattress springs made corduroy creases across his back. But he heard the calm sound of a young man Charlie knew very well, and was comforted.

Jorge counted him up, just as Elizabeth had said. His instructions were simple in the extreme. Rise up. Open his *other* eyes. And look around. And determine if there was anything important to him or the team that he should be aware of. The silence that followed these instructions was Charlie's signal to really begin.

But as soon as Charlie ascended, he knew he was not going anywhere. Even before he was fully aware of his surroundings, he knew he was trapped.

Charlie did not know if what he sensed was the same as Elizabeth's experience. But he would not have called where he found himself a room. It was more like a cage. He did not need to test his boundaries. The impression was as genuine as anything he had experienced while ascending. Charlie felt that the reason for his ascent was in fact not proper. It did not belong to the moment, or perhaps to the act of ascending. How he knew this, he could not say. But this lack of reason did not make the impression any less real.

So he hovered.

The feeling was not at all unpleasant. In fact, the longer he remained, the more it seemed that his senses gradually opened to a new dimension. He could see now that he was indeed still in the hotel room. The impression was somewhat dreamlike. He had to turn in a particular direction and focus down very tightly to see anything of his surroundings. He did this several times, then stopped. Because the physical room was not important. There was no danger. His body was resting comfortably. There was something else he needed to focus upon.

He extended his senses, probing the enclosure's boundaries. The cage seemed to follow the room's confines, as though the intention was to hold him in the here and now. Charlie reached forward, wondering if the boundaries themselves were the message. He made contact with *something*, a suggestion that he remain where he was. Charlie had the distinct impression that the boundary was pointed outward. As though it was not there so much to hold him as to *protect* him.

From what, he had no idea.

Then it happened.

Long before he realized what precisely was going on, he felt the incoming energy. A frisson that tickled the periphery of his senses. Everything he looked at became rimmed by a golden light. He did not feel fear so much as a growing sense of being prepped.

Gabriella entered then. Her presence was a reality that did not require vision to be authentic. Charlie recalled what Elene had said in the restaurant, how she had sensed his flavor.

Gabriella was with him now. In this room.

Instantly Charlie realized how close he had come to losing the chance for this moment. How weakness and doubt had almost shut him out.

He remained where he was. Which was nice in a special fashion, because it meant that she could make the move herself. Do what he had dreamed of. Close the distance between them.

If her presence could be named, it would be of meadows in a springtime dawn. A distinct flavor that was unmistakably her.

Charlie felt her love flow out, strong as a physical embrace. So powerful he felt an earthquake grip him and shake him until his senses could hold nothing more. Everything was lost to him except the feel of her love.

Gabriella spoke to him. Not in words. But in a shared impression. Their hearts were finally able to sing in a unison of conquering time and distance and all the reasons that kept them apart.

Their melody had but one word. It was the only word that mattered. *Finally.*

56

Reese told her team, "This is Amanda Thorne. She is our main ally in Washington. She has a problem, and she needs our help."

They were gathered in the control room. It was the first time her entire team had been together, at least officially, since Elene's disappearance. Reese could see the worry and the strain etched in every face. Even Jeff, the security chief, looked exhausted. Consuela sheltered behind Joss Stone, clearly uncomfortable with this arrival of officialdom.

Reese knew what they were thinking. Whatever Elene Belote had encountered in her search had so spooked her she had fled the scene. And perhaps Reese should have seen it coming and locked them down. But to what end? Either they volunteered or the whole deal fell apart. She couldn't lock them up and maintain a sense of cohesive unity. Part of the mystique was their independence. But she knew they were all tempted by the same thought. Bug out before the bad dreams struck and they landed in one of the beds downstairs.

The only way Reese could see to salvage her team was to take aim. "Our target is a clandestine intel facility in the hills of Maryland. It is run by NSA."

Neil, her gamer, was the only one who registered what she was saying. "Is this for real?"

"As real as it gets."

"We're going to break into the National Security Agency?"

"Roger that." She waited. Hoping against hope.

Neil gave her what she had hoped for. Which was a fist raised high and two words almost sung with delight. "All *right*."

Joss said, "What's the big deal, fat boy?"

"Joss," Reese said.

"Hey. I'm just asking."

"Then ask nice. He's your partner in this."

"Whatever you say." The Marine offered a mock dulcet tone. "Bro, what's the haps?"

"You don't know nothing, mister Marine. You only think you do." Reese sighed. "Neil."

Neil said, "The NSA is the Everest of hacks. And the lady is letting us go in *legal*."

Reese said, "Here's the deal. Amanda Thorne represents the White House chief of intelligence. I hope you understand what I say there. Her boss answers directly to the President of the United States."

Jason complained, "That is not information for public—"

"Jason," Amanda said.

"But Clawson is relaying—"

"This is her team. Let her handle things as she sees fit." Amanda Thorne did not need to raise her voice to squelch her aide. When he subsided against the side wall, she said, "Proceed."

Reese said to Jason, "These are frontline troops. They risk every-thing to meet your request for assistance. If you have any doubt on that score, I'll be happy to take you back downstairs and give you another chance to scope out the casualties in our clinic."

Jason only glared at the floor by his feet.

"That's what I thought." Reese turned back to find a glimmer of humor in most of the gazes. Which was what she'd been after all along. Draw them together by a shared sense of commitment. "The intel chief faces serious friction in the ranks. NSA and CIA are top of the list. They oppose the new chief's desire to draw all US intelligence under—"

"Ms. Thorne, please," Jason whined, "I must object to—"

Amanda snapped, "Zip it, Jason. That's an order. Roll with it, Clawson."

"NSA intends to arrive at the next presidential briefing with data they should have supplied to Amanda Thorne's boss, but haven't. Amanda's sources suggest the data pertains to inroads that Chinese intel has made into stealing secrets related to America's recent discoveries in cryptography." Reese examined the faces one at a time. Then she turned to Amanda and said, "Do you have anything to add?"

Amanda took her time, giving each of the team five seconds of her laser focus. Then, "Secrets are the lifeblood of our government. Whoever controls the secrets holds the only power that counts. Which means your work here is not merely important. You are *vital*."

Reese said, "This is not a test. The time for trial runs is over. This is as real as it gets."

⊹⊹⊹

Reese watched as Karla, her techie, readied her team for transition. Amanda Thorne had followed them downstairs. To her surprise, Reese did not particularly care that the woman was in the transit room. Amanda stood by the exit, a tiny silent wraith. Reese found it easy to ignore her and focus on the team.

They were still nervous. Which was natural. But the frantic tension had been replaced now by a sense of grim determination. Reese waited until Karla finished fitting the monitor cords in place, then quietly repeated the instructions for the fifth time. "Your objective is a safe in the NSA director's office. You've broken into safes before. There will be a file marked 'Priority One, Director's Briefing Report.' Your objective is to read the file and return. You have been divided into three teams. Each team will scope only their two pages. Pages one and two, three and four, five and six. This should speed up your read and help your retention. The NSA chief is known to hate lengthy reports. If for some reason there are more than six pages, which is highly unlikely, you are to ignore the rest. We're not after everything. We just want enough to arm our allies."

Reese took a breath, then started in on the words that had become rote but at the same time sounded totally new to her this time. "You will have five minutes at the target site. You will remain in complete control at all times. You will go, you will achieve your aims, you will return. You will stay safe. You will obey no other instructions, you will hear no other voice than mine."

They watched her with a singular intensity. Ten faces, ten pairs of unblinking eyes, one focus.

She met each gaze in turn. Reese said quietly, "I am so very proud of you all."

Back upstairs, the Departures Lounge held a spectral tension stronger than among her own team. Reese totally understood the mood. There was a helplessness to the moment. These were people accustomed to wielding enormous power. Yet here and now they could do nothing. They could not even observe.

Reese counted her team down. She had never felt such an intense precision to her words, her tone, her cadence. She repeated her orders for them to remain in control, stay safe, keep a tight focus on her voice. Then she ordered them away.

The clock had never moved more slowly.

She brought them home. Her heart raced. She gripped the base of the microphone so tightly her hands were chalk white. But her voice remained utterly calm. She heard herself count them back up in a drone that belonged to some other woman. Someone who did not feel as though she was stretched out there beside the others. Silent and still and unearthly.

She took the hardest breath of her entire life and said, "Open your eyes."

Reese felt the others crowd up close to the window. She did not bother to order them away. Beside her, Karla said, "They're back. All of them. They returned."

Reese fought against the tension that had gripped her throat in a choke hold. Then she found she could not rise from the chair.

Karla brushed by her as she hurried for the side stairs. Reese wanted to go with her. But she could not find the strength to rise.

Amanda Thorne leaned over Reese and said softly, "It's hard, your sending troops into Indian country. Especially when you've already faced unacceptable losses. Isn't it."

Reese tasted the air. Again. She managed, "Very. Very. Hard."

"Concern for your frontline team is not something you can teach. Either the individual has it or they don't. But I consider it vital for any officer on my watch." Amanda patted her shoulder. "Go welcome your troops home."

Kevin Hanley joined her in the stairwell. "I have known Amanda Thorne for almost ten years. I've never seen her offer a compliment before."

Reese did not respond. She entered the transit room and joined in the tumult. She felt as though she was standing at a distance, even as she exchanged smiles and shouts and laughter and high fives.

Her team.

From somewhere overhead a phone rang. Then the intercom squawked. Reese heard words shouted so loud they silenced the returning crew.

Karla was the first to look up, frowning at the windows overhead.

Jeff stood at the window, pounding on the glass with one open palm while he pressed down the microphone's button with his other.

"—emergency that can't wait! You've got to come *now!*"

Then Joss gripped her arm and started to tug her forward. But by then she was moving for the stairs.

They all were.

The redesigned prion molecule does not require a host to maintain its active state," Trent told Shane. He could not stop the hand holding the phone from shaking. "The revised form I created left it capable of devouring inanimate materials. And people. Apparently it still held on to the same traits as the Creutzfeldt-Jacob structure, because as soon as it was respirated into a human system, it attacked the host's brain."

"I'm really sorry you had to see that." Though Shane was clearly very troubled, her voice held a sense of detachment. "At least you know why you couldn't come with me."

"I have to stop them."

"Of course you do. Should I come back?"

"No, Shane. This doesn't change your reasons for going to England."

"I guess you're right."

"Is everything okay?"

"You mean, other than hearing how your research has created a totally destructive molecule?"

"You just sound, I don't know, disconnected."

"Shell-shocked is probably more like it. I got my passport in no time flat. I'm checked in for the flight. Elizabeth is here."

"Who?"

"The woman you met in the café."

"She's there? How do you know her name?"

"Because we've talked. She's explained where we're going. It's not England. It's an island in the English Channel. They're buying it."

"Who is?"

"Her team. It's a long story." A loudspeaker blared in the background. "The pilot is saying I have to cut off my phone."

"Can I speak with her?"

"What, now?"

"It's vital, Shane."

"Hang on."

There was a muffled moment, then a different voice said, "This is Elizabeth."

He recognized the hard edge instantly. "I need help."

"I know." The woman sounded more removed than Shane. As though she had been dulled by overexposure to whatever had drawn her into that Starbucks. A victim of too many close calls. "You need to speak with Charlie. You got a pen?"

"Yes. Who is Charlie?"

"Charlie Hazard is the man who . . ." Elizabeth coughed into the phone. "Sorry. Write this down."

Trent took down the number, hesitated a long moment, then asked, "Does he know how to make a bomb?"

***

Shane found she could not meet the other woman's eyes as Elizabeth handed her back the phone. Overhead the pilot welcomed them on board and ordered them to shut off all electronic devices for take-off. Shane stowed her phone in her purse and said, "I brought your briefcase-purse with me. The second one. It's in my checked bag."

"Keep it."

"That thing cost nine hundred dollars."

Elizabeth already had her eyes shut. "It doesn't suit me. Give it to Gabriella."

"Who?"

"The lady waiting at the other end. She'll love it."

The hostess walked down the aisle, offering them champagne or orange juice. Shane said, "The world sure looks different in business class."

"You don't travel much?"

"No money, and nobody to spend it with. Until Trent."

Elizabeth swiveled her head on the pillow. "Your friend seems nice."

"He is. Very."

"You're worried about him."

Shane found herself swallowing another lump in her throat. Which was very odd. When she had first met Elizabeth at the check-in counter, Shane had instantly known who the lady was. The spiky-haired blonde had stared at her with an intensity that was unmistakable. And those clothes. They were like a biker's idea of Valentino. Tight and aggressive. Like the woman. Even so, Shane had taken that first long look and burst into tears. She felt like doing the same right now. "Worried and scared both."

"Don't be. Charlie is the best there is at keeping people safe."

"That's the guy you told Trent to contact?"

"Yes. Charlie is . . ." Elizabeth's features went tight, then relaxed again. Shane had the impression it was done by strength of will alone. As though she had spent years perfecting the ability of tamping things down and locking them away. "Charlie is a professional. If anybody can keep your Trent safe through whatever comes next, it's Charlie."

Shane had the sudden impression that Elizabeth was in love with the guy. Which left her wanting to confess her own flood of emotions over Trent. Instead, she said, "I never cry."

Elizabeth closed her eyes once more. "I get that a lot."

58

Charlie found it difficult to remain stationary. His body still vibrated. His heart rate remained a trace below redline. When Gabriella came on the line, he could hear the slight tremor to his voice.

"I'm supposed to be leaving for the airport," Gabriella said.

"This can't wait."

"I'm meeting Elizabeth because you told me it was important, Charlie."

"Have someone call her. She'll be in the air. Leave her a message." His thoughts were scattered. For every word he spoke, he thought a dozen. All in different directions. What was more, he didn't care. "We have work to do."

"Just a minute, Charlie." A pause, then, "Will you tell me what this is about?"

The act of retelling calmed Charlie down. It also frightened him. His adrenaline state continued to super-divide the seconds, such that he both heard himself talk and fractioned the thoughts, granting him ample space to worry. What if she refused. What if she did not believe him. What if she analyzed it until he grew frustrated and angry. What if she asked the questions for which he had no answer.

Instead, when he finished, Gabriella did not respond.

"Gabriella?"

"I'm thinking."

"It happened, Gabriella. Just like I said."

"I need a minute, Charlie. Please."

He felt the final splinters of frisson fade away. He felt as though his body was reknitting itself at some core level of pure energy. Returning to a denser state. One of frustrated intensity. Only now there was a brooding hurt, a knowledge that he could remain here no longer. The time for waiting was over. Either she moved with him to this new level, or . . .

Charlie sighed. He was unable to shape an alternative. Either she was with him, or nothing.

When Gabriella finally spoke, it was to say, "Earlier you said something about these images carrying multiple messages."

His heart surged with an unreasonable hope. "I sure did."

She was silent an impossible amount of time. Charlie kicked at a tear in the motel carpeting and struggled to hold on to his patience.

"Forgive me for taking so long, Charlie. I am trying to bring all of this into some form of clarity. Do you think this image has multiple layers as well?"

"It wasn't an image, Gabriella."

She did not speak.

"But to answer your question, yes, I think there was an underlying message. And I also think that before we get to that, we have to deal with the first thing. The real thing. The meaning you're busy running circles around."

Gabriella remained silent.

"This wasn't some exchange between friends. This was love at its deepest level. Between a man and a woman. You need to come to terms with this. Now."

Gabriella's breath huffed slightly over the seven thousand miles.

"You came to me. I did not come to you. You loved me in a way that was both beautiful and total. And you said to me one word."

She whispered, "Finally."

Charlie felt the shivers clench his body again. He was hit by a sudden thought. He wondered if this was the only way to cry when the body's tears were no longer available. To shake through the emotions, humming like a giant tuning fork. Threatened to be torn apart by the simple act of breathing.

Gabriella said softly, "I have thought of this for so long."

It was Charlie's turn to be rendered speechless. Unable to fashion words around the tremors.

"I have a lifetime of practice at making the right moves with the wrong men. Byron was far from the first serious mistake I made." Byron had been her husband when Charlie first met her, a philanderer with enough money to buy his way out of almost anything. But in the end, it had not saved him, or them. Gabriella went on, "Byron was not even the worst. I have laid awake and thought of this. How to start with you. Whether I should risk the vital role you play in our work."

His vibrations eased to where he could say, "This is not about the team or your work. This is about us."

"Everything is about the team. These factors cannot be separated. Not anymore."

Charlie did not argue.

"When I let myself think about you, it seems like all the men I have known were there waiting and watching. All the mistakes, all the wrong choices, all the pain and sorrow and feelings that I could never . . ." She breathed across the distance, so forcefully Charlie felt the heat on his ear. "Charlie?"

"I'm here."

"Do you think we can move beyond who we once were?"

"It's the only thing that keeps me going."

They shared the music of silence. The distance between them had never seemed smaller. Finally Gabriella said, "Perhaps we should speak about the multiple layers."

"On the surface it is about us. And our love."

She breathed a quiet emphasis to his words. Then, "And below?"

"The timing itself is a message. I had almost given up on you ever being mine. I started to . . ." He did not want to go on. But she had to realize he had reached the brink. "I started to take another direction."

"Oh, Charlie."

"But I didn't. And you came. Almost as though I had earned it by my choice. And did so right at my breaking point."

Another moment's silence, then, "There's more, isn't there. Another level to the experience."

"There is, yes. And the CIA operative, Elene Belote, she's the key."

Gabriella spoke slowly. "She claims you saved her by coming to her when she was almost lost to the vortex."

He liked that word. Vortex. It fit the experience. "This is no claim, Gabriella. This is real."

"Yes. Of course. You are right. It's just . . . the thought of you going in there, it terrifies me."

"I have to do this. And you are going to do this with me. Your love is my shield."

"You have no way of knowing that this will work."

"Elene is here. I know that. And you will not let me lose myself in the storm. I know that too."

Gabriella breathed for him a moment longer, the intimacy undisturbed by the distance or his surroundings. Finally she asked, "I cannot imagine what it must be like, joining with you. Is it beautiful?"

The tremors almost robbed him of the power to reply. "Come and see."

⫶

Charlie left his room and knocked on Elene's door. His phone rang just as she opened the door. Charlie was so jazzed by the conversation with Gabriella and the prospect of better things to come, he was tempted not to answer. He stepped into Elene's room and checked the readout. He did not recognize the number. He punched the button and demanded, "Yes?"

"Is this Mr. Hazard?"

"Who is speaking?"

"My name is Trent Major."

"Should I know that name?"

"Elizabeth told me to phone you. She said you'd know what to do."

"You're the student."

"That's right."

"Okay. I'm going to pass you over to a friend. Her name is Elene Belote. She'll tell you where to come."

"Wait, I need to ask—"

"Sorry, Trent. We're running to a tight schedule here. Do you have transport?"

"Yes. At least can you tell me . . . is it safe there?"

"I'll be moving us again as soon as you arrive. Right now I have to do something. I'm going to put you on hold for thirty seconds, then you can talk with Elene."

Charlie cupped the phone and said to Elene, "You have to take over here. But first I need the names of your colleagues who've gotten lost in the maelstrom."

To his surprise, Elene had the list ready. "You're going for them?"

"I'm going to try."

Elene showed very real fear. "How can you be sure you'll come back?"

Charlie handed her the phone. "I have a secret weapon."

59

The motel room held a silence that extended far beyond the tawdry walls. The moment's power swamped Charlie. Everything his eyes fell upon shone with a luminescence that he knew was myth, and did not care. Charlie lay down, fit on the headphones, keyed the controls, and set the iPod on the bed beside his right arm.

He had no idea whether his nerves and his tension would affect his ability to ascend. All he knew for certain was, there wasn't a thing he could do about either.

The familiar hum had never sounded more musical. Jorge's voice had never been more welcoming. Counting down had never been more thrilling. The act of letting go never so fulfilling.

Charlie felt his breathing even out, recognized the gradual easing of his heart rate, which was amazing. Because the deeper he descended into calm, the stronger grew the feeling of arrival.

He ascended. And he waited.

And she came to him.

Charlie knew what was happening this time. He could sense Gabriella and he could move forward and he could meld. There was a new spice to the act, coming as it did with the knowledge that this was *her*. This was *her now*. The experience was so intense he could feel his distant body shivering in cadence. The sense of harmony redefined him.

He had no idea how long they lingered. If he could, he would have remained there forever. But he felt drawn by the sense of others needing him. As though he could only now realize the total concern Gabriella carried for her work and her team. From within.

As he started to move away, he realized that Gabriella's presence remained with him. He knew what he was going to do. It was not so much a conscious decision as stepping into a realization. He would go for Brett. He would stop Elene from entering the tempest and turn back the Marine sent to track her. Then he would go after the first name on Elene's list.

At least, that was the plan.

Charlie scarcely had time to fashion the directive pointing him toward Brett. And he was there. Back at the entrance to the maelstrom.

The mawing cavity was sharper now, furious in its silent roar. The vortex weaved and spun and sucked at him.

And yet he remained untouched. Frightened, and yet calm.

He fashioned a roar of his own, woven from his passion to leave this terror, and from his shield. He extended the force from the level of his heart. Echoing the silent power with an unvoiced cry of his own.

Brett.

He did not see the man so much as stumble upon him. The maelstrom surrounded them both, great walls of swirling smoke and raging flames, streaked with abysmal hopelessness. Charlie lowered himself to the form huddled upon the surface. He poured out the shielding love, the forgiveness, the hope. He set it as a beacon before the man. And once more he emitted his heart's cry.

Come home.

60

Reese and Amanda Thorne and Kevin and all of Reese's team jammed into the hall that ran the length of the Treatment Room. The windows were one-way glass. They could look into the clinic, but the patients could not see out. Since the patients were comatose, Reese considered it another example of bureaucratic stupidity.

The beds all linked into monitors planted in the opposite wall. Facing Reese and her team were eight sets of mirror images. Eight comatose patients lay immobile. Their faces were far too pale. Their arms were arranged outside the covers. Their mouths held breathing tubes. Cables snaked from their chests and heads to the wall. The monitors showed heartbeats that beat in military cadence.

Then there was the ninth patient.

He struggled weakly against the nurse. His mouth moved. Reese stepped to the hall controls and said, "Quiet, everybody."

She touched the speaker button, and everybody heard a hoarse voice say, "Guardian."

"I heard you," the nurse replied. "Now calm down. You've had a terrible—"

"Got to go help . . ." All strength left him. He flopped like a doll. "What happened to me?"

A voice to Reese's left muttered, "That's what I'd like to know."

"Joss."

"Sorry."

The nurse settled him back. The man continued to struggle feebly, as though lashed to the bed by his sheet. The nurse pulled a syringe from her pocket and inserted it into the IV system. She pushed the plunger. Gradually the man settled.

Amanda whispered, "Is he gone again?"

"No." Reese pointed with her chin through the glass. "Check out the monitor's top lines. His brain continues to process."

The nurse turned to the window and asked, "Are you there?"

Reese pressed the button. "Standing by."

"Has the doctor been alerted?"

Jeff said, "Inbound. Five minutes tops."

The nurse must have heard him because she said, "His heartbeat is erratic. I suppose that's to be expected, given how long he's been out."

"Stay on him," Reese said. She released the button. Rested her forehead against the glass. Sighed.

Amanda asked, "What does this mean?"

Reese kept her forehead against the glass. "I have no idea."

"Find out how it happened," Amanda ordered. "Make it happen again."

"I intend to," Reese said.

The Washington chief touched Reese's arm. "Step outside with me. Kevin, join us."

Reese forced her weakened limbs to carry her back down the hall and out into the atrium. The vast chamber echoed with a tense emptiness. Amanda said, "Jason, contact the pilot. Tell him I want to be wheels up in fifteen minutes." When her aide moved away, Amanda went on, "I have to get back to Washington. The White House intel briefing is this evening. I need you to pay careful attention."

Reese took a steadying breath. "I'm here."

Amanda said, "This connection between the student we can't find and Gabriella Speciale's team concerns me."

"It should," Kevin said. "Especially now that we know what Trent Major was working on."

"This goes far beyond the student and his research," Amanda said, her gaze still locked on Reese. "Doesn't it."

"Our team is using their system," Reese said. "Which means they have access to the same potential to unlock national secrets."

"That cannot happen. Do I make myself clear?"

"Yes."

"Can you go after them?"

Reese felt her chest unlock. It was the chance she had been aiming for all along. "I can try."

"It could be dangerous."

"I know that," Reese said. "All too well."

61

Charlie showered before emerging from the motel room. He needed to put some space between himself and what had just happened. He dressed slowly. His entire body ached as from a giant physical exertion, though he had done nothing more than lay prone upon the pallet. He tried to phone Gabriella, but she did not answer. As he walked the motel's open hallway, he smelled something rich with tomato sauce and spices emerging from the motel restaurant's kitchen. His stomach rumbled agreeably.

Elene opened her door to reveal the grad student seated by the front window. The young man had the dark hair and olive complexion of a Native American, but his grey eyes were the color of Afghan smoke.

Charlie asked, "Your name is Trent, do I have that right?"

"Yes." He wiped his hands nervously on his trouser legs as he rose. "Trent Major."

Elene asked, "How did it go?"

"We'll know soon enough. But I think good. I went after one of our own who's been MIA. Then I went for you, since you claim it was me who brought you back—"

"There's no question about that. You saved me."

"—and then I went for the guy at the top of your list. Three was all I could handle." He rubbed his neck. "Is there any way you can check in and see if your friend has returned?"

"I could try," she said slowly. "But if they're watching, I might place us and everything we're doing here at risk."

Trent said sharply, "That can't happen."

Charlie studied the young man. Trent Major carried an enormous amount of strain, but he managed to hold himself together. Charlie liked that. He said, "Let's check out of here, grab a bite, then go find another place to stay."

His phone rang. Charlie checked the readout, saw it was Gabriella, and said to the others, "I have to take this."

He stepped back into his room before answering with, "Are you all right?"

Gabriella's voice was too full of emotions to remain unbroken. "Oh, Charlie."

"What's the matter?"

"Nothing. Nothing at all." She sobbed a long breath. "Brett has woken up."

⊣∥⊢

Trent Major told them, "Prions are one of the most complex molecules ever discovered. They are often referred to as a misfolded protein, because the atomic structure is the same as the primary protein that makes up the human brain. This refolding process happens when the molecule comes into contact with what is known as an allele, which is a fragment of another amino acid. This forces the normal molecule, which holds itself in an alpha-helical arrangement, to reshape itself into a beta-pleated sheet. When that happens,

271

two events occur almost immediately. First, the reshaped molecules generate additional segments of allele, which pass to other healthy molecules. And second, they become deadly." Trent paused. "How much detail do you want?"

Charlie replied, "As much as you think we need."

"Prion forms dense plaque fibers inside an infected brain."

Elene asked, "What is the rate of infection?"

"One hundred percent."

"What's the cure rate?"

"Zero. If a person ingests the misfolded molecule, that person is gone. This transformation takes place at an alarming rate. To put it bluntly, the beta-pleated sheets eat holes in the brain. This results in a steady degeneration of physical and mental abilities, and finally death. In cows, where this phenomenon was first identified, it is known as bovine spongiform encephalopathy, or BSE, or mad cow disease. When it transited to humans, it became known as new variant Creutzfeldt-Jakob disease, or nvCJD."

Elene drew back slightly from the young man seated next to her. "They are growing these molecules in the same building where we transited?"

"So long as the scientists know what they're doing and maintain a tightly controlled environment, there is no danger." Trent spoke with the quiet authority of a natural teacher. "And tight control is essential if you are going to operate at the quantum level."

They were seated at a scarred dining table. The restaurant chairs were cheap metal and vinyl. The windows overlooked the parking lot and the highway interchange. Charlie's plate was chipped. But the food was excellent, and the place held a sense of anonymous security.

Trent pushed his plate to one side and began drawing designs on his paper mat. "Ever since the disease was proven to have mutated from cattle to humans, the CJD variant has become the most carefully studied molecule on earth. They discovered that this variant molecule possesses remarkable characteristics when electric or magnetic currents are applied. Which is why physicists began considering it as a base module for quantum computing. My goal was simple enough. We already know how the molecule becomes restructured. So why not repeat the process? Only this time, redesign the molecule so that it better suits our purposes."

Charlie leaned against the side wall and cradled his recharged coffee mug. The warmth rose through his hands. He felt himself gradually becoming reanchored in the here and now. And yet he still felt Gabriella's warmth and her strength, such that everything appeared rimmed by a special glow.

Elene asked Trent, "It never occurred to you that you might be introducing such a cataclysmic threat?"

"Not at all." Trent sounded very firm. But the hand drawing designs on the tabletop shook ever so slightly.

Charlie sipped from his mug. The way Trent contained his anxiety suggested he would remain cool under fire. And Charlie was fairly certain their task was going to require a hike through Indian country. All he said was, "Explain."

"Like I said, CJD has undergone intense scrutiny. There is only one way that the disease can be transmitted. The human must ingest the brain or spinal cord of an infected bovine carcass. In the lab, the molecule is locked within ultra-tight containers. In a quantum computing station, this includes supercooled conditions and, in many cases, further isolation through strong magnetic fields. No outside influence of any kind can be permitted to impact the molecule."

Charlie said, "But you changed the molecule. And now the disease is airborne. And able to eat its way through any container."

Trent continued to draw designs on the paper mat. "We need a bomb. A big one."

Elene shook her head. "Won't work."

"Why not?"

"Your work and the project I was assigned to are sealed inside a cube that defines bomb-proof. Setting off a device would only alert the opposition. They'd come swarming. We'd be overwhelmed."

Charlie said, "There was this beast from Greek mythology. Chop off one of its heads, seven more grow back."

"It was called the Lernaean Hydra," Elene said. "Killing the beast was the second labor of Hercules. He used a harvesting sickle to sweep off the heads faster than they could grow back, and his nephew Iolaus used fire given to them by the goddess Athena to scorch the neck stumps after each decapitation."

Both men were watching her now. Elene shrugged. "What can I say. I was a career analyst. I lived for research until I came up with the bright idea of joining their team. Now look at all the fun I'm having."

Trent turned back to Charlie. "We can't let them do this."

"That's right, we can't. But we have to fight smart," Charlie said. "All of the images we're receiving carry multiple messages, if we're willing to look beneath the surface. Finding a deeper significance doesn't make the initial message a lie. It enriches it. Makes it resonate on a whole new level."

They were both watching him now.

"Take the money you're making from these algorithms." Charlie related Elizabeth's confrontation with her family, the five million dollars, the realtor, the trip she and Shane were now making.

Trent said, "I don't follow you."

"Listen to what I'm saying. Elizabeth didn't ask about buying an island. She was after a place with sovereignty."

"You mean, like a country?"

"Effectively a place that can make its own law, yes. These days, most such places are used as tax havens. But there is one other issue. One that might be of crucial importance."

Elene was nodding now. "Extradition."

"Right. Going after a criminal who lives in a different country requires a treaty. Otherwise the laws of one country don't apply in the other, and a person cannot be brought back to stand trial."

Trent frowned over the prospect. "So now we're criminals."

"Not yet," Charlie replied. "But if things work out the way I expect them to, we soon will be."

62

Reese did not have an office as such. Offices were intended for private meetings and status and paperwork. Reese despised all three. She wanted power, and she wanted to exercise it with a team she trusted. An office played no part in her personal remit. The room they had assigned to her was used by Jeff and his security detail. Jeff assumed it meant Reese considered his work to be vital and wanted to establish that publicly. She let him think what he wanted.

She met with two of her team members in the dining area of the building's main gallery. She did not try to hide what she was doing. She had no intention of creating rivalry within her group.

Reese Clawson was after taking it to the next level.

"You don't have to do this. You're not getting any special perks. This is just a question. A what-if. If it resonates, fine. If it doesn't, we go back to the status quo. Are we clear on this?"

Joss was seated at the head of the table. He faced the room and the entrances. Typical for a frontline warrior. "You sound like a general asking me to go out and get shot at."

She liked that enough to smile. "You are one sharp guy."

"Is that a yes?"

"There could be danger. But we won't know unless we try."

Consuela demanded, "Where are the others?"

"This project only needs two of you. If either of you doesn't want to do this, I'll go find someone else. Or try to. But I wanted to ask you first."

"Why?"

"Call it a gut reaction. I think you're right for the task."

Which was both true and not true. Reese had originally planned on pairing Eli with Joss. But the youngest member of her transit team had remained isolated and frightened since Elene's disappearance. As though having someone show him the exit had left him severely rattled.

When she had gone looking for Eli about this mission, Reese found him standing in the clinic's hallway, staring at the empty bed. The formerly comatose patient had been moved to a private room on the ground floor. He was being kept away from the others and under heavy sedation, because every time he came fully awake, he freaked in an extremely noisy fashion. Eli had glanced over at her approach, then gone back to staring through the glass, studying the empty bed as though sizing it up for himself. Reese had left the clinic without speaking, filled with a burning urge to hunt down Elene Belote and stake her to the earth.

She kept her voice level as she said, "I'm looking for two people who can move in total harmony."

"I like that part," Joss said.

Consuela huffed. "Dream on."

Reese said, "We face an outside threat from a team in Switzerland. We don't know how far they've taken this. And to be honest, we don't care. The threat is enough."

Joss said to Consuela, "Here we go."

"I want to know if it's possible for my team to take them out." Reese stopped. And waited. She found herself fighting against a sudden attack of nerves. Whether it was because she was crazy to ask, or because she was finally drawing near to her goal, or because she feared a flat turndown, she could not say.

Joss said, "So we're basically your sniper-spotter team."

Consuela said, "We're what?"

"Simple combat structure. One goes on the attack. The other reads the terrain, checks the wind and elevation and everything else that impacts the strike, and watches for incoming fire."

"I'm hearing," Consuela said. "But I'm not tracking."

Reese said, "Joss is absolutely correct. I'm asking if you two would go out as a team."

Joss said, "Excuse me for asking. But it seems kind of weird, going on the hunt when we don't have firepower. Not to mention any way to carry it if we did."

"We don't know that."

Joss smiled. It was a warrior's grin. A drawing back of every facial muscle, exposing the raw power of a man who knew the business of death. "You been giving this some thought."

"Your first time out, you scope the terrain. You go in and you look around. You do *not* initiate contact. And you see if there is any way to make an attack. You *ask* this. Or I will ask it for you. You've seen how shaping the question often supplies an answer."

"Like it's already there before we ask." Joss nodded. "I can dig it."

Reese resisted the urge to gouge her fingernails into the table. "Does that mean you're in?"

Joss looked across the table. "What do you say, babe?"

"First of all, *ese*, I'm not anybody's babe."

He just grinned harder. "Always did like my food spicy."

Consuela flipped her hair at him. And gave Reese such a cold eye, she was certain Consuela was going to turn her down flat.

Instead, Consuela demanded, "I don't like this business of him doing all the sniper stuff and me just hanging back watching."

Joss laughed out loud.

"You think this is funny?"

"What I think," Joss said, "is we oughtta go with the lady, take this deal to the next level."

Reese was already rising from her chair. "Let's give this a shot."

⫶

Reese personally helped Karla ready Joss and Consuela for transit. She asked her aide to go call Jeff and Kevin and ask them to come observe a new type of transit. Reese then clicked off the mike connecting them to the lounge. She wanted to send Joss and Consuela off with an intimacy that she hoped would hold them to the course, keep them steady enough to do the job and get home. After she had repeated the instructions they had already gone through upstairs, she said, "The most important goal of all is the same now as every time. Come home."

"Roger that." Joss looked at Consuela. "I hope you're listening, sister."

"Five by five." She glanced over. "Did I say that right?"

He reached over, offering her a fist. "Just like the pro you are."

She did the fist-on-fist thing. "My man."

"I wish."

This time she smiled as she said, "You never give it a rest, do you."

"Always ready, always armed," Joss said.

"Yeah. Like you think you could handle this."

"You better believe it."

"Huh. Like I haven't heard that line. A billion times, maybe more."

"Only this time it's for real."

Reese watched the banter and knew they were using the words to knit together, get ready, amp up. She also knew she was being excluded. This was them on the front line, her seated up there in the glass box, watching from a safe distance. And there was nothing she could do about it.

Finally Joss turned to her and said, "How come you don't go hunting yourself?"

Reese tasted the air with the tip of her tongue. "I want to. But I can't."

"No offense."

"None taken."

"It's just, you don't strike me as an officer who's comfortable hanging back in the Green Zone while her troops are out taking fire."

"I'm not." She noticed faces appearing in the glass overhead. Reese reached over and switched off the monitor linking them to the Departures Lounge. "I want to go. I want it so bad it hurts. The people you're going after stole something from me."

Consuela said, "This crew in Switzerland? What did they take?"

"My confidence. And a whole lot more." Reese considered the lovely young woman. "Maybe, just maybe, if you are successful, I'll be able to take back what I lost. And then transit with you."

Consuela turned to the man stretched out beside her. "Time we go straighten these people *out*."

63

Charlie found what he was searching for five miles inland from the university. These neighborhoods formed a poor borderland that supplied cleaners and yardmen and hourly shop workers to the airport and industrial parks and university. The house had been built cheaply in the fifties and poorly maintained ever since. It was divided down the middle. One side had a "For Rent" sign planted in the front yard. The other section belonged to an elderly woman with shockingly orange hair.

When she appeared, Charlie pointed at the second rental sign taped to the neighboring screen door. "Is your place still vacant?"

The woman studied him through the screen, then said, "Step away from my door."

When he did so, she squinted at the car parked in her drive. "They gonna stay here with you?"

"They are. Yes."

"I don't run no rooms-by-the-hour place."

"I understand." Charlie motioned at the car. Elene and Trent opened their doors and walked over. Charlie said, "We're looking for somewhere quiet."

The woman was a stick figure who wore her skin like a dress made for someone three times her size. The screen mesh and the house's shadows made it difficult to determine her age. Charlie figured her for about two hundred and six. She paused long enough to light a long cigarette with a fist-sized lighter in a knitted cover. "There gonna be just the three of you?"

"We may have a few others join us. Just visiting. They won't stay long."

The woman had Charlie fit the money through her mail slot. She counted it twice. "Rent's due at the first of each month. I ain't got time for slackers. If you're a day overdue, you're out."

Charlie thanked her, then lowered his hand to the mail slot so she could drop him the keys.

He unlocked the front door, stepped inside, and surveyed the water-stained wallpaper, the flyblown window, the scarred floorboards, the weak lighting from the living room ceiling's single bulb. The sofa's burn marks were only partly covered by a fake Navajo blanket. He declared, "This place is perfect."

Elene moved swiftly through the place, opening windows. Trent grabbed a broom and began sweeping the dusty floors. Charlie walked back outside and down the front steps, surveying the terrain. A passing pickup truck slowed, and two sweat-streaked Latinos studied him. Charlie met their gaze until Elene opened the screen door behind him and said, "Coffee's ready."

Charlie walked up the front steps and accepted the mug. "Are you clear on what needs doing?"

"I follow the instructions on the iPod. I transit."

"Ascend."

Elene nodded once, a terse acceptance of more than just the word. "I ascend. I ask if there is a means for us to safely enter the building. I return."

"Any danger, any fear, any concern of any kind, you stop and you return. Safety is number one. Remember that."

She gave another tight nod. "Will you stay there in the room with me?"

"Right through it all," Charlie said. "I wouldn't have it any other way."

64

When Reese returned upstairs to the control room, she found that Kevin and Jeff had joined them. Eli had apparently followed them over from the clinic. Eli carried himself like a scared teenage runaway, slipping from one shadow to another, aware that any gaze cast his way could carry danger. Wanting to see, and wanting to escape notice. Reese sighed and turned to the controls. She could *murder* that Elene.

Reese did not risk speaking to Karla until she was certain the rage was fully suppressed. "Ready?"

"Monitors up and running. Transit tape ready to go on your word."

Reese keyed the mike. "Okay, here we go."

She ran through the instructions one more time. She saw Consuela say something under her breath, and Joss huff a laugh. She checked her sharp rebuke. That flirtatious attitude might just be the thing that would bring them back. She simply continued through the instructions and finished with, "We're beginning the count now."

·ı|ı·

Ten minutes later, it was over. Reese did not move, did not even release the microphone button, until she saw them both open their eyes.

Karla whispered, "They're back."

Reese knew Kevin and Jeff had moved up behind her chair. She could see their reflection in the glass. Eli remained in the rear corner.

She shifted in her chair, took a breath, and realized her muscles had locked. She tried to hide the wince as she worked her neck. But Kevin noticed anyway. "You okay?"

"Just tense."

"I believe it."

Jeff, however, was ebullient. "This could be some serious voodoo."

"If it works," Kevin added. "You were actually expecting them to go out and find weapons?"

"Maybe." Reese pushed herself upright. "I have to talk to them."

Downstairs, she held back while Karla disengaged the monitor cables. Joss and Consuela both exuded the same mixture of determined calm and suppressed tension they had shown before transiting. When Karla coiled the cables and stepped back, Reese clicked on the mike so they could hear in the other room, then said, "Joss first."

"It was just like you instructed. I went in. Scoped the place out. And when you said find a weapon, it was there."

She resisted the urge to turn and look up through the window. "Describe."

"Hard to say. Like a ball of fire. Or smoke. But it wasn't a bomb. Like, it was, but not . . ."

Reese gripped her arms around her middle. Reining in her impatience. "Take your time."

"It was more like a *feeling*. All these bad things wound up tight together." Joss looked at her, uncertain. "Tell the truth, it was like I had made it myself."

Reese nodded. As though she understood.

"Rage and a lot of other stuff. All bundled up tight. Waiting for me to toss it out. Then, boom."

"But you didn't."

"No, man. You said look but don't touch."

"Can you do it again?"

"Oh, absolutely." On that point he had no doubt. "Just say the word."

"Could we possibly use this weapon against people in the physical realm as well?"

"I have *no* idea. Maybe."

"Okay. Good work." She turned to Consuela. "Go."

"I could sense him working out there. But I held back. And I watched. I liked that part more than I thought. I could see, like, everywhere around us."

"Were you aware of the weapon Joss made?"

"Totally. I don't know what it was. But all of a sudden, it got really creepy. Like, I can't describe . . ."

"Try. For me."

"Like, if he'd been aiming at me, I would have been taken *out*."

"It felt that bad," Reese said. "Even though he didn't use it."

"Oh yeah. We're talking seriously nasty. I don't want to be *near* that thing when it goes off."

"Could you make a weapon like that yourself?"

"I don't know. Maybe." She turned to Joss. "You think maybe you could show me?"

"Say the word, lady."

Consuela smiled. "Least you got the name right that time."

Reese waited through another fist-on-fist, then asked, "Anything else?"

Consuela said, "I think maybe somebody saw us."

Joss frowned. "I didn't notice anything."

"You were busy with your bomb making. I was the watcher. I'm pretty sure they were there. Not directly *with* us. More like, watching from the next room. Five, maybe six of them."

"Did they see you?"

"I have *no* idea. But I think . . . maybe."

Reese noticed how the pair had coalesced into a functioning team. They had not yet succeeded at the task, but the prospect was real. Reese fashioned a smile and punched the words as hard as she could. "Good work. I mean it. This is strong."

Joss grinned and laced his fingers behind his head. "I'm thinking our crew needs a different name. Something like, I don't know . . ."

Consuela said, "Attack ghosts."

"Hey. I like that."

"You serious?"

"Totally. They hear we're coming, they spook out."

Reese turned for the door. "Get some rest. We go out for real tomorrow."

65

Gabriella said over the phone, "So this Elene woman ascended, with you guiding her."

"Reese's team calls it transiting, but it's the same process. Jorge's voice on the iPod did the guiding. I just sat in the room and kept her company."

"It's still very difficult for me, being faced with hard evidence that our process was stolen and handed over to that woman. Who has taken it and twisted it and turned it into . . ."

He felt exactly the same. But there was nothing to be gained by allowing his rage to emerge. Charlie kept one hand on the steering wheel and held the phone to his ear with the other. "It was amazing, sitting there and watching this stranger lay down and fit on the headphones and key the iPod and ascend. Like she had done it dozens of times. Which of course she had."

Gabriella said slowly, "At least we have confirmation that we can bring Reese Clawson's team over to our side, given a chance."

"Assuming they want to come." When Gabriella did not respond, he asked, "How's our boy?"

"Brett is coping. Sleeping most of the time. Full of remorse. He wants to speak with you."

"Today's already booked solid. I'll call him soon. Where are you?"

"In the waiting room at Luton Airport. I hired a Swiss air taxi to take us to Guernsey. It was the only way we could all make it there today. I hope that's okay."

"Are you kidding? It's beyond fine. There's another lady traveling with Elizabeth. Her name is Shane Schearer."

"Elizabeth told me. This jet is very expensive, Charlie."

"You ladies are going off to buy an island. You can afford a private jet to get you there in style. Matter of fact, they'll probably take you more seriously now."

She was silent long enough for Charlie to know what was coming next. Finally she said, "So you do this thing tonight."

"*We* do it," he corrected. He waited as a truck thundered past his rental car and then finished the thought. "I couldn't do it without you."

"Where are you?"

"On the freeway headed south. I need to run an errand."

Charlie was afraid she was going ask what he had to do that was so urgent. And he did not want to lie. But all she asked was, "Is that why you are entering their facility so late?"

"We're going in when Elene saw us doing it. Just before dawn. She was very clear on this point."

"Elizabeth has just come through the doors, Charlie. Perhaps we should wait and talk once we arrive on Guernsey."

"Gabriella."

"Yes, Charlie?"

"Nothing. You're right. It can wait."

"Perhaps it should." She was quiet. Charlie heard the plane engines rev up. Then she said, "I am looking forward to tonight, Charlie. Very, very much."

"Me too. That last time was amazing."

"It was more than that, Charlie." She whispered the word then. And sent fire shooting down his spine. *"Finally."*

66

Shane entered Luton Airport's private terminal behind Elizabeth. She was still scoping out the place when a truly beautiful woman rushed over and enveloped Elizabeth in an embrace. Shane could see that Elizabeth held back, as though carrying the vestiges of a quarrel the other woman had long since left behind. If the other woman noticed Elizabeth's reserve, she gave no sign. Instead, she wiped streaks off both cheeks before smiling with broken joy and saying, "You must be Shane."

Gabriella Speciale was a sloe-eyed stunner with the power to draw light from a dismal, windswept day. Her beauty struck Shane as belonging to a different era, when women wore silk gowns dyed with royal purple and were worshiped in hilltop temples and launched kings into battle. Yet Gabriella embraced Shane with the easy abandon of a woman who had traveled across continents for nothing less.

They were joined by a tall young man with a monk's clear-eyed gaze. Gabriella introduced him as Massimo. Elizabeth seemed to think even less of the young man than she did of Gabriella. But if Massimo even noticed Elizabeth's sullen hello, he gave no sign.

Beyond customs, a pilot waited for them with an umbrella and a well-paid smile. They were bundled into a small jet, which powered up before they had buckled their seat belts. Elizabeth settled into the row behind Shane and pulled down the window blind and shut her eyes to the thrill of traveling by private jet. Massimo took the lone seat across from Elizabeth and lost himself to the view beyond the window.

Gabriella chose the plush leather seat next to Shane, and once they were airborne she said, "You must have many questions about all this."

"I probably should." The jet rose above the clouds. Sunlight lanced across the interior as the plane went through a banking turn. "To tell the truth, all this is a little overwhelming."

"I understand."

Shane thought the woman opposite her had the quiet attentiveness of a professional listener. "Are you a doctor?"

"Psychologist. I started on this project because I grew tired of watching rats."

"And look where it brought you."

"Yes." Gabriella had a lovely smile. "But this is an exception. I have never been in a private jet before."

Shane turned toward the window. "All my life, I've been waiting for the moment when things finally started happening. Now all I can think of is, I wish Trent was here to make it real for me."

"Trent is your young man?"

"I have no idea. We've only known each other a few days. But with everything that's happened, it feels like years."

"He is connected to you through ascents?"

"That's a good question. He's only had dreams. He doesn't call them that, though. He says it's a completely different element, like comparing carbon and helium. He's a physicist." Shane rubbed the side of her face. She knew she was not talking clearly. But she doubted

292

she could do any better without about a week of sleep. "These images come from someone who looks like his older self."

"So Trent receives his information via experiences that resemble an intense dream state. And you ascended using the iPod that Elizabeth supplied. And now you are here." Gabriella's accent gave the impression that she delicately tasted each thought. "All this is still very new to us as well. But if you want my opinion, something happens to people who share these experiences. They discover that many barriers we often use to remain isolated become less important than we ever thought possible. If we are open to the invitation, we can join together with a remarkable force of intimacy."

"So what's happening to Trent is the same as to me."

"Logically there is no possible way the two could be connected. He dreams and receives experiences you call images. He has no control. He cannot make them happen. He is a passive observer. You, on the other hand, ascend by your own choice and actions." She smiled once more. "But I am Italian. Logic plays a much smaller role in my society. So my professional mind says, we cannot verify any connection without a great deal more study. But my heart says, we have all been drawn together for purposes beyond our wildest dreams."

⊹⊹⊹

They left the season and the sun behind when they descended into the clouds. Their little plane was buffeted and tossed as they dropped. Shane caught glimpses of savage waves and lashing rain. They landed hard.

A hotel van pulled up right to the stairs, but they were still drenched just from crossing from the jet to the vehicle. Shane did not mind. The cold and the salt air was a bracing reminder of where she was and how far she had come. The dull classes and the frustrating chains of university life belonged to a different realm.

The van drove them up a winding road, along cliffs that dropped to a sea of froth and howling wind. The hotel was a grey stone monument to another era. Its lead-paned windows and peaked doors and towers all seemed designed to defy the awful weather. Inside they were greeted by a roaring fire, hand-wrought chandeliers, and a distant ceiling painted with family shields. Even the portraits smiled complacently.

Shane's room was lined in oak paneling and illuminated by a hand-wrought iron chandelier. The ceiling was beamed. On the polished floor awaited a pair of slippers, lest the royal foot grow chilly. Shane dumped her bags and her clothes and crawled into her four-poster bed and was gone.

67

Charlie took the coastal road south as far as Ventura, then headed inland. His internal clock ticked the seconds off with impatient volume. But he took his time, driving slow enough to check the side roads. If he failed, he knew he could find a replacement at hardware stores. But mixing and building homemade explosives was a fiddling process, amplified by the need to spread out his purchases. He could ask Elene and Trent to help, but the young man was already spooked by the night ahead. And he did not want them to see the danger zone one moment earlier than necessary.

Trent had assumed that when Charlie had nixed the bomb, it meant no trouble. No opposition. But Charlie was fairly certain the night was going to end on a very loud note. He would simply prefer something easier to target than a bomb. He had not corrected Trent because there was nothing to be gained by planting the red flag of combat until it was absolutely necessary.

Most of California's truly blighted regions lay inland from the coast's serious money. But there were certain pockets where the meth epidemic had eaten away at formerly decent communities, staining the earth with a frantic cry for bedlam. Charlie found what he was looking for down a side street about two miles east of the freeway. He pulled into the parking lot of a strip mall. The bar anchoring the far corner was rimmed by a sparkling assortment of chrome and leather. A trio of bearded bikers grinned as one of their own gunned a tricked-out Harley and filled the parking lot with a bone-rattling din.

Charlie parked with his nose pointed at the bar's entry. He rolled down his window and waited with the motor running.

One of the bikers nudged his mate and pointed in Charlie's direction. They all turned to glare at him. The biker cut his motor, rose from the saddle, and sauntered over. "What're you after, meat?"

Charlie kept both hands on top of the wheel, in clear view. He did not reply.

The biker wore a stained vest and leather pants and high boots. He poked his head in the open window. A rancid odor filled the car. He snorted loudly. "Don't smell like cop to me."

Charlie said, "I'm going to reach into my pocket."

"Go for it, meat."

Charlie lifted out a folded twenty and passed it over.

"I won't wipe you off my boot for this, meat."

"I'm just offering your friends a drink. Which they'll have inside the bar."

The biker possessed eyes with no bottom. He turned and spoke to the group waiting by the rail. All but one drifted inside. The other came up to the car, crossed massive arms, and hulked over Charlie as the first biker said, "I asked what you wanted."

"Only what I can get fast."

"Time is money, meat. The less you got, the more it costs."

"I need a sidearm. Box of hollow points. And a 12 gauge. Solid round ammo."

The biker didn't speak.

"Some C-4. And caps. And a timer."

The bikers exchanged filthy grins. "Ten thousand."

"I'll give you four."

"You'll give me what I want, meat. Now let's see some ID."

Charlie had the money ready. "Five hundred now. The rest on delivery. I need it fast or not—"

"I heard you the first time." The biker stuffed the money in his vest. "There's a body shop two blocks south. I'll meet you in the back in half an hour."

"You've got ten minutes," Charlie said, putting the car into drive. "And I'll be waiting out front."

68

"Who is this, please?"

"You're the one who called in here."

"This is Elene."

"Is this a joke?"

"No. Eli?"

"Yeah. It's me. Elene, wow, people have been going postal here over your vanishing act. Especially Reese. Where are you?"

"I had to do something. I'm sorry, I thought I had called the nurse's station in the Treatment Room."

"You did. She asked me to spot her while she went for a smoke."

"How . . . how is Rod?"

"Which one is he?"

"The older man in the bed farthest from the nurse's station."

"You won't believe it. A while back, the guy just woke up."

"Is he . . ."

"He's okay. I mean, he's pretty freaked. But the doctor's treating him like a trauma victim. Serious sedation. Using antidepressants to bring him back in gradual stages. I talked with him today."

"Listen, I'm coming in. And I'm bringing somebody with me. The member of the Swiss team who supplied Reese with the technology. Is Reese around?"

"No, she split a couple of hours ago. She's been basically camped out here. Everybody's either sacked out or gone. It's just me and the guys trapped in their beds."

"When the nurse comes back, do you think you could meet us and let my friend in?"

�·|||·

Elene handed the phone to Charlie, who said, "You did good."

"He was there. Just like I saw in my transit."

"Ascent," Charlie corrected.

Elene nodded. "There is a lot more that changes than just the name."

"You have no idea." Charlie turned to Trent and asked, "You know what to do?"

Trent swallowed noisily. "Do you think this will work?"

"Elene saw it."

"She saw some guy named Eli sitting at the nurse's station. She saw us going in. She didn't say anything about getting out again."

"Yes I did."

Charlie studied the diminutive agent. "Actually, you didn't say a word about after."

"There is a lot to take in." Elene described their leaving the building, then said, "The entire ascent felt good. Really, really good. I thought the experiences in the transit room were special. This is something else entirely."

Charlie had the impression she was holding something back. But she gave him the blank gaze of a woman trained since birth to hold secrets close, and decided now was not the time to press. Either he trusted her or all was lost.

He turned to Trent and said, "You are going in and you are doing what needs to be done. Then you are coming out of there safely."

"How can you be so sure?"

"Because," Charlie said. "This is what I do."

"What, getting people into scary situations?"

"No. Bringing them out the other side."

"But you won't be with us."

"I'll be coming in as soon as I finish laying the groundwork."

"Trent," Elene said. "This is going to work."

Charlie rose from the table. "Elene, I want you to walk him through everything one more time. Then grab a bite, why don't you. We leave in an hour."

"I couldn't eat," Trent said.

"You have to." Charlie waited until the grad student met his eye. "Be strong, be rested, be prepped. You've got a busy night ahead."

69

Two hours later, Trent sat in the rental car's passenger seat. He studied the woman next to him and wondered if he could ever be this calm. Elene Belote did not appear the least infected by nerves. In fact, she seemed totally disconnected from what was about to happen. She sat and stared out at the night and talked in an utterly disconnected manner. She might as well be reading off a shopping list.

"Rod and I went through basic training together. It wasn't anything like as bad as military boot camp. But the effect was largely the same. You disconnect from externals and form a tightly knit group. Some of the ties last through an entire career. Ours did. Rod went off to our listening post in Ankara, then Singapore. I stayed at Langley. Rod came back last year. He hated working at headquarters. He called it the world's biggest fishbowl. Which is why he volunteered for this program. I signed on because I'd never before been offered a chance at ops."

They sat on the top level of a parking garage. They were high enough to look out over the roofs of the neighboring office/shopping complex and see the airport beyond. The field separating the periphery road and the runways was inky black. Lights rimmed the landing strips like brilliant jewels. The airport terminal was a distant glowing crown. To Trent's left rose a solitary building ringed by a black metal fence. The lawn surrounding the building was utterly bare, as was the structure itself. It looked like a standard white office block, four stories tall, utterly unremarkable. Elene had said the windows were fake fronts for a solid steel wall.

"So you both volunteered for this program. Whatever it is." Trent found Elene's accent both subtle and soothing, a trace of somewhere far gentler than this dark night. "Is it okay if I roll down my window?"

"Why not. We're just a couple of old friends enjoying a nighttime chat." She turned the key, her features softened by the dashboard lights. When his window was down, the car went dark once more. "It was never anything so straightforward as somebody posting a notice requesting volunteers. That's not how Langley works. If there's a direct request, there would be a chain of responsibility. A good analyst sifts through totally disconnected material, searching for the one thread that pulls everything together. That's what happened here. No official notification was ever made that this project even exists. So if things go south, which they have, there's nobody to blame."

"Deniability."

"It's the name of the game." She pulled her hands deeper into the sleeves of her sweater. "Can I ask you something?"

"Of course."

"Why is it that time doesn't seem all that important when I transit?"

"Ascend," Trent corrected.

"Whatever." She bundled the sweater up closer to her neck. "I wish I still smoked. There's nothing to make waiting go better than a cigarette."

"First of all, the whole concept of time's passage is linked to our three-dimensional senses. We are mentally and biologically wired to perceive time in a certain way. We assume that simply because time seems to pass, moving from past to present to future, that is how time must actually be. But that is totally wrong. For centuries, mathematicians tried to formulate a structure that showed how time worked, and failed. Because they looked at time the wrong way."

She had turned in her seat so that she could face him. "Do you teach?"

"Some. Why?"

"Nothing. Go on."

"Everybody who has studied the quantum formula for time comes up with their own individual way of describing it in non-mathematical terms. For me, the easiest way to view time is like the ocean on a very calm day. If you could stand on the shore of a different dimension and see time like we view, say, the planar surface of a two-dimensional field, you would see that time does not flow. Time *is*. Standing on your fifth-dimensional cliff top, you would see time as one glorious sea. At this particular point, 2:15 in the morning, we are here. Located just like we are spatially located in this parking lot beside the airport. You would observe our existence at this point on the sea of time."

Elene was watching him closely now. "I don't know if I fully get it. But I love the way that sounds."

"The problem is, so much of our experiences, our way of judging the value of things, how we look at our achievements, all are dependent upon this flawed view of time. Even the power of secrets and confidentiality are built upon the concept of linear movement in time. We have *invested* in . . . " He noticed she was no longer observing him. Her features had tightened. In the silver luminescence of the runway lights, Trent no longer saw a quietly reserved analyst. He saw danger. "What's the matter?"

"What you said struck a nerve." She turned and stared out at the airport. "I invested in a pattern of choices because I thought it would take me somewhere. One step after the other. Just like you described."

Trent listened to the distant rumble of a plane revving for takeoff. "Maybe we should change the subject."

"No. I need to be hearing this. Go on. Please."

"I've given this a lot of thought since meeting myself in those dreams. I've had to. Either this older persona has found a way to effectively prove a new construct of time, or I'm talking to aliens, or I've gone completely off-the-edge whacko."

"You're not whacko," Elene said. "About the aliens, though, I'm not so certain."

He was glad to see she had relaxed once more. "Hearing about this transit system—"

"Ascents," she corrected, smiling now. "You did that on purpose."

"This offers the first real proof of how human consciousness can be disconnected from a purely linear—"

Trent stopped at the sound of her phone chiming. She checked the readout, said, "It's Charlie."

She opened the phone, said hello, listened, said yes, then cut the connection and told him, "We're good to go."

He swallowed hard. "Okay."

She dialed another number, waited, then said, "Eli, hi, it's me. Yes, Elene. We've arrived. Could you please . . . Tunnel two. Like always. Yes, he's with me. Brett Riffkind. Sure. Thank you."

She stowed away her phone, opened her door, then glanced over and asked, "Are you clear on what you need to do?"

"Yes." Trent studied the woman seated next to him. Elene's face had resumed its hard edges. Every vestige of gentleness was erased. Even though her voice kept its slight Southern drawl, the effect now was one of a polite warrior queen. Bloodless. Capable of anything. But now, headed into the unknown, Trent found the effect very comforting. He said, "I'm glad you're on our side."

70

The building had four underground entrances, according to Elene. There were also two more at ground level—the front entrance, which was permanently locked, and a loading bay. All service personnel entered via the loading bay. It was completely disconnected from the building's main areas. Only the janitorial staff could pass through the double steel doors separating the service areas from the rest of the building, and they were chaperoned by security guards at all times. The kitchen staff connected with the building's interior through a slit in the cafeteria wall. All the service personnel were tightly vetted and their home lives monitored. There was no admin staff and just five on-site security. Everything possible was either handled off-site or electronically controlled.

Elene described all this as they walked the bare-walled tunnel beneath the glaring fluorescent lights. She called it standard ops for a high-clearance site. The design underwent constant alterations as systems evolved. But the basic construct remained the same. Elene related this in the same calmly disconnected manner she had used in the car.

As they approached an unmarked steel door, Trent asked, "How am I supposed to get in?"

"I told you. It's all taken care of." The door had no handle or controls of any kind. "I know this is all very strange. And I know you're frightened. But it's important you pay careful attention. From now on, everything you say and do will be recorded. Remember that, and everything will be fine."

Trent was about to ask how that information made anything fine when a small portal opened in the concrete wall beside Elene. He had not noticed the access panel before. It was painted to disappear in the wall. Now a blue Plexiglas sheet glowed softly within a recessed alcove.

Elene set her hand upon the panel. A line of light flashed up, then down. She said, "Elene Belote."

The panel beeped once. Elene stepped away. "Now you."

Trent stepped over and set his hand upon the panel. When the light passed up and down, he licked his lips and spoke the name Charlie had given him. The one Elene had heard him speak in the ascent. "Brett Riffkind."

The panel took a longer time scanning his hand. Elene said, "There is no record of your palm. But your name is down as someone to be granted access, so it's making a record now of who you are."

"How do you know—"

The panel beeped a second time. The door slid open. Elene said, "Let's go."

⫿⫿⫿

Eli was waiting for them just on the other side of the inner glass portal. He coded in a number, watching Trent as he did so. When the door slid back, he said, "Riffkind's name was already in the system."

"Hello, Eli. It's good to see you again."

Eli looked to be about sixteen, but Trent suspected he was older

306

than his appearance. He bore the scars of a hard early life. Eli was watching him closely. "What's he doing in the system when he's never been here before?"

"Brett Riffkind helped design the system we used to ascend." Elene caught herself and corrected, "Transit."

The kid's eyes grew round. "He's one of them? That crew in Europe?"

"Yes." She gripped his arm. "How have you been?"

"You brought one of them here? Reese is busy turning Joss and Consuela into an attack team. She's going to let them loose on that crew tomorrow."

Trent stepped forward. But before he could speak, Elene shot him a look. He subsided.

Eli caught the exchange. "Reese is going to go ballistic."

"It's okay, Eli. Brett's name is in the system, remember? You said that yourself." Elene held to the same gentle tone she had used on Trent. A means of dominating through calm. "You say you're fine. But you don't look fine. You look wounded."

Eli gave her a look that belonged on a man ten times his age. An ancient's weary cynicism. "What's it to you?"

"I'm worried about you." Her accent turned the words into a chant. "You're a very special person."

Eli huffed a very angry, "That's why you took off on us, right?"

"No, Eli. I left so I could bring Brett here. And bring my friend back from the darkness that almost swallowed me too."

The words took a long moment to register. "You brought Rod back?"

"That's right, Eli. Me and my friends. And we're going to do more." She reached over and took his hand. "Would you go with us to the Treatment Room, Eli?"

"I spend too much time there already," the kid whined, but he came along.

Trent followed them along the hallway and into a giant atrium full of muted colors and hanging plants and indirect lighting. He thought it looked like a palace of subtle control. Even the air was monitored.

He could not believe he strolled through this place like nothing was wrong. Like he wasn't a thief in the night, here to destroy everything he could get his hands on.

They entered a hallway that faced onto a long room filled with hospital beds. All but one were filled with immobile patients. A bored male nurse sat at a desk on a slightly raised dais, watching television on a computer flat screen. Trent realized the glass fronting the clinic had to be one-way, because the nurse glanced up several times and studied the patients but never once looked their way.

Elene led the kid down to stand before the last bed, the only one that was empty. "I know what you're thinking, Eli."

"What, you studied up on mind reading while you were AWOL?"

Elene touched the glass. "You're thinking this bed has your name on it."

"You're nuts."

"You're thinking it's only a matter of time. And you know what, Eli? You're right."

The kid's face was a landscape of misery. "You came back. You brought Rod back. You're here for the others."

"That's right. But you know what else is true? These pals of ours who got lost out there, they'll never leave the nightmare behind. They'll never ascend again."

"Do what?"

"Transit. They're trapped, Eli. They've lost the touch. Do you want to risk that happening to you?"

"Like I got a choice."

"But you do, Eli. And that's why I'm here. To take you back with me. Before it's too late. And have you see what can really be done with this new gift of yours."

He was watching her now. Ignoring the empty bed for the first time. "You're with them, aren't you. The ones Reese is going after."

Elene met his gaze. "Come with us, Eli."

The kid just stared at her. Trent clamped down on his impatience.

The longer he stayed in this sterile hallway, the more spooked he became. Because it wasn't the kid he saw climbing into that empty bed. It was Shane.

He was about ready to break in when Elene pointed back to where he stood. "My friend came with me to help make things right. He needs access to a computer plugged into the system."

Eli turned to study him. "You're going to wreck the place?"

"That's right," Trent said. "I am."

Eli stared at the bed a final moment longer. Then, "I can come with you?"

"I won't leave without you," Elene replied. "Count on it."

71

Reese dreamed she was in the dentist chair. The guy kept drilling in tiny spurts. Drill-drill, pause, drill-drill. She wanted to tell him to get on with it, but she couldn't speak because her mouth was filled with cotton.

Then she woke up and realized it was her cell phone. She fumbled for the light and pushed the phone onto the floor. She leaned her head over the side of the bed. Her eyes would not focus. But the screen illuminated in time to the ring. She aimed for that. Grabbed the thing. Rolled on her back. She needed both hands to connect. "What."

"This is Jeff. I just got a call from the duty officer. Brett Riffkind just showed up."

The words simply sank into the drugged sponge of her brain and disappeared. They made no sense. "Hang on a second."

Reese stumbled into the bathroom and washed her face. Again. She had tossed and turned for hours, then finally taken a sleeping pill. The one the doctor guaranteed would knock her out for eight hours.

Reese seldom allowed herself the indulgence of time off. But she had not been resting well, and her body ached with pent-up fatigue. So she had taken the pill. And now she could not scrub her face hard enough to force the blood into her brain.

She stumbled back into the bedroom. She sank onto the bed and took the phone and said, "Repeat that. Slowly."

"Brett Riffkind. He's here."

"Where exactly is here?"

"Are you okay?"

"Tired." She could not make sense of what the security chief was saying. "Riffkind is in Switzerland."

"Not anymore. The guy showed up with Elene."

"Elene Belote? She's back?"

"I'm watching her on the monitor. She's sitting in the atrium with Neil. They're drinking coffee. And chatting. Calm as you please."

"I'm going online." She shuffled across the bedroom to her desk. Her computer took forever to boot up. The clock on her desk set read 3:30. She had been out for something under three hours. The sleeping pill clogged her veins. "All right. I'm linked in. Pass me the feed."

The atrium flashed onto her screen. The camera hung from the ceiling, which was sixty feet up. All she could see were two distant figures in an otherwise empty chamber. "Draw them closer."

The view made a swooping dive, focused, and Reese stared at Elene cradling a steaming mug. She was talking to Neil Townsend, the team's resident bad-boy hacker. Reese dry-scrubbed her face. She had no idea the two ever even spoke. "Where is Riffkind?"

"Can't find him."

"What, he's left again?"

"Hold on." She heard him drop the phone, pick up a mike, ask the duty officer where Brett was. The response was rattled either by static or by her own mental state. Jeff picked up the phone and said, "He's gone off the grid."

"What is that supposed to mean?"

"I guess he's sacked out in the Barracks."

They had originally wired the team's bedrooms for light and sound. Even the bathrooms had camera hookups. But the first week Neil had been inside, he had hacked into the building's system and killed all the Barracks feeds. Security had raised a stink, but Reese had backed the kid. Giving them a little private space had seemed like a good idea at the time.

Reese said, "Go back to their arrival and show me Riffkind."

"We only have real-time feed off-site. We need to be in the duty room to access the tapes."

Reese could not quite stifle the groan as she rose from her desk. "Have the duty officer find Riffkind."

"Maybe we should wait. If Riffkind is in the Barracks, our man will wake everybody up at four o'clock in the morning checking the rooms. Riffkind's not going anywhere, and we've only got one guy on duty—"

"Do it." Her bed pulled at her like a magnet. Reese forced herself to turn away. "I'm coming in."

E li was right. Neil Townsend's computer was a treasure trove of ill-gotten gains.

Trent only required five minutes to scope the building's entire security system because Neil had it all mapped out. Neil had treated the different departments with their tightly sealed access points as another electronic maze. Each door was coded into his map. All Trent had to do was hit the various points, and his way forward was clear. "This is amazing."

"He's been bragging about this for weeks. How he can get anywhere he wants." Eli scoped the screen from his position behind Trent. "He made me promise to fry the system if he ever wound up in one of those beds."

Trent searched the system and realized, "He's only got the security system here."

"So?"

"I need access to the system computer."

Eli shrugged. "If it's not there, it doesn't exist."

Trent realized the physics research group had to be operating from their own mainframe. Which was both good and bad. Good, because it suggested any preliminary findings would be backed up only within the system itself. That made sense if this group was paranoid about keeping everything hidden away from other intel departments. Bad, because he would have to go down and access the mainframe from inside the division.

"Is anybody working in the physics department?"

"How should I know, man. I've never even spoken to them. They come, they go." Eli yawned. "I need to crash."

"Ten minutes." Trent figured it would be about that long before the kid lost any interest in sleep. "Right now I need you to go tell me when the physics department door opens up."

"Man, you're gonna set off every alarm in the state. Those security goofs don't mess around."

"Don't worry," Trent said. "It's going to be fine."

The kid cast a doubtful look as he left the room. Trent hit the various buttons by each of the departmental checkpoints, sealing the doors open and memorizing his way into the main lab.

He then went online and drew up a site he had spent hours sneaking around. He had always considered it time wasted and lost forever. Until now.

The latest generation of physicists took quiet pride in their computer prowess. They were all secret hackers at heart. Only their hunger to probe the boundaries of human knowledge kept them legal. But nothing stopped them from fooling around on their time off.

Any late-night gathering of physicists eventually descended to the point of softly whispered abandon. One of the group would cast a quick aside, merely to check the group's tone, make sure they were all on the same wavelength. Then they started talking about *other* boundaries. They snickered like kids and knew the gut-tightening thrill of sliding under the barbed wire of legality.

They loved nothing better than sneaking into supposedly hidden hacker sites. Looking around. Mostly they left little "Killroy was here" signs and snuck out. But not for the special sites. These they shared over the last pitcher of beer and pretended they weren't just another bunch of lonely nerds. Times like these, they were electronic pirates. Spies making their way through fields buckled by land mines. People of power.

Trent had not shared this particular treasure trove with anyone, for the simple reason that he had not had a chance to do so in person. He had still been working his way through the find when he received the first dream and met Shane and watched his life shoot off on a totally different course. And this site was simply too good to talk about online.

A group of Soviet hackers had built their own version of a safety deposit box, filled with every electronic worm and virus and bomb and spawn they could find. Trent had worked his way through about two dozen of their collection and come upon some real gems.

Eli popped back into the room. "The doors downstairs all just opened up."

"Great." Trent searched through Neil Townsend's desk and came up with a memory stick. He jammed it into the laptop's USB port, then selected four truly deadly specimens from the website, viruses that ate away the host system in a matter of nanoseconds. He downloaded three, then fed the fourth into the building's security system. "Okay. I'm all done here."

Kevin whined, "I still don't understand why Brett Riffkind's name is in our system at all."

"It makes perfect sense, if you'd stop complaining about getting woken up and think."

"I'm thinking as hard as I can at four in the morning." Kevin sounded almost petulant. "And it doesn't make any sense at all."

"I've told you all this, Kevin. This whole program is based on a system Riffkind helped design, then stole and sent to us. Our agreement was that he would come join us and be given the right to claim any physics-related discoveries as his own."

"Tell me you weren't actually going to let this guy go public about our work."

"Kevin, will you please wake up."

"You're the one who sounds drunk."

Reese knew she did and there wasn't anything she could do about it. The drug left her feeling like her blood was congealed, her brain still mostly asleep. The road in front of her windscreen swam in and out of focus. The only reason she had made it this far was because she had the roads to herself. She had the cell phone hooked to her car's Bluetooth. She disliked the way her voice rang in the empty vehicle. "Riffkind wouldn't be allowed to do anything without my approval. Which he wasn't going to get. But we needed him on-site. Who knows how far we can take this thing? If anybody can help us refine the process, it's the guy who made it work in the first place."

"I still say it was a bad idea."

"And I'm telling you, it was the only logical course. Riffkind was coming over. We had his room ready, lab space, the works. Then he vanished. Now I'm thinking I shouldn't have called you at all."

"No, no. I just didn't get much sleep, is all."

"That makes two of us."

He made a rustling sound. Reese realized he must have dragged his hand across his unshaven cheek. He asked, "Where are you?"

"Just pulling into the parking garage." Her phone chimed. She checked the readout and said, "Hang on, I've got a call coming in from Jeff."

The security chief said, "The building's whole security system has just gone down."

His laconic tone was the only thing that kept her from flipping out. "That can't happen."

"I wish. This is the third time in eight months. It's always been some glitch that the techies take hours to find. Which is why they should have stuck to human monitoring."

She didn't have the time or the mental energy for this. "What do you mean, down?"

"Cameras, monitors, door-locks, the works. Same as before." The security chief sounded almost satisfied, as though having an electronic error confirmed his own worth. "Always happens in the middle of the night. Which is good, if you think about it. The landline phones are okay. My guy's done a check. Everything is cool. Eli and Neil are still in the atrium talking with Elene."

Reese stepped from her car. The parking garage was utterly silent. The night air tasted almost sweet. "I thought you said it was just Neil."

"Eli's been drifting around. I saw him before I left. He never sleeps much. But I've pulled the duty officer off searching the bedrooms. I want him walking the beat. Let Riffkind sleep."

She took as much comfort from his tone as his words. "I'm parked and going in."

"Not through the tunnel, you're not. I told you, the doors are out."

"How do I get inside?"

"Go back to your car and drive to the loading entrance. I'm two minutes out. We'll do it the old-fashioned way. We'll walk around to the front door and I'll use my key."

74

Trent strolled through the building's physics department. The place was drawn from his fantasies of where he'd always wanted to wind up. It was made up of eight large chambers. Everything he saw defined pristine. The eight rooms were linked by glass panels and sliding doors, all open now. The labs were jammed with equipment, a lot of which Trent figured the physicists probably didn't need. It was like somebody had gathered a bunch of geeks together and tossed them a checkbook and said, make a list. Three electron microscopes fed into the largest flat-screen monitors Trent had ever seen. A Cray supercomputer stood in its own room. The iconic tower rose from its cooling unit like a polished black sculpture in a pool of glowing water. They had *everything*.

Trent was jolted to see his formula scrawled across a wall-length greaseboard. He picked up the eraser to wipe it away. But his hand would not obey.

He jerked at a sound drifting in from outside. Somebody might have laughed. Or perhaps they called his name. He had no idea how long he stood there. Staring at two years of work. Wishing he could do away with the whole nightmarish scenario.

He rubbed the writing so hard he knocked the greaseboard off the wall. He jumped back, then just felt it all come apart. He stabbed the board with his heel. Again. Stomping down over and over, smashing it into a billion pieces. Just like his thesis and his dreams and his life. Gone.

His chest heaving, he walked from room to room, moving farther away from the entrance. His stolen hard drives were in the admin desk's top drawer, just as Elene had seen in her ascent. He used a nickel-plated sampling hammer he found in the same drawer to smash them to a pulp.

Also as Elene had described, he found a computer station by the isolation chamber that was still up and running. The screen was turned away from the front rooms. A weary physicist had obviously neglected to walk back and power down. It happened all the time. Only today it meant that Trent could sidestep the security system and access the mainframe. He found a standard USB port located on the keyboard and uncapped the memory stick containing the viruses he'd downloaded from the Russian website.

It didn't take long. The mainframe gave off a sound that was almost like a human sob. And the screen went blank.

Trent left the rooms without a backward glance. There was nothing for him here.

Consuela followed Joss slowly through the Departures Lounge. "We could get in serious trouble."

"Hey, what are they gonna do, dock our pay?" Joss reached the stairs going down to the transit room and grinned back at her. "This could be a gas."

"I'm thinking more like a disaster."

"And I'm telling you, it's time we see how far we can take this."

Consuela took her time going down the stairs. Wondering why she followed him at all. When she arrived in the transit room, Joss was already bouncing on the chair. Like a kid testing out bedsprings.

She said, "You're a fiend."

He laughed out loud. "No argument there."

"I should go."

"Come on, lady. See, I remembered and I'm talking nice. Who turned you into a mouse?"

"Reese is who. Don't tell me the woman don't scare you too."

"Absolutely. But here's the thing. She's got her own ladder to climb, right? She'll have us waiting, like, weeks before they green-light this deal. Believe me, I know all about officers and how much time they can waste." He gestured at the empty chair beside him. "Come on, lady. The motor's primed and running."

His smile convinced her more than his words. "You are a wicked, wicked boy."

He only grinned harder. "Tell me you don't love it."

"I hate you."

"Like I believe that for one minute."

"How can we do this without, you know, Reese and the sounds and everything?"

"I got Karla to show me the ropes. I go upstairs, I turn the stuff on, then I come back and we go. I've done it, like, a million times."

"You're such a liar."

"Okay, five."

"For real?"

"I get bored sitting there in my room waiting for the next shot. So I go up alone."

Consuela found herself drawn by the prospect. "You're not fooling."

"What, you think I'd drag you down here to pretend?"

"Or something."

Joss grinned at her. "That's an idea."

But she was caught by the prospect of a secret transit now. "That means you get control."

"Go where I want, when I want. I figure maybe they know about this all along. Karla checking with Reese, the lady deciding why not, give it a go and see how it flies. I think Elene's done it by herself too, but I didn't get a chance to ask her. Tell you the truth, when I did it the first time, sitting down here all by my lonesome, I was one scared little puppy."

"I can't imagine you being scared over anything."

His grin returned. "Except you."

"Yeah, well, you got a good reason there." She settled back. "So what do I do?"

He popped out of his chair. "First we figure what it is we're going to do. Then I go upstairs and set the stuff up. I say we transit, meet up here, then go straight for the target."

"The woman and the guy and the team in Switzerland."

"Name the name, that's rule one in sniper school. You ID the target and you build your scenario around the situation at hand."

"You scare me, talking like that. It makes everything so real."

"Real as it gets, lady. You in?"

She reached for her headphones. "What is it you guys say before action? Lock and load, is that right?"

76

The knocking at Shane's door was as unwelcome as it was persistent. Shane moaned and rolled over and found her mouth was so dry she could not tell them to go away.

The knocking stopped, then started anew. Shane groaned a second time and forced herself up and crossed the room and said, "Not now."

"It's Gabriella. I'm sorry to disturb you."

"Hold on a moment." She shuffled into the bathroom, found a robe hanging from the back of the door, slipped it on, then came back and let Gabriella in. "How long have I been asleep?"

"Three hours. Not long enough, I'm sure. But I left this as long as I could." Gabriella entered bearing a tray with a silver thermos and sandwiches and linen napkins and two cups. A leather briefcase was slung over her shoulder. "I need your help. If you are willing."

"Sure. Is that for me?"

"Yes. I thought you might need something."

"Let me get on some clothes." When she emerged from the bathroom, Shane discovered that Gabriella had made the bed and re-

324

arranged the furniture. The coffee table had been drawn over beside the bed. The chair from the desk was pulled up beside the table. The tray was set on the dresser by the door. On the coffee table was a cluster of electronic gear. "You want me to ascend?"

"No. I must do this. I need you to guide me." Gabriella lifted a sheet of paper. "I have written out everything that is required. We can go through this while you eat. Timing is very important. I must begin in . . ." She checked her watch. "Precisely eighteen minutes."

Shane drank a cup of coffee and ate a sandwich standing up. Gabriella stood beside her, walking her through the instructions. The process followed the same pattern as what Shane had heard on the iPod but was much more tightly controlled. She set down her cup and said, "I can do this."

"I am certain you can." Gabriella hugged her very swiftly, then walked to the bed. "Elizabeth should be the one helping me. But I cannot ask her."

"You two have argued."

"Never. But she is in love with Charlie. And I am ascending so that I can go to him. And join in a very special way." Gabriella settled onto the bed. "Elizabeth would help me. But I would rather not have to ask. I hope you can understand that."

"Absolutely." Shane watched her fit on the headphones. "So all I have to do is press this button, then speak into the mike."

"Be sure and follow the clock exactly. The timing is essential." Gabriella used both hands to adjust her pillow. "Which is why I could not ask Massimo. He is a wonderful young man. But he and his friends have become increasingly, how should I say, disassociated. They ascend together as a group. For them, it comes natural. These days I feel they are tethered to earth by the thinnest of threads. One hard wind, and poof, they would drift away. I cannot rely on him to even notice the time, much less follow it. How long do we have?"

The laptop screen showed a numerical clock in the upper right-hand corner. "Six minutes."

"The others of my team think Massimo and his group are just adolescents who play at ascending. They are very helpful and do much of the kitchen work and the cleaning. Yet they only seem to play when they ascend. Then occasionally Massimo says something, usually to me in private. And I am left wondering if perhaps he is why we are here at all."

Shane found the woman on her bed invited confidences, both by her words and the manner in which she spoke. "Are you in love with Charlie too?"

"So much I have spent a year running from him. In truth, I have two professions. I am a psychologist. And I am a specialist in choosing the world's worst men."

Rain and wind pounded on the window. Shane asked, "You think Charlie is wrong for you?"

"Of course not. If he was, I would have invited him in long ago." Gabriella's smile was piercingly sad. "It is so hard to break bad habits, no?"

"Terrible."

"Do you know, I think we are to become the very best of friends." She studied Shane a moment longer, then reached for the phone. "It is time for me to join with Charlie."

Charlie used his fake ID to take yet another motel room. He had spent a small fortune over the past few days on temporary residences. This particular suites-only motel stood where the main airport road met the avenue leading back to the facility. Charlie made a thorough check of his room on the second floor. He disliked being off the ground floor, but this was the last room they had. The night manager had charged him the full rack rate. Two hundred and seventy dollars plus tax. A lot of money for a ninety-minute stay. But from where he stood on the balcony, Charlie could look out over the dark airport runway and straight into the compound where Elene and Trent were now.

The building where Reese Clawson worked was a featureless block that shone pearl-white under the security lights. Dawn was about two hours away. The roads and airport were still. Charlie knew the quiet was an illusion. He had known the instant he heard Reese's name that this confrontation would end with a bang.

When his cell phone rang, Charlie went back inside and shut and locked his door. He slid the security bolt in place. Shut the drapes more tightly. Jammed a chair under the doorknob. "This is Charlie."

"Hello, my darling."

He should have realized a soul-shimmering joy, hearing her speak those words. Instead, his voice sounded flat to his own ears. "Gabriella."

"We are all here on Guernsey. Elizabeth arrived with Shane. You did not tell me how lovely Shane is."

"I never met her."

"Of course. Shane is here in the room with me. She has agreed to help me ascend. I wish you were here too, Charlie. Shane's room is in the tower of a castle that was built three hundred years ago. It is storming. Listen. Can you hear the wind?"

"Yes."

"I walked out to the veranda after we checked in. The waves are crashing against the cliffs below the hotel. They tell me the weather is like this most of the winter and spring, with strong winds and storms and waves that make the whole island shake. Will you keep me warm, Charlie?"

He felt a palsy grip his frame. He forced himself to utter the words, as calmly as he could, "There's something I need to tell you."

"Can't it wait until we are together?"

"Not this." He walked over to the wall. Pressed it with his fist and his forehead. "I think I realized the first moment I saw you that you had come to change my world."

"Charlie—"

"Let me finish." He swallowed hard. "I had learned to be content with never feeling satisfied. Never fitting in. Never knowing a happiness lasting longer than the next adrenaline rush. That was my world, and I was stuck with it. Then you came. I've discovered new words to describe a universe I never knew existed before. Words like chivalry. Sacrifice. Living for a higher cause. I just want to say thank you. For everything. But most especially for waking up my soul."

"You've made me cry."

"I love you, Gabriella."

"I love you as well, Charlie Hazard."

"Are you ready?"

"Wait, let me blow my nose. All right. I must ask you, Charlie, do you really think you can handle bringing back all eight lost ones?"

"Yes."

"But you were exhausted after doing it for just three."

"That was the first time. I need to bring back as many as I can."

"As many as you can *safely*."

"Roger that." He checked his watch. "I make it as twenty minutes past four in the morning, West Coast time. We are go for launch in ten minutes."

"Take care, my darling. My heart races from the thought of joining with you again."

He hung up the phone. Stood staring at the blank wall. Wondering if somehow she knew how this was probably going to end. Gabriella was the most intelligent person he had ever met. Perhaps she surmised at some deep level that he would probably not survive the coming assault on Reese Clawson's compound. And this was why Gabriella could allow herself to love him now.

78

At the appointed time, Charlie ascended. And waited.

Gabriella came to him almost instantly. There was no hesitancy this time, no lingering at the borders of his awareness. Instead, she rushed at him. If there was a word to describe their joining, it was hunger.

Charlie indulged himself for a time beyond time, reveling in the union. Then he knew they had to move. As did she. Gabriella did not release him so much as simply acknowledge his departure.

He formed the impression of his destination. Not of a specific name. But of the handwritten list Elene had given him. All eight remaining names.

He had no fear of this. It was almost normal now. He had been in storms before. Desert winds so strong the grit threatened to blast away his skin and whittle down his bones. Hurricanes lashing the Georgia coast, one tearing apart the barracks where he was sleeping. He had

330

already survived his first encounter with this particular tempest, and his second. He was utterly confident that Gabriella's shield would hold.

The danger was not here. It was in what came after.

The vortex raged at his approach. His ready defiance only strengthened the maelstrom. Charlie could not see where he was or where he went. But he kept stumbling upon forms. Each time he silently called a name, he shifted position and found the next one. They were all the same, sprawled and inert. Then he reached out with Gabriella's love and his own strength, which proved enough to awaken them even here. They rose. And he took them back. And then he returned. Each time, the tempest was stronger. It was not dust that blinded him but the fragments of wasted lives. He could sense his own mistakes and wrong deeds flashing at him, hot as lava spewed from a volcano, hurled by a banshee wind.

It did not touch him. He remained sealed within Gabriella's protective embrace.

He restored the eighth person and returned. He enfolded himself more tightly within Gabriella's loving energy. He lingered there, her love lighting him up like a beacon, a flame so strong he felt able to handle anything that came next. Even his own end.

If only their union could have lasted a little longer.

79

When Gabriella left him, Charlie allowed himself to be drawn along by her sweet fulfillment, the answer to what felt like a lifetime of hopes. Wishing he could have more, and have it for longer.

He traveled with her to the Guernsey hotel. His awareness of the physical surroundings was vague. He sensed the room and the presence of another woman at Gabriella's bedside. As the woman started the return sequence, Charlie was fairly certain Gabriella was still aware of him.

Which was when he spotted the incoming threat.

A dark mass drifted in from the realm of nightmares and death. A wraith, followed at a distance by a second form. Both of them carried shadows with them. As though they formed a mini-vortex through their intent and took pleasure from their dark handiwork.

The wraith cast something at Gabriella just as she was returning to her physical self. Charlie had the sudden recollection of a day in

Iraq, and hearing the tick of a bomb, and through it the countdown to a friend's demise.

Just like then, he did not think or hesitate. Charlie extended himself in a manner that he did not even know was possible. Perhaps it had not been until the need arose. He stretched himself out like a covering whose dimensions enclosed both women. Enveloping them entirely. Sheltering them beneath his strength.

The bomb landed on top of him. He knew instantly that was what it was. A compressed ball of fury and psychic fire.

And then his world exploded.

80

Shane followed the script to the letter. Holding to a tranquil tone had never been easier. The room was filled with a serenity so strong she could smell it, like walking through a field of desert blossoms, their petals open after the first rainfall in centuries. Shane's senses felt utterly open, wholly awake. The intensity carried an alien edge, as though she was party to something that was intimately not her own. And yet she was welcome. She counted the silent woman on the bed back up and felt certain she had found a new and dear friend.

Then it happened.

As Gabriella took a first long breath, the room's atmosphere shifted. The wildflowers were replaced by a stench of death.

"What was *that*?"

Gabriella reached over and gripped her with frantic talons. "You have to count me back."

Shane would have bolted from the room except for the grip the

334

woman kept on her arm. She could not have shifted those claws without a wrench and a Taser. "That *scared* me!"

"*Listen to me.* Charlie is in danger. I have to go back *now*."

Gabriella lay back down. Resettled the headphones. Took a pair of long breaths. Said, "Restart the controls and read the sheet just like the last time. Do it now."

The scent of sulfur left Shane fighting nausea. Terror dripped from the walls. But Shane did as she was told. "I'm starting the count."

⫴

Charlie drifted in a no man's land. He felt as though he had been ripped away, not just from the room, but from life. He remained aware, but barely. His perception was flooded by a shattering tide of rage and hurt. He searched for something that would keep him intact. But he knew it was a losing battle.

He sensed that the two attackers were readying another assault. Another bomb was incoming, and Charlie knew he would not survive.

Then Gabriella was there again. Filling him with her love. Reconnecting him with the goodness and strength that was hers to give.

Charlie absorbed her might as he would an elixir. He filled and filled and refashioned her love as his shield.

The attackers moved in. Thanks to Gabriella's presence, Charlie was able to look beyond the psychic pain and realize that the attackers had shaped the charge from a wasted life, with the same deliberate care as a human bomb maker. He watched it sweep toward them and, in that timeless awareness, knew precisely who was behind it all.

Charlie found himself developing battle-honed tactics at this new level. But where his warrior's senses had required years, this new advance took no time at all.

His awareness stretched time. He had experienced this before, when the adrenaline rush amped his senses to an impossible degree. Only now there was no outlaw rush, no flood of terror and rage. Charlie extended a shield of impossible potency. He deflected the incoming attack.

335

The two wraiths were confused but reacted swiftly, preparing yet another attack.

Charlie moved forward as he had for the other lost ones. He extended himself as he had to protect Gabriella and Shane. And enveloped both the attacker and the one who hovered on the perimeter. At the instant of contact, he had the sense of confronting a sniper and his spotter.

He felt them struggle against his hold. His own returning strength and Gabriella's love were strong enough to keep them in place, at least for a moment. He extended a message crammed with a love-filled wrath.

Come with me.

Charlie held them fast and extended himself to a new destination. He turned them about and revealed what lay just beyond their field of vision. For now.

The maelstrom's fury had never seemed fiercer. The sucking draw of remorse and guilt reached forward and tried to haul them away.

Charlie's grip remained strong enough to hold them there. He extended another message. *This is waiting to swallow you.*

He realized the spotter was a female. She fought him with genuine terror. The other was a warrior, trained and battle-hardened, and his own panic was more contained. As though he could search beyond the fear and the vortex, seeking to understand who Charlie was. Charlie recognized both the tactic and the attitude. A sniper's first duty was to determine who was the foe, the threat. Charlie held them in place until he was certain this second attacker had the chance to rethink his destiny.

Then Charlie drew them away and offered a final message, one shouted against the vortex's silent fury. *There is a different way to use your talent.*

As soon as Charlie released his grip, the female spotter fled in a wild panic. The warrior lingered a moment, checking him out. Still coming to terms with the shift in his world.

When the second attacker departed, Charlie followed close behind. He saw the room where they ascended. He knew they called it the transit room. He left them there and moved out. Saw the entire Departures Lounge. The empty electronically controlled lobby area. The position within the building. The group that clustered around Elene down in the atrium. He saw it all.

Charlie drew himself away and back to where he lay in the motel room on the airport's other side. He rose from the bed. Went into the bathroom. Washed his face. Stared at his reflection. Told himself to lock and load.

Nothing had changed. He had known from the outset he was going to have to go in there and end this thing. Only now his reason was far stronger.

He was going to stop Reese Clawson once and for all.

81

Reese was waiting with Jeff for the duty officer to unlock the building's front door when Kevin hurried up. He wore a raincoat over jeans and a candy-striped pajama top. Kevin said, "I didn't even know this opened."

The main security station stood where a normal building would have a receptionist. The curved desk was rimmed by blank screens.

Reese said, "This can't be good."

"It's typical, is what it is." Jeff did not even bother to glance over. "They could have hired an army for what this system cost. These techies ought to be lined up against the wall."

They entered the atrium to find her team clustered around a table. Elene sat at the head. Everyone but Joss looked over as the trio entered. Their expressions were grave. Consuela looked terrified. Joss held one of her hands, his gaze locked on some grim and distant horizon.

Elene Belote showed neither surprise nor real interest in their arrival. "Hello, Reese."

Reese struggled to fashion a response. She needed to be sharp, but her brain simply would not function. Something was seriously wrong with the picture. Five o'clock in the morning, and all of her team were awake and gathered. And focused. Not on Reese. On Elene. Who should not have been here at all.

Kevin asked, "Where's Riffkind?"

Then pandemonium erupted.

Wails filled the atrium. The vast chamber echoed with the sound of very real human anguish. Screams and howls and moans, a chorus of bedlam.

The male nurse came flying through the clinic's entrance, his eyes round, his face bleached white. "You got to get in here!"

Before they could recover, the patients stumbled out. All of them. They shrieked like ghouls, waved their arms, tore at their hair, their clothes, shouted nonsense words. And headed straight for where Reese stood.

Reese and Kevin spotted Trent Major at the same moment. He walked out of Kevin's lab. Trent showed no surprise at the commotion. Just stood looking at Kevin. Who gaped in reply.

Reese shouted for security to grab him. But she could not make herself heard.

82

"Charlie?"

"Thank you for coming back, Gabriella. I couldn't have made it without you."

"What just happened?"

Charlie shut the motel room door and walked along the outside passage toward the stairs. "Reese is forming attack teams."

The news almost broke Gabriella. "She is using my own work to destroy everything I stood for."

Charlie unlocked the car and slipped behind the wheel and started the motor. "That's not going to happen, Gabriella."

"What are you going to do?"

The answer was, what he had aimed on doing all along. Only now there was an added urgency to his work.

He burned rubber out of the parking lot. "What I do best."

·||·

Charlie left the car across the street from the compound. Any front-line warrior would say the best time to hit a protected site was the hour just before sunrise. The darkest hour of night had passed, and with it the soldiers' concentration. The world rested. The night beasts were in their burrows, the day creatures not yet up and moving around. The streets held an almost breathless quality.

The compound was typical for a top-secret operation. At first glance, the fence was a decorative affair, with black metal posts forming a pattern around the compound's periphery. Charlie knew the razor edges continued down to chest height, making it impossible to scale or attach any sort of line. The spacing allowed the internal security to observe any approach. The security lighting was intense and illumi-nated an utterly bare lawn. The only adornment was a blank granite block waiting for some company's name. The ground was laced with unseen sensors. The place was a hidden fortress. The guards would be numerous and armed and highly skilled.

And Charlie was going in alone.

He could feel his strength already sapped by the attack during his ascent. He wanted to crawl under these bushes and sack out.

Two cars were parked to either side of the perimeter gate. The gate opened into a concrete strip that ended at the loading platform. The presence of those cars was both good and bad. Good, because it confirmed that the perimeter gate operated on its own backup power, which could be accessed even when the security system was down. Bad, because it meant the security team had been reinforced. He reminded himself that he was a combat vet and a highly trained security specialist. This was just another assignment. He would tough it out.

Charlie slipped behind the shrubbery at the sound of a lone engine. He raised his head a fraction and saw a delivery truck trundle down the street. The vehicle was just as Elene had described from her ascent. Charlie gripped the black duffel bag. The contents clinked softly as he tensed for the leap.

As soon as Elene had described her escape from the compound, Charlie had known it would come down to this.

Elene's images had been vividly clear. She had seen herself lead a group drawn from Reese Clawson's team out of the building. They emerged together. Unchallenged. And they made their escape in a white grocery truck that was drawn up to the loading platform.

Simple. Except for one thing.

Trent Major had already cut the security system. Elene had described that as well. And as any operative knew all too well, when the system went down, the exterior entries instantly locked. It was an automatic response. Each portal carried its own emergency battery pack. Even an instant's interruption to the energy supply resulted in the place turning into a fortress. The security chief would hold a key. His duty officer would have another. The only access was via a dual unlocking system. It could be done from inside or out. But both keys had to access the same door, and only one door worked. Charlie assumed it was the front portal. Which meant the loading bay was sealed for the duration.

This left him with just one option. Because refusing this challenge was not in the cards. He was going in. And they were coming out. The fact that they came out unchallenged meant he must have stayed to duke it out. And did not escape with them.

Charlie ran at a crouch, using the shrubs to shield his acceleration. The truck slowed and halted before the compound gates. He waited until the driver reached out his window to tab the security panel, then opened the passenger door. The driver was alone.

Charlie held his revolver up where the lone driver could see and asked, "Do you speak English?"

"Sí—yes."

"Good. Now tell me you want to live."

83

Charlie moved the driver to the back of the truck and used silver duct tape to lash his wrists and ankles and mouth. The driver, a chubby Latino in his fifties, watched him with eyes swimming in fear.

Charlie drove through the open gates and swung the truck in a tight circle. The truck peeped its warning signal as he backed up to the loading dock. He climbed down from the truck, leaving the driver's door open and the motor running. He dumped his duffle on the raised loading platform, then jogged back out through the open gates. The silenced pistol gave sharp coughs as he shot out the front tires and windscreens of both cars.

He vaulted up the stairs to the loading platform, crouched, and unzipped the duffle. He inserted a fresh clip into the pistol and put two more full clips into his left trouser pocket. He hefted the shotgun, checked to ensure the chamber was filled, opened the box of shells, and put six more rounds into his right pocket.

The bikers had not come up with his requested C-4 plastic explosive. Charlie had asked for it because he wanted the bikers to assume he was a burglar, in town to make a head-on assault of some high-security compound. Instead, they had supplied him with a dozen flash-bang grenades. Which was what Charlie had wanted all along. He slipped four into his jacket pockets and strung the remainder to his belt by their handles. When he stood, he clinked. But Charlie was way beyond the point where he needed to worry about making a little noise.

·|||·

The back of the loading platform contained three reinforced metal doors. Charlie levered a round into the shotgun, braced himself, and fired at the first handle. The boom slammed through the concrete cavern. He stomped open the door and faced a chilled larder with floor-to-ceiling shelves.

He stepped to the next door and fired again. The shotgun's solid rounds kicked him back on his heels. He hammered the door open and faced another concrete chamber. Only this one was filled with wires and cables and electronic controls. Charlie smiled with adrenaline mirth, unclipped two of the concussion grenades, tossed them inside, shut the door, and planted himself down the wall. The resulting explosion blew the reinforced metal door off its hinges and into the loading area, where it rocked and smoldered.

He aimed at the next door-lock, fired, kicked, tossed in another flash-bang, and then replanted himself on the side wall.

Combat soldiers had their own special term for Charlie's tactics. Shock and awe.

84

Even before the first of the patients appeared in the passage leading to the Treatment Room, Elene was up and moving. "We have to go now."

Eli remained where he was, trapped by Reese's presence even though the woman stared away from them, across the atrium, to where the din steadily increased.

"Eli."

He turned slowly.

"If you are coming, you have to move now."

He remained where he was.

Instead, it was Joss who said, "What do you need?"

"We must move everybody into the sleeping quarters," Elene replied. "Don't take the elevators. The power is about to go out. Use the stairs."

Consuela whined, "We'll be trapped there. We'll never get out."

Elene said, "That is not going to happen."

She shooed them up and got them moving just as the first patients staggered into the atrium's opposite corner. The shrieking cacophony accelerated their departure. Elene remained where she was. She might as well have been invisible, for all the attention Reese and Kevin Hanley and the security personnel showed her. They were all focused on the screaming patients and on Trent.

Reese pointed at Trent Major and shrilled, "*Get him!*"

Then the atrium was filled with the sound of a sonic boom.

Though she had expected it, Elene still flinched as the air around her compressed tightly. The security personnel and Reese were caught completely off guard. They were still recovering when the second explosion rocked the building.

All the lights went out.

Two seconds later, the atrium was filled with a spectral illumination, more silver than white. Emergency lights glared from all four corners of the ceiling, too intense to be stared at directly. It cast the giant chamber into bizarre shadows.

The patients wailed and writhed and formed a macabre procession about the atrium.

At that point, Elene could have ridden bareback on a silver unicorn around the atrium and gone unnoticed.

Trent started toward her just as two further blasts shook the chamber. Elene resisted the urge to pluck Eli bodily from his seat. The young man sat staring at his hands, totally detached from the insanity that filled the chamber.

His choice.

Elene met Trent by the stairway. "Second floor. Hurry."

Trent gasped from behind her, "What was *that*?"

"Charlie Hazard."

"He's here? I thought—"

"You thought Charlie would do his ascent and then leave us alone." Elene gripped his arm and urged him along the landing. "Charlie Hazard is a pro. He is coming to make sure you all get out of this safely."

From down below, someone shouted her name. Elene assumed it

was Reese. She pointed down the stairs to where Joss led four of the others up toward them. "Joss Stone is a former Marine. Tell him—"

Elene's words were lost to another boom, this one louder. Elene assumed Charlie had just breached the kitchen exit. The lights flickered, and when they restabilized, Elene realized that the duty officer had started up the stairs behind them. He was in the process of crouching and aiming his pistol back toward the cafeteria area when the ground floor erupted in light and noise.

Elene staggered into Trent and they both tumbled to the floor. She had heard of concussion grenades her entire career, but this was the first time she had felt their impact. Even from two stories up, the assault scrambled her brain.

But the adrenaline surge gave her the strength to focus. She forced herself to her knees, gripped Trent's shoulders, and shook him. Hard. "Are you with me?"

He floundered a minute, then with her help made it back to his feet. Elene risked a glance over the railing. Joss was standing over an inert security guard and helping Consuela stand.

She turned to Trent and said, "Tell Joss the truck is waiting for you at the loading platform through the kitchen. He'll know what to do."

"What about you?"

"There's something I have to destroy."

"But—"

"*Listen to me.*" From below came the sounds of gunfire. The patients' screams tore at Elene's vision. "Get everyone out of here, Trent. That's what you and Joss must focus on now."

She turned and ran.

85

As far as Charlie was concerned, he could not have dreamed up a better kill zone.

The emergency lights were planted into the ceiling, which was miles overhead. The designers had tried to overcome the atrium's size by strengthening the lights' power. This resulted in an almost strobe effect. Whatever was directly in the path of the illumination was lit up with laser-like intensity. But everything else was lost in impenetrable shadows.

Charlie spotted Reese Clawson standing next to a blue-jacketed security specialist. The specialist was in a regulation crouch, his pistol held in a two-armed grip. Another man, portly and scared, gaped at the insane scene. Charlie discounted him immediately. Reese screamed something at the security guy. The man paid her no notice. He searched the periphery. Ready. Charlie knew as soon as he started up the stairs, he'd be spotted.

He plucked another three concussion grenades from his belt and lofted them high. They clattered down in the atrium's far corner, behind the trio.

The flash was monumental, the response even worse.

The patients all screamed in renewed panic. They raced about, weaving back and forth with arms outstretched and necks taut with the effort to bawl even louder. Charlie evaded the clutch of one bug-eyed young man and bolted up the stairs.

Two bullets whanged sparks off the railing. Clearly the security guy knew how to recover under fire. Charlie vaulted the final three stairs and rolled.

"Here! In here!"

Elene crouched inside an open door and waved frantically. She winced but did not retreat as a round struck the panel directly overhead. Charlie leapt inside. Elene pointed at the inner access. "I can't get it open!"

"Stand back." Charlie slipped the shotgun off his shoulder, aimed, and blew the door off its hinges. They stepped into a smoldering room. Directly ahead was a glass viewing station fronted by a control panel that ran the entire length of the wall. "These are the main controls?"

"Reese sits by the mike, her technician by the computer station there."

He knew there might be backup somewhere else. There was nothing he could do about it. Charlie pumped new shells into the gun and demanded, "Where is Trent?"

"With the team. Heading for the truck."

"Move back into the lobby."

"I want—"

"Go!" He levered a fresh round into the chamber, aimed at the controls, and fired. The round dug a smoldering cavity into the station and shattered the glass wall. Charlie fired three more rounds, his ears aching from the noise in the enclosed space. He stepped forward, gripped two of his remaining four grenades, pulled out the pins, held them over two of the newly excavated holes in the console, dropped, turned, and flew.

And ran straight into a three-way battle for control of the security man's gun.

At first glance, Elene looked totally outmanned. She was the smallest by far. Reese appeared to be almost twice her size. The security guy was a giant by comparison. But Elene fought with a ferocity that stunned both her opponents. She gouged the security guy in the eye, gripped his gun hand, and bit deep into Reese's shoulder.

Reese screamed and fought to free herself. Elene just bit down harder.

Charlie flipped the shotgun over and clipped the security guy above his left ear. The guy blinked and struggled to stay upright. Charlie was going in for a second blow when the wall behind him erupted.

They were blown completely through the wall and landed in a dusty heap in front of the elevators. Charlie felt something warm dribble down his neck and assumed one of his eardrums had burst. He sifted through the rubble and came up with Elene. The security guy was out. Reese struggled feebly. Charlie gripped Elene by the collar and stumbled for the stairs.

He definitely needed to rethink his take on analysts. He'd always assumed the only reason anybody ever became one was because they were attracted by the lure of danger, so long as the peril was directed at somebody else. But this was one stand-up lady. Charlie intended to tell her that, soon as he managed to wash the dust from his throat and relocate his voice. Right now, though, it was all he could do to cough and walk down the stairs.

To his astonishment, Elene chose that moment to wrestle out of his grip and race back *up*.

Charlie wheeled about and saw Reese reaching over the banister, taking aim with the security man's gun.

Reese's hair was a witch's brew about her face. Her features were pulled back in a feral mask, turned white by the dust. Her eyes burned at him as she fired.

Charlie threw himself toward the railing directly below Reese, limiting her target area. He felt a searing burn score its way down his back. He arched in agony, which drew his head directly into her line of fire.

Then Elene attacked.

Charlie needed both hands to haul himself back up the stairs. He arrived at the top to find the two women scrambling in the debris, all four hands locked on the pistol. But Reese now matched the smaller woman for ferocity, particularly after she spotted Charlie's approach. She snarled and pried the gun down. And shot Elene.

Charlie gripped the gun with one hand and hammered Reese with the other. Her eyelids fluttered. He punched her again, a straight right to the jaw. Her eyes swam back and she slumped.

Charlie cradled Elene in his arms and tumbled down the stairs.

He followed his course of entry back down the rear hallway and onto the loading platform. A dozen hands helped him off the dock and into the truck's rear hold. A young man with a compact military build and a killer's eyes helped ease Elene down to the floorboards, then shouted, "Go, go!"

But as Trent gunned the motor, Elene murmured, "Tell him to stop."

Charlie did not understand it, did not even agree. But he saw something in her gaze that caused him to shout the order forward.

When the truck ground to a halt, Joss complained, "There's an army breathing down on us."

"Do as she says." Charlie sank down beside the stricken woman. "Hang on now."

But her lips were tinted pink, and her eyes held a fevered awareness. "For what? I'm checking out, and you know it."

Charlie held back on the trite words that would only shape a lie. Instead he said, "You saved my life back there."

"Just repaying the favor." She coughed, and it cost her.

"Easy now. We'll get you to safety."

"No you won't. You've got to take me back and set me on the loading dock where the police will find me." She stopped his protest with a smile. "It happened just like I saw. But I couldn't tell you this last part because I knew you wouldn't agree." Elene coughed once more and managed, "Heroes don't like being saved. Do they."

Then she was gone.

86

They stopped at a pharmacy. Though Joss wanted to handle it, Consuela took Charlie's money and went in alone. She returned ten minutes later, carrying two bulging plastic bags. As Trent drove them inland, Joss handed Charlie a bottle of Advil and a liter of water. Then Charlie lay on the truck floorboards and Joss went to work. He did a thorough job of swabbing out the wound, used three bottles of the spray intended for children's sore throat as a local anesthetic, then stitched Charlie shut. "It ain't gonna be the most perfect job. But it's not like you don't already got your share of scars."

Charlie's back already felt better. The piercing burn was diminished to the constant ache of a healing wound. "You're Ranger?"

"Naw, man, I don't got no time for those fidos. Marines all the way, baby." Joss padded the area with alcohol and taped a field dressing into place. "You're good to go. But you want some advice, I'd say let somebody else take the next punch."

Charlie rose to his feet and shrugged. The stitches and field dressing shifted comfortably. Now if only they could do something for the wound to his heart. "Thanks, Joss."

"Okay, now it's my turn." Consuela tried to cover her own distress with a scowl. "Hold still." She used a bottle of hand disinfectant and cotton swabbing to clean Elene's blood from Charlie's face and arms. Then she handed him the second shopping bag. "It's not what you'd call high fashion. But it's clean and it ought to fit."

"It's great." Charlie stripped off his dusty and bloodied clothes and put on the Santa Barbara T-shirt and sweatpants. Then he eased himself down beside the trussed Latino driver. "Consuela, could you give me a hand here?"

"No problem." She moved back beside him, taking care not to touch the still-wet bloodstain by the rear doors. The other passengers watched them with the slack expressions of bomb victims. Which, Charlie supposed, they were.

Charlie cut the tape away from the driver's wrists and ankles. Then he called through the sliding front window, "Trent!"

"Yes?"

"You still got our money belt?"

"Around my waist."

"Pass it back, will you?"

When the nylon belt made its way back, Charlie unzipped one compartment and held the cash before the driver's face. Then he pulled the tape from the man's mouth.

The driver said, "Please, *señor*, I want no trouble."

"I want to apologize for what's happened. And I'm going to make it up to you." Charlie counted out fifty hundreds. "Here's five thousand dollars."

"Please, there is no need—"

"Is this your truck?"

"Yes. Is mine. And my brother's."

"So yours is a family business."

The driver's T-shirt was bound to his body by fresh sweat. "Yes, is true. Nine of us."

"They must be worried. Do you have a phone?"

Through the sliding window, the young man in the passenger seat said, "There's one here on the dash. It's rung maybe half a dozen times since we started off."

Charlie asked the driver, "Will you call them and say you're all right? Tell them you will be coming home a little late, you've had an unexpected job. But you're fine, and you'll be done around midnight. Until then, they shouldn't expect to hear from you."

"Of course, *señor*." The driver accepted the phone, but his trembling fingers made a hash of dialing. He gripped the phone with both hands, hung his head, and huffed a fearful moan.

Consuela touched his arm and spoke to him in Spanish. The driver did not look up, but he managed to dial the number and speak to someone. Consuela nodded to Charlie.

When the driver cut the connection, Charlie said, "I'd like to offer you another five thousand. To vanish for the rest of the day."

The driver lifted his head. "Please?"

Charlie waited while Consuela translated. The driver's gaze shifted back and forth between them. Clearly the man was having difficulty understanding what he was hearing. Charlie went on, "We're going to be getting out in a little while. All I want you to do is hold off contacting anyone else until tonight. Drive somewhere and park. Then at midnight, you go home. Do anything you like. Tell anyone anything. Or not. It's up to you."

The driver's forehead creased. "*Señor*, excuse me, but the business where you just left. There are security cameras everywhere."

"They're all out," Charlie replied. "Nobody saw anything."

The driver looked from one face to another. "Of this you are certain?"

Trent called back, "They didn't see a thing. Not today."

"As far as they are concerned, you didn't show up today. If you want to change that, fine." Charlie stuffed the ten thousand dollars into the driver's pocket. "It's your choice."

87

s Trent took the highway into the Central Valley, Charlie
reached out to contacts he had developed over the years.
They arrived at the Bakersfield airstrip just after two. The
plane was waiting for them. As they crossed the lot, the man leaning
against the stairs called over, "One of you named Hazard?"

"That's me."

"A buddy said you needed a lift to Albuquerque."

"That's an affirm."

"I'm your man. I didn't hear how many of you there'd be."

"We are . . ."

"Eleven," Joss said, joining them.

The pilot was about what Charlie had expected, an overweight vet
with solid arms, a few faded tattoos, and a moustache he took great
pride in cultivating. His pale blue eyes twinkled in the fierce inland
sun but showed no humor. Only steel.

Joss turned and surveyed the perimeter. "Is it always this quiet?"

"Pretty much." The pilot surveyed the group straggling toward his plane. "Looks to me like your crew's seen enough action for one day."

"Joss, why don't you go help them load up." The plane was a twin-engine King turboprop, a common workhorse among independent pilots. "Maybe you and I should talk business."

"Sure thing." But the pilot hung back far enough to survey Charlie's wound and announce, "You're leaking."

"I'm okay." Actually, his back had started protesting against the jouncing ride an hour earlier. Charlie's head swam from the Advils he had swallowed. But the wound hurt enough to shout through. He wanted to get the business done now in case he fogged out later. "Our mutual friend told me a price, but I want to make sure he got it right."

"Eleven passengers to Albuquerque, you got any luggage?"

"No."

"Call it fifteen. That sound right to you?"

Charlie continued to walk away from the plane and the group. "How does fifty sound?"

The man's grin held no more humor than his eyes. "Sounds like serious trouble."

"I want you to fly us to a commercial strip near Nogales."

"As in south of the border."

"That's right."

"And you don't got no ID's."

"No. But I have a friend who runs a hotel. You get us down, he'll get us in."

The pilot kicked at a pebble. "Trip like that, I'm thinking seventy-five would sound a whole lot better."

Charlie knew he should argue the man down. But he just didn't have the strength. "Twenty now, the rest when we land."

The pilot started to slap Charlie's back, then thought better of it. "Mister, you just bought yourself a taxi."

Shane awoke late to brilliant sunshine and the sound of her ringing phone. When she answered, Trent's words were, "We don't ever need to visit Nogales."

When she came downstairs, Shane still floated from the joy of reconnecting with Trent. She entered the dining area to find Elizabeth and Gabriella seated together by the window. They stared out over the sunlit sea, talking with the quiet ease of old friends.

Shane said, "I just spoke to Trent."

"And we have talked with Charlie. They will join us here in a few days, as soon as he manages to find everyone papers." Gabriella smiled at her. "From the look on your face, I must assume your young man had something nice to tell you."

She blushed her way into a seat. "I'm starving."

"Please eat fast. The realtor meets us in half an hour to take us to our new home."

⫰⫰⫰

Sea froth from the passing storm blanketed the beach and clung to the cliffs. They left the Guernsey harbor on a boat built to resemble an Edwardian launch, a broad-beamed wooden craft whose wheelhouse was a glass-sided affair lined with embroidered settees. An empty brass champagne bucket was fastened to the underside of the center table. A metal vase held six blooming roses. Shane felt as though she should be dressed in crinoline and bows.

The sea was a crystal blanket that lied in its promise of endless calm. Gulls sang a discordant shanty overhead as they sliced through the eight miles that separated Starn Island from Guernsey.

Their guide was a local realtor named Edith, a blowsy woman who accented her bulk with a pleated ankle-length dress and matching navy jacket. Once they were under way, she unpacked a wicker hamper and offered them cheese and grapes and biscuits and wine. "Starn Island is a place for growing myths. It's not much good for anything else. Even the sheep tend to bed down hungry. I probably shouldn't be telling you such things. But you'll find out soon enough."

The front of the wheelhouse was made of doors that folded back in accordion style. The air was spiced with sunlight and seaweed and the water's biting chill.

The woman continued, "My granddad fished these waters since he was a nub. The island has known many names over the years. A number of the locals still call it Realta. My granddad prefers Reannig. Realta, Reannig, Starn, they're all old Gaelic, don't you know. They all mean heaven. Or star. The Gauls used the same word for both. The three words come from three different strands of Gaelic, or Celtic as it's known in these parts. The Celts once had kingdoms that ringed these waters."

The closer they drew to the island, the punier it became. The sea looked immense, capable of swallowing it whole with one decent blow. Starn Island was dominated by a single peak that rose in emerald splendor from an atoll that scarcely seemed large enough to support its weight.

The island was rimmed by a beautiful beach. A few pleasure boats were anchored along its length, visitors taking advantage of the calm day. Shane counted eleven parasols sprouting like seafront blossoms. Sheep dotted the hill's lower reaches. Stone cottages and one larger manor adorned the single expanse of flatland.

The realtor expertly maneuvered their vessel into the rock-walled harbor and docked by a barnacle-encrusted mooring. Otherwise the port was empty. Fishing nets dried from a collection of lobster cases. They alighted to the welcome of bleating sheep. Shane saw a few people emerge from the cottages to stare their way.

"Nowadays the only legends these residents care to speak of relate to the most recent occupants of Starn Manor." The realtor waved carelessly at the locals, who replied by shrinking back inside their homes and shutting the doors. "The latest owner, one Horace Talburt, was rather fierce by all accounts. He renamed the island the Royal Seat of Talburtistan. After one particularly bad meal in La Rochelle, he officially declared war on France. Quite mad, of course. But a gentleman to his friends. The islanders adored him."

The manor appeared genuinely decrepit. Its stone walls were liberally dosed with lichen. Several windows were cracked and patched with tape and wood. Three shutters hung like flags of defeat. The front steps were cracked and pitted. The door did its best to resist the realtor's efforts to unlock it, then shuddered and moaned as it opened. The interior was dim and dusty and smelled of mildew and cats.

The realtor led them from one massive room to another, her voice echoing off the high ceilings. "The island's history is really quite unique. In 1828, a sea captain and merchant prince performed a great service for King George the Fourth. In return, the king granted the captain the title Magistrate of Starn, along with sovereignty for two hundred years. The title passes with ownership. As does the royal charter, which has another seventeen years to run."

The kitchen was in horrid condition. A stone Victorian sink was topped by a hand pump. A wood-burning stove dominated one wall. Opposite this rose a massive fireplace whose interior was shaped such that two stone benches hugged the side walls. The benches were worn smooth with use.

The realtor led them back to the broad central staircase. "Upstairs you'll find twenty-six bedrooms and three baths, one for each floor. I suppose you want to inspect the lot?"

"Not really," Gabriella replied. "Elizabeth?"

"I've seen enough."

The realtor sighed with relief. "That suits me, I don't mind telling you. When I heard you were coming, I brought over the finest builder in the Channel Islands, Murphy's his name. He didn't like trusting those stairs any more than I did. Talburt didn't spend a quid on this place in thirty years." She walked over and rapped her knuckles on the oak-paneled wall. "Still, the place is sound as a bell. But you don't need me telling you that everything needs redoing. Murphy's still busy preparing his quote, but he doubts you'll see a penny back from two million pounds."

Gabriella walked over and took Elizabeth's hand. "What do you think?"

Elizabeth stared down at their intertwined fingers. "You're asking me?"

"Of course. It's your money."

"No it's not."

"Elizabeth. You brought us here. I need your wisdom."

In the interior shadows, her white-blonde hair looked as ethereal as sea foam. "Everything so far has been totally on target. I say we go for it."

Gabriella turned to Shane. "You agree?"

"We have a million dollars sitting in the bank," Shane replied. "I need to get Trent's take on all this. But I think he'd say the money came to us for a reason."

Gabriella turned to the woman and said, "We agree to the asking price. On one condition. We will make a down payment of five million dollars. We will make no further payment for five years. At which time the entire remaining sum will be due."

The agent opened her mouth and shut it several times. "You have clearly given this some considerable thought."

Gabriella glanced at Elizabeth. "You have no idea."

"You received word?" Elizabeth asked.

Gabriella nodded. "I think the word you used was *image*."

"When?"

"Last night."

"After Charlie rescued you?"

"Yes. It was waiting for me."

The agent clearly was flummoxed by the exchange. She cleared her throat and asked, "You are saying the current owners must carry the note?"

"Yes. This is a firm offer and not open to negotiation."

"Well, it's not my place to say, really. But if you want my opinion, given the current state of the market, they would be utter fools not to accept."

"In that case, we'll take it."

89

Murray Feinne had never been to Langley before. He was astonished at how much the foyer resembled the images he had seen in countless films. And how simple it was to enter the CIA's main building. There were guards everywhere, of course. And the level of vigilance was very high. But he was permitted to stand inside the foyer and watch the tide of people hurry through the turnstiles, flashing their ID's at the electronic monitor and then once more at the guard station. They were perhaps more silent than in a normal corporate environment. There might be a higher level of tension on the faces he saw. But otherwise it was just another governmental office complex. Except of course for the seal embedded in the floor. And the wall of stars representing unnamed fallen agents.

"Mr. Feinne? Jack Parrish. Sorry to keep you waiting." A young man with a military buzz cut offered Murray a visitor's ID on a lanyard. "I don't need to tell you to wear this at all times, do I."

"No." Murray followed the young man to the guard station, where he showed his driver's license, was photographed, and signed in. Then he was led down a series of halls and into a large waiting room that held three clusters of quietly urgent conversations.

The young man said, "Wait here, please." He disappeared into the inner sanctum, then returned to say, "The director will see you now."

The current director of the Central Intelligence Agency carried himself with the rumpled disdain of a tenured professor. Murray had seen him on television for years. The director had served as advisor on international affairs to an earlier president, then been brought back by the current administration to clean up an organization whose greatest talent had become its ability to waste time with infighting.

The director spoke softly on the phone as he waved Murray forward. He hung up and offered his hand without rising. "Have a seat, Mr. Feinne. Coffee?"

"No, thank you."

"You are here because allies within the intelligence community vouched for you. Mind if I ask how a corporate lawyer in LA became so connected?"

"An associate set this up. I have never been anywhere near your world."

The director glanced at his assistant, who had taken up station by the side wall and was frowning at Murray. "That is extremely odd, since these contacts insisted that this meeting was of the highest possible importance."

"It is."

The director's gaze carried the impact of supreme power. "Mr. Feinne, you have thirty seconds to explain."

"You have a dead agent on your hands by the name of Elene Belote."

The aide stiffened slightly and came off the wall. The director stilled his staffer with a glance. "I'm listening."

"You also have another agent who is probably still missing. His name is Rod Aintree."

The aide said, "Mr. Aintree is in the mental patients wing of a secure facility outside San Francisco."

The director asked, "As of when?"

"Day before yesterday. We received word of his admission last night."

When the director's attention turned back to him, Murray went on, "The chief of national intelligence has an assistant by the name of Amanda Thorne. She has been operating a clandestine facility outside Santa Barbara. The operation has two divisions. One is run by a gentleman named Kevin Hanley, a theoretical physicist formerly with military intelligence. The other division is headed up by Reese Clawson. Maybe you've heard of them."

"And if I have?"

"I've traveled here today," Murray said, "to hand you their heads on a platter."

The director inspected him a long moment, then turned to his assistant and said, "Clear the rest of my morning."

READ AN EXCERPT FROM
BOOK 2 IN THE

FAULT LINES

SERIES

COMING

SUMMER 2016

The officer who came for her was the one Reese Clawson thought of as Flat-Face. Female inmates tended to know their prison guards far better than male prisoners. This was part of staying safe. Abuse among female prison populations was fairly constant. Not that Reese had much to worry about on that score. Word seemed to travel with her to each of her new locations that she was to be left alone.

The guard was short and wide and had freckles that were stretched into a second coloring. Her face looked smashed by a frying pan, flat and utterly round, her nose a miniature indent. Most of the guards shared two things—odd physical appearances, and gazes as dull and flinty as old iron.

"Clawson, you've got a visitor. Bring your gear."

She still had an hour before the morning claxon. So Reese took her time closing her book and rolling off the bunk. Inmates did everything on their three-by-six foam mattress. Hers smelled bad, but it was not the worst she had known in her fourteen months of incarceration.

For most inmates, visitors meant a sliver of activity in their dull grey existence. For Reese, it meant something else entirely. She pulled her sweatshirt over her prison blues, then filled the front pouch with her meager belongings. The book she left on the empty bunk. Her hand lingered on the blank notepad, then she decided to leave that as well. Why she had spent prison money on a journal was a mystery.

369

She would never have dared write down her recollections. Even so, she had found a sense of bitter glee over the havoc she might have caused. But the thoughts remained locked inside, where they belonged. Because if she started writing down what she knew, she would sign her own death warrant.

Her cellmate was a huge Native American, so big she jammed onto the wall and spilled over the lower bunk's rim. She asked sleepily, "Going somewhere?"

"Out of state, most likely."

"What, you read smoke in the sky?"

"Something like that."

The woman shut her eyes. "See you when you wake up, girl."

Reese followed the guard down the concrete alley and through the buzzed security doors, down another hall, past the main security point, ever closer to the forbidden outside. Reese was good at pretending she did not care about ever breaking out. But now and then she caught a whiff of the world beyond the wire. And her heart skipped a beat. Like now.

She had assumed they were leading her to the narrow concrete-lined quadrangle where vehicles parked for prisoner transfers. Instead, the guard led her into an area she did not know, another windowless hall, another series of metal doors. But as far as Reese was concerned, any change in the routine was interesting.

The guard stopped by a door with a wire-mesh window and waved to the security officer in the bulletproof cage. The door buzzed. The guard opened it and said to the person waiting inside, "Rap on the glass when you're done."

"Thank you, Officer." The visitor did not look up from the file open on the metal desk. "Sit down, Clawson."

Reese did as she was told. Not because she was good at following instructions. Because she caught another faint whiff of a fragrance from far beyond this realm.

The woman on the other side of the desk turned a page in the file she studied. She wore a pin-striped suit and a white silk blouse with a frilly bow at the collar, which on her looked absurd. She was bulky and mannish with long dark hair clenched tight inside a gold clip. The frilly collar appeared odd, like she had intentionally dressed to draw attention away from her expression, which was cold and hard and calculating. She turned another page in the file and continued reading.

Reese had no problem with waiting. She had been doing little else for fourteen long months.

Since her arrest, Reese Clawson had been relocated four times. When they had first picked her up, she had been sent from Santa Barbara to Raiford Women's Prison in central Florida. Then Tennessee. The last two had both been in Virginia. Endless trips in the backseat of cars that had smelled worse than her mattress. It was enough to drive her insane. Which was perhaps what they had intended.

The woman reached into her jacket pocket and pulled out what at first glance was a digital recorder. Which was probably why prison security had let the woman bring it inside. But Reese knew better. She had used the exact same device. The woman flipped a switch and waited until the light glowed green. The device sent out a jamming signal, intended to blanket all frequencies. Such meetings as this were supposedly protected by attorney-client privilege. But it was this same code of ethics that stated no American citizen could be held without charge for over a year.

The woman had still not looked up. She turned another page. "Do you know where you are, Clawson?"

The obvious answer was, the Lawyer Room. It was the inmates' name for the security chamber, the only place in the entire prison not wired for sight and sound. At least, not on record.

Reese Clawson had not been here before. Which was hardly a surprise. Since she had also never been charged. Or had any need to ask for a lawyer. Up to this point, she had been fairly certain that any such request would have made that day her last.

The woman turned another page. She seemed to find nothing

wrong with Reese's silence. "You are at the verge of the only chance you will ever have."

Reese did not respond. There was nothing to say. Yet.

"My name does not matter, because I am not here. We are not meeting." The woman looked up and revealed a gaze as hard as a prison guard's. "Clear?"

"Yes."

"I have one question for you. Answer correctly, and you will move on to a different status. What that is, and where you will be operating, does not matter. Yet."

The woman liked holding this life-or-death clout, Reese could tell. There was a glint of resentment in those eyes, brown as muck, dark as the life Reese had come to call her own. She detected a tight anger and realized the woman was here against her will. At any other time, Reese might have found that humorous.

The woman went on, "Answer incorrectly, and you will be swallowed by the federal system. Permanently. Tell me you understand."

"Perfectly." All four of the prisons where Reese had been held were run by state penal systems. In each case, cells were rented by the federal government to house prisoners convicted in federal court. Federal prisons were so overcrowded they could no longer ignore the public outrage. It was easier to house the overflow in rented cages than build new facilities. But this also meant it was possible for the government to falsify documents and claim this particular inmate had been tried, convicted, and sentenced. To a life without any shred of hope of parole. Which was no life at all.

The woman's actions were overly slow, deliberate as an executioner. She tapped the pages back into order. Settled them into the file. Shut the cover. Placed the folder in her briefcase and snapped it shut. Rested her hands on the table. Gave Reese ten seconds of the eyes, cold as a cell door. "What would you do to earn another chance at freedom?"

Reese gave the answer as much force as she could. "Whatever it takes."

The woman cut off the jamming device. She rose to her feet and hefted her briefcase. She walked to the door and rapped on the security glass. "That is the correct answer."

⫶

A black Escalade was waiting for them outside the prison gates. Reese was directed into the rear seat. The woman slipped in beside the driver, a bulky guy dressed in a tailored suit of slate and silk. He asked, "Any trouble?"

"No. Drive."

Everything Reese saw or sensed carried an electric quality. Even the woman's hostile silence was pleasurable. The world spun and the road unfurled and every breath took Reese farther from the existence she had feared was all she would ever know.

The woman said her name was Vera. Reese assumed it was a lie, but just the same she wanted to thank her for the gift. To offer any name at all suggested a future and a purpose big enough to require further contact. The Escalade was not new and smelled vaguely of disinfectant. The leather seat was seamed with the sort of ingrained dirt that no amount of cleaning could pluck out.

Vera said, "There's a briefcase behind you in the rear hold."

Reese turned around and pulled the heavy Samsonite case onto the seat beside her. The briefcase contained four thick files. Reese estimated their weight at between twenty-five and thirty pounds. Their contents were divided into a logical sequence—finance, product development, legal and human resources, clients. She was deep into her initial read-through when, an hour later, the Escalade pulled into the parking lot of a cheap highway motel, one that probably catered to the prison visitors.

Vera kept her face aimed at the front windscreen as she said, "There's a key in the case. Your room is straight ahead of where we're parked. Go inside. Go to work. Don't leave the room. There's an envelope in there with cash. Order takeout. Don't make any other calls. If you try and run, federal marshals will be given a shoot-to-kill order. You have seven days to memorize the contents of those files."

Reese felt her face constrict into an unfamiliar expression, but at least she could still name it as a smile. Not because of the command or the warning. Because this woman thought she would need a week. "Will there be a test?"

"Absolutely." Vera did not bother turning around. "Fail, and Jack here will dispose of you."

Thomas Locke is a pseudonym for Davis Bunn, an award-winning novelist whose work has been published in twenty languages. Critical acclaim for his novels includes four Christy Awards for excellence in fiction. Davis divides his time between Oxford and Florida and holds a lifelong passion for speculative stories. Learn more about the author and his books at www.tlocke.com.

COMING

SUMMER 2016

BOOK 2 IN THE

FAULT LINES

SERIES

DON'T MISS IT!

"An explosive read."

"A thrilling ride . . . groundbreaking fiction."

"A gripping and intense experience."

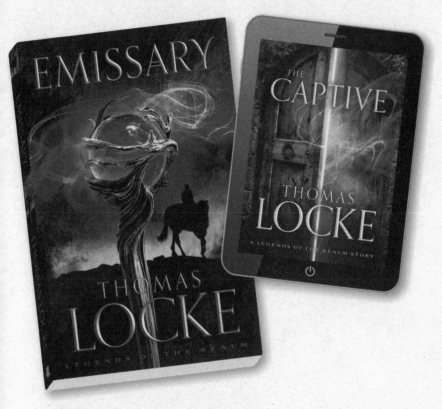